NEON STREETS

BY

VIN SMITH

ISBN: 1-4033-3434-X (e-book)
ISBN: 1-4033-3435-8 (Paperback)
ISBN: 1-4033-3436-6 (Dustjacket)

Library of Congress Number 2002093765

This book is printed on acid free paper.

Printed in the United States of America
Bloomington, IN

1stBooks – rev. 08/21/02

We gratefully Acknowldge permission to reprint lines from Love You Forever by Robert Munsch, Firefly Books, (1986). Firefly Books Ltd., 250 Sparks Avenue, Willowdale, Ontario Canada

"Jealous Heart," by Jenny Lou Carson. (BMI) Arista Records, © 1994 "Flasco Jimenez" C 8772

"Looking for my love in the Pouring Rain," by Tish Hinojosa (ASCAP), Warner Brothers © 1994 "Destiny's Gate." 9 45566-4

Author Photo by Terrell Lloyd, RTL Photography, P.O. Box 8086, Foster City, CA 94404

And pluck till time and times are done
The silver apples of the moon,
The golden apples of the sun.

William Butler Yeats
The Song of Wandering

To my wonderful Ginger; my soul mate, the one who makes it all worthwhile.

CHAPTER 1

Sunday, June 9, 1991

The rotund hacker in the foursome just ahead lagged far behind his party, seemingly ensconced in the rough. He sported passe parrot green polyester slacks and what he must have thought a complimentary canary yellow golf shirt with an animal logo perched over the left breast. He appeared to be less than steady on his Foot Joys.

"Who's that clown?" asked a tall, wiry dentist wearing John Lennon specks, who went by the unlikely name "Pudge." Jeffrey "Pudge" Elliot not only lived next door to his golfing partner, but had been his best friend since kindergarten. Elliot was pudgy as a small fry, only to do the jack-in-the- beanstalk thing as a teenager.

Cox Delaney grinned. Pudge was far too hyper to have the patience of the saints on the golf course. Up ahead, the hapless duffer trickled the ball a few feet with another inept swing. "That's Tubb. He's just taken up the sport. The classy thing, you know. Word has it he runs a 200 average bowling, and perhaps about the same on the course."

"What's his real name?"

"That's it. Jonathan Tubb. Everybody calls him Tubb. Managing Editor at the Plain Dealer."

"I didn't know those guys have the time to golf," Elliot observed.

"They can't work seven days a week."

"Think we can play through?"

Jonathan Tubb took that moment to pick up his ball and wave them on to the first hole. Cox Delaney and Pudge Elliot were playing alone, having signed up for a very late tee time.

Elliot teed his Titlist. Staring down the perfect turf of the 377 yard par four first hole at Shaker Heights Country Club, Pudge let go a tremendous shot down the middle of the fairway.

"Show-off," muttered Delaney.

Delaney's drive wasn't a whole lot shorter, perhaps 280 yards, and slightly hooked left of Pudge's straight and narrow 290 yard blast.

The pals slowly walked their way up the fairway. Neither would use a cart under any circumstances. A comfortable breeze wafted off Lake Erie, or perhaps Shaker Lakes. Maybe both. Greater Cleveland, and Shaker Heights in particular, were enjoying a fabulous late spring day.

Selecting a 4 iron, Delaney sent a shot that approached the cup, threatening to drop for an eagle two before it died six inches away.

"Now who's showing off?" laughed Elliot.

Pudge picked a 5 iron, and dropped the ball fifteen feet from the cup. "If I'm lucky I can stay within a shot of you, my boy."

1

They could see Tubb washing his ball at the second tee. Delaney wondered what kind of score he'd claim for the first hole. "If history is any indication, you will."

Cox Delaney was the Director of Computer Systems Analysis for his father-in-law's company, High Data Associates. He was a compact looking six foot, chiseljawed redhead, with the kind of muscles only a fitness club could provide. He never could understand how the lanky Elliot could consistently outdrive him.

With Pudge away, he picked the putter from his bag and began a test stroke or two. On the second tee, Delaney noticed Jonathan Tubb taking a miserable swipe at his ball. Again he chuckled.

"Laugh at my form, will you?" Elliot growled with mock severity.

"Probably should. Actually, I'm amused at Tubb over on the second."

Overhead, gulls performed a flying/gliding exhibition. Patches of blue from the lake could be seen peeking through the trees.

With practiced nonchalance, Pudge Elliot sank his fifteen footer.

"You devil."

With his marker six inches from the cup, Cox Delaney lazily matched Elliot's birdie.

"You seem preoccupied today, old friend," Pudge observed. "In spite of your feeble attempts at jocularity. Almost as if you were waiting for me to do a root canal."

They were in for several minutes worth of waiting, the foursome in front of them also seemingly bogged down. The sun was beginning its downward ride in the sky. They would probably finish just before twilight. If other foursomes didn't hold them up. As if reading minds, a couple of the players in front of them waved them through. Tubb walked off to the side and leaned against a tree. Delaney had the impression that for all of his miscues on the links, he seemed to be having a fine old time.

"I've got to talk to you one of these days, Pudge. Something's come up. I don't know how to handle it."

"I'm ready good buddy. When you are."

The club bar was packed with nineteenth holers. Outside, the deepening twilight brought with it a spring chill that hadn't yet surrendered to the fast approaching summer solstice. A gorgeous brunette deftly brought Cox Delaney and Pudge Elliot VO and water. A combo played light jazz; the trumpet man seemed in a blue funk as the music alternately soared and sank with contrasting passions.

Cox was in a pensive mood. Once again, Pudge had come roaring back with a birdie on the eighteenth, trimming Delaney by a stroke. For not the first time, the computer analyst figured Elliot had been toying with him.

"You ready to spill gut?"

Delaney grinned. "Not here. Not now. We need to take lunch this week, but certainly not at one of your heartburn parlors."

"Remember, Coxy. God invented antacid."

"You also claim he invented Novocain."

"No. I never said that. We dental gurus came up with that one."

2

Blue Moon tripped from the trumpeter's lips, curling around the room and touching at the human core. A look of concern crossed Elliot's lean features. "You been havin' problems, Coxy?"

"Not me. But I mean it, Pudge. Not now. Not here."

"All right. How's Cherie and the babes?" A survivor of three failed, childless marriages, Pudge Elliot always worried about Delaney and his family. He seemed to figure if he couldn't be a family man, things had to always be perfect for his friend.

Delaney's face lit up immediately. "Tomorrow's her birthday, you know. I'm taking the day off. The big 3-0."

"You don't deserve her, ya big lug."

"God. Don't I know it. Nor Tina and Tonya. I'm never home enough, but that's gonna change."

"Oh, retiring, are we? At what, thirty-two?"

"Next month. On the sixteenth. Birthday, I mean."

"I had the pleasure of reaching that milestone a couple of months ago. I notice you didn't even take me out for a drink."

"I did forget, didn't I? In that case, the drinks are on me."

"They're on you anyway, loser. Speaking of which, I need another VO."

"You'd think drinks would always be on the wealthy. People like TV repairmen, plumbers. DENTISTS."

"You ain't doin' too bad, podnuh."

Delaney became quiet.

"What'd I say?"

"Nothin' really. How's that blonde you've been seeing? The one with the bazooms."

"All women got bazooms, Coxy."

"Possibly true."

"However, to put an Orwellian twist to it, some are just more equal than others."

"Gloria? Is that the lady's name?

The brunette brought refreshed drinks to their table. Her smile, and perhaps cleavage seemed to baptize them both in sensuality.

"Now, now, Coxy. We mustn't allow libidos to...ah...rise, one might well say."

"Things like that don't...bother me...bother me...bother me...bother me..."

"Randy. I mean, that's her name, and yes she is."

"The cocktail waitress?"

"No. My latest flame."

"Bimbo."

"Coxy. The utter insensitivity of your words."

* * *

The Norman-style, two-story house on Woodbury, in an appropriately tony neighborhood just down the street from Shaker Heights High School, was large, luxurious, and paid for by Daddy. Cherie's Daddy. It never bothered Cox; the hours he spent making Maurice Devereaux richer seemed more than adequate as payback.

It was nearing nine-thirty; perhaps the twins—eight months old today—would still be rug ratting about the playroom. Cherie had overhauled the upstairs activities room, installing duckies and rabbits and everything stuffed in a play area that measured twenty-four feet by twenty-two. Tina and Tonya were almost three weeks into creeping and crawling. Into every nook in the room. The thought caused a broad smile to play across Cox Delaney's face.

Pulling into the spacious garage, he lined the Park Avenue next to Cherie's Beamer. Borf gargled a bark Cox's direction; greeting his master was the high point of the Heinze 57 mutt's day. The dog's vocal chords had been injured years earlier, before the bedraggled animal limped into the lives of Cox and Cherie Delaney. One day the dog simply appeared in their yard. You couldn't feed him. Try and approach, and he'd croak out a warning, all the while backing off. When a friend tried the same, the dog charged. The friend barricaded himself inside the house, all interest in the strange looking creature diminished to nada. It had taken a long while, but the dog finally responded to them both. Not so with anyone else. Borf could, and possibly would, decapitate a stranger if it seemed called for.

Delaney lowered into a squat, scratching Borf's head. The dog answered with a dolorous, but deeply affectionate threne. "I don't know how you got this far into Shaker Heights, old boy, but I'm glad you did. What you must have gone through."

Delaney entered the house from the garage, going straight to the wash room. Washing his face with his hands, he was annoyed to still feel itching eyes from the grasses at the country club. The wash room was done in a purple; he conceded Cherie had chosen a gentle purple. Garish colors displeased him.

Refreshed, he passed the clutter room, circled the huge kitchen, accented in brick tones, with copper utensils, pots, pans and assorted paraphernalia suspended on hooks. He cut through the dining room, its massive oak table the centerpiece of a wood grain decor. A substantial crystal chandelier winked in the muted lights, bathing the room with rich, though understated luminescence. His pace quickened through the foyer, and he bounded up the curved stairway.

Cherie Devereaux Delaney was waiting for him on the balcony. The twins were on the floor behind her, trapped by mesh netting in the entryway of the revamped playroom. Tina seemed to be practicing backwards mobility. Tonya had fisted a rattle toy, and was giving it a good shake.

Cherie melted into his arms.

"Were you a duffer today, handsome?"

"Pudge beat me by one stroke, if that's what you mean, beautiful."

"I missed you."

"Is that right?" Delaney proceeded to French kiss her. "Remember, I have improved, new, powerful kisses. Nowadays."

"The old ones weren't all that bad."

"Think so?" The kiss was getting steamy.

"Hey, big guy. You don't want to give your daughters ideas they might use at playschool." Tina and Tonya weren't paying the slightest attention. Tina was now trying to get the rainbow-hued rattle toy away from Tonya.

Cox Delaney's kiss intensified.

"Definitely new and improved."

"Don't forget powerful," he gasped.

"That, too."

After the babies were bedded for the night, with but a minimum of fuss, the two repaired to the dining room where Cherie had fixed a late dinner for Cox, consisting of his favorite, chicken Kiev. A browned rice and baked Italian squash complimented the meal, with his favorite blue cheese dressing on a lettuce wedge. A fine Cabernet Sauvignon complimented the dinner.

"You spoil me, Cherie."

"Have to. It's in the manual. 'The way to a man's heart is through his stomach.'"

"If the vehicle is chicken Kiev, I believe that old saw might be somewhat accurate."

Cherie matched him chew for chew. "More wine?"

"I think not. I mustn't dull my edge. One never knows what later will bring."

"I wouldn't say that. I think I know what later will bring. Very predictable." Cherie's dark eyes were dancing, framed by lovely chestnut hair. Her perfect body poised, her mellifluous voice teasing. "That's what I love about you dear. You never keep me guessing."

"You like that?"

"Sure. I can guess at the weather. I like my men steadfast."

"Sounds boring."

"No, never. Comforting. For example. In ten or twenty minutes, you are going to ask me for the keys to my BMW and drive to the store and buy some Death by Chocolate."

"You mean we're out of it?"

"Yep."

"God, I must be transparent."

"Like Windexed glass." Cherie's eyes were still dancing. Her smile was the smile of Universal Woman. Earthy. Warm. Come hither.

Cox Delaney had to try three stores to get a half gallon of Death by Chocolate ice cream.

Shaker Heights is one of the richest communities—perhaps the richest—in all of America. When Moses Cleaveland, of the Connecticut Land Company, founded the town that bears his name (now sans the a), where the Cuyahoga river empties into Lake Erie in September of 1796 (he spent all of one month in the Western Reserve of the Ohio country), he laid out four townships on the outskirts of Cleveland. They were Euclid, East Cleveland, Warrensville, and Newburgh. It was in 1822 that a religious group known as "The United Society of Believers in the Second Coming of Christ" picked out fourteen hundred acres in Warrensville

Townships's northwest section. There they built a utopian society; a sort of Theistic communism. They called their enclave North Union. They often referred to it as "The Valley of God's Pleasure." The spot is high ground, not a valley in the real sense.

Due to the dancing, agitated movements of some of their rituals, they were dubbed the Shakers. They soon excelled in producing home remedies and tonics. The products were world renown. One of their best known concoctions was Corbett's Shaker Extract of Sarsaparilla, widely prescribed in the last century for those who suffered from syphilis.

They had many new notions about agriculture, which produced among other things, improved livestock breeds. They had a funny notion about breeding among themselves. They banned conjugal relations, which forced them to recruit from the outside to keep their numbers up, and to survive as a colony.

It didn't work.

Enter real estate siblings, Oris Paxton Van Sweringen, and Mantis James Van Sweringen. After the original Shakers had dwindled to but a few, at around the turn of the century, the men who would change the face of Cleveland discovered the opportunity that awaited the enterprising developer at North Union. Enter Shaker Heights.

Cox Delaney turned onto Woodbury, a happy overlay partially occluding the deep sense of ominous dread that had permeated his very essence over the preceding weeks. He knew what he had to do. He knew that he had to do it. It might mean shaking hell loose from its moorings. So be it.

Cherie had that marvelous ability to leaven his moods. Not even the obligatory Sunday round of golf with Pudge had worked this day. It took dinner with the light of his life to accomplish that.

Perhaps everything would work out all right after all.

Armed with nature's mightiest weapon, Death by Chocolate ice cream, Cox Delaney entered the mansion. What a vision of loveliness awaited him.

Cherie Devereaux Delaney in a stretch lace tanga bikini. Victoria wasn't keeping any secrets. Cox's heart nearly stopped, seemingly next to his Adam's apple. "That sure isn't predictable," Delaney croaked.

"Of course not. I never am," she, or perhaps, the ghost of Mae West said.

Ice cream as aphrodisiac. Lovemaking as affirmation.

The black van might have belonged to a neighborhood youth. Except that it didn't. How to describe the occupants. Central casting is accused of much stereotyping, and of course, there is a grain of truth to every cliché. Inside the vehicle, the muscle was burly. Always is. Together, the pair might be described by the average person as possessing the intelligence of a fence post. That would be a mistake. Both were college grads. Each possessed a keen, calculating mind. Neither would please an ethics Prof.

Watching and waiting. Patience bordering on the infinite.

No one questioned their right to park on this stretch of Woodbury. With vans, pickups and SUV's proliferating as if they were vehicular rabbits, it wasn't likely the gendarmes from Shaker Heights would check it out. And if they did, the two large fellows would scrunch down, out of sight. And the registration. The registration was solid gold Shaker Heights.

* * *

"In a mere one hour, six minutes, you, my dear, according to my oldest brother Jake, cannot be trusted."

"Coxy, I never could be trusted. And I've never been predictable. Now what kind of mysterious woman would aspire to that?"

"That's simple. One that turns thirty in sixty-five-and-a-half minutes."

"So now we're doing a new year's-style countdown?"

"Turnabout is fair play. You practically barked the seconds a couple of years ago when I had my geriatric crisis. And the present you gave me. Grecian Formula? I'm surprised you didn't buy it in a fifty-five gallon drum."

"They didn't have any in stock."

Cox Delaney reached over and gently kissed his wife.

"No."

"No? What do you mean no?"

"Coxy, you are now way over thirty. If I'm to have you at the stroke of midnight, you must conserve your strength."

"I know how to do that."

"Oh? Perhaps you might enlighten others. Maybe with a letter to the editor of Modern Maturity."

"The secret is more ice cream."

"Death by Chocolate," they said in unison.

"Last one to the fridge is a rotten egg," Cox said, as he attempted a leap from the bed.

Cherie Devereaux Delaney tripped him up nicely, spinning him back on the king size bed. "That will be you, dear."

The corpulent, big-boned man, mountainous of flesh, and sporting an arrogance that frightened mere mortals, sat back at his desk in the opulent office and weighed the measure of the rapidly unfolding night. All the bases would be covered. Well, they always were. You didn't hold a Masters degree in management and allow piffles to roar through a strategy meeting. You don't allow loose strings to dangle from every rafter. Above all, never be equivocal. Issue the ukase, and hold your lieutenants responsible.

That's how an organization performs up to standard. Didn't America's corporate cretins understand that anymore? Simply full of hand-wringing morons, eyes riveted to the short term performance, oblivious to the larger picture.

Plan your work, and work your plan.

Simple.

If stogies were his style, he would have taken a satisfying puff about now. Instead, he stabbed another smoked oyster with his fork.

*   *   *

"What do you think? How does it feel. Now that you are officially thirty, I mean."

"About the same as the first time, Studly. Maybe better. Definitely better." Cherie rolled over and sighed. "God, we ought to market Death by Chocolate. It works."

One of the twins gave out a piercing cry.

Cox shot out of bed like a cannon. Cherie followed in the controlled way mothers do when they have decoded a babies plea. Tina seemed like a bag of tears that had burst from the seems. Her face morphed into a prune-like symbol of profound displeasure. Tonya awoke with a start. Upon surveying her twin's displeasure, she too decided a lachrymose protest was in order. Cherie said, "Burp 'em, and I'll get a bottle going."

With a daughter over each shoulder, he gently burped them cross-handed. Nothing. Tina seemed simply to be hungry, as her little mouth made sucking motions. Cherie had weaned them a mere six weeks earlier. Tina, especially, hadn't quite got used to the bottle.

Soon, two bottles of formula were ready. Cox held Tonya, and Cherie comforted Tina. Both babies fed happily. Delaney reached for a book. "I'm going to read to them."

"That's good," Cherie said dreamily.

"By the way," he said matter-of-factly. "I'm staying home tomorrow."

She smiled.

Cox Delaney had cried the first time he picked up a little book by Robert Munsch, illustrated by Sheila McGraw. Love You Forever. He began to read:

> "A mother held her new baby and
> very slowly rocked him back and forth,
> back and forth, back and forth.
> And while she held him, she sang:
> I'll love you forever,
> I'll like you for always,
> As long as I'm living
> my baby you'll be."

*   *   *

The passenger door swung slowly open, followed a moment later by the driver's side. The burly, erudite thugs emerged from the black van into the darkness; patient shadows garbed in dark power suits. The driver, a gentleman named Fairly, was armed with a cellular phone. This he flipped open, punching numbers with practiced fingers. Fairly hated violence with a passion. Violence was something Fairly felt should be tightly controlled. So he spent his time controlling it.

8

His partner, a man named Tomajac, sported a Valmet M76 Bullpup carbine, which uses a Kalishnikov AK action, with .223 caliber bullets, a semiautomatic. Tomajac was almost incapable of missing a target at most any distance. Unlike Fairly, Tomajac liked violence. He loved violence. He lived for it. He'd practiced murder on every continent with the exception of Antarctica. One day he hoped to rectify that.

It was a rather strange thing. Fairly and Tomajac, like two peas in a pod, were yet as different as night and day. Though they might look interchangeable, they were chosen by the ones who called the shots because of their remarkable ability to compliment one another. Synergistic.

"It's time…" Fairly mumbled into the phone.

Affirmation crackled into the ear piece.

Fairly liked to confine wet jobs to the witching hour. Even later. Things went smoothly that way. Professional killers are almost always meticulous, though Fairly didn't see himself as a killer. He thought himself an expediter. It was his job to see that business was well-oiled. He might drive a visiting businessman to the airport in a limo one day, and retire a competitor the next.

Tonight he had an early retirement plan for Cox Delaney, though the plan was noticeably short of benefits.

"You've been uneasy about something lately," Cherie said, laying next to him in the king size Select Comfort bed he'd bought for her a year earlier when she'd turned twenty-nine. It had immediately relieved lower back pain, exacerbated by pregnancy.

"What makes you say that?" he asked.

"Oh, you try to mask it, but I know."

"The transparent thing."

"Of course."

A grandfather clock could be heard striking the half hour. Cherie wriggled her toes against the satin top sheet. A single down comforter was all they would need to keep warm. Tina and Tonya were once again in the arms of Morpheus.

"Are you going to talk to me, or not?" she finally asked, tiring of his silence.

"I am. Just not now. I'd like to get you and Pudge together, perhaps over fettucini Alfredo and a Zinfandel. You two are the best sounding boards a man ever had. That's my best chance to work through what I have to work through. Deal?"

"No. Never. Not in your lifetime."

"Why for not?"

"Lousy menu. Now, if it were Perigord truffles, with a fabulous Chateau d'Yquem, the king of Sauternes, and perhaps a little foie gras and pate, then you'd have a deal, Coxy."

"Frenchy to the core, aren't you Devereaux?"

"Mais, oui.".

Always meticulous, Fairly set himself up against a white ash tree, and surveyed the Norman-style mansion occupied for the moment by the Systems Analysis Director of High Data Associates. His wife and the two babies. While this kind of

9

termination was rare, sometimes there isn't a choice. Fairly accepted that. He might not like it, but you march to the orders of your superiors, or perhaps become the victim of termination yourself. Delaney must have really screwed up, Fairly figured. Probably went into business himself. Espionage. It happens.

Tomajac was already heading toward the left, around the garage, in back of the wash room, where he would enter the gathering room with a thoughtfully provided key. With any luck, his entry into the master bedroom would be silent and undetected. The custom silenced Bullpup would do its work. Two people would die. Fairly didn't like that. He felt there was no need to off the woman. He had been told, succinctly, "…no loose strings."

So the two of them would die. In their beds. The babes would be spared. Thank heavens for small favors. Fairly might have balked at wet work that involved infants.

Fairly muttered into the cellular phone. It crackled back. They were mere minutes away from carrying out the mission. Then they could go home and sleep. With less than five years until retirement, he figured he could put up with the occasional annoyance the job sometimes included. Two million dollars in retirement money masks a lot of annoyance.

Randy loved to spoon. Her new suitor, Pudge Elliot, the rich dentist of her dreams, seemed to like it too. She labored her mind overtime to try and find a strategy to snare the lanky three time loser. She worried that she was not winning the battle. Elliot had been remote at dinner. Chinese take out. One thing Randy didn't do was cook. She was no more competent with oatmeal than she was with beef Wellington. She often burned TV dinners in her little apartment. No wonder they saw her a lot at Burger King.

She knew Elliot liked her. Especially her tits. The classic tit man. No doubt about it. Men were such children. So easy to manipulate. It was almost laughable the way she had played him like a cheap fiddle at a mutual friend's cocktail party. As easy as spreading catnip with a shovel.

"What's a matter, hon?" she couldn't hold it any longer. She had to feel in control. Silences frightened her.

"Something's wrong," he said, adjusting the covers.

Now she was really worried. She had to get the upper hand again.

"What, honey?"

"Coxy. Something bad is wrong."

"What do you mean?" she could barely contain her sigh of relief.

"I don't know what I mean. We've been friends forever. He's the worst actor in the world. He couldn't mask a fart. Something has happened, and I haven't the slightest idea what."

"What did he say?"

"Not much. Wants to do lunch. Guess I'll know then. God, if it's something to do with Cherie. They're the nearest thing to a brother and sister I'll ever have."

In spite of innate cynicism, Randy Duran was actually growing fond of Pudge Elliot. She'd have to watch that. You can't surrender the upper hand. Fondness, she had found, is a weakness that usurps advantage. Now that she was past thirty, perhaps she was beginning to soften up.

Naw.

"Turn around," she murmured huskily. "Randy can make you better."

*   *   *

Tomajac had what he called "Indian feet," perfected in Southeast Asia, among other places. Without the slightest sound he was inside the gathering room. Another eight yards, and he would reach the foyer. Just around the corner would be the master bedroom. Some technicians made the mistake of charging like a bull in a china shop. Tomajac considered that artless. Also dangerous. Nowadays, homeowners were armed to the hilt. More than one intruder had been aerated by high-powered fire from the likes of a 357 magnum. Not a few spent hours on the range, perfecting their marksmanship.

Most pros used a well-balanced hand gun, for quickness. Not Tomajac. He liked maximum stopping power, high-level accuracy, and outright intimidation. Many of his targets froze, their little pistols useless when they saw his Bullpup.

A man and his tools.

Fairly waited patiently. He wouldn't hear a thing. Neither would the neighbors. Covert. That's the way you executed a contract. Not to mention the mark.

A Dodge Caravan lumbered down Woodbury. Probably a domestic heading home for the night. The van was heading toward the high school. Crickets were soundtracking the night with their time honored symphony. It was balmy, in that way the Great Lakes could be in the last couple of weeks of spring. A three-quarters moon was too low in the night sky to much illuminate Fairly, but he eased around the tree nonetheless.

Once he'd accompanied Tomajac on a procedure. He'd nearly lost his stomach. He much preferred directing the show and acting as a lookout. The only thing that made him nervous was the waiting. He trusted that Tomajac would make short work of the assignment. Gazing up at the home, Fairly could see that the house was completely dark.

As smooth as butter, Tomajac entered the master bedroom. Within milliseconds he produced three nearly soundless plinks with a squeeze of the semiautomatic. The bullets pounded into the mattress.

Something wrong.

The bed was empty.

Had he been compromised?

He frantically surveyed the room. A penumbra encased space that showed not a sign of life.

"I think you're addicted."

"Am not."

"Are too."

11

"One can never have too much Death."

"You're the worst chocoholic I've ever known," said Cherie. "And that includes my father."

They were sitting in the attic, above the garage, faint illumination from a street lamp down the way streaming through the mullioned windows; all they needed to eat their umpteenth helping of ice cream. Unable to sleep, Cox had wanted to search boxes of childhood keepsakes for a book about a tugboat. Since the attic had no light fixtures, he was using a penlight to check titles. "I think it was called Scruffy the Tugboat, but I'm not sure."

"If you still have it, it's there," she said matter-of-factly. "You've probably kept your first diaper."

"Think I'm a pack rat, do you?"

"What do you think?"

"I think I'm a collector."

Cherie Delaney smiled at her husband. Sometimes she couldn't believe her happiness.

When you have been in his business for awhile, you develop keen hearing that would rival a piano tuner's. Tomajac was no exception. He could sense conversation, before he actually heard it. From somewhere distant in the six thousand square foot house.

Into the hunter mode.

Fairly continued to lean against a tree. No more traffic came down Woodbury. A street lamp down the street was partially obscured by a chinaberry tree. The position of the house and the size of the parcel it sat on made it extremely unlikely that his position would be seen. He began to wonder what was keeping Tomajac. It should be a quick, surgical hit.

Better call in. They liked play-by-play contact.

"Do you have any plans for this attic?" Cox asked his wife, as he continued to rifle through his old children's books.

"Yes, actually. The exposure is fantastic. I'd like to make a studio out of it. I took art classes in high school, and have always thought I should pursue that sort of thing."

"I could finish the room, install track lighting, and you could hire a decorator to make the room your own special place."

"I'd like that."

Cox frowned, barely visible in the soft incandescent/moonlight mix.

"What's the matter?"

"It's not there. Scruffy's not there."

"Oh, no. Pack rat failure."

Tomajac was getting closer. You can't elude the true hunter. The true hunter homes in like a smart missile and finds his prey. This was a game. Tomajac loved the game. And to think that they paid him for this. Paid him to off a cheating asshole. Life couldn't be better.

Now he distinctly heard voices. Above. Climb the stairs. These hoity-toity, presumptuous spiral staircases. Well, the spiral wouldn't do any good. Tomajac could hear them just fine. Still some distance away. So what. Stalk the prey. Stalk the prey. Bead in. Plink.

Really quite simple.

* * *

Next time, Fairly decided, they would use headsets. The technological age, for God's sake. With a headset, he could keep in constant contact with the operator. Tomajac wouldn't like it.

So what.

Tomajac was inside the attic.

The piercing scream.

Eyes adjusted to the light, Tomajac squeezed a message of death into the screaming figure. A star burst of red spread over the chest. The screaming was suffused, muffled, dragged into a moaning plaint.

Cherie Devereaux Delaney sank to the floor, as the red river of life poured and drained to the hardwood surface.

The momentarily startled Cox Delaney threw himself at the attacker, grabbing onto the semiautomatic rifle. With incredible swiftness, Tomajac wrenched the Bullpup out of the hands of the enraged husband. He squeezed two rounds into Delaney's side before Delaney could club him with a forearm.

Tomajac sank to the floor, a crumpled, sleeping ball.

Bleeding like an open spigot, Cox Delaney ran from the room.

\#

CHAPTER 2

September 2, 1996 Labor Day
McAllen, Texas

Patrice Orosco arose to the ding dong song of her new electric alarm clock radio. Birthday gift. First the dings, then the conjunto music of Flaco Jimenez wafted over the ether. Her sister Yolanda's choice of going away presents would help her in her new job. Lord knows, she'd have to arise early. In Cleveland. She still couldn't believe she'd agreed to report to the Plain Dealer, located in "The Mistake on the Lake."

Her friends couldn't understand it, either. Her parents flat ordered her to forget it. The Daily Oklahoman had also beckoned. The Baltimore Sun would have hired her in a minute, according to Mel Dones, her advisor at the University of Texas, at San Antonio. He was close to the managing editors of all three papers. Strangely, the San Antonio Express News had shown no interest whatsoever. Could be because Dones had once punched out their managing editor, an irritating gentleman by the name of Quick.

Jimenez, accompanied by Radney Foster, were in the turnaround. Patrice moved languidly to the edge of her childhood bed, and listened closely to the lyrics:

> Sin tu amor es como mi conciencia
> Sin tu amor no me deja dormir
> Dime que es falso, vida mia
> Sin tu amor me voy a enloquecer

Patrice loved the song, Jealous Heart, by Jenny Lou Carson. It kind of spoke to her. It explained her life. Gave her a sense of closure. Perhaps, her own jealous heart had sent Pablo to his death. She couldn't shake the feeling. Pablo Morales was dead. He'd left in a rage when she announced she'd be going to school in San Antonio. Why should she stay? Pablo was seeing other girls. She wanted commitment. Not playing the field. He wanted to be sure of their relationship. Give it time.

So she enrolled at UTSA, became an avid Roadrunner fan, played on the tennis team, and concentrated her studies in the Department of English, Classics, Philosophy and Communications.

Two weeks after her matriculation, he was dead, wracked in pieces, enveloped by the crunched steel of his Ford F-150 pickup.

Jimenez and Foster closed out with the English verse:

> Jealous heart, oh, jealous heart, stop beating
> Can't you see the damage you have done?
> You have driven her away forever
> Jealous heart, now I'm the lonely one.

14

Now, four years later, she had to join the real world. College was history. Armed with her BA in journalism, she had become serious in mid-July about finding employment. The usual course was to work for a small paper. Patrice managed to bypass entry level employment by selling some three dozen articles to various magazines, some of them major, in her four years at UTSA. She'd won awards. Made money. Been there. Done that. The life of a freelancer was not what she wanted. She longed to hone her skills with the crucible of deadlines. The chance to have a mentor. Mel Dones emphasized that above almost everything.

It was her choice. Dones was emphatic about that. At the same time, he hinted strongly that the Plain Dealer would be her best bet. "Cleveland is the emerging city in the so-called Rust Belt," he'd told her. "They've got the Rock and Roll Hall of Fame and Museum, a new ballpark for the Indians, and I know you love baseball; Jacobs Field, The Jake, as they say. There's the Terminal Tower, the Tower City Center, Gund Arena, where the Cavs play. I know. I know. You are a Spurs fan. Habitue, of the Alomodome. So root for the Spurs when they come to town. Nobody will kill you. At least if you don't make a nuisance of yourself."

"Mel, I just don't know," she'd sighed. "It's a long way from home."

"I'm not trying to influence you, now. Far from it. I'm just being practical. There's the Great Lakes Science Center. The Cleveland Museum of Art, The Western Reserve Historical Society, with a Napoleonic collection that is second to none. And you like old cars. Only girl I ever knew who drove a Model A Ford."

Patrice laughed. "That was two years ago. I sold it."

"Well, you like 'em. And the Crawford Auto-Aviation Museum has every old car in the world, practically. I'm talking cosmopolitan city, Patrice. Home of the world-famous Cleveland Orchestra. But the best reason for choosing Cleveland as your first real newspaper job is the fact that the Plain Dealer is a great newspaper. And Jonathan Tubb will take care of you. I guarantee it. I'm not trying to influence you, remember."

"Mel, you'd try to influence a dining room table."

"Never. On that I'd draw the line. A hutch, maybe."

And so Patrice Orosco accepted a position as a feature writer on the Plain Dealer. "I won't try to stop you, Mija," Ruben Orosco finally told his oldest daughter, coming to grips with the situation. "I couldn't, I'd guess."

Patrice flashed her blinding smile. "Oh, Papa. You are the one who always told me I could conquer the world!"

"Yes! It is our proud heritage! Conquistadors!"

She would be leaving the next morning, rumbling north in her Jeep Cherokee, a 1488 mile drive from San Antonio. She'd leave McAllen that evening, after Labor Day festivities at her father's restaurant. She'd spend the night as the guest of Mel Dones and his wife.

Ruben Orosco was born on May 19, 1944, in McAllen, Texas, a war baby; a "bohunk," to a German mother and a Mexican field worker father. The father, Manuel, dead now just eighteen months, was a native of nearby Reynosa, a charming Mexican city of a quarter million souls, just over the Rio Grande river, eight miles from McAllen. Ruben grew up trilingual. To this day, he maintained mastery of English, German and Spanish.

His mother, Stella, a taciturn lady of a certain amplitude, arrived in America in 1936, from Argentina. She, too, spoke Spanish fluently, as well as her parent's native German. She learned English late in childhood, and had a pronounced, though hard to define accent. She was still very active, at seventy-two, and oversaw the hospitality at Padre Orosco's. Ruben had actually named the restaurant after his father, a fact that had made Manuel very proud to his dying day.

A stint as an army cook during the ill-fated Vietnam War led to extensive study in hotel/restaurant management, and later cooking school.

Ruben opened Padre Orosco's in 1975. It was wildly successful from day one. The entire family worked the eatery. Well, with one exception.

Patrice loved her mother. In some ways, Audrey was distant. No question. She married Ruben to get out of her family. That happens. Then she spent the years after the marriage trying to distance herself from her new family. And yet, when the chips were down, Audrey Orosco was always there. For everybody. In ways that Patrice could never quite understand, Papa Ruben seemed not unhappy with the arrangement. Many times, Patrice had reflected on the truism that no one knows what goes on inside a marriage except the partners.

Vitally interested in the art world, Audrey Orosco became a world traveler nonpareil. With her husband's money, it hadn't been a problem in years. Lately, she'd begun to make money brokering art deals. That seemed to be leading to a decision to open an art gallery.

Patrice finally escaped the solace of her canopy bed. Her room was decorated in eclectic teenager, not yet readjusted now that she was twenty-two. Posters. The New Kids on the Block still occupied a corner. Hammer had his spot. So did Garth. The poster she was most proud of, however, was Tish Hinojosa. Something about Tish's singing. And the lady was gracious. After a UTSA concert, Hinojosa had been most kind to Patrice, the hospitality coordinator. Patrice had seen celebrities up close before. Many were distant, or outright rude. Not Hinojosa.

Her room was practically a greenhouse, to boot. A lover of plants, Patrice Orosco especially admired cacti. She had a crown cactus, a rose-plaid cactus, the pale green Mexican brain cactus, a rattail cactus, a bishop's cactus, a star cactus, and an old man cactus; all from Mexico. From Argentina, she had the peanut cactus. Alas, these she would leave. They would not see Cleveland. A new wave of sadness passed through Patrice. She was still not sure her decision to go to Cleveland was the right one.

A tap on her door. That would be Yolanda.

"Yo, Pat.".

Patrice hated to be called Pat. It made her cringe. This her eighteen year-old sister knew. In spite of that, Yolanda would test the envelop from time to time. The way she got her name was sacred to Patrice. Grandpappy Manuel took Grandma Stella to the Metropolitan Opera in New York. Stella had been with child for four months. It was December 4, 1943. Stella had been exposed to the coloratura repertory at a very early age. Manuel's young wife was ecstatic. So was Manuel. When Patrice Munsel made her debut as Philine in Thomas' Mignon that night,

Manuel Orosco fell in love with opera and the eighteen-year-old soprano. Manuel and Stella would have just the one child, Ruben. As a small boy, Ruben agreed to name his first daughter Patrice after the star, and the memory.

"Yol."

"Mom wants us to pick her up at the museum. Seems she ran out of gas again. My car is dead, so I guess it's your Cherokee. She'll be ready in about an hour. She coasted into their parking lot, then went to the meeting. Didn't want to wake you, so she waited to call until now." Audrey had a certain susceptibility to empty tanks. She seldom remembered to fill up. Mostly, Ruben picked up the pieces.

"We can head to the restaurant from there, then."

"That seems to be the plan."

A few minutes later, the shower gently massaged her aching back. Patrice had taken up late night jogging with the realization that her tennis career was over; at least on a competitive level. She had had some success with the Roadrunners at UTSA. Now the pounding of the road seemed to be aggravating a back condition that had plagued her for years. She surveyed her body in front of the full length mirror that graced her bathroom. Ruben Orosco allowed his daughters to decorate to their own specifications. Patrice color coordinated everything. Blue ruled the place.

Patrice was gratified that her body was hard, lithe, slim, and with a certain musculature. Soft females? Patrice couldn't buy it. The human body was made to be hard. Her hispanic and her teutonic forebears had been hard of body, though she acknowledged the German females were often kind of well-endowed. "A little fat," she'd once remarked. Grandma Stella only laughed. "Well upholstered, Liebchen."

She liked her body. Five foot seven, small breasted, but that was okay. Some men even preferred that. Dark hair, brown eyes, a full mouth; others had called her strikingly beautiful. For herself, she dared not say. One boy on campus had insisted on calling her Queen Quetzalcoatl. It amused her to picture herself the wife of the great feathered serpent god of the Aztec and Toltec cultures. What Patrice knew for sure was that beauty today, was faded looks tomorrow. She would have to find a workout regimen once she arrived in Cleveland...

A few minutes later, Patrice turned the heavily loaded Cherokee onto Nolano and cruised to the 1900 block, where the McAllen International Museum contained a terrific Mexican folk art collection, among other things. Audrey's Volvo sat crookedly in a parking spot near the street. Testament to its empty fuel reserves. Audrey, herself, was nowhere to be seen.

"Want me to go find her?" asked Yolanda.

"Naw. I won't get to see this place for awhile. Think I'll go in. Come if you want."

The girls caught up with their mother near the Earth Science Gallery.

Yolanda was in many ways, a less formed Patrice. Not a few people had recognized one sister or the other, even though never having met, thanks to an acquaintanceship with the other.

The former Audrey Meadows (same as the actress) on the other hand, was California bred, with sandy hair, and quite pretty, but perhaps not classically

17

beautiful in the sense that her daughters were. Her father built bridges for a living, and though he himself had grown up in warm Southern California, had joined the Winter Texans as soon as he retired. That eventually led Audrey to school at Baylor. It was while visiting her mother and father, wintering in McAllen, that she met the dashing Ruben Orosco. It was love—a curious love to be sure—but love nonetheless, at first sight.

"I really do think that gas gauge is on the fritz," Audrey Orosco said with a certain bit of petulance. "Your Daddy really should fix it for me."

"All gas gauges go on the fritz," Yolanda said.

"They do?" asked Audrey.

"Oh, yes," said Patrice, winking at Yol. "Especially when you fail to feed them."

"Oh, my," Audrey said. Was that alarm in her voice?

The three ladies walked across the parking lot to what Yolanda liked to call the Patricemobile.

"Maybe some of the cousins will bail out your Volvo," Patrice remarked.

"Oh, dear. Are they going to be there?"

"Yes, Mama. Everybody's going to be there. They all have to say bye bye to Patrice. Though, frankly, I think it's stupid. She'll be back inside of three weeks. Mark my words."

"You're a lot of help, Yol," said Patrice.

"Your Dad's people all think I'm such an idiot. A..."

"Gringo?" Yolanda supplied.

"Perhaps Grandma Stella doesn't think that," Patrice laughed. "She probably thinks, oh, I don't know..."

"Verruckt," Yolanda supplied.

"I was gonna say dummkopf," Patrice said, "but what do I know."

"Probably nothing," Yolanda said. "Verruckt is the right word. Crazy."

"Let's talk about something besides my in-laws," Audrey sighed. "That's a troublesome enough subject to think about, let alone verbalize."

Patrice steered into the parking lot of Padre Orosco's, on North Main Street. Some of the Orosco cousins' eclectic mix of Low Riders and other chariots were already lined up in back, where employees parked. They would be all too glad to gas up the Volvo and drive it back. To a man, the male cousins were tinkers, some gifted, some suspect. But all could gas up cars.

"What is Dad serving at this bash?" asked Yolanda.

"Algo que comer." Patrice replied.

"Funny. Real funny. Like what? Hay algo de particular?"

"Albondigas con arroz. Alcochofa. Maiz," Patrice replied.

"On the cob, I hope," Audrey said. "And I hope he has mayonnaise for the artichokes. I hate butter so. That is, on artichokes. Butter just isn't civilized on artichokes. On corn, yes. Doesn't his people know anything?"

They entered the rear door of the restaurant. Out front, they were busy with Labor Day diners. It was in the private, back room, where the family would dine, and say farewell to the pride of the Orosco's, Patrice Maria.

Ruben Orosco hugged his daughters first, lingering over the departing Patrice a little longer. Then he held his wife in a tight hug. Audrey seemed to melt into his arms.

The spacious back area of Padre Orosco's was overflowing with relatives, over forty in number. The age range was awesome. From babies still swaddled, all the way to the very elderly. About eighty percent were of Mexican heritage, the rest Germanic.

Grandma Stella was in her element. She had, of course, mastered many hispanic dishes. One of those, Albondigas con arroz, actually originated in Peru. She also had a number of German and Yiddish dishes prepared, including a number of wicked blintzes; some with cheese, some fruit, and one in particular, featuring strawberry, that was always wolfed down by young and old alike.

Patrice sought out two of Ruben's cousins, brothers by the name of Alex and Jose. They seemed the best bets to expedite the problem with Audrey's car. She quickly explained the problem. Amused smiles played across their lips. Alex pointed to Jose. "Entiende todo cuanto se relaciona con la mecanica."

"It's just out of gas, boys. No big breakdown."

"Vaya!"

"You know Mom. They called her ET, even before the movie? Empty Tank."

"Debemos irnos! El caro!"

Alex and Jose skipped happily out the back, happy to show up the loco wife of cousin Ruben.

Ruben Orosco finally had his oldest daughter alone. With full bellies, the group was dancing to salsa music. At least the young, uninhibited ones. The older members watched silently. Alone with their thoughts, a kind of Hispanic inscrutability.

"You know I'm against this move of yours," her father finally said. "What am I supposed to think? Descuide Ud. que no le pasara nade?"

"You've made it perfectly clear, Papa, what you think of the new job. And don't worry, nothing is going to happen to me! I'm a big girl. You gave me the tools, Papa. You gave me the tools. You've trained me from day one to tener buen exito. You sent me to college. You encouraged me all the way. Who was it who held me in the night when Pablo died? It was you Daddy. It was you!" Tears fluxed down her beautiful face. "And now, would you hint that I am not up to such a life choice? That I am somehow, indigno?

Now they were both in tears. "Vaya con Dios, Mija. You are, of course, right. As your grandmother might say, "...in den Zwanzigern sein. To be in one's twenties. I believe in you, my daughter. It's just others I do not necessarily believe in. Creo que no. It is a cruel world, Patrice. Cruel world. There are monstruos out there."

Patrice hugged her father. "I'll stay in touch, Papa. I will."

"With that in mind, my daughter, I have this regalo for you. A phone card. I will send you lots of phone cards. And you will call your old Papa. Please. Puedo contar con Ud.?"

"You can count on me Papa," she said softly. "You can always count on me."

Patrice Orosco left for San Antonio three hours later, deluged with warm fuzzies from the doting crowd of folks who loved her from the very center of their souls.

Alex and Jose revived Audrey's Volvo. Gas, of course.

Yolanda actually cried as she hugged Patrice. Then she looked embarrassed. Audrey shook her hand. Her handshake contained five, hundred dollar bills. Then she kissed her daughter. "I'll be visiting the Cleveland Museum of Art next month, honey. We'll eat at the Palazzo. I always do when I'm in Cleveland."

"Okay, Mama."

"And don't listen to your father. I've decided you'll be just fine."

Patrice found it hard to keep her eyes dry. Affirmation. Maternal affirmation. Her heart filled with gratitude.

Grandma Stella leaned into the driver's side window. "Now, remember, Liebchen. Don't neglect eating. You are anything but fett. You can't spare a single pound."

"Yes, Grandma Stella. I'll eat. I don't know what, but I'll eat. Eine feine zunga haben."

"Yes! Yes! That's the spirit! To be a gourmet! I'll ship you some fine German sausage! You love German sausage!"

Patrice licked her lips. "I'll miss you, Grandma Stella. I'll really miss you."

"And I you, Liebchen."

Tears streamed down the old woman's face.

Patrice had to get out of there. Quickly. It was getting too much to bear. What had she gotten herself into, going all the way to Cleveland, Ohio?

It was a hundred and ninety-three miles to Mel and Martha Dones' house. Less than three hours and a speeding ticket later, she arrived in time to be taken out to dinner.

"At your favorite spot, I dare say," Mel Dones said.

"Mine, too," added Martha.

#

CHAPTER 3

It had been gently raining, the smell of ozone wafting through the late summer breeze by the time Patrice arrived at the outskirts of San Antonio.

The Tower of the America's loomed in the skyline like the Colossus of Apollo at Rhodes, bathed in the dwindling daylight like a deliberately underexposed photograph.

Mel Dones drove them in his Lincoln Continental, keeping up a patter of nostalgic whimsy as he parked the car just off Commerce Street.

Mi Tierra Cafe was crowded. Located at 218 Produce Row, in the heart of Market Square, the place was known as the "Granddaddy of Mexican restaurants." It never closed.

A Mariachi band serenaded the guests. A three dimensional mural by Jesus Garcia in the west dining room where the Dones' and Patrice were seated after the customary wait, depicted Henry Reed, the paterfamilias of the family, and sire of the owner of the Old San Francisco Steakhouse; General John "Black Jack" Pershing, Pancho Villa and Emiliano Zapata.

Upon reflection, Patrice decided something light would be in order, considering the bounty served at her father's place earlier in the day. "Quiero comer algo ligero," she said to the waiter.

It took but a few moments. Chalupa Compuesta, a bean and cheese chalupa, topped with guacamole, accompanied by an enchilada and rice seemed to do the trick. Dones, always a heavy eater, chose the Steak a la Tampiquena, an eight once ribeye, with guacamole salad, green chicken enchilada, refried beans and the ever present tortillas, served inside a warmer. Dones, like his wife, was rail thin, wiry of muscle, and unbelievably strong. Martha had been an NCAA gymnastics star. Both could put the food away without gaining a milligram. She nearly duplicated her husband's order, but at the last moment chose the Mi Tierra Deluxe Mexican Dinner. It consisted of a beef steak ranchero, tamal, guacamole, cheese enchilada, crisp beef taco, Spanish rice and refried beans.

"You are about to embark on the adventure of your life, young lady," Mel Dones observed, after their food arrived steaming hot. He reached for the warmer and removed a tortilla, which he proceeded to butter. "There is simply no better way to get a perspective on the human condition than writing for a daily paper. You'll see everything. Hear it all. Feel emotions you've never known existed. Leave it to Carl Jung: 'Emotion is the chief source of all becoming conscious. There can be no transforming of darkness into light and of apathy into movement without emotion.' Write your stories with a clear eye to detail, and accuracy. But do not spare the emotion. Do not hide behind the dry twigs of fact."

"My father would agree with you and Carl Gustave."

"Of course," observed her counselor. "He has Toltec and Teutonic blood coursing in his veins. His genes understand the power of passion."

"That's why Mel got out of newspapering," Martha said. "Newspapers have abandoned passion. They often sneer at good writing. Especially local papers. What is often wanted today is McPaper. USA Today style newsspeak."

"Don't discourage the lass, Martha. You'll make her flee the newspaper wars."

"She has an advantage, Mel. You really do, Patrice," said Martha. "UTSA doesn't really have journalism students. What we have are educated students. When they are through, they know how to communicate."

"Come Ud. con gana?" asked their waiter.

"Tal bueno," said Patrice.

And good it was. Often a respite from her classroom work, Mi Tierra never failed to satisfy. They left with a bag of bakery goods for Patrice to take with her on the trip north.

"Let's walk some of this off," suggested Martha. "Anybody else feel like stretching?

"River Walk, anyone?" Mel Dones chimed in.

"What a great suggestion," said Martha. "Glad you thought of it."

"I'm game," said Patrice.

"Of course, we'll avoid Hooters," said Martha.

"Of course," laughed Patrice.

"Oh rats," Mel Dones muttered.

They left the Lincoln in a parking garage.

Descending a stairway, they were now below street level, along the San Antonio River, moseying along the famed River Walk. "You've got to ride a river boat again, Patrice. To not do that would be like eschewing jazz in New Orleans. Like ducking corn in Iowa. Dodging slots in Vegas."

"She probably gets the picture, Martha."

"Again, I'm game," said Patrice. "As long as we walk a lot. My tummy feels like a wholesale food warehouse."

Waiting for them to load was the river boat Angela, docked at the Paseo del Rio Boats ticket office, across from the Hilton. The San Antonio River runs from about four to twenty-five feet in depth. There are about thirty-four boats and ninety some drivers.

There were only about eight other passengers. The three of them got as far away from the commentating boat captain as they could. As they passed the Palacio del Rio, a wonder of modular construction, Patrice sighed. "I'm going to miss this town and its twenty-seven major ethnic groups."

"So fly back. Frequently. You can make enough money with your freelance writing to catch the Spurs now and then at the Alamodome," Mel Dones said. "And if you want to justify the cost, do stories on San Antonio and the Gulf Coast. Maybe you can even get Jonathan Tubb to spring for a trip."

Patrice continued to watch the passing points of interest, remaining silent.

"What are you thinking?" asked Martha Dones.

"I'm thinking that as much as I love South Texas, I need to get away. I need to know that I can make it in the outside world."

"That's what I've been trying to tell you," said Mel Dones.

"Oh, oh," said Martha. "Hooters. Don't look, Mel."

"I'm only looking at Tony Roma's, actually."

"Really? Then how do you explain the fact that you are looking left, when Tony Roma's is facing right?"

22

"Stereoscopic vision?"

*   *   *

After walking the entire perimeter of the developed River Walk, the three of them emerged topside on Commerce Street, and headed toward the River Bend Parking Garage. They passed several homeless people lurking in front of a cheap all night eatery, screaming neon persuading the hungry to test the vittles. "I think my parents have finally accepted what I'm doing," Patrice interjected between Mel Dones' comments about faculty politics. "They obviously wish I had changed my mind, of course. Mom has decided to visit Cleveland next month. It's hard to say if it is one of her regular forays into Museum Land, or if she added it to an itinerary just to check up on me."

"Does it make any difference?" Martha asked.

Patrice laughed. "Not in the least. The fact that she wants to be part of my support team suggests to me that she is taking this seriously."

"Exactly," said Martha.

On the way to the Dones' house, Mel took Alamo, passing the Alamo Plaza and the famous fortress itself.

"God, what a city," murmured Patrice with reverence. "Mi tierra. My land, my country, my hometown. Well, my adopted hometown."

Mel Dones had the kindness to not pass by the Alamodome.

It was one o'clock in the morning before Patrice managed to nod off to sleep. The guest room of the Dones house was a marvel of comfort. Even so, she slept fitfully. She dreamed of big lakes, big monsters and the curse of impossible deadlines. After what seemed like a six-week bed struggle, the alarm canceled whatever alpha waves continued swimming inside her head.

A breakfast of biscuits and gravy, sausage and eggs over easy fortified Patrice Maria Orosco for her journey. When she couldn't delay her departure any longer, she lingered briefly in front of the Cherokee, suddenly realizing she didn't quite know how to say good-bye. This wonderful couple had taken her under their wings in her Freshman year, right after Pablo's death. Without any fuss, they simply invited her into their lives. They had become a combination of second parents, older brother and sister, and best friends. You couldn't ask for more from your fellow human beings.

"Hang tough, kid," was all the emotional Mel could say.

"Mel," she uttered in someone else's shaky voice. Surely she was tougher than this. First, teary with her father. Now with Mel and Martha Dones. Get a grip, girl.

"I want postcards," Martha said. "And the occasional call. Don't be a stranger."

"Never," was all Patrice could say.

And she wrenched her body inside the Jeep and began the trip to the Western Reserve country of Ohio.

\#

CHAPTER 4

Wednesday, September 4, 1996 Cleveland, Ohio 11:37 p.m.

Cleveland Teachers Walkout is Averted: Negotiators headed off a school strike at least temporarily last night as district employees agreed to continue working while bargaining goes on. Students are to report to classes today."

> Scott Stephens and Patrice M. Jones
> Plain Dealer Reporters.

A new town is always an adventure in negotiation when cruising a four wheeler into the city limits for the first time. Without an onboard computer (such as truck drivers sport) finding an address is a bit chancy. Patrice Orosco found that out royally after locating the Cleveland Memorial Shoreway and getting off the Shoreway near Whiskey Island, close to the Cuyahoga River. The very name means crooked, and crooked the river is. She then cruised Division Avenue until it ran into River Road.

No Dick's Last Resort ("You Can't Kill a Man Born to Hug").

Jonathan Tubb would be waiting for her with keys to her new apartment. Food would be ready for her. Steamer's and chicken. With corn on the cob. Clam chowder. Her stomach rumbled.

She'd called from a truck stop on I-71, getting Mrs. Tubb. Jonathan took the phone, confirmed the obvious guess that she was hungry, and invited her to the place that had catered to legions of Cleveland Brown's fans before Art Modell broke the hearts of people all over Ohio. Thirty-five years into owning the team founded by Mickey McBride in 1946, and coached by the legendary Massillon High School and Ohio State Buckeye coach Paul Brown from the beginning through the 1962 season (Modell shocked Clevelanders on January 7, 1963 by summarily firing the coach many called a genius), Modell succumbed to greed and expediency, and slinked off to Baltimore.

Still no Dick's Last Resort.

Which meant food to the hungry, traveling, Patrice Maria Orosco.

Finding a convenience store, Patrice discovered that Dick's Last Resort was not, in fact, on River Road. It was on Old River Road. She was instructed to cross over the once fiery Cuyahoga River (the Shoreway turns into Main Avenue), take the offramp, and when she did she found Old river Road.

And Dick's Last Resort in The Flats.

Live music made the place jump ("No Cover! No Dress Code! No Rules No Class (ever)").

Patrice took an instant liking to Jonathan Tubb. The portly Managing Editor greeted her with a hug. "You are supposed to hug here," Tubb pointed out. After leading her to their table, he made arrangements for her dinner. "You made good time from San Antonio. Not so good from the truck stop."

"I got lost."

"Figures. Inside of a month, you will be an expert on Greater Cleveland. I guarantee it."

Patrice smiled wearily. "I'm sure you're right. At the moment, I don't think I could find my way around the corner."

"You won't have to. I'll lead the way to your new apartment. I hope it meets with your satisfaction."

"I'm not that particular. At least not at the moment."

The food arrived. Almost from the first bite, Patrice began to perk up. The clam chowder was excellent. The steamers almost indescribable. The chicken superb. The corn-on-the-cob would make you cry. There were even yams.

"I feel guilty bringing you out at this time of the night."

"Routine, my dear. Routine. Gloria would have come, but her dadblame mother dropped in at the last moment, just before your call. The biddy would show up at the deflowering of a virgin if she knew the starting time. Oops. Sorry about that."

"I'm not that much of a prude, Mr. Tubb."

"No, No. Don't call me mister. Call me Tubb. Everybody calls me Tubb. And I like it that way. I've earned every pound."

Patrice laughed. "Tell me about you and Mel Dones."

Now it was Tubb's turn to chuckle. "Mel Dones. God. What a guy. I'd have fallen for Martha if I'da just met her first. But that's okay. Martha introduced me to Gloria, and while we've had our problems, often concerning her mother, the rest, as they say, is history. I wouldn't trade the old girl for any woman in the world. I'd trade her mother in a New York minute. For anything, even a thousand miles of bad road. But, that's not what you asked.

"Mel Dones is, or was, a newsman with an almost lost touch for the story. Other journalists have a real problem getting the angle and the slant just right. Even the play. Dones knew just when a story would run out of poop. He knew when a source was equivocating; he knew how to unravel posturing; he could get unvarnished truth from a pathological liar.

"We were great friends. Still are. Thing about Mel is, if he likes you, he likes you. If he don't, watch out. You've got an enemy for life. And he don't forget. I guess I'm kinda the same way. Can't say I got it from Dones, just seems the right way to be. You know. Unwavering loyalty to those who treat you right. Constant vigilance when someone proves to be an asshole."

The house band took a break between sets. Patrice was getting full.

"I've sure eaten a lot the last few days. Dad pulled a shindig as a going away thing on Labor Day. Mel and Martha took me out to my favorite restaurant in the whole world. Now this. The food is going to make me come back again. I didn't know this sort of place could be this great."

"We'll do it again, as soon as Gloria can send her mother packing to haunt another one of her children."

"I'd enjoy that. Next time, my treat."

"We'll see about that. I'm awful fast at grabbing checks."

Again, Patrice laughed. She found it very easy to be in Jonathan Tubb's company. After she finished, and he paid, he walked her to the Cherokee.

Patrice followed Tubb's Buick LeSabre, rubbernecking at the Cleveland skyline. They passed Public Square, and near the Terminal Tower and Tower City Center; got a glimpse of Jacob's Field; managed a peek at Gund Arena. When they passed by the Plain Dealer building, Tubb honked and pointed. An electric, bolt-like thrill coursed through Patrice Orosco's body. They soon turned off Superior and jogged right onto Chester Avenue, which is also US 322. Chester spilled into Euclid Avenue, passing Case Western Reserve University on the right, and the world famous Severance Hall to the left, home of the superb Cleveland Orchestra, before turning right onto Mayfield Road, all the way into Cleveland Heights. The apartment complex was on the tree-lined Mayfield Road, near Alescis Imported Foods. Patrice pulled in behind Tubb in front of the loft townhouse.

"You don't have to stay here any longer than one month if you do not like it," Tubb said, as he escorted her to her building. "I kind of leaned on them. They wanted $650 for the two bedroom unit you specified. I got them down to $600. It has an indoor garage. That'll help when the weather turns cold."

"I've been kind of wondering about cold weather. It is kind of mild in South Texas."

"Mecca for Winter Texans," Tubb observed.

Tubb produced a key and let them in the loft townhouse unit, apartment number eight. It was an attractive building, perhaps eight years old. It appeared to be newly painted and well-maintained.

"Nice," Patrice remarked. "I like it. It helps that you have already had it furnished."

"Got to if you want to attract talent."

Patrice blushed.

"Do you like the style?"

"Sure. I told you I'm not that hard to please. Besides, oak is my favorite, which I told you, and you and the rental people obliged."

Patrice quickly checked the loft, the kitchen area, the bathroom, and the guest bedroom, finding it all to her liking. It even reminded her a little of the apartment she had maintained in San Antonio for her four years at UTSA.

"Let me help you unload your Jeep."

"I could use the help. I'm really bushed."

Patrice drove the Cherokee into her allotted spot in the covered garage. Tubb was waiting for her. They had the vehicle unloaded in a jiffy. It had taken her much longer, with Yolanda, to load it.

"I don't want to see you until Friday," Jonathan Tubb told her, as he prepared to leave. "You actually start Monday. On the payroll."

"I'll be in some time tomorrow," she answered.

"But I won't give you any work. Not until Friday. I want you to hit the ground running. By the way, you aren't the only Patrice we have."

"I know. I bought a Plain Dealer at the truck stop. Story about a teacher's strike."

"Nasty business. Let's hope it doesn't come down to that."

"You want me to write a feature about education? Is that it?"

"No. We got that covered. The only thing I might do is a story on voucher students at Hope Ohio City Academy. But I think you'll be too busy for that. Anyway, I'll tell you Friday what I want." Tubb's grin was infectious. "I'm serious. I want you rarin' to go. Newspapers are stressful places. I want you to find your rhythm. I don't want a burnout case, either. So, we'll see you Friday. Tomorrow, if you insist on looking around."

"I insist."

Suddenly consumed with nervous energy, Patrice put all of the belongings that made the traveling list away, in what she hoped were appropriate places. And if they weren't, she would simply rearrange at a future date.

She remembered a promise to call her father, but the phone would not be connected until the next morning. Unable to suppress the need to call, and to not leave Ruben Orosco up in the air, she found a pay phone a block from the apartment complex.

"Papa?"

"Mija! When did you arrive?"

"About three hours ago. I'm all moved in. At least, I think I am."

"You don't know?"

"Well, I put everything away. I hope I can find things. Maybe I'll rework it later. I wanted to feel at home."

"I've decided you'll do well, little one."

"You've been talking to Mama?"

"Of course. What do you think?"

"Well, Papa, I am going to make it. And I will be visiting often. I hope you will visit me here, in Cleveland."

"I might even visit the museum."

"Papa!" Patrice laughed. "You hate museums!"

"Perhaps, if the museum is located near my Patrice, I can learn to at least tolerate it."

"I love you, Papa."

"And I you, Mija."

A couple of minutes after talking with her father, Patrice collapsed on the futon thoughtfully set up in the main bedroom by the rental folks. It had been her plan to brush her teeth, take a shower, and don some nightwear. A momentary lay-me-down lasted until ten-thirty the next morning. Encased in rumpled traveling clothes, she slipped to the floor to greet the old morning.

"Boy did I sleep in," she yawned at the mirror.

For some reason the reflective device refused to picture Patrice the way she preferred to look. As the somewhat late Edmund Spenser uttered four hundred years ago, she mused, "Sleep after toil, port after stormy seas, Ease after war, death after life does greatly please."

A revivifying shower; briskness of toothbrush; coffee from powders; all worked their magic. Wide eyes. Alert. No food. Curiously empty belly. The late night repast from Dick's Last Resort obviously history.

Traveling a short way down Mayfield, Patrice found a Finast Supermarket in the 3600 block. She would have to start from scratch. Boy, would she. It took forty-five minutes to fill a shopping cart full of staples and a few items to make a complete dinner for several evenings.

At the checkout counter, a friendly redhead smiled a warm greeting. "Looks like rain," she said. "Wouldn't doubt it any."

"I don't know the weather yet," Patrice answered. "Guess I'll learn about it, though."

"New, huh?" The redhead was incredibly efficient scanning the grocery items.

"Just got in last night."

"Where you from?"

"San Antonio, and McAllen, Texas."

"I lived in San Antonio! I was there for five years. With my then husband. He left. So I left. Came to Cleveland to study law at CWRU. Working my way through. What brings you here?"

Patrice blushed. "I graduated in June. UTSA. Now it's my first real job, outside of working for my Dad."

"One forty-one thirty-seven," the redhead said, when the total popped up on the monitor.

Patrice counted out the amount with travelers checks, and a buck with change. She gazed at the checker's name tag. Norma. A box boy already had her groceries bagged. "It's like old home week," Patrice said with a smile. "A fellow South Texan."

Norma handed her a slip of paper with her address and phone number. Norma Darling. The address was the same as her own. Same complex. Apartment ten, two doors down. "If I can ever do anything for you, just let me know. Show you around. Introduce you to people."

"We live in the same building! How neat. I'll take you up on that. I've got to get my phone up and running today. I'll call you this evening. I assume you're off? They don't work you around the clock?"

An elderly black gentleman pushed a cart into Norma's station, followed by a young Asian housewife. "I get out of class at ten. Call me at ten thirty and we'll lollygag."

"I'd like that," said Patrice.

It didn't take long to put the groceries away. Huevos revueltos for breakfast took a little longer. Chorizo on the side. Some liked the spicy pork sausage mixed in with the eggs. Not Patrice. Perhaps, as a friend at UTSA had suggested, the breakfast wasn't exactly health food. Patrice laughed when she thought about what the Center for Science in the Public Interest would say about her morning repast. Oh, well. Granola the next morning. Time to check out the paper.

Patrice was greeted by a receptionist in an outer lobby. After announcing her presence to Jonathan Tubb, she was buzzed inside the frenetic building. A beehive of activity. Tubb was overwhelmed. The deadline for Friday morning's bull dog, the early edition, was less than three hours away. He seemed to bob in his chair behind the horseshoe. "Gimme a take-and-a-half," he shouted into a receiver. "Watch the slant. I'm tired of phone calls. Do it straight." A pause. "I know what you think, and I don't care. Keep bias outta here."

He grinned at Patrice. "Don't you wish I'd hired you for a beat?"

She laughed.

He grabbed another phone. "Is Theodore anywhere in the building? You don't know? Why don't you know? You know everything that ever happened anywhere in the Western Reserve. When you find him, tell him to get his ass over to the 'shoe." Slam.

The city editor, a short man named Blowers, leaned over, a sheaf of papers in his hand. He seemed to wish them on Tubb. "The budget changed," he said simply."

"Then do something about it! Send it to copy! I don't care if it's a lobster shift! Just do it!"

A very old, very small, elfin-like man glided precisely into the command center, known as the horseshoe because of its shape. The newsroom's open configuration of numberless desks, gave the impression of vast space. Patrice might have noticed the man had she not been on sensory overload. Tubb picked him up while he was still twenty yards away. His face lit up like a Roman candle. He boomed, "I knew you were here!"

"Can't stay away, not with you incompetent boobs running the place!" the elfin bellowed.

"Patrice, this curmudgeon is Theodore O'Reilly, who would tell you he's the best reporter who ever covered a beat."

"Damn straight," said O'Reilly, in a voice that would do Darth Vader proud.

"The Damon Runyon of Cleveland," Tubb added.

"At least," O'Reilly agreed.

"They retired him twenty years ago, and he's never noticed, in spite of getting paid zilch."

"What's money amongst friends?"

"Indeed. Very important, I'd say. You owe me a sawbuck. Remember your ridiculous bet in which you said Art Modell had too much integrity to sell us down the river? Where's my money?"

"In your dreams, Tubb. Wet dreams, maybe."

"Now, now, Theodore. There is a lady present."

"This the tomato you told me about?"

"The very one. The very one."

O'Reilly looked up at a precipitous angle and gazed straight into Patrice Orosco's face. "Va va va voom!"

"If you wish to get along with this scalawag, Patrice, you must call him Theodore. Never Ted. Never Teddy."

"If you are in awe of me, you can call me O'Reilly. As in Runyon, Reston, Considine, Cannon, Winchell. Buds, all." Was O'Reilly leering?

"Are you kidding?" Tubb snorted. "You were out of the business before they even started. Try Sam Clemens, if you are searching for contemporaries."

"Never heard of 'im."

"Patrice, Theodore is going to take you under his considerable wing, and walk you through all of your paces. He'll not only give you a thorough tour of the building, he'll accompany you on your journeys. Probably forever, because there's no getting rid of him."

"I know karate," said O'Reilly.

Patrice was grinning, from ear to ear. She said, "Then, let's go look this joint over, top to bottom."

She hooked her arm around O'Reilly's, and they glided away. The old reporter glanced at Tubb over his shoulder and winked. He said, "Sweep 'em off their feet every damn time."

The twins were cleaning up a finger painting mess. Piles of paint plopped to the desk top. Scrub it up. That was the rule in Miss Dandridge's room. Dandridge was an old-time, veteran teacher, nearing retirement age. Maybe two years more, and she would hang them up. No nonsense. Yet, she was reasonably playful. Well, you had to be with this age. There would be plenty of years to make them toe the line academically. Let them enjoy the educational experience, before things like SAT scores and GPA's clog the picture. But discipline was still king in Miss Dandridge's class. Listen to the teacher; do not hit anybody; respect other people's things; clean up your own mess. A substantial woman, badly abused by her father as a child, Miss Dandridge had about as much use for men as a miser for a March of Dimes canister. With a great head of silver hair, she was a handsome, if formidable looking woman.

With twenty-three students, Miss Dandridge had one of the smallest classes she'd had in years. The Thompson school, private all the way, bordered the Shaker Heights Country Club on Fernway Drive. The school had been around for sixty years, and was immaculate in every respect, with ivy covered walls, manicured lawns, and lush shade trees.

Tina Devereaux finished ahead of her sister, Tonya. That made her feel superior. "Tonya, get the lead out! It's in your shoes!"

Miss Dandridge could barely suppress a smile. Tina was a corker. Her identical twin was more serious in every way; she'd be bookish one day, Dandridge could tell. Meticulous. Things had to be just right for Tonya. Tina, on the other hand, was a straight ahead type, and if it wasn't right, well, so what.

"There, I'm done. And my side is cleaner!" Tonya retorted.

"All right, children," Miss Dandridge interjected. "Let's get ready. Bus students may go as soon as their station is clean. Make it quick!"

Children as whirling dervishes. Clean it up, and outta here.

Bus students soon scrambled aboard the lone yellow school bus. Most students either walked the few blocks to their homes, or were picked up by parents, sometimes doting parents in a limousine.

Maurice Devereaux's driver, a burly man, was waiting with the white limo. Tina and Tonya scrambled into the back. "I want the back back," Tina screamed.

"No, it's my turn," Tonya shrieked.

"Why don't you both sit in the back back?" asked the burly chauffeur.

"Because Tina will hit me," said Tonya.

Well hidden behind a somewhat generic conifer tree was a lone man. This was the third day of school at Thompson. He'd been there each day. Clutched in his hand was a prop used for disguise.

A lunch box.

As soon as the limo made its departure, the roughly dressed man appeared to head for the section of the Heights where most of the day laborers and domestics lived. This particular day laborer continued going. All the way to The Flats. Deep into The Flats. To an industrial section of The Flats not yet gentrified. You could sure wear out shoe leather that way.

The lunch box worked well again. A Shaker Heights radio car cruised by, barely noticing the man. They'd seen him all week. Workers have to work. And of course they pack their lunches.

Norma Darling didn't have a class at CWRU until seven. Home from her job at Finast, she zapped a TV dinner in the micro, which would serve as a very late lunch; she'd eat dinner out with friends after class. She changed out of her working clothes and into her student chic. She was in the process of flipping the television set to channel 23, and General Hospital, which was already in progress, when the phone rang. "Darling," she answered.

She listened for a few moments. "Then, why not come over early next week for lunch? I'm off Monday and Tuesday. I'll fix sandwiches or something. I don't mind, Randy. What are sisters for?"

After a few more ticks, Norma smiled and said into the receiver, "Then it's settled. Monday, noon."

Jonathan Tubb left the Plain Dealer building. He was disappointed that he had been too busy to reconnect with Patrice Orosco. He knew old buddy Mel Dones would be calling in the next couple of days. He wanted to make sure she would be ready to roll. He wanted, hoped, he could reassure Dones, especially since Mel's original reaction to Tubb's plan seemed to be that he was throwing her to the wolves. True, what he had in mind for Patrice would tax a neophyte. But with her track record as a freelancer, perhaps she wasn't so new to the game.

Time would tell.

She had one ace in the hole. Theodore O'Reilly. Maybe he was an old, old goat, but he could see that she got the job done.

Patrice downed the convenience store coffee, courtesy of Theodore O'Reilly, as they sat in her Cherokee at A J Mini Mart on Euclid. After getting the two bit tour of the Plain Dealer building, a tour that lasted all of five minutes ("You'll get to know this place all too well. Starting tomorrow," O'Reilly had muttered in a dismissive way), he'd insisted on her driving the Cherokee to points of interest.

At the North Coast Harbor, she was able to see the Rock and Roll Hall of Fame and Museum, and the Great Lakes Science Center. "Go take them in at your earliest convenience, otherwise you never will. People don't visit what is just down the street," O'Reilly had said. She glimpsed the "Grand Old Lady," Cleveland Municipal Stadium, scheduled for the wrecking ball in just two months. Next they walked around University Circle, which features more than fifty cultural institutions, with the Cleveland Museum of Art the centerpiece. They visited Public Square, where Patrice was awed by the Old Stone Church, which would celebrate its 176th birthday soon.

And of course the Terminal Tower, and Tower City Center.

Now Patrice was chewing on a slice of beef jerky with her coffee, sitting in the convenience store parking lot. O'Reilly had a pickled egg to go with his java. "This is what I like," he said, "a cheap date."

Something about the basso profundo delivery from this small elderly man caused her to laugh. "I'm sorry. I'm not laughing at you. Well, I am. I mean, you keep me in stitches."

"Better that than tears! Say, Seattle comes to town tomorrow. Maybe we can catch the game at the Jake! Your treat!"

"You know something? I'd like that!" she said, still laughing. "My treat, huh?"

"Ya. The Polish dogs. You couldn't buy a ticket if you wanted to. Always sellouts at The Jake. I got season tickets. Always have had, ever since Bill Veeck owned the Indians. We Clevelanders love our baseball, you'll find out. And we're gonna love our Browns again, by '99, when we get either an expansion team or an existing one. That damn Modell. At least we own the name and the colors. What's in a name? I hear you saying?"

"Ya, O'Reilly, what's in a name?" She chawed on the piece of jerky.

"They named the Browns after the coach, is what's in a name. Paul Brown. We did that before, here in Cleveland. The Indians used to be called the Naps, after Napolean Lajoie, who was their manager. Great player, too, powerful hitter. They were also once called the Blues, also the Forest Citys and the Mollie McGuires. They once played in the National League, when they were known as the Spiders. Before 1900. Before there was an American League. Tubb would say I remember it well."

Patrice let out an involuntary laugh.

"I'm not saying," he said, eyes sparkling. "Hey, would you like to go kick around The Jake? I can get you in!"

"What I'd really like to do is open a checking account. You have any suggestions?"

"Boy, do I! Head back to East Ninth Street. The Star Bank. Why, there's this moll in there, with gams a mile long, she has feet that look so neat, like she threw away her shoe in the summertime!"

Patrice, still laughing, steered onto Euclid and pointed the Cherokee toward the 2000 block of East Ninth Street, and the Tower Branch of Star Bank.

They arrived at 3:30 with just a half hour to spare before closing time. "You coming?" she asked O'Reilly when she'd parked the SUV.

"What? Stay behind? Miss that wench's heavenly legs? Besides, maybe I can get you a cheaper rate on your checks."

32

Patrice linked her arm in O'Reilly's once again.

The lovely bank employee of Theodore's dreams was nowhere present. After rubbernecking the entire visible working area of the bank, he turned to Patrice, wide-eyed. "See? See? What have I always said? When you want something, go after it! Now she's probably in Tahiti, a mai-tai in one hand, or perhaps in a maison de sante, an insane asylum in France, heart crushed to powder that I never showed up, and swept her off her feet. You never know about these things! It can go either way!"

Patrice opened up a Star Select Interest Checking Account.

Most park playgrounds in America are smaller than the private play area Maurice Devereaux had built for Tina and Tonya. There were monkey bars, jungle gyms, swings, a covered plastic ball pool, and a covered, all weather heated kiddy pool. There were balance beams, crawl tunnels, sand boxes and parallel bars. There was a kiddy car track, with gasoline powered miniature autos. And the *pièce de résistance,* a miniature riding railroad.

Tina and Tonya Devereaux couldn't wait to go outside and play. For the moment, reading readiness homework was the order of the day. Playtime came only when the work was done. No exceptions. Four days a week, it was piano practice. Piano lessons came on Saturday. Ballet lessons were Monday. Art lessons Tuesday. Sunday school and church were followed by a formal dinner in the dining room; full dress, no exceptions.

The rest of the time, Tina and Tonya were free to be little children, but always under the watchful eye of the nanny, Virginia Compton. The rather severe woman called it indirect structure, one of those new, experimental methods of child rearing that self-described gurus always seem to invent.

For now, Compton was drilling the girls on the first eight letters of the alphabet. Tina gripped a pencil in her small hand, trying hard to make a capital D, block style. Finally, in exasperation, she glared at Virginia Compton. "Why can't we go ride the train now?"

"You certainly can, as soon as you get to H. Your grandfather was most emphatic about that."

"I want a drink," said Tonya.

"You can both have some juice, as soon as you finish."

Tina tried to buckle down and get the job finished. She was very frustrated. Her right hand hurt, in a kind of kindergartner's version of writer's cramp. She finally shrieked, "I can't do this today! I can't!"

Virginia Compton was about to make a withering pronouncement, when Maurice Devereaux bounded into the room. A tireless man, always optimistic, Devereaux spotted the impatience of the small child wishing to play before the weather prevented it. It was rather cloudy, with rain imminent, according to the weather forecasters. Compton was about to draw Devereaux into her disciplinary strategy, when the silvered hair tycoon flashed his brilliant smile. "Girls, how about a train ride?"

"YES!" One word. Two voices.

Compton fumed.

Devereaux zoomed around the tracks, granddaughters, pigtails and grandfather stuffed inside the pygmy locomotive.

*   *   *

The comfortable house on Grand Road, just off Buckeye Road, had been home for more years than Theodore O'Reilly would ever admit to.

His Mary had decorated the house soon after its purchase, only three years after their marriage. Though she'd been gone for almost ten years, Theodore had not touched a thing. Forever it would remain a monument to Mary O'Reilly's impeccable taste. Theodore liked to be thought of as a man of the world; a rogue, really. But never once had he strayed from Mary. Never once had he wanted to. Some people are lucky in this life. They find their soul mate. Theodore O'Reilly thought of himself as one lucky man. He had found the woman of his dreams. Right next door. She'd been there all along.

He hadn't known it. At least not at first. He'd matriculated to Ohio State University, became a sportswriter for the student newspaper, and came home to the waiting Mary Kelly, not really knowing he had. His first clue came when she took him to a furniture store to pick out furniture. That was midway in his senior year. When he asked her what they were doing, Mary had simply said, "What do you think?"

The wedding was five months later. Mary Kelly always had said she would be a June bride. And that she would be Mrs. O'Reilly. This, of course, she said behind Theodore's back. "Never give a man a clue," her mother had always insisted.

Theodore loved being a ribald old man. He thrived on it. It was one of many tricks he used to prevent himself from traveling down that dusty road of deterioration old reporters seemed to take. Old anybodies, in Theodore's opinion.

But now, Theodore O'Reilly was upset. So he called his friend, and onetime protégé Jonathan Tubb. Gloria answered.

"Glory, that old goat home yet?" asked O'Reilly.

"You got that right, Teddy." Gloria Tubb was the only human being still on Earth who could get away with calling Theodore O'Reilly, Teddy. The other had been her older cousin, Mary, O'Reilly's late wife. "He sure smells like a goat."

"Well tell that so-and-so to get his carcass on the phone."

"He's sittin' in the hot tub, reading the New York Times. Serve him right to interrupt him at his crossword puzzle."

"Atta girl, Glory. Keep him in line."

"Have to. I'll take the cordless to him, Teddy. Are you taking care of yourself, these days?"

"No need to worry, Glory."

"Hear you've got a new kid under your wing?"

"That old goat of yours flaps tongue, does he?"

"Oh, always. He learned that from you, you know."

O'Reilly's stentorian tones erupted into a deep guffaw. "Get the goat, Glory."

When Jonathan Tubb took the phone from Gloria, he was greeted by an irate Theodore O'Reilly.

"I don't mind the assignment you are about to give Patrice, Tubb, but I don't like the way you want her to go about accomplishing the task. There is an element of danger. And you know it."

"I don't think so, but that's one reason why you are going to be her mentor, Theodore. Why you are going to be her shadow. That should prevent her from getting into trouble. And if it looks dicey, call those nephews of yours. That'll even any playing field."

"Tell you what I'm afraid of," O'Reilly said. "I'm afraid you are going to ruin a perfectly good candidate to become a force for the much maligned fourth estate. Also, there is no reason to put her in such an active position. I never have agreed with a journalist becoming a part of the story."

"I have a reason, Theodore. A very good reason. It involves a very good man. That's all I can say for now."

"This kid better not be hurt," said O'Reilly.

"I hardly think there is any real danger, Theodore."

"There better not be."

Since dropping Theodore O'Reilly off at the Plain Dealer, Patrice got busy with several more details involved with the move. She wanted a post office box; that she accomplished at the main Cleveland branch. Jonathan Tubb's people had already set up the utilities for her. No problem there. She did want cable, however, so this she managed to accomplish before the cable office closed. The Super had agreed to assist in letting the phone installer in. She wanted a jack in the bedroom. Another in the kitchen.

Now she was back home.

Call her mother. She might be home. You just never knew with Audrey. She wasn't. Only the answering machine was.

For the first time, she was really lonely. She now knew just three people in Cleveland, if you discounted the hastily introduced folks earlier at the paper. She picked up the Plain Dealer. Perhaps a movie would fill the bill, fill the emptiness that seemed to gnaw at her insides. Perhaps she could go to the Lakeshore 7, on East 226th Street, near the Lakeshore Shopping Center. Perhaps do a little shopping later, if they were open. If she hurried, she could catch The Island of Dr. Moreau.

Done deal. If she stayed around in this home that wasn't quite home yet, she just might contract cabin fever.

Rain splattered the windshield as she headed out Euclid for 222nd Street, on her way to Lake Shore Boulevard. She inserted a Tish Hinojosa tape. It was fitting that the tape was cued to the song, Looking for my Love in the Pouring Rain.

> There's a burstin' cloud above my head
> Need to find a hold on dryer land
> Didn't we ignite an eternal flame-
> Looking for my love in the pouring rain
> Looking for my love in the pouring rain

She couldn't help thinking of Pablo Morales. And the night that they met. In the pouring rain.

#

CHAPTER 5

Friday, September 6, 1996 6:30 a.m.

(Columbus)
Lawmakers Proposing White Take Over Schools: Two Greater Cleveland lawmakers say they will introduce legislation today to put Mayor Michael R. White in charge of the 70,000-student Cleveland school system.

> Mary Beth Lane
> Plain Dealer Bureau

Threatening skies. First thing the bleary-eyed Patrice Orosco noticed when she cracked the curtains upon awakening. "No need for this," she mumbled, reaching for a jar of instant coffee. "Better stop."

Then she looked at the mess on the counter from yesterday's breakfast and a hasty feeding after the movie. "Better clean this up before I have an instant kitchen midden." Get a grip, Orosco, she thought. Talking to yourself again.

If the rains came seriously, and wiped out the first pitch, at 7:05 p.m., Patrice would miss out on her first major league baseball game. A longtime fan of the minor league San Antonio Missions, Patrice had never been to the Houston Astrodome, once called the "Eighth Wonder of the World." Many a night she'd sat in the intimate ballpark at Highway 90 and Callaghan Road in San Antonio, roaring her lungs out. If only Mike Piazza had seen her! What a dream boat. Of course, she'd still been in high school when Piazza played in San Antonio. Papa had taken the girls regularly, all of their lives. Baseball. Just about the only thing that ever took Ruben Orosco's mind off of business. Same for Patrice. Well, basketball and baseball. In that order.

Her day with O'Reilly would begin early. He insisted on taking her out to breakfast at one of his haunts, before she reported to Jonathan Tubb at nine. Insisting he was a great cook, O'Reilly had maintained that only great cooks had the privilege of eschewing cookery. All others had to constantly practice.

After Patrice returned home from the movie the previous evening, and after a lengthy phone conversation with Norma Darling, Patrice did her midnight jog. "What a way to get mugged," Norma had said, upon learning of the plan, and refusing an invitation to join in. "You got guts, kid."

To which Patrice answered that she'd always taken midnight jogs in San Antonio, without incident. "Besides, Theodore O'Reilly and I have one important thing in common. We both know karate."

"Don't know the guy, but I hope he protects you. By the way, you'll like my sister. She used to be a little wild. Marriage settled her down, though. Married a dentist. Her little girl might have a chance to be seen by a specialist. I'll tell you all about it before Randy arrives if you want to come over a little early on Monday."

"Have a good time in Toledo," Patrice said as the conversation wound down. Norma was going with her new boyfriend to visit his parents over the weekend. She was understandably nervous. "It'll all work out."

"Thanks, I appreciate that."

It was going to be fun having someone to do girl things with. Patrice was deeply grateful for the lunch invitation on Monday. Only after hanging up did it occur to Patrice that it was odd to be lollygagging on the phone with someone only two doors down. They wouldn't do it that way in Texas.

At precisely seven, Theodore O'Reilly tapped on her door. He had his cherry red '57 Chevy parked out front, and insisted on driving. "Only way to alert my cronies that I'm there. You're gonna love the diner. Only problem is, I can't decide which one we're goin' to."

"Lead the way, Theodore."

O'Reilly turned expertly onto Prospect Avenue. When he parked the classic car in the 1400 block, he turned to Patrice, a warm smile playing across his features. "I wonder if you would do me a little favor, Miss Texas?"

"And what would that be?"

"I've been thinking. Since we're gonna work closely together, and get to know each other all too well, perhaps it would be best if we dropped a little formality. I would be proud to have you call me Ted or Teddy. And I'd like to call you Treece."

Patrice's eyes got a bit misty. "My grandfather, Manuel, called me Treece. The only one who ever did. I like it. You may call me that. And I think Teddy is a great name. Especially for you. You're kind of like a Teddy bear."

"I'm a bear, all right," O'Reilly said gruffly. "Besides," he grinned, "that will make everybody at the paper go bonkers. They know I'd bite their heads off if they called me Teddy. It's the art of intimidation, Treece. Control. Never lose it."

They were standing outside a diner. "Only two places I'll eat breakfast. A & B Diner, some ways down Prospect, eight hundred block, and here, at Ruthie & Moe's Midtown Diner. Get out of the Egg McMuffin habit, and I'll buy your breakfast a couple of times a week. Do me good to be seen with you."

"You're trying to spoil me," said Patrice.

"No, you'll spoil me. I may eat ten Polish dogs tonight at The Jake. All on you."

"You ever have huevos rancheros?"

"Not often enough."

"Then I'll have to make you some."

Soon they were seated in a window booth of the narrow diner, menus at the ready. "Order a lot," O'Reilly said. "First days can be murder."

Same frenetic news room. Same Jonathan Tubb, a regular Mexican jumping bean behind the horseshoe. "Get hold of a board member. I want reaction to Forbes' attack on the school talks. Do it now," he blasted into the phone. "And while you're at it, see if Stokes has any more to say."

Tubb smiled at Patrice, grinned at Theodore O'Reilly, if there can be a difference in facial expressions. "See you brought in my prize new writer, Theodore."

"She's ready to work. She ate right."

"Which means one of those diners of yours. I hear you. I wish I had a decent breakfast in my considerable belly, instead of the yogurt and granola Gloria made me swallow. Go ahead. Call me fat!"

"You're fat," said O'Reilly.

"Thank you. I needed that. Blowers?" he croaked across the expanse of computer-laden desks. "WHERE THE FUCK IS BLOWERS? COFFEE BREAK? I'LL GIVE HIM A BREAK! THE OBIT PAGE! BLOWERS! GET YOUR ASS OVER TO THE 'SHOE!"

The short city editor appeared, well, shortly, and settled silently behind the desk. Blowers glared at Jonathan Tubb.

"Whatsa matter, Blowers? Not up to the job?" Tubb bellowed.

Blowers continued to glare.

Tubb led the way to a conference room, off to the side. The walls were glassed, affording a perfect view of the working area. The Managing Editor barked into the phone a quick message aimed at holding all calls, even from the President. "Sharon Stone would be an exception," he said, by way of signing off.

When they were seated, Tubb glanced out at the crowded news room. Blowers was deeply engrossed in a mountain of copy. "You know? He's the best I've ever had as City Editor. A natural. But he has to be kicked in the butt every so often. He tends to coast." Tubb looked at Patrice for a few moments. "Patrice, do you tend to coast?"

Patrice eyed Jonathan Tubb levelly. "What did Mel Dones tell you?"

Tubb laughed. "That you give as good as you take. That you'd probably knock my block off if I ever felt I had to kick you in the butt."

"That about says it," Patrice said coolly.

"And he called you a bulldog. Actually, a mama bulldog. They can be vicious when the call comes for it. That's why I hired you. I want tough. I want caring. I want commitment to an issue. Whatever story you are on. I want fairness. I demand it. The Plain Dealer demands it. I happen to think it is the best damn daily paper in America. And I read the New York Overrated Times."

Theodore O'Reilly was giving his best impression of the late Sam Hayakawa's tam-o'-shanter-framed senate snooze.

"You can break in here, any old time, Theodore, to pep up our new friend here."

"You're doing fine; almost verbatim. I wrote that speech in ought...oh, never mind. Why date myself?"

Patrice laughed.

"You're dated, all right," Tubb agreed. "But, forgive me for the compliment, more like a fine wine."

"God! I hate it when you make nice!" O'Reilly bellowed. "Stay the same sour, fire-breathing fright monster I trained, or I'm outta here!"

"Is that a threat, or a promise!"

"Humph!"

"Patrice," Jonathan Tubb finally said, after the snickers died down a bit. "I'm going to give you an assignment."

"Ah!" she said, chin resting in the palm of her hand.

"And only one assignment. For all of time. When you complete this assignment, you will generate all of the rest of your stories quite on your own. That's what helps to make this paper great, when it comes to features. Our reporters are close to the community. They bring in an idea, we give the go sign, or the stop sign, as the case may be. That gives them a vested interest. Sometimes, of course, a newspeg dictates a feature story."

Patrice nodded.

"I want you to do a series of stories on the homeless."

Patrice had no reaction.

"At first, you will talk to experts. Write an overview."

That same level-eyed Patrice Orosco gaze.

"Then I want you to go underground. For a month, perhaps. Live on the streets. Live as if you were homeless. Experience the life. Feel the pains. Digest it. When you have finished the living research, and the features for the paper, a lucrative book deal awaits you. It is already arranged through a book editor friend of mine. He's seen all of your clips. It's a done deal. That is, if you approve. If you do not approve, there are garden society stories you can do. Or you can go back to old San Antone."

No reaction. Patrice continued to eye Jonathan Tubb.

"Well?" Jonathan Tubb seemed even more fidgety.

"Why didn't you tell me this from the very beginning?"

"Good question," O'Reilly rumbled.

"To which I have no good answer. It just seemed better this way. To take your measure, perhaps. But I think you'll jump for it."

A strange smile spread across Patrice Orosco's face. "Well, Tubb, if that is what you thought..." she patted Teddy's leg with her right hand, as she rose to her feet, and gave him a wink, "...then you were quite right."

"Great! That's great," Jonathan Tubb said enthusiastically.

"Only one thing," Patrice said, with a gigantic smile on her beautiful face. "You are going to rewrite my deal with the Plain Dealer. Fifty bucks more a week. And next time you have a scheme up your sleeve that involves Patrice Maria Orosco, heir to Toltec and Teutonic thrones, involve me in it at the very beginning. It's cheaper that way."

Jonathan Tubb was sputtering.

"She's got you by the short hairs, Tubb. Face it."

Jonathan Tubb continued to sputter.

#

CHAPTER 6

Friday, September 6, 1996 11:00 a.m.

Forbes Echoes Stokes' Attack on School Talks: For the second time in three days, an influential black leader has blasted Cleveland school officials for their handling of teacher contract negotiations.

George L. Forbes, president of the Cleveland chapter of the NAACP, yesterday echoed Rep. Louis Stokes' contention Tuesday that the district's negotiating posture was "heavy handed."

> Scott Stephens
> Plain Dealer Reporter

"I'd love to go with ya, kid, but I gotta get my dahlias going," Theodore told Patrice on the way out of the Plain Dealer building.

"Your what?"

"The Dahlia Society of Ohio. I'm a member. Tomorrow is our sixty-sixth annual show at Randall Park in North Randall. I've been to all of them. Gotta get my shit together, as you young people say. Dahlias take a lot of work. Look, just walk in there and start firing questions."

"I don't mind going alone. I'll just miss you, is all."

"Ah, they all fall for me, sooner or later. Usually sooner. I'll call ya this afternoon. No, I'll wait 'till I pick you up for the game. Maybe we can set up a plan for next week. Save some wild goose chases."

"Sounds good, Teddy."

With a gigantic roar, the cherry red Chev mowed its way down the road, an amused Patrice Orosco watching him zoom away as she stood at curbside in front of her building. Meanwhile she had a few moments to kill before her appointment with a Mr. Anderson at the Cuyahoga Metropolitan Housing Authority. The idea of starting there seemed sound to Patrice. Get some solid information on the state of affordable housing. Find out the reasons people were losing their homes, if in fact, that was what was happening. She might even start the series with a backgrounder on the difficulties of buying a home, or even getting into a rental property.

Once inside her apartment, Patrice flipped her small color TV to Regis and Kathie Lee on channel five. She decided against making herself a sandwich. It was too early for lunch, she figured. She could stop at a deli somewhere and buy something later. She went bored quickly, and switched to Donahue on channel three.

Talking heads. She killed the idiot box.

The cardboard condo had seen better days. Once the protective shield for an Amana refrigerator, it was now home to Oscar Somebody or Other. That's what Oscar called himself. He didn't know his last name, or if he ever had one. On the street, they called him Oscar No Name. He didn't like that. He had a name. First name, anyway. So he probably had a last name. He just didn't know what it was yet.

Now his mother was dead. She didn't last. That's what Oscar told people on the street. He was confused. He knew he was confused. He didn't know why Mama didn't last. Didn't she always say she'd be there for Oscar? As far as a father was concerned, Oscar knew some people who had fathers. Some had mothers. Some had both. He didn't feel bad about being one of those folks who didn't have a father, since mothers seemed to know more about food. If he'd had to have only a father or only a mother, he was glad he'd had a mother. She'd cooked many a meal in the occasional cold water flats they had lived in. Good stuff. Some of the restaurants she'd washed dishes for gave them food. That was good food, too.

Since Mama died, meals had become less frequent. He was excited when Mama told him they would become campers. That was an awful long time ago. He'd been smaller. Years before that, the boy scout troop had taken him camping. That's when they lived in a small place on West Thirty-Sixth, near a cemetery. There had been a lot of rough kids in the troop. They picked on Oscar. Even though he was bigger than any of them. They called him a cream puff. The scoutmaster had been nice, though. A gentle, white-haired priest.

This was a different kind of camping. At first it had been okay, kind of like a survival trip to the wilderness. Then reality hit. Right along with the cold weather.

Mama always said don't trust the government people. Not cops. Not social workers. Especially not social workers. They played a game with you. They made you do all sorts of things, much like dog tricks, causing you to jump through hoops. All for the pleasure of turning you down for something. They didn't need that, Mama would say. They would be just fine. They didn't have a house, maybe. But what they had was much bigger.

A whole city.

Well, maybe not a whole city. "We're West Siders," Mama would say. "Always have been, always will be."

Without understanding anything about it, Oscar almost never ventured east of the Cuyahoga. Things were just different there. Scary. In that way that bigness, brightness and shininess can be scary.

Oscar's stomach told him it was lunch time. He longed for the days when Mama would make a sandwich in some small home she had secured. They would only stay a short time. It was great while it lasted. He would have lunches, and breakfasts, and dinners, and treats, just any old time. No special occasion. Just because Mama was, well, Mama.

The city of Cleveland fought with Detroit in the early part of the century for auto manufacturing supremacy. Somewhere around eighty different makes of cars were spawned in Cleveland, including the famous Hupmobile. Word on West Fifty-Second Street was that this stretch of residential/commercial mix had once housed one of those auto plants.

Tucked into the back corner of a roofless, partially-walled warehouse where West Fifty-Second ended, was Oscar's cardboard home. Not far away was where

Red Dog lived. His place was more elaborate, made of an old wooden crate that had once housed a metal-working lathe. Red Dog, who sported an incredible mop of red hair to go with a similar beard, actually owned a dog. A dog so vicious, so ugly, that nobody dared to mess with his master. Or his master's friend, Oscar No Name Something or Other.

But Red Dog wasn't home. No telling where he was. He never said. When he was gone, Oscar was frightened. He was scared of what some of the people on the street would do if he scored. Whether he scored a lunch, or something to recycle. Sometimes it seemed that hunger was so great, waiting for an evening meal at St. Herman's, or the West Side Catholic Center, that food scrounged during the daytime went only to the strongest. Oscar was not, by any means, one of the strongest. He knew that. For the most part, he accepted that. His size sometimes intimidated others. But not always. Certainly not the truly tough.

But Oscar was hungry. Really hungry. He would have to find something to eat soon. That might be why Mama didn't last. Toward the end, she hardly ever ate. Oscar wished she was around to fix him one of those old-time sandwiches. Or feed him whatever the lunch special was at one of those restaurants she used to work at.

But Mama was dead.

He had to go find food. And it was too early for West Side Community House. Could he make it until dinner? He might have to. He could forage in a Dumpster. If he wasn't seen. Last time he tried that, on Wednesday, they had jumped him. Robbed him for scraps. Two huge black men who called themselves brothers. But they weren't. Brothers. Oscar knew that for sure. They might have been cousins, but weren't brothers. So many things confused him nowadays. Things like, where was Red Dog during the daytime? All of a sudden, and Red Dog was gone early in the morning, before the sun peeked over the skyline. He wouldn't return until late, missing an evening dinner at one of the five or so churches, or like on Fridays, the community house.

He had to find food.

If they jumped him, they jumped him.

Arnold Anderson was finishing up a report on housing inventories in the Greater Cleveland area. It always depressed him. As a mid-level operative at Cuyahoga Metropolitan Housing Authority, his lack of power often gave him an uncomfortable, impotent feeling. What can you do when funding is nonexistent? "Not a whole hell of a damn lot," he had once told his wife, Madge.

And now, Jonathan Tubb's new writer would be paying him a visit in a few minutes.

About a decade ago, the regional Emergency Shelter Coalition had asked the Housing Authority to make available something like 3,000 empty housing units to relieve the homeless situation in Greater Cleveland. Only problem: No money for renovation. No renovation, no way to meet codes.

With the country lurching to the right; with programs getting axed by conservative politicians on the federal and state level; with taxpayers poised on the brink of outright revolt; with compassion fatigue being the norm; Arnold Anderson felt things would only get worse before they got any better.

Madge was on line two. What a great woman. Probably still worried about him. Ever since last night's roast beef dinner, he'd been having one of his unstoppable headaches. "Madge," he said when he'd picked up the phone, a deep feeling in his voice.

"How are you doing, Hon," she asked. Her husband of seventeen years, still youthful looking at thirty-nine, was obviously a stress case. "Your head still hurt?"

"Ya," he said, rubbing his forehead with his left hand. "I've just taken two more Excedrin, but it isn't touching it."

"When you get home, I'm going to draw you a hot bath. I'm going to dump you in the tub, and see if that doesn't clear your head."

Anderson gazed around the Spartan office, stuffed with commercial issue office furniture, in and out baskets, and the now indispensable PC, connected not only with the mainframe, but also to a modem and America Online. Now he could connect himself with counterparts in most every city in America. Strange. It didn't make him feel linked. It made him feel isolated inside an electronic brig.

"I'll try anything," he said evenly, still rubbing his head.

"Did you eat your roast beef san?"

"And the pickle. I love your homemade pickles."

"We Polish girls know how to make them."

"Isn't that the truth."

"When is your appointment?"

"She'll be here any minute, I guess. Maybe her story will help just a little bit. Lord knows we need something. What kind of society is this, when the federal government, not to mention Columbus, cuts programs, instead of expanding them? In the long run, it will cost us. Decay is never the answer, and the private sector can't pick it all up."

'You're not helping your headache, Dear."

"I know, I know. It's this Goddamn report, more than anything."

"I love you, Arnold."

"I love you, too, Madge. Always have, always will."

If he was a big boy, even a man, and Mama had said that he was; then what he had to do was take a tour of the back alleys behind the cafes on Lorain Avenue. Eating once every twenty-four hours just didn't make it. There would be scraps. He might find cans and bottles to recycle. Perhaps something else usable. But would he get away with it?

Oscar certainly hoped so.

Back alleys are always dingy, even in the best neighborhoods. This locality, the Near West Side, once called Ohio City, before annexation by Cleveland proper, was a good mix of Appalachian whites, Hispanic, and African Americans thrown together in a quintessential multi-cultural melting pot. Most were hardworking lower to upper middle class citizens, but gentrification had the unintended consequence of pushing the poor further and further away from urban rehabs. Some of them became homeless, in a sort of top down osmosis. A few of them were mingling in the particular back alley Oscar No Name was now passing through. None of them were familiar.

That was good. If those two big guys didn't find him, then they couldn't take anything that he would find. Oscar smiled. He felt like he had a tremendous insight. He approached a Dumpster. Nothing much. Cardboard slabs, torn and smashed flat. Oscar laughed. No wonder. A paint store. Nothing there he could chew. He laughed again at his personal joke.

A few feet away, he came across an old boot. Only one. Wrong size. He could use a new pair, that is an old pair, of boots, if he could find any. Oscar hated new shoes. When Mama bought him new shoes, his feet hurt. Shoes, boots, whenever they were new, they just hurt. Everybody knew that old is better. Mama said that's because they are already worked in. It's amazing what Mama knew.

The alley was paved, but the pavement buckled everywhere. Must have been years since it had been macadamized. Much litter, and many tin cans were strewn everywhere. The usual malt liquor, ale and beer cans, but a lot of them were bean cans. Oscar had learned that baked beans taste just as good cold as they do hot. An easy meal. Sometimes Mama found enough soda and beer cans to redeem them for a can of beans. That's before she was bad sick. Maybe long before. It had been awhile since Oscar had had a can of beans. He wondered if he could do it himself. Red Dog did if for him sometimes. Bought him beans. But, again, where was Red Dog, when a guy needed him?

Pay dirt.

A bag of what Mama had called dead soldiers. Probably tossed in back of the wooden outbuilding by kids out for a buzz. You could get money for glass. Oscar knew that. He'd been with Mama when she scored with glass. Could he get enough to buy a can of beans?

He didn't know.

Better not take a chance. Have to find more.

The skies were once again threatening. Last night's rain had really soaked the cardboard. Staying dry was sometimes chancy. Oscar Something or Other knew instinctively that the summer was limited. Soon the leaves would turn, then they'd fall—Mama said that is why they called it fall—and rain would come more often, and then the bitter cold.

Sometimes they had found space in a shelter, when there were available beds. Other times, a grate kept them warm as it spumed steam upward to a grateful body. Then there was the fifty-five gallon drums that some folks got hold of. By lighting a fire inside the drum with whatever refuse you could find, you could sometimes stay warm, if the night was fairly balmy.

Sometimes folks came by with blankets. Unfortunately, other street people sometimes stole the blankets. That made Oscar sad. Why do people want things that aren't theirs? he had asked Mama.

She had thought about that one for a long time. "Maybe," she had said, "because they hurt so bad they can no longer tell what is right and what is wrong."

Oscar No Name had thought about that one himself, for a very long time.

Patrice Orosco decided to get an early start for the Cuyahoga Metropolitan Housing Authority office at 9520 Detroit Avenue, in the Near West Side. Just after she crossed the Lorain-Carnegie Bridge (The Detroit- Superior Bridge, officially known as the Veterans Memorial Bridge, was closed for renovation and wouldn't open until late November) she began to wend her way to Detroit Avenue.

"This is it, Orosco," she finally muttered to herself and the car, as the nondescript government building loomed into view. "My first interview."

It was one minute past the hour when she arrived in Arnold Anderson's office. A secretary showed her in promptly.

Anderson was as nondescript as the building. He looked like every other human being who ever worked for an agency. Probably dedicated, undoubtedly overworked, definitely underpaid, judging by his cheap suit and obligatory tie, a paisley affair that no one would pick out on purpose. He looked vaguely Scandinavian, but Patrice wasn't sure.

"Miss Orosco," he said, holding out his hand. His smile seemed tight and forced.

"Thank you for seeing me on such short notice," said Patrice.

"It wasn't that short. Tubb mentioned several weeks ago that you would come today." Anderson attempted a smile, but it seemed pained.

"That sounds like Jonathan Tubb," Patrice said, not knowing whether to be miffed or amused.

"Would you like some coffee?"

"Sure. Black, no sugar."

Anderson himself got up from the desk and went out of the office and across the hall. Soon he returned with a Styrofoam cup full of scalding institutional coffee. "Maybe I'll just start filling you in on background, then you can ask any questions you might have."

"That works for me."

Arnold Anderson seemed to study the drab walls, decorated only in a token fashion. The office was not large, Patrice noted, and it was definitely crowded with books, journals, papers and general clutter. Finally, he cleared his throat, and took a sip of his own coffee. He seemed to grimace. "If people think homelessness has been a problem in the past, say, fifteen years, they haven't seen anything yet. The President capitulated to the mood of congress, which may or may not be the mood of the country. Time will only tell. I personally think congress will be swept out again in two months, but I could be wrong. Once people realize that budget cuts that have swept every level of government will produce gigantic dollar costs in law enforcement, degraded infrastructure, environmental havoc, health care and suffering..."

Anderson cleared his throat and slowly shook his head.

"When you say the President capitulated, you mean..."

"He's a man wholly without principles. He's not a conservative, he's not a liberal, he's not a libertarian, he's not a socialist, he's not a fascist. What he is is a man totally motivated by a self-serving agenda. He's not out to protect middle class taxpayers; he's not about helping the downtrodden; he's not propelled by any mind set. He's driven only by the desire to be reelected. That has resulted in pandering to the lowest common denominator. If he had any concrete belief system, I would at least respect his position, wherever it landed on the political spectrum. As a result

46

of his flip flops and vacillations, the country is rudderless. Therefore, we haven't the slightest idea how to handle any of our social problems. This includes housing."

"Tell me more about cutbacks in funding."

"I can fax you statistics later this afternoon. But first, let me give you the overview."

"That would be fine."

"There is no intelligent argument against the statement that unbelievably massive federal cutbacks in housing assistance have pushed people out of their homes. At the same time, slashes in welfare payments have forced some people to decide whether to eat or pay the rent."

"Some would say that is simplistic."

"Some are into denial, Patrice. May I call you Patrice? Just call me Arnold, if you will."

"That would be fine."

"When I fax you the stats, you do the arithmetic. See if funding cuts are motivational tools to wake people up into being self-sufficient as the conservatives say, or if the cuts are so deep that economically, housing has become out of reach for blocks of people. Then talk to others in other disciplines, such as experts on homelessness, or social workers; the ones in the trenches who see the problems up close and personal."

"Surely cutbacks have been necessary. We've gone through some hard economic times in recent years."

"That's very true. America is no longer a rich country, some people say. We've spread ourselves thin overseas, according to some critics. We've drained our coffers with military spending, others say. A frisson of truth in every stance. But, Patrice, let me ask you this: How do we explain the children? Throwaway children. Abused children. How do we rationalize malnourished kids right here in the States, children not of some third world country that refuses to embrace freedom and democracy, but American young people. How do we come to grips with rampant crime, when in our heart of hearts we know it comes from the breakdown of family. Homelessness represents the ultimate breakdown, an almost total breakdown of function.

"Where the conservatives say the answer is building prisons for criminals, and the liberals claim the answer is increasing self-esteem to prevent young people from becoming criminals, the real answer is too many people chasing too few resources."

"Now you are getting Malthusian."

"Oh, definitely. I plead guilty. I noted a few years ago that the Catholic Bishops suggested the Earth could support some forty billion persons. Bullshit! We have, what, six billion now? That's probably three billion too many."

Patrice was taking notes in shorthand at a furious rate. "Is there a real housing shortage?"

"It depends on what you call real. There are probably enough structures in Cleveland to put up all of the homeless. Or at least there were a few years ago. A lot of them are getting gentrified. But most of the vacant units that exist violate code. And not just some petty, ridiculous bureaucratic thing. We're talking uninhabitable."

47

"Certainly they could be rehabed."

"How? Where would the money come from? More taxes? That's about as popular as dandruff. Private sector? Bankruptcies are at an all time high. Foreign competition has made it necessary for corporations to get leaner. Greed has caused them to become meaner. It gets back to your Malthusian ethic. Good old Thomas Robert Malthus. We have a population bomb, Patrice. And guys and gals like me are charged with finding ways to provide housing for people.

"And there are so many more things to factor in. The cost of lumber, and building materials in general. Environmental concerns make the lumber situation dicey. Environmental impacts make it harder to build any kind of development. The savings and loan fiasco didn't make it easier to finance housing. Middle class families are finding the American dream, that picket fence and bungalow, almost unaffordable. Legions of speculators are cleaning up in real estate, driving up prices. Rentals are going through the roof. Some people drop through the cracks. Viola. Homelessness.

"Lifetime employment is no longer a given. Especially here in the rust belt. When the ax comes, good people filter down to lesser paying jobs. That displaces less desirable workers. They filter down to the most menial of positions. That displaces more workers. The bottom rung worker becomes unemployed, and perhaps, unemployable. When their benefits run out, there goes their housing.

"And then there's technology. Fewer workers are needed to produce the nation's goods and services. Those workers needed have to have more skills. Again, the bottom rung takes the biggest crunch.

"Offshore jobs. There's another factor in the mix. Low skill employment goes to other countries, and you see the results here. More unemployment. More hunger. More homelessness.

"So here we are. There is an abominable lack of low-income housing. Fewer than half of LBJ's six million unit War on Poverty housing goal ever got built. Some of the babies that would have lived in those houses are now in their thirties. And some of them are homeless."

Arnold Anderson wiped his brow, whether from the over warmth of the office, or frustration, Patrice didn't know. Perhaps both.

"What is the private sector doing?"

"Habitat for Humanity has done wonders, building homes for the homeless. Jimmy and Rosalynn Carter have been instrumental in that. Check it out. Comic Relief is another, though I'm not sure if they build houses. I've gone beyond my area of expertise, here. Getting into the social aspect. But, perhaps, if you expand from just the housing inventory side of homelessness, your purposes will be better served."

"I thank you, Mr. Anderson. Arnold. Can I call on you again, if I have any more questions?"

"By all means. Anytime."

"Hey No Name! Stop, asshole. If we run afta yo' ass, gonna get mo' shit 'n y'can handle!"

Oscar No Name Something or Other broke into a frantic run. Legs churned like freewheeling pistons. Arms chugged almost like a swimmer. For all of his effort, he was not going fast. Crossing Lorain, he hightailed it toward West Forty-Eighth Street. Clutched in his right hand was a can of baked beans purchased from a mom and pop grocery on Lorain Avenue.

"Red Dog! Red Dog!" he muttered under his breath.

He must elude them. He must. Hungry. He was hungry.

"Stop, asshole."

It was those fake brothers! It was them!

"It gonna be hard on yo' ass, muthafuckah."

They were gaining.

Oscar No Name almost reached West Fiftieth before he was overtaken. Tackled in a weed infested empty lot, he hit the ground hard. "We tol' ya, muthafuckah. We tol' ya. Now we gonna teach yo' ass the way things is."

One of them sat on his legs, while the other, perched on his back, methodically lifting his head by the long neck hairs and smashing it into the dirt. "Yo' tryin' ta hol' out on us. You not be tryin' that agin."

After awhile, the two brothers grew tired of their sport and took their leave. With the can of beans.

Oscar No Name lay in the field. Face a bloody, dirt-caked mess. Quietly he sobbed. "Mama...Red Dog... Mama..."

#

CHAPTER 7

Saturday, September 7, 1996 6:00 a.m.

Teachers Criticize Guards Brought Into Schools for Strike: Teachers at several high schools are charging that security forces, hired to police schools in the event of a strike, intimidated students and faculty members and made a mess of some classrooms.

The Cleveland Teachers Union gathered several teachers and students at a news conference yesterday to air the claims. Several said they believed they saw guards with guns—an accusation the district vehemently denies.

> Scott Stephens and Patrice M. Jones
> Plain Dealer Reporters

Groggy. And why not? After a late night with a man purported to be old, but actually ageless, Patrice Maria Orosco nonetheless answered the bell—an insistent, persistent, alarm clock bell—on the beginnings of a new day. Not that she wanted to. A sleep-in would have been preferable.

Not to be.

It was at Afterwards on Bridge Avenue that Theodore had given her a plan for an early Saturday that she couldn't refuse. Why not, he had asked, tour some of the areas where homeless people congregate? Get a feeling for the reality before the fact of experiencing it?

"But I've barely scratched the surface with interviews, though Arnold Anderson was very helpful."

"You're not going to get very far interviewing officialdom on a weekend," was his succinct answer.

"Hadn't thought about it. You're right. I'm getting the impression you are always right, Teddy."

"I have a theory about that. Anybody is going to be right fifty percent of the time. The secret is to get the edge on the competition. Be right sixty percent of the time. I've always strove for that."

"I'll try to remember that," she said, laughing.

The live band struck up I'm so Lonesome I could Cry.

"Tell me. What was your impression of Anderson? I've heard of him, but I've never actually met him, though we've occasionally been at the same functions, but only since the Plain Dealer sent me to pasture and forced me into the role of city character gadfly."

"He struck me as being different. You wouldn't notice him in a crowd, of course. His opinions, as he wraps them around facts, seem somewhat amorphous. One minute he seemed to see the conservative viewpoint, the next the liberal. I was quite astounded."

A waitress brought them freshened drinks. Patrice, never one to go ritzy, was quite content with one of the beers that had made Milwaukee famous. O'Reilly was nursing a foreign ale with an unpronounceable name.

"Someone told me he's a brilliant man. Thinks the conservatives are cretins, and the liberals are idiots."

"Equal opportunity disdain," Patrice said dryly.

"I'm really sorry about the game," O'Reilly said, with the sadness only the true fan can bring to the reality of an interrupted contest. "You can go with me anytime you want. The Indians are going to win the whole tomato this year."

"Not really," Patrice grinned. "It's the Rangers' turn."

"Why, you provincial wench!" O'Reilly exploded, eyes dancing up a storm. "Next time I'll eat twice as many Polish dogs!"

"That wouldn't be hard considering they called the game after three innings and a rain delay of over two hours. No wonder I feel slightly wet."

"What's worse is we were trailing the Mariners two zip."

"It didn't count, Teddy. They reschedule rainouts. Say, you got gambling shekels, O'Reilly?"

"Have I! You are going to have to put your money in front of your nose! Say, a C note!"

"You're on, big guy!"

"Hey! I like that! You can call me that anytime! Sure beats short stuff, runt, shorty, tiny, munchkin. Now there's a moniker. Munchkin. Much preferred by the dowager crowd. And my dahlia people. Speaking of the dahlia thing, too bad I won't be with you tomorrow, when you breathe in the local flavor."

"That's okay, Teddy. I've got to practice my craft. You won't have to hold my hand, but I can tell you that you are welcome to come with me anytime, and always. I may even fly you to the Gulf Coast one day. I plan to do an article on Vietnamese shrimpers some time next year. I have one more article on contract for a magazine that requires a Gulf Coast angle."

"Haven't been there since the war."

Now it was Orosco's turn for the dancing eyes.

"Do not. Do not. I repeat, do not ask which war!"

"Why, Teddy," Patrice said, voice choked with innocence. "I wrote this paper, you see, for American History. I'm an expert on the War of 1812."

Theodore O'Reilly glared at her lovely brown eyes for several heart beats. "That does it! Your next beer was going to be something good, like a Michelob. Now you'll have to settle, instead, on the swill you're drinking."

"Is that a threat, or a promise?"

Now Patrice was faced with the diurnal problem of morning ablutions, literally hours before her mind, soul and spirit were ready. Never an early riser by habit and choice, she found the mornings to be a staunch adversary to her circadian rhythms. A night owl. Ruben Orosco had always called her that. Time after time he'd caught her studying with the midnight oil, or writing an article until all hours, stereo softly serenading her every effort.

Another thing Papa had never understood. She didn't drink coffee because she liked it. She drank it because she needed it. Always instant. That alone affronted her father's generation. They only liked full-brewed coffee. Mexican coffee, at that. Rich. Full throated. Sleepily, she reached for her jar of instant coffee and began to stir in the requisite amount.

Idly, she wondered what kind of day she would have.

Oscar No Name wondered the same thing.

The afternoon before, Red Dog had found him encased in his own blood-leak, sitting Indian style in the middle of the vacant lot. "Hey, podnuh," his mellow voice had intoned, "looks like somebody got to you. How long you been sittin' here?"

"Dunno, Red Dog. I got no beans."

"You went out tryin' to find somethin' to eat?"

"Ya. I bought a can a beans. Those fakey brothers beat me up and took the beans. They ain't brothers, Red Dog. They ain't."

"You want we should go get you a can? T'hold you 'till dinner?"

"Can we, Red Dog?"

"Sure, kid."

Wouldn't have happened if he had been around the digs, Red Dog thought sadly. But for the foreseeable future, he had no choice. He had to do what he had to do.

Now as a false dawn reflected in the skies, Oscar lay awake, peeking through the cardboard structure Mama had fashioned that he still called home. Red Dog had cleaned him up as best he could. The beans helped, but he felt so sore. Later, when dinner time rolled around, Oscar was again hungry, but he didn't want to be seen with a badly battered face. Red Dog quietly brought him a paper plate of food from Westside Community House. "Eat up, podnuh. Gotta keep up the strength. We'll find the so-called brothers you talk about and see if we can reason with 'em."

"You gonna beat 'em up, Red Dog?"

"Now, Oscar, that's the trouble with the world today. Everybody wants to beat everybody else up. Keep those kind of thoughts out of your mind, my friend. Thoughts like that will only eat you up."

Now, with morning at hand, Oscar wondered what he would find to eat for this day. He felt confident that he would get to eat. Red Dog said he wasn't going anywhere because it was Saturday.

Oscar decided he liked Saturdays.

Early morning conferences at High Data Associates had always been de rigueur, and the work day always du matin au soir. This Saturday was no exception. As usual, the impeccably dressed Maurice Devereaux presided in his imperial way, hand-carved teak partners desk dominating the spacious office. A deep pile carpet, sound absorbing material on the walls acting in both decorative and functional capacities, and a seemingly unlimited supply of Capodimonte gewgaws completed a scheme that was both understated and overstated at the same time.

"I don't like the leakage," Devereaux said by way of introduction. "I refuse to allow dishonesty inside this organization."

Sitting in uncomfortable chairs that surrounded the teak desk were three minions. Well, two minions. Two slim brothers in button down suits, Harvard MBA's by the name of Gary and Gerry Orson, and their immediate supervisor sitting between them. The Orson brothers were factotums without much personality. They each had their areas of expertise, though they were counted on to be versatile. Had to be. The Devereaux empire spanned the globe. Maurice Devereaux didn't believe in specialization. Specialization was for his competitors. Integrated management techniques required a grasp of an entire industry. All the better to spot trends.

The man Gary and Gerry Orson flanked, the porcine second man in charge, Todd Englewood, was decked in a specially tailored Armani suit that slimmed his physique markedly. The quintessential organization man. There wasn't a single component of the Devereaux empire that he didn't have his finger on. He could boot up any computer in the world and access whatever information that he had to have. He answered only to Maurice Devereaux, who, with him, owned every share of the company that was surely headed onto the Fortune 500 list. Englewood had been with Devereaux from the very beginning. At first, they were equals. Slowly, Maurice Devereaux gained the upper hand. Englewood seemed content to have things that way. Pragmatic people often think like that. Give the baton to the hot hand. Devereaux had proven to have a hot hand. The company was now worth a good hundred million dollars. The sky, as they say, would be the limit.

"Would you mind elaborating?" Englewood asked, in his calm, measured tones. "This comes from out of the blue."

"I'm sure that it does," Devereaux said with a small smile. "And I do not blame any of you three. It is not something you would have been aware of. In fact, the information comes from a friendly competitor. Someone with whom I have an understanding. It seems a party that is part of our, shall we say..."

"Cabal..." Englewood supplied, with a straight face.

Devereaux winced. "Such a primitive word. I would prefer the term...consortium." His eyes sparkled devilishly. Business as fun.

The three men seated at Devereaux's feet smiled their understanding.

"So, what I would like is a merger," Devereaux said in a reasonable tone. "That would insure the growth of both companies. His and ours. Certainly he would wither on the vine if we didn't step in..."

"And save him..." said Gerry Orson.

"Really, from himself," Gary Orson supplied.

"Of course," said Maurice Devereaux.

"With extreme prejudice?" Englewood asked.

"Naturally," Devereaux replied, handing Englewood a Manilla envelope.

"And I suppose you want us to do the usual, as regards the acquisition?" asked Gerry Orson.

"Including rerouting the acquisition's business?" brother Gary added.

"You gentlemen have an extremely clear view of things. En realite. C'est bon."

Patrice couldn't believe that she was heading for a diner. Who cooked better than one of Ruben Orosco's daughters? Maybe only Grandma Stella. Hunger is a funny thing. It goes way beyond the needs of nutrition. It is above mere mental abstraction. It can get down to the visceral in a hurry, especially in the morning with only coffee sloshing in your veins.

The Broadway Diner was doing a brisk early morning business. Patrice managed to be seated quickly. The menu made her mouth water. In a short amount of time, hash browns played on her plate with a slice of ham, eggs over easy, toast and jelly.

The factory packed landscape made her feel comfortable. Nowhere in America, she figured, was there a mightier concentration of industrial might than right here in Cleveland. U. S. Steel loomed in the skyline. Nearby, LTV Steel Corporation. The engines of commerce had always fascinated her. She considered herself to come from working-class stock, regardless of her father's success as a restaurateur.

And then there was the winding river. The Cuyahoga. She knew about Whiskey Island salt mining, on the banks of the river near the old mouth. What she wondered was what impact dwindling industry had on employment and homelessness. She figured she would begin to find out shortly.

She left the Broadway Diner with a full and satisfied belly.

Darcy might have been eleven years old. It was hard to tell. The years had snowballed, one on top of the other. Her mother, Lottie, didn't precisely remember the year, let alone the date of Darcy's birth. Lottie knew she wasn't young when Darcy came along as a big winter surprise some time in the mid 1980's. She knew who the father was, that was for sure. That no-good Darnell, that's who. Sumbitch. Fucked her up for his own pleasure, then he split. Like as you will. Left her high and dry in the holler.

That's a man for you. Wring you dry like a twig, and then, poof, they're gone.

Lottie protected Darcy good, she always said. Kept her away from men, boys, or anything that moved on two feet and grew peach fuzz. Kept her away from school, too, where they just take your mind and cram it full of nonsense. Things that boiled out of the big cities and bled out into the countryside. Highfalutin' notions that did no body good. Now Lottie and Darcy were in the big city. All the more work to protect Darcy.

As intermittent morning showers began to diminish, with the sun threatening to peek through to the world, Lottie began to think about her daily rounds. Rounds the two of them would undertake together. Best way to protect a young 'un, as they called 'em in the holler. Kentucky. Seems like a long way off, she thought. Rain in the Kentucky woods was a good thing. Here in the city, not so much so.

It had been several years since Lottie and Darcy had come north, past Cincinnati, past Dayton, and Springfield, and Columbus, and all the way to Cleveland. Money was hard to come by back home. Especially since old Mrs. Dilbest had accused them of stealing silverware. Nobody would hire a thief in rural Kentucky. And thieves are what they were branded. Good-bye to the life of a domestic. Good-bye to the holler. Hello Cleveland.

Lottie sat haunched in the corner of their makeshift shelter, a leaky old tarp for a roof. Their closest neighbors were Oscar No Name and Red Dog. Both were gone as the sky lightened. Darcy had been beating a couple of sticks together, keeping time like a drummer she'd once seen. Now she approached her mother. "Mama, they're givin' doughnuts away at a Laundromat. Can we get some?"

"Lead the way, child."

Mother and daughter went out hopefully in search of a morning repast, such as it was.

Red Dog and Oscar rifled through the trash deposited in back of a pizza joint. Sometimes you struck gold. Uneaten slices of pizza discarded from table leavings. Salad makings that were headed to wilt city. Wily homeless folks had come up with a ploy a while back: Phone in an order for several pizzas. When they were not picked up, they got tossed out the back door. It didn't take long for the restaurants to get wise to the scam.

Oscar No Name found a calzone that looked promising. Perhaps a party of folks with eyes bigger than their stomachs. It didn't take him long to wolf it down. Red Dog had to content himself with bread sticks, similarly discarded.

"That takes the edge off," Red Dog noted. "Almost like having a meal. You ever do a doughnut thing in the mornin', podnuh?"

"Mama used to. When it was leftover."

"Where do those guys hang out, Oscar?"

"I think that way."

From the direction Oscar pointed, Red Dog decided it had to be about West Forty-Fifth Street. Sounded about right. Adrenaline edged through his veins. Even when he was a kid, Red Dog liked to attempt to talk reasonably to the bullies in his life. By example of his logical discourse, he would show them to be so unbelievably ignorant, that when it came to crunch time, it was downright pleasurable to smash them to smithereens, all the while talking calmly, explaining why they had to hurt. It was a high so profound that no words could describe the feeling Red Dog was getting. "Let's go, Oscar. We've got us some guys to talk to."

"Oh, ya!" Red Dog said happily. "They won't bother Oscar no more!"

"Well, that's the idea, anyway."

* * *

Shaker Heights Country Club had seen a lot of Jonathan Tubb over the years since his doctor and boyhood chum, Harrison Varris, had strongly recommended; ordered actually, that golf, sans the cart, become a part of his life. Cardiovascular. The Varris watchword. As a general practitioner, Varris more and more encouraged prevention among his patients, instead of radical measures to chase after disease. "Think life extension. Think exercise. Think low fat diet. Think adequate rest. Think stress reduction.

"You think too damn much!" Tubb had barked with exasperation.

"And you, my friend, too little! You'll join me at my club this weekend!"

55

And Jonathan Tubb, fresh off a lousy physical exam, had done just that. Surprisingly, what had once been a reluctant hacker turned into a dedicated golfer who slowly improved his way into a respectable handicap.

A midmorning tee time was fast approaching. Tubb and Varris were waiting patiently, three foursomes ahead of them. Tubb was sipping an orange juice, much to Dr. Varris' approval. Varris himself had used a blender at home to prepare his own juice, an unnatural concoction of eclectic elixirs that no tree could ever produce. Varris always intoned, "Much better for you. You really need one of these machines. All the difference in the world. More vitamins. Many more vitamins. The factory stuff is better than nothing of course, and infinitely better than soft drinks, which leach all kinds of things from your body. Then there's your former booze habit; the hard drinking journalist. My God. Death to brain cells."

And so, frequently, went their conversation, Varris taking a personal role in keeping his lifelong pal kicking. That both bothered and reassured Jonathan Tubb. His regimen, now over five years in place, had been a fairly painless one. Painless, because he had learned to tune Harrison out, while still minding his health care fiats.

"So, how is your new writer coming along?" Varris asked, as they waited to tee off.

"She's gonna be great. You know, I've been bucking the trends lately. What with downsizing, cost cutting, mergers, even closures, not to mention increased competition from electronic outlets. The newspaper business is not like it used to be. And it probably will never be that way again. Newhouse is actually putting money into the newsrooms of its twenty-six papers, including the Plain Dealer. But the trend now is to public journalism. In some ways that's good. Reader polls, focus groups. Close, touchy-feely community relations. What I want to do with Patrice Orosco is to have her use a combination of old-fashioned investigative journalism, and something back in favor, personal journalism. Then we'll expand on that with so-called public, or civic journalistic techniques."

"Thanks for the seminar."

"I know. I told you how to build a watch."

"Ah," said the good Dr. Varris, "I would be willing to discuss procedures for any operation, were you of a mind to listen."

"No thanks."

"By the way, if it isn't a state secret, what are you sending her out on?"

"The homeless problem."

"Interesting you say that. I've begun, with a dentist friend of mine, a bit of store front medicine in the Near West Side."

"Maybe I'll sic Patrice on you. Who's the dentist?"

"Do you know Pudge Elliot?"

"Oh yes. Met him about five years ago. A mutual friend supposedly killed his wife."

"I remember that. Guy named Cox Delaney. You don't think he did her?"

"Not on your life."

The first tee was now vacant. Jonathan Tubb sent a shot straight and true, two-hundred-and-sixty-five yards down the fairway.

*   *   *

Patrice parked the Cherokee on Carroll, near the Lutheran Medical Center. A short walk, and she was back on Lorain. Culture clash, she thought. People who were making it, thrown in together with people who weren't. And yet, wasn't that the story everywhere in America in the fin de siecle year of 1996? The rich getting richer, the poor getting poorer, and either nobody knew how to reverse the trend, or the people in power didn't want the trend to be reversed.

Patrice squirmed, a little involuntary shudder that she did at times when something was way bigger than she was. So much poverty in America. It's easier to turn a blind eye.

Some seedy shops; merchants just hanging on; hardware stores; a few record shops; news shops; used book stores; used clothing stores; cafes; all with the timeless look of the inner city. Most with neon signs in the windows. Even though it was now about mid morning, Patrice could imagine what the avenue would look like at night. You'd have a neon street.

"Pretty lady..." said a voice in front of a dry cleaners. "Pretty lady come a slummin'..."

Patrice stopped. She was not afraid. The man (she doubted she would have noticed him if she were not on assignment) was unprepossessing, and Hispanic to boot. She decided to affect attitude. "Me? You talkin' to me?"

"Who else? You are not of this vecindario."

"Is it that noticeable?"

"You have uptown, is that the word? written all over you. So why don't you go back to your comfortable home and leave us be."

"Siento mucho molestarle." Patrice started walking up Lorain again, wondering if her trip draped in mufti had been such a good idea. Next time she came to the Near West Side to get a glimpse of the street people, she would wear their uniform. Grunge. Certainly not a pantsuit.

"Wait. You aren't bothering me," the young man said. "Perhaps it is the other way around. I did not mean to be disrespectful. I was not raised that way. But a girl like you in a neighborhood like this...tener cuidado."

"Oh, I'm always careful. How about you?"

The young man was matching her stride for stride heading west on Lorain Avenue, storefronts looming and retreating in her vision. At a home improvement store on the corner of West Thirty-Second and Lorain, a forklift was barreling down the entranceway toward the street.

"Cuidado!" Patrice shouted, grabbing his arm.

The young man let out a whooping sound, reminiscent of a high-school football game. "Well, the tables are turned, Senorita Uptown Girl. Turned they are. Now do you mind telling me what you are doing in this neighborhood? If we are to be each other's guardian angels, perhaps we should introduce ourselves. My name is Juan Antonio Samaranch."

"Exacto! I'm Amy Van Dyken."

"Well, I am an amateur, at least. Actually, at most. I didn't make it as a ballplayer, so here I am. The failed Juan Sanchez Prieto, unemployed Dominican."

They were nearing St. Ignatius High School. A senior courtyard could be seen, to the side of the brick building. Rank hath its privileges. Prieto pointed to the courtyard. "Let's go over there."

"Indiqueme el camino."

"Let's speak English. I'm still practicing."

"Like hell. You speak English like an English teacher."

"Cleveland State. What's your real name, I mean, now that I've admitted mine."

"You don't buy Amy Van Dyken?"

They were sitting on a stone bench in the Senior courtyard at St. Ignatius High School, beneath the shade of a poplar. A pair of northern flickers were hungrily devouring the remains of a bag of sunflower seeds.

Juan Prieto laughed. "Not for a minute, Uptown Lady."

They were at West Forty-Fifth street. A one-time factory that had manufactured protective coatings for the space industry, now piled into a kind of apocalyptic rubble. The yard seemed to say, 'I am the future of your great societal enterprise.' Red Dog shook his head in dismay. What he saw were lost jobs.

Oscar No Name was pointing to a trashed picnic table. "That's it, Red Dog! That's it! Those fake brothers live under that table! They're mean Red Dog! Real mean! Beat 'em up!"

No one was around to talk to, or to beat up for that matter. Not a soul could be seen amidst the caput mortuum.

"They gotta be here, Red Dog!"

"Well there not, buddy."

"Can we wait?"

"You bet. This is top priority for today, my friend."

"You talk like those guys in suits," said Oscar No Name.

"Used to wear 'em. 'Bout a million years ago."

"This is the place, Mama."

Darcy led the way into the building, Mama Lottie close at her heels.

The Laundromat was under new management. They hoped to compete for business in the community better than the previous owner had. Old management had gone belly up, thanks to a petty attitude. The street had picked up on that fast. New management didn't care if you drove a Cadillac or a grocery cart. Everyone's quarters spend just the same.

The building was old, in a general state of disrepair, all except for the machines. Hobie Strauss, the hopeful new owner, had made the machines his top priority. It was said that Hobie could repair anything that man can manufacture. His plan was to upgrade Hobie's, until it matched the East Side places where the college students frequented. He was off to a good start.

Now, Hobie was behind a laundry folding table, open cardboard doughnut boxes displaying just about every variety available. Styrofoam cups of hot, black coffee, sweeteners and creamers available, stood at the ready. Hobie was filling cups for an appreciative trade.

"Hello, Hobie," Darcy said by way of greeting. "This is my mother. Her name is Lottie."

"Hi," Lottie said shyly. "How you doin'?"

"It's coming along. The machines are in good repair. Place needs some paint."

"You know, I can paint," Lottie said hesitantly. "I'm pretty good."

"How about tonight? I'll pay five bucks an hour. Legit. Pay stubs and everything. We close at ten. You interested?"

"Ya. God, ya. I really thank you...Hobie. Can I call you Hobie?"

"If you called me Strauss, I wouldn't answer." Hobie Strauss was a medium sized man of about fifty, brown hair, brown eyes, nothing out of the ordinary. Except for the smile. The smile was what got you.

"What you doin' in the 'hood, Uptown Lady?"

"Ah. His English deteriorates," laughed Patrice.

"I can talk the talk. Any talk. Languages are easy for me," said Juan Prieto.

A few teenage couples strolled across the lawn of the high school, hand in hand, a timeless tribute to the attraction of the sexes. On the street, Saturday morning chores were being run by Clevelanders, even as they do in any city.

Patrice eyed Juan Prieto levelly. "You've had some college, right?"

"I'll be a Sophomore when I return. And I will return."

"I'm doing a story on the homeless. Stories, actually."

Juan Sanchez Prieto didn't say anything for a long while. When he turned back to her, the pair of northern flickers took wing and vamoosed. "No shit," he finally said. "And I won't ask you to pardon my French. Why would uptown lady Patrice Orosco want to come to the West Side and dig around the 'hood and talk to us homeless freaks?"

"Homeless freaks? Is that what they...did you say us, as in, including you?"

"Ya. I'm homeless. Been that way since the Indians cut me from A ball. And yes, that's the way people see us. So we repeat it. Like when the blacks, or is it African Americans? call themselves nigger. I don't have African blood, I guess. So I'm just a spic. I hear that a lot. Do you?"

Now Patrice was taken aback. Did she indeed? "Only in a joking way. I'm only one fourth Mexican, anyway. One fourth German, and fifty percent some sort of European mongrel. Anyway, South Texas is where I'm from, and we do the multicultural thing pretty well."

"I understand this country," Prieto said after another bout of silence. "It is all based on money. Making it, and spending it. If you have it, you are somebody. That's why I sell drugs."

Patrice felt a wave of shock pass through her body.

"I just started last week. A nickel bag here, a nickel bag there. Maybe I'll be able to afford a house for my mother and three sisters. And for me. Soon, I'd think. Maybe, since the Norte Americanos demand crank and crack and skag and maybe even magic mushrooms, I'll be performing a valued service. When State suspended me 'cause I couldn't pay; when the mill sent me packing, because of downsizing; and the landlord evicted us because he has bills to pay too, well, your country made this here Dominican a criminal. Now my green card is no good, my visa long since shot to hell, and all I could get would be a sweatshop job. Forget it. Worse than the Maquiladoras back in the Dominican Republic. And they are awful places to work. Take my word."

The protected daughter of Ruben Orosco was too stunned to speak.

"You are shocked."

"Why would you deal?" she asked quietly.

"I thought I just told you. Okay, I'll elaborate. The Major Leagues come to the Dominican, and throw nickels around like manhole covers. They sign a bunch of guys for a couple of grand each, not ever thinking they will let them play Major League baseball. They are used to give the prospects someone to play with and against. But they don't tell the Latino players this. They fill them full of hope, and send them to minor league cities all over America. They send them to fail. What do you think is the attitude of the players when it is time to go back home?"

"They don't want to go."

"Nine out of ten of them don't go back. We are a small island of poor people. Eight million strong. There is no economy. No hope. Nothing. No way to climb out. In your country, you can move out of the barrio so much easier, and even then, it is hard. In the Dominican, no way."

"So, you've given up your dream of playing baseball."

"In our country, young men say, you cannot walk off the island. You have to hit your way off. As in baseball. It is for us, fuente de vida, truly the fountain of life. I play in a semipro league. I still think I am going to get my chance. Am I a dreamer, Patrice?"

"As far as the baseball goes, not according to the late Berton Braley. In The Thinker he said, 'Back of the job—the dreamer/ Who's making the dream come true!'"

"I like your Berton Braley."

"As far as the drug dealing goes, to quote another great thinker: 'I do plainly and ingenuously confess that I am guilty of corruption, and do renounce all defense.' That was Francis Bacon. He went on to say, 'I beseech your Lordships to be merciful to a broken reed.'"

"You think I should turn myself in."

"That wouldn't serve much of a purpose. I think you should find a better way to take care of your family."

"Uptown Lady, it is easy enough for you to say. It is much harder for me to do."

Back came the brothers.

The defunct factory, their home and castle, made them feel so proprietary, that in their own eyes the mere presence of the interlopers justified an angry response. The taller of the two, they were both towering, let out a snarl like a maddened bear.

"Yo' asses grasses, an' we's the lawnmowas." He and his partner started to advance. Accompanying the two tresspassers was the ugliest dog the 'hood bros had ever seen. The dog looked vicious to a fault. Strangely, the menacing animal seemed totally composed.

Red Dog held up his hand as a sign of caution. Perhaps not so surprisingly, considering the dog from hell's presence, the two homeless thugs stopped in their tracks. Red Dog was shaking his head slowly, as if in amazement. A funny grin was splayed across his face. "Now, is that any way to treat friends? I think not! Oscar and I want to talk with you gentlemen about a cooperative venture. We wish to obtain much needed supplies by banding together!" The silly grin widened. "Together we are strong! Apart, well, bad things happen! We all know how tough it is on the street. If we band together there will be no need for your boorish behavior of the past, like when you beat Oscar here to a frazzle!" The grin disappeared. "That can only lead to your undoing. 'Come, let us reason together,' as a great president once quoted the Bible." Now the smile flashed again, brilliantly. "Let us work together in a kind of Rainbow Coalition. Brothers all!"

The tallest of the two grimaced. "Whitey talkin' trash," he rumbled. "He spittin' ina face a th' brothuhs. Le's get 'em."

"I think they turned us down," Red Dog said sadly.

The tallest fellow advanced rapidly, an extra long blade materializing in his right hand. He waved the blade menacingly. In a most blinding way, Red Dog blurred inside the blade and produced two quick hand movements.

The thug hit the ground like a bale of hay kicked over the side of a moving pickup truck. The knife clattered harmlessly to the detritus capped ground.

Red Dog turned on the second man, moving practically into his face. The thug clutched a lead pipe in his right ham bone fist. Ten feet separated the standing thug from the quaking, retreating Oscar No Name. The grin returned to Red Dog's face. His voice was musical. "You want to give me the weapon?"

The pipe clanked to the ground.

The homely canine uttered an undoglike rasp, perhaps a sound of approval.

"That's good. Now, let's continue our conversation. Your friend will be okay, as soon as it wears off. I want you guys. I need you. I need you two to help me make things easier on the street. I know you can do it." The grin was absolutely magnifying. "Whaddaya say? Can we be friends?"

The shorter, standing thug, practically breathing Red Dog's breath, was completely motionless, gripped in a wholly strange petrifaction.

His prone, taller pal, began to wreath and moan.

Red Dog's grin was beatific. "We really must get on a first name basis."

A half block away, a junk yard dog began to howl.

The ugly mutt croaked an answer.

#

CHAPTER 8

Saturday, September 7, 1996 Midmorning

Westbrook Ready to Fight NFL Over Tax Stance: City Council President Jay Westbrook says he is dismayed that the National Football League doesn't want to play by the council's rules.

The league this week refused to give binding assurance that it will pay property taxes on any restaurant or other development next to the new football stadium that is to open by 1999.

> Alison Grant
> Plain Dealer Reporter

Then the rains came.

In the aftermath of Hurricane Fran, perhaps seven inches of rain blew into Greater Cleveland, drenching the Cleveland Metropolitan Zoo, especially the zoo's Monkey Island. Picnic tables were smashed, fences were damaged. The storm wreaked great havoc, including power failures throughout the Western Reserve.

It was wet.

At the moment she sagged inside the apartment on Mayfield Road, Patrice felt like the proverbial drowned rat. But not for long. A hot shower basically solved that problem in short order. A nice long nap helped her to regain her equilibrium. Without her rest, Patrice didn't function well.

At four, she turned the TV to HBO, and Hugh Grant's hilarious performance in Nine Months. She'd seen it before, but that's okay. She knew what was coming, so she knew she'd like it. That reasoning never failed to annoy either her father or sister Yolanda. As far as Mama Audrey was concerned, you could play it a million times, she'd never pick up on it. As long as Patrice could remember, she'd had her head immersed in some art book or other.

When the movie ended, she felt so lonely she decided to call her mother. Who knows? They might have a decent conversation.

And maybe not, she thought, as she was dialing.

*   *   *

Reno, Nevada, Mid-Afternoon

Pink neon proclaimed the civic logo over Virginia Street: The Biggest Little City in the World. Divided north and south by the Truckee River, Reno, Nevada, is one of those cities that never sleeps. You can fritter your cash in casino after casino, pay a night lady for store bought sex in Sparks, and eat surprisingly good cheap meals at the hotels.

None of that for Fairly and Tomajac. For them, it was all business. From the moment the Lear jet touched down at Reno-Cannon International Airport, the job at hand was all that they thought about. When the job was finished, that would be the time to let down the hair, take a deep breath, and enjoy the wonders of the town surrounded by the Sierra Nevada mountains, and watered by Lake Tahoe by way of the Truckee.

Fairly settled himself behind the wheel of a Ford Escort. What a touch. Most firms would give you a Lincoln. Or a Cad. All the easier to trace. Furthermore, the plates were forged. Now that was really operating. Stamp out your own license. Fake as a strippers double D cup.

"I want some doughnuts," Tomajac rumbled ominously, perched in the suicide seat. They were passing in front of the spectacular dome of the Silver Legacy, the Circus Circus and the El Dorado hotel casinos. "Gotta have energy when I'm working."

"You always want doughnuts," Fairly muttered.

"That's not true. Sometimes I want scotch on the rocks."

"I'll hand you that," Fairly said, with a laugh.

A couple of minutes later, Fairly turned onto Keystone and then West Seventh Street, and found a Raley's Supermarket. Their gear was stored in the trunk. They left the car unlocked. Smash and grab insurance.

"God, I'm gonna miss your doughnuts," Fairly mumbled, as they headed inside the store's doors.

They had to dodge a ratty looking mother with four kids and a basket filled sparingly with prepackaged groceries. A container of Gummy Bears stuck out of the sack. Her two-year-old shrieked, "I want a Gummy Bear."

"You're gonna hafta wait, Anson," his mother bellowed.

When they were gone, Tomajac looked knowingly at Fairly. "Trouble with the world today," he whispered. "Controlled by bratty kids. When I have a litter, they're gonna be disciplined."

"Bet they won't eat Gummy Bears."

"How d'you figure?"

"They'll eat doughnuts."

"Bet you continue eatin' 'em. When you retire next month."

"I'll have to. To remember you by."

The doughnut aisle. Variety pack. Chocolate covered. Powdered. Old-fashioned. Tomajac chose the variety pack. That would make Fairly, the professed non-doughnut eater, happy.

"You eat your share, and then some," said Tomajac.

"What can I say. We do hungry work. Makes me hungry."

"That's the truth."

They each chose a quart of chocolate milk to wash it all down with. And they each contributed four quarters to the slot machines.

Fairly won five dollars.

On the way out of Raley's parking lot, bellies full, ready to get down to work, Tomajac spotted the Starlight bowling alley from Keystone Avenue. "What say we roll a couple lines, for old times sake, when we finish business?"

Fairly, driving beneath an overpass, approached a changing light and was about to answer a quick no. But then he reconsidered. This might be their last out-of-towner together. Why not make it memorable? "Scratch?"

"Sure. Who's got an up-to-date handicap? I haven't had one in years, myself."

"First, I gotta have some of that Basque food at the Santa Fe."

"Ya," said Tomajac. "I can go for that."

The house was close to the Upper Peavine Creek Dam, just off the Avenida De Landa. Down an unnamed, winding dirt road, partially cloistered by pine trees. Fairly was not surprised to see carefully cultivated desert flowers and the de rigueur cactus treatment. The house itself was fifties ranch style, knotty pine, complete with wagon wheels, old buckboard, cow skull, and an old-fashioned wheel barrow competing with salvaged track and a mine car to scream "...this is Old West Reno, yessiree..."

"Western kitsch," Fairly muttered. "This Stanley Kremintz guy has questionable taste."

Tomajac snorted. "I wouldn't know. I'm an Easterner."

Fairly parked the Escort in the circular driveway. The two burly partners approached the house. They looked like representatives from the AFL-CIO, or perhaps Mormon converts spreading the good message.

A grinning man of lanky frame and sparse blond hair, perhaps in his mid-forties, opened the door. The grin slowly faded. The grin died. The man slumped, as if his body had formerly been inflated by an air pump. His voice had an emptiness to match. "Oh, God, no..."

"Oh, yes!" said Fairly with a smile. "Yes, indeed! We are here. We are here, now, and you are going to enlighten us Stanley! You will tell us all that we need to know. Now, Stanley," Fairly and Tomajac glided into the house, the lanky man involuntarily shrinking away, "I'm a fairly good interviewer. Yes, I am. But, Tomajac, here...he's a real card. He could get the story from a mummified deaf mute. Yes, he could. He can show you his techniques, or you can use the short form! Cut to the chase! Spill the beans! Get it off your chest! Capiche? I like that word! I'm not even Sicilian! But I love it! Do you capiche, Stanley?"

Stanley's stupefaction prevented him from occupying any spot on the verbal spectrum. Before either Fairly or Tomajac could apply any sort of motivation, Stanley Kremintz fainted dead away.

"You scared 'im," Tomajac muttered. "For a guy who claims to like finesse, you sure fall far short, my friend. And you're not gonna get any better, 'cause all you wanna do is retire! You just want to bask in the sun, roll in your dough, eye the broads, stick your wick in a few, and golf in Key Biscayne. That ain't no kind a life! Far away from commerce! From the action! Guess I'll hafta show you how to process this guy!"

Tomajac marched to the kitchen. When he returned, he stood over the fallen mark. "Stanley Kremintz! Arise!" Tomajac shouted, tossing a glass of water into the prone, pale face. Just a twitch. "Stanley Kremintz! Arise!"

Kremintz opened his eyes. Fright swam from the depths of his soul.

"Now, Stanley, we aren't gonna hurt you," Tomajac said in an avuncular voice Fairly had never heard before. "No way. We think you can be of use to the organization down the line. You're a genius, Stanley. We know that! You know it! You can still make us big profits. And yourself! Your fine little company can continue to prosper, Stanley. You will, of course, wish to return to the organization that which belongs to the organization. You can do that with a few key strokes, Stanley. You can."

Gingerly, Tomajac brought Kremintz to his feet. He patted the frightened financial genius' shoulder like an older brother soothing a hurt.

"I'm sorry. I'm sorry I did what I did," Kremintz said softly, as he sat down in front of a terminal. "I'll make it right. I really will."

"I know you will, son," Tomajac said softly.

Fairly was watching with an amused expression. He wanted to drink in every moment. At least every preliminary moment. He could walk outside when he needed to. And he would need to.

"You know," Kremintz said, as he booted the computer program, "I didn't skim at first. It was the gambling. I got in the hole. I'm out of it now. My operation is profitable again, and I'm through with the crap tables." He made a few more keystrokes. Column after column of figures on the screen were being electronically transferred back to the organization.

"I am now restoring the funds. Every cent that I...skimmed. How did you people find out? I was going to restore the funds in a couple of days, I swear I was."

"I know, Stanley. I know. No harm done," said Tomajac.

It took a few minutes. At last, Kremintz was through. He stood up, a tentative smile on his face. "That should do it, I would think."

Fairly stood. "Think I'll take a walk. You two finish up your business."

A puzzled look came over Kremintz' face. "I thought that was it?"

"Not quite," said Tomajac, after Fairly had exited the premises. "I'll need all of your codes. It would be helpful."

"But, why? I made it right. I returned all the money."

"Because if you don't give me the codes, it will take me about two hours to pull them up. I'd much rather go eat."

"It never was part of the deal that I share my codes with your people."

"I know, Stanley. But deals change."

Something about Tomajac's eyes.

At that moment, Stanley Kremintz knew the truth.

"You aren't going to give them to me, are you?" Tomajac asked, something like genuine sadness in his voice.

Fairly heard the muffled pop inside the house, as he listed against the buckboard enjoying a cigarette. A few moments later, Tomajac emerged from the house and moved directly to the Ford Escort. He opened the trunk, pulled out a small black box and scowled at Fairly.

"Wouldn't give you the codes, huh?" Fairly asked.

"No. The prick."

"Want me to run the program?"

"No. Do the search, as you planned."

It actually took Tomajac less than two hours to strip Kremintz's computer system of every dollar, secret, and ounce of his business' lifeblood.

Fairly tossed every square inch of the ranch house. Both finished up at about the same time. Fairly had a huge smile plastered across his face, as he emerged from a back room. "Guess what I found?"

Tomajac took a Manilla envelope from Fairly, opened it, and again frowned. "Where did you find this?"

"Behind a loose knotty pine board in the sewing room." Fairly was beaming. "The boss will be a happy man. We'll get a bonus."

"You'll retire with your only loose end wrapped up."

"Exactly. You know, it's weird..."

"What?" asked Tomajac.

"He never left Cleveland."

#

CHAPTER 9

Monday, September 9, 1996

Going, Going, Gone: Steelers fans are left to grumble without rabid browns supporters to hate: Blue skies of sighs and the whispers of history surrounded Three Rivers Stadium yesterday morning…Most fans said the signs of a rivalry gone belly up were just too hard to ignore. It wasn't so much what was there as what wasn't— Cleveland fans, for one, and that old "take no prisoners" spirit.

> Brian E. Albrecht
> Plain Dealer Reporter

Her desk was crammed way back, deep in a corner of the newsroom, almost totally out of the way. Isolated from the hustle and bustle of the city desk; divorced from the national editor; nowhere near the area where the paper's columnists toiled; out of sight of the sports desk; Patrice wasn't even close to the art department, which itself was stowed out of the mainstream.

"This is where we put the interns," said the tall, stiff, pageboy coifed lady from personnel, one Gerry Andrews, who had just shown Patrice to her desk. It had taken awhile to do the routine task of filling out the required paperwork, on this, her first official day on the payroll. "I know you're not an intern, but space is at a premium." The lady footed back to personnel on clacking heels without another word.

"No problemo," Patrice muttered, staring at the scratched metal desk. An identical battered unit abutted against hers.

"Mine's right next to yours!" said the happy elfin, Theodore O'Reilly, who miraculously materialized at her side. "I've been asked to edit your stuff. Think of it! You have your own personal editor! They're even paying me! Not that I need the money. Hell, I've got so much I'll never spend it all!"

"Then give me some of it, you Irish miser!" bellowed a graying, stoop shouldered man in his late sixties. "I know how to spend!"

"Right, Mulligan," boomed O'Reilly, "you'd spend yourself to the poor house. Like a million Micks before you. Patrice, this Gaelic rascal, One Michael Mulligan, has been here forever. No one knows what he does. He never appears in the paper, so one has to assume he can't write. Figures. He can't think, so how could he write? Rumor has it he works with the bean counters. But I'm not sure."

"Miss Orosco, I'm glad to make your acquaintance. Don't believe much Theodore has to say. Trouble is, he has a lot to say, and most of it makes no sense. I take it Mrs. Andrews took care of you?"

"Yes, Sir."

"Call me Mick. What should I call you?"

"Call her Patrice, Mick. She's one of the boys."

"That okay with you?" Mulligan asked.

"Sure."

"Now, about you Theodore. I think we can designate you as an independent contractor. That okay with you?"

"Nah. Put me on the payroll. I don't wanna mess with anything other than a W-2 form."

"Very well. You wanna make a bet? Indians and Yanks?"

"Go away, Mick. Last time I bet you, in '54, the outcome was not good for me, you dumb New York outcast!"

"How 'bout we catch a breakfast this week. It's been awhile."

"I'll be at A & B tomorrow."

"My turn to pay."

"You're damn right it is!"

The storefront building was about as unprepossessing a building as you could find in Cleveland. Shabby. Possibly always had been. A new coat of paint would not have crossed anyone's mind in this land of unrelentless graffiti. Tucked just behind West 105th Street in an alley near the corner of Oliver and Dixon streets, it had once been an auto upholstery shop. Several junkers on blocks could be seen in the area. The mixed commercial/residential area had seen better times. Or maybe it hadn't.

The African-American lady reading Time Magazine in the waiting room could have been a poster woman for Intact Dignity. If you'd been acquainted with her for awhile—she wouldn't tell you—you'd know she'd once killed a live-in provider (She never viewed him as a boyfriend) for the supreme violation of her ten year old daughter. A racist DA had tried for all the world to fry Almeda Peres. Murder is murder, he'd said. Intolerable. Send her to the Big House. But a compassionate, streetwise jury let her walk. The conservatives roared. The liberals wrung their hands and pontificated, waxing eloquent about historical injustice.

While Almeda Peres rambled the streets, renting her sex, beyond the sphere of the political spectrum.

An older woman, dressed in traditional nursing white, waved Almeda Peres into the inner sanctum of examination rooms. Amy Walker acted as nurse, receptionist, dental assistant and medical records technician. Low budget operation, Near West Side Medical. That Harrison Varris and Pudge Elliot would even offer the money losing service was a marvel of the modern medical community, in a day and age of HMO driven service contraction.

"How are you, Almeda?" Amy Walker asked, genuine concern in her voice.

"Stiffer 'n a board, actually. How are you Amy?"

One of the inviolable rules of Varris and Elliot's practice was everyone, including the providers, be on a first name basis. Close community ties, they felt, could be better fostered if artificial barriers were removed.

"I suppose I have the same complaint!"

A new electronic thermometer indicated there was no fever. A blood pressure cuff was not so reassuring. "You are shaking your head, Amy."

"Are you taking your Vasotec?"

"I try."

Walker rolled her eyes. "Harrison will be right in. I think he'll want to scold you."

"I know he will!"

The outer room was now empty. The morning session had gone smoothly. Twice a week, Monday and Thursday mornings, Varris and Elliot saw patients. Amy Walker hated acting as a dental assistant, but, you did what you had to in storefront medicine. Walker, fully retired from her position as a charge nurse at a convalescent hospital, enjoyed the twice a week service she provided. Somebody had to do something. In her opinion, a country as rich as America that would allow a subculture to languish in its streets was something less than civilized.

Harrison Varris bounded into the examination room. Everything about Varris was moderate. Height, weight, hair, skin, voice. A man easy to ignore in a crowd, but with a personality so vibrant you would always remember him. Pudge Elliot always said he was a man of a thousand faces.

"I don't like this," Varris said, glancing at Peres' chart. "160 over 110. Shouldn't happen with the Vasotec. Almeda, hypertension is nothing to toy with. So many things can happen. Brain attack, what we used to call stroke. That leads the list. Not to be overlooked, is heart and kidney disease. You've got to watch it. When did you last take your prescription?"

"Late last week, I guess."

"You're taking one five milligram tablet, once a day, when you manage to take it. I want you to double that for two weeks, then come back in here and we will evaluate it."

"Once in the morning, once in the evening?"

"No. Vasotec acts for twenty-four hours. Take both tablets, once a day."

"I've been pretty stiff lately, Harrison. I'm sure it's just rheumatism. But it's getting worse. With cold weather coming up, I thought maybe I should check on it."

Varris examined her joints very closely. After finishing with the rubber hammer, he jotted notes on her chart. "Are you taking any anit-inflammatory drugs?"

"Tylenol."

"No. That won't work. Doesn't touch the inflammation. I'm going to call in a prescription. Nothing major. Just Ibuprofen. You could buy Advil or Motrin, but the county will pay for the prescription. If that doesn't work, then we'll get you something serious."

"Thanks, Harrison."

"Take the Vasotec, kid."

"I will."

"Where are you going to eat tonight?"

"St. Malachi's, I think."

"Vegetables, Almeda. Vegetables. Think vegetables."

After Almeda Peres left, Varris waved good-bye to Amy Walker, and stepped briefly into Pudge Elliot's office. Elliot was examining some X-rays.

"Through for the morning?" Varris asked.

"Not quite. Got a guy coming by in a few minutes. You want to hit the links Wednesday afternoon?"

"Sure. Buck a hole."

"Better have some cash, sucker."

Amy Walker stuck her head in the door, a few moments after Harrison Varris left. "I'm outta here, Pudge."

"Thanks, Amy. See you Thursday."

After Elliot finished with the X-rays, he transcribed notes for a few minutes. When he looked up, his last appointment had arrived. He locked eyes with the man for a few moments. He drank in the mop of red hair, the scruffy, unkempt, burnt sienna beard, the jaw still chiseled, the same muscular frame.

The eyes haunted.

"Hello, Coxy."

Patrice finished typing her notes into the computer. She used her own outlining system, something that she'd worked out while at UTSA. She was off to a flying start. In her spiral notebook, she had listed almost a score of people to run down and interview.

"You want to let me suggest something?" Theodore O'Reilly asked, as he returned to the adjacent desk, clutching two steaming coffees.

"What suggestion would that be?"

"Take a trip to the morgue. You can get copies of everything the Plain Dealer has published about homelessness."

Patrice smiled. "Be a dear, Teddy. Go down to the morgue. A guy named Rex said he'd have them ready for me, in say, about three minutes from now."

"You always this fast?"

"Even faster, Teddy. I'm a whir. A blur. De pronto."

Theodore O'Reilly grinned, bounced to his feet in the most agile of ways, and began to dart for the morgue. "In that case," he rumbled in his well-modulated voice, "Estoy pronto para empezar!"

Darcy was the first to awaken. Mama Lottie was still gripped in a state of segnity, an exhaustion caused by nonstop painting Saturday night and most of Sunday. They'd managed three hours of sleep in the middle of the marathon brush work. Hobie Strauss had matched them stroke for stroke.

When they'd finished, the Laundromat looked like a different place. Late Sunday, installers laid down an indoor-outdoor carpet. New soap, change and soda vending machines would be installed early Monday.

Finally, Lottie's eyes flickered. The first thing she noticed was Red Dog's ugly canine. The animal licked her face, making a raw and rusty mewling sound. She smiled. "Good morning, Borf."

The dog had taken a liking to Lottie, Darcy and Oscar No Name. Anyone else should be advised to keep their distance.

"Mama, we gotta go see Hobie. He's gonna pay you this morning."

"We gotta find somethin' to eat."

Red Dog approached. "You two want some breakfast?"

"They given somethin' away?" asked Lottie.

"Gentleman gave me some cereal, milk and paper bowls. Got some coffee cake, too."

"I'm sure. You gone out an' spent yer money, again, Red Dog."

"Mama..."

"Now you shush, child. It's not fair for Red Dog to feed us."

The chiseled jaw worked itself into a smile. "I'm not. 'Course, I could hoard this stuff. But it wouldn't taste as good that way. Taste kinda bad, eatin' it all alone. Anyway, this gentleman gave me enough for several. Anyway, the milk'll spoil if y'all don't help me use it."

"Aw, Red Dog. What'm I gonna do with you?" But Lottie was smiling. "Tell you what. Tonight, instead a findin' some chow line, I'll take the three of us out fer a pizza."

It was hard for Red Dog to not tear up. He looked away. Borf was scratching in a puddle, near a spot where new cars might have stood. Showers looked imminent. Their home was hopelessly muddy from several days worth of rain. The roofless shell of a factory warehouse looked as if it had been hauled up from Lake Erie. Water logged walls from hell. "I can go for that. But only if I get to treat later in the week. I made a few bucks moving pianos the other day. Best way to spend it is on something that tastes good."

"Tacos?" Darcy asked.

"You got it, Little Lady!"

"You're too much, Red Dog," Lottie said with a laugh.

The three of them began to eat a box of generic wheat flakes from the paper bowls, moistened with one percent milk. The coffee cake was delicious.

A sad sack of a man, with a face stamped with the map of Liverpool approached the three of them. A defeated looking woman with a small child in her arms dragged behind. The man cleared his throat. "Excuse me?"

"Yes Sir?" Acknowledged Red Dog.

"We're looking for a place to crash."

"Where you from?"

"Flat Rock, Kentucky."

"What are you doing in Cleveland?"

"Came here for a mill job. But the mill was full up last week."

"You going back to Kentucky?"

"Can't. Lotsa reasons."

"We're from Kentucky," said Lottie. "Me an' Darcy. Not too far away from you."

"I'm not," said Red Dog. "But I've been there. Pretty place."

"No work."

"Don't reckon there is," said Red Dog.

"I hear you control this area."

"Have to. Keep the mean ones out."

"I'd better introduce myself. I'm Claude Johnson. My wife is Margie. Our baby, Madge, is three years old."

Red Dog walked over to Margie Johnson. He held out his arms. "May I?"

Without hesitating, Margie Johnson handed the little girl to Red Dog.

"I have twins. Just a couple of years older. They're in kindergarten now. I see them sometimes. From a distance." He cradled the little girl for a minute. When he spoke, his voice was musical. "Would you like some cereal, Madge? And some coffee cake?"

"Oh boy!" the little girl giggled.

"Feed Madge, here, and her parents," Red Dog said to Lottie, handing the toddler back to her mother, "I'll help Claude build a shelter."

Claude Johnson seemed relieved, embarrassed and nervous, all at the same time. The way human beings look when they might see some light at the end of an extremely dark tunnel. "I'm much obliged, Mr. Red Dog."

"You'll have to cut the Mister stuff. Just Red Dog."

"Sure."

"The only rule around here is that we help each other. You understand that?"

"You bet. It was like that back home. Only, nobody has anything to help anybody out with."

It didn't take long to find some materials to fashion a shelter. Red Dog used a still sturdy section of unused warehouse wall to anchor a lean-to made from old boards and heavy cardboard. When the two had finished, Red Dog excused himself. "You stay with your family, Claude. I'm gonna go get some blankets and stuff. I'll be back shortly."

There might have been a tear in Margie Johnson's eyes as she helped Madge with the cereal.

Hobie Strauss was waiting for Lottie and Darcy when they arrived a short time before noon. The gleaming new vending machines; the new carpet, laid down after the finished paint job, made Hobie's a truly transformed establishment. Once again, Hobie was passing out doughnuts. The place was packed. Every machine in use.

"Lottie, Darcy. My painting phenoms. Guess I have something for you." He handed Lottie her check. Eighty dollars.

Lottie and Darcy beamed.

"Oh, rats," muttered Hobie Strauss. "I almost forgot. Darcy was there every second of the time, usually keeping up with everything we did."

He reached into his coat pocket and produced a second check.

For an additional eighty dollars.

"I couldn't give her a payroll check, because of her age. So it is a business check. Officially, I've bought her jacket. The one she left here yesterday. Then I lost it. I got to thinking that wasn't right, so you'll find a replacement jacket in the back room."

Darcy bolted for the rear storage space.

"I think you should take your checks to a bank," Strauss told Lottie while Darcy went after the coat. "Open an account. Get an ATM card. You'll have access to your money, without losing it to ruffians."

"I've never had a bank account, Hobie."

"I'll be glad to go with you, help you open one up. You'll need it, anyway. Because I want to hire you to run the place on Saturdays and Sundays. After all, I need a little time off."

"You want to hire me?" Lottie's eyes were getting misty.

"You heard me right. You are one hard worker. Can't find that every day."

Darcy appeared out of the back room. Wearing a brand new blue coat.

Patrice Orosco made it back to her apartment with fifteen minutes to spare before lunch with Norma Darling. Norma had requested she come a little early, so Patrice went straight to apartment ten.

The redhead was dressed retro sixties, complete with pedal pushers, bobbed hair, and fuck me shoes.

"This a masquerade lunch?" Patrice asked. "Oh, that was unkind."

"Not at all! Actually, though I never thought of it that way, it kind of is. Randy and I always dress like we used to as kids when we have lunch together. We really work at keeping close. We only have each other. All of our relatives are either dead or long gone and lost."

"Makes sense to me. You were going to tell me about your sister's kid?"

"Yes. I wanted to prepare you for it. Randy is bringing Midge with her. She's almost four. She suffers from something called Moebius Syndrome. The upshot is, she can't smile. She and Pudge, her husband, have contacted a specialist. They think they can give her a smile. It will involve two separate operations. For each side of her face. The child is very affectionate. I think you'll like her. I'm anxious for you to meet Randy. We seldom run into South Texans. Fortunately, we have a lot of Hispanics in Cleveland, so we can get something of our culture. But not so much of South Texas; know what I mean?"

"Oh, yes. I miss it already, even though I've only been gone a week. Cleveland is nice, in a strange, vibrant, phoenix from the ashes, rust belt kind of way. But in my heart, it will always be San Antonio."

"Do you think you will return?"

"Of course. My family is relatively close by."

A tap on the door.

The sisters embraced. "This is Patrice Orosco, Rand, Patrice, my sister Randy Elliot. One half of the former Duran Sisters. Hoofers. We tap danced our way around Brownsville as kids. Made it to McAllen a lot of times. I don't know if I mentioned that."

"I don't think so."

"And this is Midge."

An altogether lovely child. Something tugged at Patrice's heart. She crouched down and smiled at the little blonde girl. Midge's eyes danced.

It was Midge's smile.

Jonathan Tubb sat in the glass-enclosed conference room, door closed to hustling reporters and frenzied editors. An executive from the Newhouse owners group was the only other person in the room. The man, Erickson, wore a frown. He hated to uncover a convoluted agenda he'd known nothing about. And he hated anything that might involve the Plain Dealer in legal hassles.

"When you go after a corporation," Erickson was saying, "it is never an easy sail. You know that, Tubb. And this Orosco. Sending a woman into a viper pit. I don't like it. Not one bit. You should have cleared it with me."

"You'd have squashed it, Tom. And I'm telling you, High Data is bent. It used to be a newspaper's purview to root out corruption. At least it was when I started in this business."

"It still is, Tubb. But not the way you are going about it. You should have presented your case to the Grand Jury. Then reported on the Grand Jury's finding."

"The Grand Jury would have quashed it, too, Tom. Don't you see?"

"What I see is you are about to fly into a hornet's nest. And with that girl as your point lady."

"'That girl,' as you call her, is as tough as nails. As compassionate as Mother Teresa, as smart as every whip ever manufactured in this country. She did a series of articles on the Vietnamese Dragon influence on the Gulf Coast. One of their versions of a hit man tried to take her out. Patrice made him into a mince meat pie. She was a legend before she ever graduated from UTSA. She's the right man for the job, to bend the gender a bit."

"So exactly what is your plan?"

"She's having lunch as we speak, with the lady who is acting as the conduit into the homeless population, where my man has been living for five years. The homeless articles are for real. What Patrice doesn't know, is she is going to also have a shot at breaking High Data Associates and their underworld money laundering. If she doesn't make her career and win a Pulitzer in the process, I'll be very mistaken."

"But there is already a casualty," said Erickson.

"Kremintz…"

"How many more are there going to be, Tubb?"

"There won't be, Tom. What Patrice won't know is she will be shadowed. I hired professional bodyguards this morning. That, along with her considerable skills in survival, should make this gig a walk in the park."

"On the way to a Pulitzer."

"On the way to a Pulitzer."

Tom Erickson seemed to relax. "It has always been my policy to go with a man's track record. Yours is a good one."

"Damn straight."

Norma served up a choice of six kinds of sandwiches. Chips, dips, condiments. White soul food. Conversation was lively, especially from Midge, who turned out to be a very humorous little girl.

"Daddy almost died from laughter!" Midge said after she'd finished the last bite of her sandwich. "He said, 'Why am I making you a dinner, when I'm so hungry myself?' I said, 'Because, Daddy, you're the past, and I'm the future!' He was rolling on the floor!"

Patrice nearly choked on a pickle, as she roared from the belly.

74

"Then it is set?" asked Randy Elliot, as the luncheon was about to break up.

"Sure. Tomorrow evening at six. Your house. Norma picks me and Theodore O'Reilly up at the Plain Dealer, skips class for a night, so I won't get lost in Shaker Heights somewhere. And your husband will give me an in-depth interview on the homeless situation."

"That's it," said Elliot. "Dinner will be at seven, so we should have plenty of time for Pudge to fill you in."

"Now, if I can just remember this long enough to write it down in my daybook."

"I'll write it down on a slip of paper for you," said Darling.

"That'll help."

As Patrice was about to make her way to the front door, Midge walked over to her. Again, her eyes were dancing. "I like you. You're very pretty. I'm going to be pretty someday."

Again Patrice crouched down. "Oh, Midge. You already are. You will just get even prettier!"

Midge Elliot was positively glowing.

#

CHAPTER 10

Tuesday, September 10, 1996

Black Leaders Want Say in Schools: Minorities 'deprived' of voice, Stokes says: The contract standoff between Cleveland school officials and teachers has magnified the concern of black leaders that they have been ignored by the state officials who run the predominantly black district.

Last week, Rep. Louis Stokes and George Forbes, president of the local NAACP, blasted school officials for taking a hard-line stance in negotiations and for cutting the community out of decision making.

> Mario G. Ortiz and Scott Stephens
> Plain Dealer Reporters

Gunfire erupted as the sun's rays peeked through the Cleveland skyline, a perfect quotidian celestial ritual blemished by human rhythms out of sync.

"Yo, Red Dog, cocksuckuh. Le's even out th' fight, white devil!"

Standing in the middle of the factory rubble, was the tallest of Oscar No Name's ornery 'hood bros. He wielded not a knife, but a lethal looking Universal Enforcer model 3000 Automatic. The hulking hoodlum had everyone's attention. Except for Red Dog, who was nowhere in sight.

Claude Johnson peered out from his enclosure. Oscar, bleary eyed and frightened, peeked through a small opening in his cardboard condo. Lottie stepped into the weak, fog-shrouded sunlight.

"You don't go scarin' kids like that, Mister," she snarled in the kind of angry voice that spoke of long experience dealing with bullies. Darcy cowered behind her mother.

Claude Johnson stepped out into the open. "Why don't you leave before we have a problem?"

"Who're you? Think you c'n hide b'hind that chickenshit Red Dog?"

The Enforcer started to rise to a level plane.

The thug's legs gave out before he could cause the automatic to stutter its death message. They say the knees are the first to go. Red Dog made sure that was the case. In what could be described as a crack back block, Red Dog's blind side smash destroyed the right knee. Kicking the Universal away, he turned the thug over in a blur of motion, and stomped the left knee to ruin.

His voice was soft. "Now look what you've done for race relations. You come in here with a gat, discharge it, scare the life out of these fine people. I can only think you will do it again! You would, wouldn't you?"

"Fuck...you...Red...Dog..." the wounded man mumbled through the pain.

"We must prevent that, brother. We have to. We really do. I take no pleasure in this, friend. You want to be friends?" Red Dog viciously smashed the man's right hand with a muscled stomp of his right booted foot.

A horrific moan.

"Nah...that's not enough." Down came the jackboot again. An orthopedic surgeon's nightmare. "It'll be hard to fire a gun in anger with that hand. But I've still got a worry, friend. We friends yet? No? You know what my worry is? Ambidexterity! Know what that means? I can just see you coming around, a horrible gimp, a no good right hand, but clutching a damn heater. With your left. Murder in your heart. We gonna save ya, brother. We gonna give your heart to Jesus! We're gonna make it impossible to clutch a rod. God, don't ya love gangster movies? You love gangster movies, friend? Here's what they do next..."

"No..." Through the impossible pain.

"See! You're gettin' religion! Yes! We are doing a conversion here! You will live a humble life, my friend. Let's take that left hand..."

"NO, RED DOG!"

It was Lottie.

"You mean, you don't want me to do this?" said Red Dog. With two vicious kicks, he destroyed the left hand.

"You didn't have to go that far, Red Dog," said Lottie. "You could have turned it over to the police."

"Well, of course I did!" He gently cradled the now unconscious gangbanger's head. "I may have just saved the man's life! He might well have been shot, even by the corrupt police this very day! Now, he has very little choice but to live a righteous life. Yes sir, it's Red Dog's ministry. Face the evil down, eye to eye, and show the error of its ways!"

Lottie had Darcy by the hand. "You're just like the rest of them, Red Dog!"

She marched away. Perhaps in anger, but mostly in sadness.

Oscar No Name slowly walked up to Red Dog. "That was great, Red Dog!"

"Nothin' great about it, kid."

"You saved my life, Red Dog," said Claude Johnson. "I've never seen such courage. You came from out of nowhere."

"Red Dog's not afraid of anything," said Oscar.

"Quite the contrary. I'm afraid of everything. I'm afraid of a mad man like this killing me in my sleep before I do what I have to do. I'm afraid of hurting good people like Lottie, or you Oscar, by just trying to stay alive. But most of all, I'm afraid of extinguishing any spark of goodness I might still possess."

"Ah, Red Dog. You're not afraid!" said Oscar.

"Gentlemen. Help me roll this man up in that ragged old carpet in back of the corner wall over yonder. I'm gonna hoist him on my shoulder and take him to his digs. Unless I'm badly mistaken, we won't be bothered by these guys or anyone for awhile. Not until someone new rolls around and wants to fight over turf."

A totally exhausted Patrice Orosco rolled out of bed at the crack of nine. A long day at her desk researching from the morgue had ended with a long night of jazz at Nighttown in Cleveland Heights with the irrepressible Theodore O'Reilly.

Two numbers into the set, a gentleman by the name of Marcus Deutrieve stepped out of the combo and brought Teddy a saxophone.

"I keep it here, like some folks keep their bowling ball at the alley. Now, Treece, I want you to listen closely. My man Marcus here, is going to make you weep with his licorice stick. I'm gonna back him with the sax."

"Is Teddy any good?" Patrice asked, as Deutrieve and O'Reilly turned to join the combo.

"Teddy is it?" laughed Deutrieve.

"Don't even think about it," rumbled O'Reilly.

"He's good for a honky," grinned Deutrieve.

The combo did the Tommy Dorsey ballad, I'll Never Smile Again, which gently reverberated through Patrice like a lonely threnody lamenting lost souls. Deutrieve was smooth with the vocal, and O'Reilly absolutely nailed his backup role with the sax. They played three Goodman tunes, Swing Time in the Rockies; Sing, Sing, Sing; and the melancholy closing theme Benny always featured, Good-bye.

"You never fail to amaze me, Theodore O'Reilly. You grow dahlias. You drive a classic Chevy. You blow a saxophone at a storied jazz club."

"Mostly, we were playing swing. But, yes, jazz is a great part of my life. What music do you like?"

"I like most everything. I suppose I listen most to conjunto, which is a kind of mix between German polka and mariachi music. And tejana. Tex-Mex. Labels. Everybody is always trying to categorize everything."

"Same with us. Is it swing, is it jazz, is it bebop, is it blues. Basically, it is music. Only two kinds of music. Good music, and bad music. And speaking of music, did you know that Cleveland was once a Mecca for jazz?"

"I didn't know that."

The combo, sans O'Reilly, went into a lively John Coltrane number.

"From the thirties until the mid-sixties, we had guys like Fats Waller, Art Tatum, Charlie Parker; they called him "Bird." Oh, let's see. We had Billie Holiday, the always loquacious John Coltrane, Duke Ellington, Miles Davis. Satchmo, that's Louis Armstrong. Treece, it was heaven on earth, I tell you. We had clubs along East 55th Street, Cedar Avenue and Woodland Avenue. Nobody paid no mind the color of your skin. The thing was, could you play? If you could play, you sat in. You jammed. You lived, you soared. You went down. When the times were hard, you went down. Down to the depths of human despair. But then, just like that, the music would save you. It would pick you up on a great, high draft of emotion, and make you see something that only a true jazz lover can see."

"I can see that you love it."

"When Mary was alive, we often took these guys, the majority of them Black, into our home. Neighbors once made a do about it, so I made sure they were investigated by every agency from the fire department to the tax collector. Miraculously, the neighborhood grew more tolerant. A fight with City Hall, or Columbus, or Washington, when they knew the source of their troubles, tended to do that. They hated me. That's okay. I didn't like them. I have always hated bigotry, from whatever source." He paused.

"Big names. They'd come into Cleveland for a gig, and be consigned to the ghetto in Cleveland's East Side. There was a flop house near East 123rd Street and

Imperial where many of them stayed. Not fit for man or beast, and especially not for a star. So, when we could, we let them room at our place while they were in town. We often jammed into the early morning hours on Friday's and Saturday's. Couldn't the other days. I had a beat to cover.

"I usually cooked. I did a gumbo that made the New Orleans crowd jealous. Never would divulge the recipe."

"Would you tell me, Teddy?"

"Hell, no."

A gorgeous African-American waitress brought Patrice another margarita, at a hand signal from O'Reilly. Teddy was drinking Glenfiddich Scotch Whiskey. On his third. The minimally lit room, walls covered with photos of the famous, seemed to Patrice to be steeped in a Zeitgeist not unlike her own.

"If I were to explore jazz," Patrice said after sipping her latest margarita, "where should I start?"

"Benny Goodman. Because he is so accessible. Do yourself a favor and get Benny Goodman: The RCA Victor Years. You will branch off from there. Bix Beiderbecke, Charlie Barnet, Louis Armstrong, Fats Waller, Count Basie, Duke Ellington, Dave Brubeck, Miles Davis, Bing Crosby…"

"Bing Crosby?"

"You've seen his movies on cable?"

"Yes."

"He was also a great jazz singer. Practically invented microphone singing. Also, Frank Sinatra. And your generation is getting to know and love Tony Bennet. Best friend a song ever had. Oh, God. There are hundreds more. Ella Fitzgerald, Bessie Smith, Billie Holiday."

The combo played Goodman's bop flavored Stealin' Apples.

"I remember when that came out," O'Reilly said, his face a nostalgic mask. "Had to be 1948. Mary…" His voice choked. Obviously embarrassed, Theodore O'Reilly worked to compose himself. "Mary had just been to the doctor. We were at the Aragon Ballroom, at West 25th and Clark Avenue. I had just bought a new four door Plymouth. Green. Mary picked out the color.

"The band played Stealin' Apples, made famous by Goodman, Fats Navarro, and maybe a guy named Gray and a few others. Goodman used to do that. Small group pieces. Not with the whole band. Anyway, we danced. We bopped to that song. Then the band took a break. We walked back to our table in the corner. Just like that, Mary says: 'Doctor Mason says I'm barren." O'Reilly now had a tear slowly trickle down his face, in spite of himself. "Just like that. 'Teddy,' she said, 'Dr. Mason says I'm barren.' Like it was her fault. God, I'd a loved that woman if she was the mother of twenty. Or just the mother of our collection of mutts."

"She sounds wonderful."

"I wish you could have known her, Treece. I only wish you could have."

It was way too late. Way too late to hold in a macho reserve. Now the tears were seriously falling down Teddy O'Reilly's cheeks.

Outside Nighttown, the streets picked up the blinks of neon; the image of buildings reflected in rain puddles; the bouncing of halogen lights off window glass; all an urban collage imprinted on the collective mind.

Almost lost in the flickering penumbra of a deserted, gutted building, a stones throw from the jazz club, was a lonely figure huddled for warmth against the chilling air of Lake Erie. A tattered coat. Frayed canvas shoes. Soiled watch cap. Dead soldier hooch bottle. Had anyone been listening, they might have heard the last gasp of a death rattle.

In front of the club, a late model burgundy Buick Park Avenue slammed to a stop in front of the entrance. The driver punched the horn without patience. Shortly, a platinum blonde raced from the building and jumped into the passenger seat. The car bolted as if the atmosphere of Cleveland Heights contained a virulent infection. In the distance, a fire engine's wail pierced the night. Inside, the music played on…

Now Patrice was struggling with her usual circadian rhythms. She zapped some water in the built-in micro, spooned in the instant coffee, and in deference to her dad added pan dulce, sweet rolls, to the tentative breakfast mix. She'd save the Mexican coffee for another day.

"One too many margaritas…" she muttered to the empty apartment, while downing two Excedrin. "Maybe two…"

What a night. Deutrieve found out she'd taken music courses in college, and had warbled with the glee club. Next thing she knew, she was on the stage, singing from Marcus' charts. Deutrieve taught her to bend notes in a bluesy way. Theodore blew the sax in counterpoint to Deutrieve's clarinet.

She still felt bleary when she arrived at the offices of the Plain Dealer. Good thing she didn't have to punch a clock. She greeted a number of the employees by name, and reached her desk, only to find the Elfin One already waiting.

"Banker's hours, Orosco?" O'Reilly asked, with mock severity.

"Can it, Teddy. Early risers make me puke."

"You missed a good breakfast at A & B Diner. Mick was there."

"Oh, God… I could barely down a cup of coffee. I tried to have pan dulce, and I about choked on it. That, Teddy Early Bird, never happens to me. Do you always do this to the girls, O'Reilly? Take them out, liquor them up, cause them to make fools of themselves by crooning songs they don't know on a stage they've never set foot on before?"

"Oh, sure. Sometimes we give them peppermint schnapps to loosen them up."

"Well, I had a good time, Big Guy. But I think I will stay with margaritas."

"I never criticize a gal's poison."

"I just wish we could do it again tonight."

"Tell me about this dinner."

"Norma Darling is picking us up here at the paper," said Patrice. "At six, I think."

"You think?"

"I can't think. But I have the note here someplace. I was supposed to jot it down in my daybook." She began to rummage in her purse. Finally, she found the note that Norma had given her. "Ah. Norma picks us up at five fifteen. We get to the Elliot's at six, and then we spend an hour talking about the homeless. We eat at seven. Then we leave. I go home."

"No Nighttown?"

"No, you reprobate. A girl's gotta sleep now and then. But you're on for tomorrow night."

"Atta girl, Treece. Say, you here the news?"

Theodore O'Reilly gestured around the newsroom. "This place is primed to have its greatest years ever. You are working for the greatest newspaper in America. They announced today a new labor contract that guarantees no work stoppages for the next ten years."

"That's great."

"In a day and age of El Foldos in the news biz, I would think that this would give you something to think about when you get lonesome for ol' San Antone."

"I'll keep that in mind."

Juan Sanchez Prieto leaned back against the old brick wall of a tire warehouse in the Flats, a bottle of muscatel lubricating his lips. It was very early in the day. He was very drunk. Ordinarily, Juan would not do that on game day. But ordinarily, he didn't suffer from a possible torn rotator cuff. Possible, because it was undiagnosed. Nobody to foot a medical bill. Not for a bajo amateur. The day before, he'd made a hard throw from deep in the hole at shortstop. A pop.

"...Like this stuff..." said his companion. "Stops the pain, sometimes all the pain."

"Almeda, you don' know pain," said Prieto. "Pain is when your game is gone to the birds like guano. Like Caca."

"Pain is all over, Juan Sanchez Prieto. All over. You don' have a lock on it. None a you besbol hombres got no lock on pain."

Almeda Peres gazed through a liquored haze out at the humongous industrial might of the Flats, but saw only internal scenes. The violation of her daughter when she was ten. Her daughter, now fourteen, and in the life. It was okay that Almeda walked the streets. She could live with that. But not her daughter. Not Shaleen.

"Little more muscatel, an' I won' feel no pain," said Prieto.

"I wan' you to ask aroun', Juan. Fin' out who is runnin' Shaleen. I wan' her outta the life. You hear?"

"I'm not involved in whorin', Almeda. I got no in'trust in that." He took another chug of muscatel. "'Sides, I do that, an' the guys in it gonna won'er why I'm askin' questions. That not good."

"Juan. You like Shaleen. I knows you do. I knows, 'cause you nevuh use her." Almeda took a swig herself. "You respec' her. That mean somethin'."

"Maybe I could. Maybe I could do somethin'. We'll see."

"I knows you would..."

It is hard to walk on sore feet. That almost never happened to Red Dog. Walking was his stock in trade. He'd have to remember to make stomping guys a rare thing. Now, every step was torture.

He was entering Shaker Heights.

That's when the cruiser pulled up, slowed, and stopped. Two officers partnered. A window rolled down. "Can we help you?"

VIN SMITH

The patrolman who spoke was a blond fellow, not over thirty, with the kind of arrogance that is taught at the police academy.

"I'd love a ride," said Red Dog.

"Don't be a wise ass, son."

"Didn't expect you're a cab service. Thought I'd try."

"What's your business, here, son?"

"Movin' pianos today. Wanna help?"

"You're tryin' my patience, son."

"And you're tryin' mine. You can check with Shaker Keyboards, if you want. Meanwhile, unless I'm mistaken, it's not a crime to walk to work."

"You always have attitude?"

Red Dog leaned closer to the cruiser, lunch pail clutched in his left hand. "Sir, I got attitudes you've never explored. Now, I suggest, if you want to run me in for walkin' to work, then have at it. Otherwise, drive on, and get outta my face."

"We'll be keepin' an eye on you, mister."

"And I on you."

The cruiser drove on. Red Dog continued to stride toward the piano store, adrenaline coursing through his veins. "Proactive, schmoactive," he muttered. "Assholes..."

The two officers, George and Canady, had barely turned the corner when Canady began to check with dispatch about a mangy looking guy with red hair and Shaker Keyboards. Red Dog quickly checked out.

"Another loser with muscles," Officer George said.

"Ya. One of these days, we'll ID him. Run 'im through NCIC," said Canady.

"Hafta catch him jaywalking."

"Then we'll catch him jaywalking."

Tina and Tonya Devereaux were swinging with three of their friends, the Thompson School playground a mass of small humanity. Best subject in school. Recess. However, Tina loved finger-painting more than anything, that's why her fingers were purplish. With maybe hints of red on the backs of her hands. Tonya had spent the morning working on her picture book with scissors, glue and construction paper. Tonya hated finger-paints, too messy.

It was Claudine Demarco, coming from halfway across the playground, who started in. Sidling up to the twins, the blonde, almost too beautiful girl snickered. "Well, well. Too bad Tina and Tonya don't have a mommy!"

"We do too, she's just in heaven," said Tonya.

"You'll never get there, Claudine Demarco," growled Tina.

"And your father is a murderer! Running loose somewhere!"

Tina was off the swing like a shot. Down went Claudine Demarco, rolling in skirt tumbles, blonde hair and dust. A loud chorus of partisans. The comic sight of Miss Dandridge hot footing across the schoolyard.

Tina's small fists were pumping like pistons, most strokes reaching the targeted Demarco face. Claudine was crying like a banshee. Tina's face was screwed into a mask of resolve.

82

"Children! Children! Stop that!"

Miss Dandridge collapsed in a heap, still twenty feet from the ruckus. She lay still. Now children raced to the teacher.

Milton Thompson III, callow generation X grandson of the founder, current Headmaster, and owner of a reputation few would wish to have, namely of being an idiot, was standing in front of the bay window in his office overlooking the campus. When he saw Miss Dandridge drop, he dropped the Who's Who book he was holding. Had his own bio, in which he was inordinately proud. Match that, at twenty-seven, anybody!

Thompson raced out into the yard. He panicked. What to do? Stop the fight! Which was still going strong. He'd check on Miss Dandridge, and what was probably only a sprained ankle, after he restored order! Nobody is disorderly at the Thompson School! Not with Milton the Third on duty! He could, he would, he did run the school with an iron hand, just like Grandpops!

"Let's break it up! Break it up, now!" shouted Milton Thompson III.

University of Texas, San Antonio

"I don't like it," said Martha Dones. "I don't like it at all. I think the whole thing was too risky from the start. Now Kremintz is dead, and that changes the whole equation. I want Patrice out of Cleveland!"

"You give the girl too little credit. She's a fine investigative journalist. Learned more on her own than we ever taught her at the University. And I don't think a corporation trying to maintain its good public image is going to mess with a journalist. It seldom happens."

"It happens a lot, Mel. More than you'll admit. Journalists are becoming targets all over the world."

"You're reading way too much into Kremintz' death, Martha. You know you are."

"I know nothing of the kind. I have half a notion to call Ruben Orosco, and tell him what is going on. Maybe his little girl is getting the opportunity of a lifetime, but maybe the price she might pay is too much!"

"She's poised to do a Woodward/Bernstein, Martha. She stands to bring down a group of thugs masquerading as a Fortune 500 company."

"If anything happens to Patrice, Mel, I swear you will never breathe easy the rest of your life!"

Mel Dones gazed around the office he maintained on the campus of UTSA. Book lined. Cluttered. But with a perverse kind of organization, like the man himself. "Martha, if anything happens to Patrice, I wouldn't want to breathe easy. But, I can tell you this: Nothing is going to happen. She's probably going to win a Pulitzer. It will make her career as a writer and as a journalist. We will expose a vile organization. And we will return a good man to the topside world. A man who sat on my knee as a toddler."

Martha Dones said nothing.

Cleveland, Ohio

Todd Englewood sat comfortably in his office, spreadsheets before him. It was good. Kreminitz' slice of the business was now safely in the fold. The Orson brothers had just made their reports. It seemed nothing could go wrong for him, he reflected. Something on the order of Branch Rickey's dictum: "Luck is the residue of design."

He picked up the phone. Dialed direct to Reno. Room 114, Santa Fe Hotel.

"Fairly."

"Englewood. The instrument, five large, should arrive at your drop within seventy-two hours. Also passage to zone nine. It's a bit wet, and might take two weeks in the mud. This will require a larger instrument. Possibly as big as ten. I'll talk to the engineer. I'll get back to you."

"Fine."

Disconnect. Englewood smiled broadly. Everything on course.

*   *   *

Few men know how to move pianos. All lads of muscular frame think they can. The telltale sign of bad piano moving is when the bottom of an end panel is gouged. Pros, using either a four wheel dolly or regulation piano dollies, manual or hydraulic, know how to avoid this.

Red Dog was a quick study. Within one day, he had not just the basics, but the nuances of the piano move down to a tee. Balance points in the dead lift. Staircase technique. Tipping strategies. Grand piano skid procedures.

"Glad to see you Red," said Skip Omyer, the owner of Shaker Keyboards. Skip was in his seventies, balding, thin, pencil mustache. Omyer had once been the leader of a dance band. Of course, he played the piano. After dance bands went by the wayside, Skip opened a piano store. Over the years, he reluctantly added furniture organs, until they began to go sour. Then the synthesizer and keyboard industries began taking the silicon chip, then the microchip technologies to new heights. The result, many domestic makers of acoustic pianos went under. "Hear you had trouble with George and Canady?"

"That their names?"

"Well, don't worry about it. It's taken care of. I can't have my piano movers hassled."

"'preciate it, Skip."

"Today, we've got a new Schimmel grand going to Parma. Also, an old Lester upright to East 120th, just off Eddy Road. Jason will be in this afternoon about three. Too bad you don't drive, Red. But I don't mind. Long as Jason is at State. When he graduates, I'll need another driver. Sure you don't want to try again for a license?"

"Not really."

"I understand. Guess I'd feel the same way."

In Red Dodge's laconic way, he had made it clear that a traumatic experience behind the wheel had turned him into a pedestrian, or a passenger at best.

"I'll be back before three, Skip."

"Thanks, Red."

Skip Omyer headed for the office, as Red Dog strode out the door. On his way back, Omyer stopped to flick some dust, real or imaginary, from the Schimmel grand.

"Betsy," Omyer said to the aging, heavyset bookkeeper when he reached the nerve center of the business, "I'm sending Jason Kirk and Red Dodge on those two deliveries. Cut 'em both a check." Omyer gazed past the keyboard laden floor to his powerful piano mover, now proceeding up the street. "Imagine that: The guy won't drive, for love or money, yet he seems to be named after a car."

"Honey, we're gonna use th' money to save for a real place. So we gotta save." Lottie's eyes were sad. "I'm afraid t' stay out any longer than we hafta."

"I know, Mama. But I sure would like some in-line skates. I could run errands quicker."

"I promise I'll get 'em for ya. Just as soon as I can."

"Mama. Why you mad at Red Dog?"

"There's too much bad stuff, Darce. Way too much. People hurtin' people real bad. Red Dog seemed t' enjoy it. That's not right."

Lottie and Darcy were sitting on a picnic bench at Fairview Park. Only about half a dozen people were sharing the spot of green with them. One was a man of about thirty, tossing a Frisbee to a brown setter. Down the way, a radio was tuned to a rock station. The day was somewhat overcast, with a valiant sun trying to win a celestial war with the clouds.

"Darce, what'd you say if we moved away. Maybe the West 38th Street area. We could still be close 'nuff to Hobie's."

"No, Mama. Red Dog is good. I know he is. He saved us, Mama."

"He brought it on hisself..."

"No, Mama."

Red Dog arrived at the Thompson School just before Tina and Tonya's room, one of two kindergarten classes, was dismissed. On a whim, he decided to go into the front office. He had no plan as yet. His friends thought the time might be right to start to make his move. Of late, according to his sources, a certain recklessness born of arrogance had begun to infest the organization. If so, the onetime invincibility of High Data Associates might be showing just enough of a crack to bring it down, once and for all, and reunite him with his daughters. His first move would be to reveal himself to Miss Dandridge, his onetime kindergarten teacher.

What a wonderful year it had been! Before his father had been transferred to San Antonio to head up his company's South Texas regional office. How ironic, years later, to be again living in Shaker Heights. To meet, and fall in love, with Cherie Devereaux.

Then they killed her.

They would pay.

Red Dog Red Dodge Cox Delaney would find a way.

The secretary shook her head sadly. The nameplate on her desk said her name was Mary Sarong. A plain lady, devoid of humor, sparing of smile, she had enough sorrow in her spirit to rise to heroic levels when things hit rock bottom. Today, she was in her element. "I'm sorry, Sir! What did you say your name was?"

"Red Dodge."

"You couldn't have picked a worse day, Mr. Dodge. Miss Dandridge collapsed on the playground about an hour ago. They took her to University Hospitals."

For a moment, it didn't register.

"I'm so sorry. Have you known her long?" asked Mary Sarong.

"I…she…was my kindergarten teacher." He almost said, and his daughters' teacher as well. "I'll have to visit her."

"Do you know where University Hospitals is?"

"Yes."

"Mr. Thompson said she's resting comfortably. They'll be doing tests. I'm sure the family will appreciate it if you pay a visit. They may not let you in, of course."

Red Dog turned silently to go.

"I'm sorry, Mr. Dodge."

*   *   *

Patrice Orosco admired Theodore O'Reilly's deft handling of the cherry red '57. He seemed to know all the easy ways to negotiate Cleveland. Soon, they were in the Near West Side, downtown skyline to their backs.

Cleveland Health Care for the Homeless was located in a very ordinary building. Functional. Not that Patrice had expected a marbled bank-style building. The man on the phone, Jim McGraw, had been most friendly when Patrice had broached the subject of a face-to-face.

"I've got a little time in the early afternoon if you want to drop by," he'd said. "I might be able to enlighten you a little."

Inside, they had less than five minutes to wait.

"I suppose you want an overview," McGraw began, settling himself in the swivel chair behind his desk. Patrice and Theodore tried to relax in uncomfortable client chairs.

"Sure," said Patrice. "I'll just break in if I have any questions to clarify something. Then, I'll fire away when you've finished."

"I'm just going to observe," smiled O'Reilly. "Watch a real talent in action."

"Teddy! Don't build me up. I'll just have farther to fall when I stumble."

McGraw smiled. He was a slender man, kindly, but with an obvious underlying strength and competence that would make you hesitate to cross him. His hair was graying, his eyes bright with intelligence.

"Well, the first thing I should make clear is that homeless people suffer from the same problems the rest of the population suffers from. I don't have to enumerate, I'm sure. Plus, a lot of things directly attributable to living on the street."

"Like what?" asked Patrice.

"Conditions are often crowded. Sanitation lacking. Many skin diseases result from seldom bathing. A portion suffers from mental illness. To my mind, it can almost be a question of which came first, the chicken or the egg? Are they homeless because they are mentally ill, or did homelessness make them mentally ill? The stress is unbelievable."

"Some would say," said Patrice, "that there is very little difference between this generation of homeless and what we used to call hobos, tramps, bums, vagabonds. and gypsies."

"Of course, that element, the extremely peripatetic, always have, and always will exist, throughout time and all the ages to come. In fact, there is an honorable history to much of the nomadic, itinerant history of mankind. But this, Miss Orosco..."

"Call me Patrice."

"Sure. Call me Jim. But, as I was about to say, this phenomenon, the American Homeless, is a horse of an entirely different color. From Single Room Occupancy, or SRO, hotels, to mainstreaming, to the rude welcome home we gave the Vietnam vets; from battered single mothers pushed out into the street; to the jobless parents who loose a home; we have brewed a social prescription that will lead to chaos, anarchy, class warfare, pitched battles in the streets; a real-life Road Warriors."

"Whoa," said Patrice. "Isn't that a rather extreme, and certainly a dim, view of the actual problem?"

O'Reilly chuckled. Elfin eyes dancing.

"I certainly hope so," said McGraw, "for all of our sakes. But consider this: The French Revolution. France was quite wealthy as a country, yet the government was always on the edge of bankruptcy. Why? The rich, who had the ability to pay their taxes, shirked that responsibility. Sound familiar? How about the scion of that famous soup company, who lives out of country, and avoids his fair share of taxes. Our government always has a shortfall, be it from tax loopholes opened up by rich conservative lawmakers, or the underground economy. Ergo, budget shortfalls, program cuts, social misery.

"But, back to the French Revolution. The Nobles were always granted fiscal privileges. When Louis XVI requested the French aristocracy pay their fair share, they resisted. Much like today's tax protesters. I won't bore you with the rest of it, the fall of the Bastille, the limitations of the Monarch, the reduction of the Nobility to the level of the common man. Liberte, egalite, fraternite. The execution of Louis XVI in January, 1793. The civil war between the royalists and the republicans, the hate, fear and panic that led to the Reign of Terror.

"The point is, there are parallels, two centuries ago in France, and today, in America. The rich are getting richer, the poor are getting poorer. And nowhere in the culture of poverty is the issue greater than in housing and health care. My field is health care, obviously, and I see things getting so bad they are despicable. How many plagues can rise up out of such poverty? Out of America's own Black Hole of Calcutta, the inner city?

"We have many physicians out there who are busting gut to bring medicine to the homeless. There's the Volunteer Doctor's Medical Clinic that meets Tuesdays and Wednesdays at St. Patrick's here on the West Side. There's Near West Side Medical that just opened up a while ago, run by Dr. Varris and Dr. Elliot, who is a dentist."

Patrice raised her eyebrows. "Pudge Elliot?"

"That's the one."

"Okay," said Patrice. "You've given me an overview on a lot of things. What other agencies or organizations are doing anything about health care for the homeless?"

"I've mentioned two. There is also the Health Care for the Homeless Program, which is sponsored by the Robert Wood Johnson Foundation. There is the Pew Memorial Trust. The U.S. Public Health Service has funded over a hundred clinics to provide free services to the homeless. St. Vincent's Hospital and Medical Center in New York has done a lot of research about medical problems with the homeless. The Salvation Army has always been in the thick of the fight. So has the American Red Cross. There are many others, but it is not nearly enough."

"What are some of the specific health problems the homeless face?"

"The main thing is, many types of illness that are relatively easy to treat in the beginning, become difficult, at best, to treat when they have been neglected. Leg ulcers come to mind. The cause is almost always unsanitary conditions. Left untreated, amputation is sometimes the only recourse. Scabies, which is caused by mites can be easily treated with lindane lotion. Trouble is, you have to get the lotion to the people. Then you have to raise their level of hygiene, by getting them to wash their clothes in hot water. Left untreated, you think you are going to scratch yourself to death.

"Then there's body lice. Once in a while, crab lice. Head lice. All hard to eradicate when there is a distinct lack of sanitary facilities."

Patrice sighed. "What about shelters?"

McGraw snorted. "Sometimes people have to line up for hours for a washing machine. Sometimes the showers hardly work."

"What about serious illness?"

"Street people walk and stand a lot. They sit a lot. Sometimes that causes phlebitis, or blood clots. Or maybe inflammation, swelling, or sores. That can lead to the leg ulcers I mentioned. High blood pressure is a problem with the homeless. Their diet is lousy, stress is awful. How can they always take their medication? For many, it is very hit and miss. Pulmonary disease is rampant. Tuberculosis is now out-of-hand, and some of it is not touched by antibiotics any longer.

"Lifestyle diseases are endemic. Heart disease. Diabetes. You wouldn't believe how many homeless people go into a diabetic coma. Others go blind. Blind. That's what we are." There was now a serious catch in Jim McGraw's voice. "It's almost as if the homeless are invisible to the rest of us."

"Thank you, Jim. If I have any more questions, can I call on you again?"

"Of course. And I'll send some literature to you by courier just as soon as my secretary gets back from vacation. Be a couple of days."

"Didn't I tell you she was good?" asked Theodore O'Reilly as the two of them got up to leave.

"That you did, Sir. But I seem to remember you were pretty good yourself," said Jim McGraw.

"Still am!" O'Reilly bellowed.

On the ride back to the Plain Dealer building, Patrice spent the time viewing the landscape. A silent viewing.

"You're crying…" Teddy finally observed.

She was silent for a long moment. "He's right, you know. I never saw them. Never saw them at all…"

With a final, gigantic lift, Red Dog gave the final shove, sending the Lester upright to the top of the stairs. At least it wasn't a spiral. He and Jason Kirk rolled the dolly into the family room, and positioned it just in front of the spot the homemaker specified. Then, with another heave, Red Dog dead lifted one end of the heavy vertical piano. Kirk slid the four wheel dolly out from under.

Another successful, back-wrenching move, this one somewhat tougher, due to the stairway, than the Schimmel grand had been in Parma.

Back in the truck, Kirk was talking excitedly about his plans to get laid at Cleveland State. "Bazongas out to here, tight little pussy, gawd, what a bod…"

"Hey, Jason. How 'bout dropping me off at University Hospitals?"

"Dontcha wanna get paid?"

"Pick it up tomorrow," said the man known as Red Dodge.

"Whatever…"

Red Dog was surprised, and relived to find no restrictions on visiting his old teacher. He found her with her brother, in room 434. He hung around outside for several minutes. The brother approached him as he was leaving. "You're a neighbor, aren't you?"

"No. Miss Dandridge was my teacher."

"Oh, Ethel will appreciate you coming to see her. I appreciate it, too. She hasn't had any other visitors. Yet, anyway. She keeps to herself, you know. Not that she's unfriendly. She's really not. Just, I don't know. Lonely. Shy. Maybe a little insecure. Well, I'm not going to give you our life histories. Thanks for coming, Mr.?"

"Red Dodge."

"Thanks, Mr. Dodge. I'm Harvey Dandridge. Well, I'll be seeing you around, hopefully. Really got to get going. Glad to have met you."

"Same here."

Red Dog walked inside the austere hospital room. A single flower arrangement, probably from Harvey, was on the rolling table. He was surprised she wasn't hooked to tubes of some kind. No IV. The television, perched high on a wall stand was tuned to Jenny Jones on channel nineteen.

She followed him with her eyes, as he walked to the foot of her bed.

"I was wondering when I'd see you," she said quietly, her voice tired. "You're Cox Delaney."

"How do you know?"

"I've seen you watching your girls."

"Yes."

"I knew Cherie, you know. She and I were in the garden club."

"Yes."

She smiled. "You never came to visit your old teacher."

"No..."

"I know you didn't kill cherie."

Tears dribbled down Delaney's cheeks.

"I know who did," she said simply. "Did you know that Cherie had begun to have suspicions about her own father?"

A sledgehammer to the gut couldn't have winded Cox Delaney more surely.

"Oh, yes," said Ethel Dandridge.

The two were silent for awhile.

"I've had a bit of a scare. A heart problem, the doctor says, though not an attack, thank heavens. I'm to rest for several weeks. But right now, I imagine, we need to do something about allowing you to see your daughters. I know you play the piano. We have a piano in the room. I'll tell that pipsqueak Milton the Third that I have a special music teacher coming in to help. You will get to know your daughters that way. Until you can find a way to straighten this mess out. By the way, what do I call you?"

It is very hard to speak clearly when your throat is swollen into an emotional knot. But he managed to mumble, "Red Dodge..."

Old teachers have good hearing. And good memories. She said softly, "After that toy car you used to play with."

It was hours later before he headed back to the old abandoned car factory. The long walk, cooled by the breezes of Lake Erie, refreshed him from the day's labors.

For the first time in half a decade, he felt a sense hopefulness.

#

CHAPTER 11

Saturday, September 28, 1996

Hurricane Helps Make This Month The Wettest Ever: Forget April showers and July cloudbursts. September storms have drowned them all out.

This month is the wettest on record at Cleveland Hopkins International Airport. And it's not over yet.

The Plain Dealer

"Mija...I have never interfered with your trabajo!" roared Ruben Orosco.

"Sick einmischen! Never!" shouted Grandma Stella.

"But what Martha Dones tells me is absolutely unacceptable!"

Unfortunately, the day and age of fiber optics made it impossible to claim a bad connection. Patrice would just have to sweat through the conference phone call. Audrey and Yolanda were also on phones at Padre Orosco's.

"Honey! Whatever would possess you to go out and live among the homeless!" asked an exasperated Audrey Orosco.

"I have to do it, people!" Patrice roared back.

"Stick to your guns, big sister!" said Yolanda.

"Yolanda! Silencio! You are not helping things!" roared Daddy Ruben.

"Honey, you've gotten stories before, without so much personal involvement," observed Audrey.

"I said nothing when you fought with the Vietnamese Dragons, sabe Dios!" Ruben Orosco continued to roar. "What's a little karate, now and then! I always taught you we descend from warriors! But even warriors can freeze to death! Or be felled by germs in dirty places! Cielos!"

"I have studied the problem academically until I'm blue in the face," said Patrice with evenness, hoping to diffuse her angry father. "I have spent eons in the paper's library. On the Internet. Tete-a-tetes. Group sessions. Seminars. With every organization in the Western Reserve that works in any capacity with the homeless. Now it is time to taste the streets."

"It is a gusto you will not savor, chiquita. Amargo! Mucho amargo! Very, very bitter taste!"

"I don't suppose it will be a walk in the park..." said Patrice.

"Oh, honey! Why can't you just interview some of them?" asked Audrey.

"It would be sterile, Mama."

"Gott will watch over her, Ruben," said Grandma Stella, with finality. "If this is what my Liebchen wants to do for the people, Gott will be there for her!"

"Not you, too, Mutter!" Ruben wailed. "First Yolanda, then you! We must talk this nina into some sense! For the good of her life!"

"Now I know I'm coming to Cleveland!" said Audrey. "Next week!"

"Can I go, Mama?" asked Yolanda.

"You have school."

"I can get the assignments!"

"I thought you were planning to come all along, Mama," said Patrice.

"They want to give me an award in Florida," she said. "But I can postpone that. I'll be there, Patrice."

"So will I," said Yolanda.

"We'll eat at The Palazzo," said Audrey.

"I know a couple of diners," said Patrice. "We'll eat at one of them."

"A diner?" asked Audrey, the sound of horror in her voice.

"Yes," said Patrice. "Remember, I'll be homeless."

"Dios Mio!" Ruben croaked. "I'm coming, too!"

"I'd love that," said Audrey. "I'd really love that."

"You can't keep me home," said Grandma Stella. "The cousins will watch the restaurant for us."

"When you guys get here, contact Theodore O'Reilly at The Plain Dealer. He will know how to contact me at all times."

The lump in her throat made her voice husky; the tears, her eyes wet; the love in her heart, her soul fulfilled.

Her family had always been there for her.

*   *   *

It had been an amazing couple of weeks. Not even at UTSA had Patrice ever been so snowed under with a glut of information. None of the articles she'd ever published even came close in complexity. She had interviewed a score more experts; read every book on homelessness ever written; digested her own paper's library. Of all her sources, Pudge Elliot had been the brightest light. It amazed her that the dentist had taken up the cause of street people with a vengeance. In the past two weeks, she had occasionally reflected on his reasons. With that in mind, and two hours to spare before Teddy would drop by in Cherry Red (her pet name for his classic chariot) to take her to the streets to experience the life first hand, Patrice picked up her notes of the dinner meeting at the Elliot house.

Randy Elliot met Patrice, Theodore and her sister Norma Darling at the front door, dressed in a kimono. The luxurious house on Woodbury Road in Shaker Heights was decorated to the nines. Randy threw herself into the art of household furnishing from the moment she became Mrs. Elliot. She had more than a dozen subscriptions to magazines to help her along the way, including Architectural Digest. She watched half-a-dozen shows on cable to increase her skills. Lynette Jennings was her favorite. Like Sarah Winchester and her house in San Jose, California, Randy Elliot always had a project brewing, as if to stop might mean the whole thing might end.

When you start life with nothing, you become an instant conservative when you finally have something. In some respects, Randy was no different than other newly prosperous people. She wanted to hold on to her husband's money. But she supported his charitable work, without question.

"The budget cuts are ridiculous," Pudge Elliot began, after all were seated with drinks in their hands in the large family room. The space was decorated in an eclectic, yet satisfying way, with leather covered overstuffed sofas, divans and a love seat, facing a sunken fireplace. In back of the seating was a full-sized pool table. Three video arcade games lined one wall, with a Cinzano umbrella shading a round Plexiglas table. "For one thing, only one in eight persons needing low cost housing is ever going to get it. A decade ago, the waiting list in New York City was 18 years long. After another round of budget cuts, it is now 25 years and stretching."

The original idea had been to have Pudge Elliot one-on-one with Patrice. But the more she thought about it, the more she wanted Teddy and Randy and Norma to sit in. Patrice had perfected a kind of non-direct questioning technique that seemed almost as if she were barely in the game. The result: Invariably subjects talked their heads off.

"I'm a bloomin', bleedin' liberal Irish hand-wringer," O'Reilly interjected, "yet I can't see where the money is. How are we going to erect hundreds of thousands of low-cost houses, many more apartment complexes—and those tend to become instant slums—when the GNP, or whatever they call it now, is stagnant."

"GDP, Gross Domestic Product. The President wouldn't agree with that," Pudge said, "he'd point to all the jobs his administration has created."

"Low pay service industry jobs," said Patrice.

"There you have it," said Pudge Elliot. "Even with a new increase in the minimum wage, you cannot afford a mortgage, let alone rent on a decent place at the minimum wage. To think otherwise is shear lunacy."

"I don't know how people can live working for minimum wage," said Norma Darling. "If I hadn't found a way to confiscate my ex-husband's assets, I know I couldn't."

"Do you like my picture, Patrice?"

Again Midge Elliot was smiling with her eyes.

Patrice looked carefully at the farm animals grazing near a barn in Midge's picture. Her throat caught. "It's tremendous!"

"Can I sit with you?"

"You certainly may! Hop up on my lap, honey." Patrice set her margarita on a coaster, conveniently placed on a clear Plexiglas end table.

"You realize the root problem, do you not?" asked Pudge Elliot.

Patrice thought about it a moment, while she bounced Midge on her knee. "Obviously, today's payroll, on the bottom rung, does not match up with the cost of living."

"True," said Elliot. "But, why?"

"It's complex. Why don't you give me your insights?"

"This girl is good," Pudge said to the room. "Okay. Here goes. The most insidious tax in the history of mankind has decimated the working poor."

"All right," said Patrice.

"Inflation," said Theodore O'Reilly.

"Precisely," said Pudge Elliot. "As the wage/price spiral has gotten out of hand, it has forced industry to send jobs offshore to remain competitive. This means, the third world ends up getting a lion's share of low wage, low skill work, that once went to, say, Appalachian whites in this country. Also to rural African-Americans. Ditto, big city workers."

"Don't forget union busting," said Theodore O'Reilly. "That creates a top/down employment squeeze. Those on the bottom end up jobless. Or they work in clandestine sweat shops. Or they go on welfare. Or they drop out, even out of the housing loop."

"I think real estate speculation plays a part," Randy said. "People force up the price of homes when an area becomes a hot spot for jobs, or an escape from crime. I know some people who used to live in central California. They were priced out of their house. It started with the increase in assessed valuation. Then higher property taxes. Finally, they couldn't afford to refuse an offer on their house.."

"Where was that?" asked Patrice.

"San Luis Obispo."

"That all plays a part," said Pudge. "Poor economic conditions. Lack of affordable housing. Budget cuts that make social services less available to the poor. Runaway jobs. Another factor that few people will admit to: Environmentalism. You spoke of California, Rand; the entire west coast is reeling from restrictions. You have the Northern spotted owl perhaps needing protection in Washington, Oregon and parts of California. But at what cost? Locking up the forest? The price of lumber has skyrocketed. The cost of new construction has sent the price of low-cost housing through the roof. Then, at times, interest rates soar. How does that affect the poor? Federal housing subsidies have shrunk. Another stress. The breakup of family. Perhaps eighty percent of homeless families are headed up by women. Wife beating. That sends some women and their children—and the kids are frequently under five years of age—out into the streets.

"And then there's dental care. I'm sure somebody has talked to you about medical care. Here's an overview of the problems I see. Abscesses that haven't been seen since the middle ages. Gingivitis. Almost an epidemic. Untreated, the teeth fall out. The best treatment is hygiene. They don't get that. Some don't have enough teeth to properly masticate their food. That leads to all sorts of problems. Carries—you'd call them cavities—left untreated can eventually lead to poisoning the system. Let alone loss of teeth."

"Which is why you opened the clinic with Dr. Varris," said Patrice.

"Partially." Elliot gazed into her eyes.

Patrice said nothing, but held eye contact.

"I also know somebody living on the streets."

Patrice remained silent.

"I'd like you to meet him."

"Okay..."

The dinner was unquestionably superb. Chicken fajitas. South Texas style. Patrice was enchanted. The former Randy Duran had learned to cook.

But it was Midge who stole the show.

"I'm going to smile for you in a few weeks," the tiny girl said to Patrice when dessert, cocada pudding, was being served.

Pudge Elliot's grin was wide. "Harrison Varris has a friend who is one of the three best surgeons in the world for Moebius Syndrome. It will take two operations. One for each side."

"I've heard of it," said Patrice.

"I'll be like other people," said Midge.

"You know what?" said Patrice. "I can tell when you are smiling. That's because you have beautiful, smiling eyes! Then when you can smile with your lips, it will be even better!"

"Will I still have beautiful, smiling eyes?"

"Oh, yes! Even more so! Because then the smile will be all over your face!"

"Would you like to play Mr. Potato Head?"

"That's a great idea!"

Later, Midge insisted Patrice help tuck her in bed. After a great big hug from her daddy, Patrice wrapped the little girl in her arms. Admiring the unique color patterns on the walls of Midge's bedroom, and the framed cartoon characters that livened the room, Patrice said to the little girl, "You know what? You remind me of my little sister."

"Is she pretty?"

"Yes. Just like you. She's almost all grown up now, but I miss her very much. Especially when she was little, and was afraid of the dark. I'll bet you aren't!"

"I'm not! I'm a really big girl! So why do I remind you of her?"

"'Cause I couldn't beat her in games, either."

"Aren't you very smart?"

"I don't know!" said Patrice. "Do you think I am?"

"Well, maybe. But you couldn't put Mr. Potato Head together! And you didn't win Chutes and Ladders! I did!"

"Yes, you did!"

"Will you visit me in the hospital, Patrice?"

"Would you like me too?"

"Yes! I'd like that!"

"Then I'll be there."

On the drive back to her apartment, Patrice fell silent in the back seat, where she insisted on riding, while Norma drove and carried on with Theodore about the St. Ignatius/Lake Catholic football game on Saturday.

"My boyfriend Larry's brother plays for the Cougars." Norma remarked. "Jason is a second string tackle. He's only a Junior. Jason came to live with Larry to escape the neighborhood in Toledo. Isn't that a gas? Cleveland safer than Toledo?"

"Depends on the neighborhood," said O'Reilly. "By the way, that puts us at odds. My nephews played with the St. Ignatius Wildcats some years back. I never miss a game, when the weather is good. St. Ignatius has a running back, Matt Bunsey, who I'd like to see play for the Buckeyes. He ran for a school record 321 yards last week."

"It's going to be a great game," said Norma Darling. "The Cougars have a quarterback named Jason Battung who can really throw. Say, why don't we all go to the game? Me and Larry, you and Patrice?"

"What do you say, Treece?" asked O'Reilly, craning his head over the front seat.

"What?"

"Hello in there?" said O'Reilly.

"Sorry. I was thinking," said Patrice.

"Theodore asked you if you wanted to go to a football game Saturday night."

"Last time I went with Teddy to a sporting event, it rained cats and dogs. The Tribe got rained out against the Seattle Mariners."

"It will not rain Saturday night!" said O'Reilly. "I guarantee it!"

It poured.

Lake Catholic stunned St. Ignatius 21-12, in a virtual mud bowl.

"You're the King of Bad Weather!" a thoroughly soaked Patrice Orosco groused to Teddy O'Reilly on the way out of Mentor Stadium.

It was a hard two weeks. Patrice suffered one of her infrequent colds. While it didn't put her down, it did make the interminable research that much more uncomfortable.

The two hours were nearly up. Patrice finally put away her notes in the filing system she'd created for the homeless series. She looked around her apartment, wondering for the umpteenth time whether or not she was about to embark on something stupid.

She was all packed. The sum total of her street persona's possessions was bundled in a bindle.

Teddy O'Reilly smiled that avuncular grin that had so captured the hearts of women all over the Western Reserve. "You look awful. And of course, that's wonderful!"

"If I didn't know what you were saying," said Patrice, a chunk of ham on her fork, "I'd say something was lost in the translation." Ruthie and Moe's Midtown Diner always did ham right. Not too salty. "In fact, everything would be lost. You'd be batting zero."

"Oh? I have a batting average?"

Patrice smiled that disarming smile the Orosco girls learned from Grandma Stella. "You know what I mean!"

"Ya. I'm te…twe…thir…forty years too old…"

"Teddy, Teddy, Teddy. You are the youngest…"

"Codger…"

"…Whatever…"

"Curmudgeon…"

"…I've ever known…"

She was laughing so hard, small pieces of ham were Salad Shootering on her plate. Her scrambled eggs were beginning to resemble an omelet. "Now…look…what…you're…making…me…do…"

96

O'Reilly was in the grip of mirth himself. The waitress, Francisca, new to the job, fresh from Northern Italy, light of hair, blue of eye, looked like she was viewing a real life Ken Kesey novel. She seemed at a loss as to whether to intervene with these two pazzo americanos, or return to Venice and enter a convent. "Mi scusi," she managed to croak. "Ah...Excuse me? Will you require anything more?"

"No, no, Signorina!" said Theodore O'Reilly, still choking on laughter, "Nicente. Especially not carrot cake. Treece, you should have known him! Lester Buster Bismark. Went to school...with...him..." Teddy was losing it. "Every time he ate carrot cake, I'd crack him up with a joke. The carrots... shot out of his mouth...like buckshot!"

Patrice practically collapsed onto her plate.

The remains of the ancient auto plant at West 52nd were nearly deserted as the sun climbed high in the sky. Sitting in the back seat of the parked Cherry Red was Pudge Elliot, scooped up from his clinic to make the introductions.

"I'm going to stay right here," said O'Reilly, shutting off the engine. He gazed at Patrice on the passenger side. "Don't forget your rucksack."

Patrice got a glimpse of a great mane of red hair, a face obscured by a sixties beard; a powerful looking man emerging from behind a fragment of decrepit, crumbling wall.

"That's him," said Pudge Elliot. "Calls himself Red Dog."

"I'll always be available," O'Reilly said. "Twenty-four hours a day. If it ever gets too much for you, we'll call it off. You've got my number."

"Don't be silly," said Patrice. "I've never been a quitter."

"You've also never been homeless," said Elliot.

"I'm not now either. I've got a nice apartment to go home to."

"Not real soon," said Pudge.

"Keep that warm apartment in mind," said O'Reilly. "You'll make it."

The crusty old curmudgeon had to look away, lest his misting eyes give him away.

"Why, Theodore O'Reilly!" purred Patrice Orosco. "Are you getting emotional on me again?"

"Never!" he growled. "Never in a million years! Irishmen are the most stoic of the stiff-upper lipped crowd you'll ever see! Stolid, phlegmatic, stone-cold-sober stuffed shirts, uptight automatons all!"

"Is that Glenfiddich in your flask, Teddy?" asked Patrice.

"Of course! I take it just to steady myself!"

"...and sometimes we get so steady we can't move..." Theodore and Patrice sang in chorus.

"If you two have finished your George Gobel routine, I'll introduce Patrice to Red Dog," said Pudge Elliot. He wasn't very successful in stifling the laughter in his voice.

"This is Patrice," said Pudge, as he and Patrice stood with Red Dog in front of his makeshift shelter.

"Patrice..." said Red Dog, locking eyes with the beautiful journalist.

"Orosco," she said filling in her last name. "And what might your actual name be?"

"We don't ask questions on the street. You won't be asking them either. And 'Patrice' will have to go."

"I beg your pardon?"

"You'll have to lose the name. On the street, you'll be known as Kat."

"Like hell I will!"

"And your hubby threw you out. Beat shit outta ya"

"What the fuck?" roared Patrice.

"You're my second cousin, and any guy wants you for a squeeze gotta go through me first."

"You listen to me you asshole! I'm not going to follow your script! I'm going to do things my way!"

"Then you'll die," said Red Dog. "Dealers get one whiff there's a newspaper woman on the street, you'll face a smorgasbord of death. Maybe a hotshot. That's a lethal injection of illicit drugs. Maybe an old-fashioned shiv. Maybe a nine. Or piano wire. A garrote. Ice pick. Perhaps right through the ear. Maybe they'll lace a drink. Beat you to death with a sap."

Patrice stared him down. Pudge Elliot had the good sense to say nothing. Heavy rain was in the forecast. Light drops began leaking from the sky. The wind was picking up. Patrice caught a glimpse of Theodore O'Reilly, a hundred yards away, leaning back in Cherry Red.

"It is my intention to keep you alive, Patrice," said Red Dog. "If it will help, when we are alone, I'll call you Patrice. It is a beautiful name."

She continued to stare at the hirsute onetime computer analyst.

"Kat?" she finally managed to croak.

"Probably short for Katherine. You can say that if you have to."

"And where am I from?"

"Search me. The rest of it you can make up as you go along. Once you construct a fiction, just remember to stick to it. Nothing arouses suspicion on the street more than when a story changes."

"Is that all?"

"No. When Lottie gets back, I'll have her fix you up. That is, if she isn't in one of her moods. She's been a tad angry with me for a while."

"Gee, I wonder why!" said Patrice.

"Hasta be my charm, or lack of it."

"And what do you mean, 'fix' me up?"

"You don't look much like a street person."

"My clothes are grunge...I look like a mess..."

"You look like an actor dressing for a part. Lottie will fix you up."

"He always like this?" Patrice asked Pudge Elliot.

"The streets have their own rules, Patrice. Listen to him. He'll take care of you. Now, if you two don't mind, I've got to get back to the clinic and do an emergency root canal. Supposed to be off. I'll be in touch."

Pudge Elliot began walking back to O'Reilly and Cherry Red. Patrice stood, bindle in hand, watching him go. Well, here it was. Now it was time to put up or shut up. She'd been in tight scrapes before. But as Pudge Elliot had pointed out, never in a homeless situation.

"Let's get busy," said Red Dog.

"Doing what?"

"We've got to build you a shelter. Maybe even check out the shelters. If it rains as hard as I think it might, we'll have to go indoors. When you do, go indoors that is, only go with me. That's the only way to keep you safe."

"I can take care of myself, Red Dog."

"No," he shook his head emphatically. "Nobody can. We take care of each other. That's the first rule of survival on the streets. Learn that today, and you will be ready for a tomorrow."

"Were you ever charming?" A hint of a smile.

Red Dog gazed at her for a long while.

"I don't know. Nobody's left to tell me whether or not I was."

Now she gazed at him for a bit. "I know. I know. Don't ask questions."

"You're learning, Kat."

"Hey, we're alone."

"Just practicing. You're learning, Patrice."

"That's better," she said.

The Deli sandwiches from Dave's Deli on West 32nd were what deli sandwiches always should have been. That was Fairly's considered opinion. Tomajac wasn't so sure. "Delis are delis, fer crissake. Just eat it. Sandwich is just working-class food. I prefer it. Goes back to my roots."

Fairly knew better than to wax philosophic for very long with Tomajac. It sometimes surprised him to remember Tomajac had a college education. Hit man as scholar.

"Fact is, that's why I like Cleveland. Ethnic place. Working-class place. Like me. You got Poles and Czechs; Hungarians and Germans; Serbs and Croats; Russians and Slavs. There are a lot of Russians around Mayfield Road. Did you know that?"

"You've told me," muttered Fairly, stretching in the small corner booth.

"I'd like a bowl of borscht right now. Go good with this sandwich."

"Topped off by a doughnut, I'd imagine."

"Good suggestion. Let's go," said Tomajac, picking up the half sandwich he had yet to eat. "We'll go to the Russian House. Get some borscht. Then stop in at a Dave's and get some doughnuts. Give us another place to drop off these pictures of Delaney."

"Do you even know what goes with white wine, and what goes with red wine?"

"Naw. Who cares?"

"Only about twenty million wine connoisseurs."

On the way out, Fairly admonished the young man behind the counter to be sure and call if they saw the man in the pictures. "Might be a reward," he added. "But the important thing is to do your civic duty."

"Stone killer, huh?" said the kid.

"You got it," smiled Fairly.

Raindrops chased them all the way to the car.

"I'm sorry to say there has been no movement on that front," said Todd Englewood. "But Fairly and Tomajac are staying with it. Fairly is somewhat miffed. He was supposed to retire a couple of days ago."

Maurice Devereaux sighed. "I promised to pick up the girls myself. I've got to leave, Todd. Do stay with this. I want the asshole run down. God. Here in Cleveland all this time! Ridiculous."

"We'll take care of it, Sir."

"Do that. Where is Avery? He's not half the driver Fairly is. Wish I could keep that stubborn sonuvagun. But a promise is a promise. He wants Florida sun, he gets Florida sun."

Avery walked through the door at that moment. A small, compact man of indeterminate age, Avery had been reassigned from groundskeeping and given a crisp new uniform. "The limo is ready, Sir."

"Very well," said Devereaux.

Devereaux followed the new chauffeur through the labyrinthine maze that was High Data Associates.

It was a short, quick drive to the Thompson School.

Arriving a few minutes before the brand new Saturday Computer Camp dismissed, Devereaux himself went inside the school. He went straight to the offices of Milton Thompson III.

The obsequious smile. "Monsieur Devereaux! Comment ca va?"

"Stuff it, Thompson! I pay you big bucks to educate my granddaughters. After the unfortunate incident a couple weeks ago, I want to know what you have been doing to rectify the matter."

"Ah, well, as a matter-of-fact, we have things well in hand! Yes, we do! Miss Dandridge is back, and starting Monday, we have a new music teacher coming in! Quite a delightful fellow. This will give our students a sense of self-esteem they haven't had before."

"Sounds like a left-wing concept, Thompson."

"I assure you, Sir, it is not. 'Music has charms to soothe a savage breast,' as William Congreve wrote. I guarantee it will be a boon to our curriculum."

"Thompson, I want you to hear me, and hear me clearly. If any other tyke annoys either of my granddaughters, I will pull them out of this school and sic my lawyers on you. I will win. I will own the Thompson School. Are we clear on this concept?"

"Yes, Sir, we are. It will not happen again."

Devereaux's smile was gritty. "No, Thompson, it won't! Good day, Sir."

When the bell rang a minute later, Tina and Tonya spied their grandfather positioned in front of the school, and scampered after him, whirling balls of arms and legs, cheeping voices vying with the reverberation of wind and splattering rain bouncing off their waterproof coats.

"Grampa! Grampa! We got to get on the World Wide Web!" said Tina.

"Oh, spider webs are awful!" laughed Maurice Devereaux. "Sticky, and just terrible!"

"No, Grampa," said Tonya. "On the computer!"

"You've got cob webs on your computers?" asked Maurice Devereaux, face contorted in alarm.

"No, no," said Tina, laughing.

The girls piled into the back of the limo, Devereaux following.

"Grampa, you're silly!" said Tonya. "Don't you got computers at your work?"

"Well, maybe! But nobody as beautiful as you two to work with them!"

"Oh, Grampa!" said Tina. "You just say that!"

"'Cause you love us!" supplied Tonya.

The limo headed for Mrs. Cronemiller's house and the Saturday piano lessons. A relaxed Maurice Devereaux would accompany them. Nowadays, the only thing that allowed him a moment's rest was when he was in the company of Tina and Tonya.

The twins turned their high voltage smile on the doting gentleman. "Grampa? Can we have a banana split at the ice cream shop if we get good lessons?" Tina was the spokesperson.

"C'est mon voeu le plus cher!"

"Merci grand-pere! C'est bon!"

The two scruffy, vacant-eyed hooligans had Lottie and Darcy cornered behind a now closed co-op grocery near West 38th Street. Both men, sallow of skin, emaciated, reeking of rotgut, lousy hygiene and a fear/anger cocktail raging inside evil eyes, loomed like hungry predators sure of the kill.

Lottie stood absolutely still, Darcy her shadow.

"Now we gonna get the money, honey," said the rusty voice of the closer of the two. "Why don' you hand it over, little lady, 'fore we take it from ya with a blade. Then we's gonna let ya go. But only if yer good!"

"No," said Lottie. "I worked for it."

"She worked for it, Moe! She worked for it! Ain't that a blast? We'll, we's workin' for it, too, it seems! You don' seem to wanna give it over! So, I'll just cut ya! How's that? I like my work!"

"No," she said.

"I tried, Moe. I tried. Thought I'd get away from blade work."

"You did try, Billy. You really did," said Moe. "I'm prouda ya, Billy. But sometime ya gotta just do the blade work, boy!"

"I think you guys better go away," said a new player in the game.

"Y'think?" said Billy, eyeing the big, boy-man. "Y'think? I know ya. You that kid with the bitch that died!"

"That's him," said Moe. "I rec'nize him, missef, now."

Oscar No Name shook his head sadly. "You shouldn't of said that. You shouldn't."

"Tell ya what," said Billy. "I'm gonna cut this boy first, then I'm gonna cut the bitch, and her snivel nose kid after that!"

A tire iron appeared in Oscar's hand.

"Y'gonna try that play, are ya?" said Billy.

Billy and Moe advanced on Oscar. Both sported six inch blades. They didn't appear to have enough vigor to last a day, until they went into an agile, knife man's crouch. Slowly they swayed closer to Oscar No Name. Oscar backed up. They continued to come.

"This here pig sticker gonna spill yer guts, boy!" said Billy.

Oscar was against the wall of the co-op. The sound of traffic was as loud as the surf on a rocky beach. Neighborhood dogs yapped at each other. Overhead, jets could be seen leaving Cleveland Hopkins International Airport.

Oscar No Name suddenly lunged toward Billy and his cutter. The tire iron came swinging from a side arc. It missed, but Billie lost his balance getting out of the way of the iron, and stumbled into Moe.

"Whoa, boy!" said Billy. "I was on'y gonna scratch ya a bit. Now, I'm gonna hafta carve ya up!"

"Le's stop flappin' gum, an' do this boy, Billy," said Moe.

Billy and Moe began to circle, in opposite directions. Oscar No Name had never been so calm in all of his life. The only things in his mind were the simple questions: What would Red Dog do? How would Red Dog handle this?

"I don't wanna hurt you," said Oscar. "I really don't."

"Y'got it all wrong, boy. Y'ain't gonna hurt us. We gonna hurt you," said Billy.

Billy and Moe coordinated their attack like a pack of jackals. Moe dropped to the ground a foot away from Oscar No Name, a hideous groan rising up from his throat. Lottie stood in back of Moe, gripping a four foot length of two-by-four.

Seeing his comrade splat to the ground caused Billy to hesitate just a fraction of a second in his attack. Just enough for Oscar to take a good round house swing.

He missed again.

Billy was simply too quick, side stepping the awkward Oscar's hack.

"Oh, you hurt m'brother, bitch."

With surprising speed, Billy moved around Oscar and went for Lottie.

"Run Darcy!" shouted Lottie.

Oscar seemed glued to the spot.

Billy was making his thrust.

It seemed a miracle that Lottie parried the blade with the chunk of lumber. She stepped away.

"This gettin' int'resting," croaked Billy's rusty voice.

Oscar advanced.

"Get away, boy! Maybe I'll spare ya," said Billy, as he prepared to dance around Lottie and her club.

Oscar kept coming.

Billy spun around.

Oscar's timing was superb. The tire iron landed on Billy's left shoulder. A shriek of pain like a mortally wounded animal. Billy stepped back five paces. He breathed deeply.

"Didn't think ya had it in ya, boy. No matter. Me an' my brother gonna hurt a few days, but you gonna be dead."

Slowly Billy circled Lottie and Oscar. He carried his left shoulder stiffly. He seemed to be timing his adversaries every breath.

"I don't wanna hurt you..." Oscar repeated, sadness in his voice.

Billy made a quick move. The knife began a thrust. It missed Oscar by the narrowest of margins, as he pivoted at the last minute and began to thrust his own weapon.

The tire iron struck Billy's right shoulder. Much harder than the blow to his left shoulder. Lottie's board planked him in back of the head at almost the same moment.

Billy hit the ground like a rock.

Soundlessly.

"Let's get outta here," said Lottie. She grabbed the small bag of groceries from the co-op and began a visual search for Darcy.

The little girl emerged, shivering, from the corner of the building.

"Mama? You okay?"

Red Dog stood with Patrice, admiring the new shelter. It was a hodgepodge of materials that just might prove to be moderately leak proof. But then, maybe not. Hard rain has a funny way of penetrating supposedly well-maintained roofs.

"If I can just think of this as a camping trip," mused Patrice.

"Good as any way of thinking, I guess," said Red Dog.

Soon, she'd unpacked her bindle, spreading out the bedding to test the space for a living configuration. Finally, she was satisfied.

Red Dog peeked inside the makeshift structure. "You'd better find a spot to stash your goods, Kat. They'll disappear otherwise."

"I hadn't thought of that," she said. "Back to Kat, huh?"

"Guess I'd better. A slip of the tongue might cause you problems."

"I guess."

"How do you like your assignment?"

She chuckled. "They're paying me."

"There is that," said Red Dog.

"This is what I worked for."

"Any regrets?"

"What else could I do? I might have just begun teaching grade school. I could have been a dental assistant, cleaning teeth. I wouldn't have needed UTSA for that. I might have embarked on a climb up the corporate ladder. But that seemed boring."

"Want some advice?"

"I have a feeling I'm going to get some."

"Drop the cultured tones. Develop a patois. Kentucky would be good. Texas, which you're familiar with, might be easier," said Red Dog.

"Why? About four percent of the homeless are college graduates."

"Not around here."

"You are."

"I'm the exception that proves the rule."

"Then I will be, too."

"Not if you want my cooperation," said Red Dog.

"God! You really are an ass, aren't you? Is that why you hit skid row? Couldn't get along with anybody?"

"Here comes Lottie. I'll have her smooth over your uptown image."

Lottie, Darcy and Oscar No Name were walking quickly, nervously into the ad interum compound.

"Funny," said Patrice. "Somebody else called me uptown."

But Red Dog wasn't listening. With the senses developed in a jungle, he knew intuitively that something was very wrong.

#

CHAPTER 12

Sunday, September 29, 1996

HOPING AGAINST HYPE: Indians Fans are Impatient for a World Series Title but Try to Keep Optimism disguised with Caution: The courtship, it seems, has been leavened by expectations.

Indians fans have moved from last year's dewy-eyed rapture to a foot-tapping impatience. Forty-eight years is enough already.

Lou Mio and Tom Breckenridge

Rip roaring headaches are never welcome. When Patrice awoke in a strange place, temples trip-hammering, ersatz bed hard like a sharp-edged rock pile, it was touch and go whether panic would set in.

Then Patrice remembered.

She was now undercover. Only Red Dog knew of her real identity. She wondered about Red Dog. Why would a man so smart, so competent, so drop-dead gorgeous, be so down-and-out?

She would keep an eye on Red Dog.

Amazing, the day before, how he had calmed Oscar No Name, Lottie and Darcy! From terror so profound the three had barely been able to tell of their experience, to an orderly recounting of events. Always, he spoke in measured tones. Unflappable. He gave each of the three his undivided attention when it was their turn to speak.

Then Red Dog took the little band out for pizza. With the three Johnson's, Claude, Margie and little Madge, he managed to brighten the day of seven people.

"I'll beat up more people, Red Dog, if I can get pizza!" said Oscar No Name.

Red Dog smiled. "Let's hope it doesn't come to that, Oscar. As I've told you before, there is too much violence in the world, as it is."

"He really was a hero," said Lottie.

Claude Johnson smiled, in between bites of pizza. "Oscar reminds me of m'cousin, Bill. If it hadta be done, Bill did it."

Oscar grinned, feeling good about himself for perhaps the first time since his mother had died. Darcy placed another slice of pizza on his plate.

"He was a good man," said Margie Johnson. "But they killed him in Cincinnati. Just broke 'is spirit, an' he died." She was quiet for a moment. "I'm scairt a big cities. Ain't no place t'raise younguns."

"There are problems everywhere," said Red Dog quietly.

It was comical watching Madge try and cope with a slice of pizza supreme. Red Dog had insisted on everything but the kitchen sink for toppings. The pizza parlor, which had just opened a week ago in a long abandoned but now refurbished Googie-style building on Lorain, was nearly empty. Patrice hoped the place would catch on. The pizza was great.

"I'm going to try and get us an old SRO building just off Detroit," said Red Dog, when the two giant pizzas had nearly been consumed. "It was condemned in '87, and they were going to raze the place and build one of those gentrification projects, complete with yuppies. Financing fell through, and we just might be able to work with a man named Arnold Anderson at the Cuyahoga Metropolitan Housing Authority. He might be able to grease some wheels. I don't know if I can pull it off, but I'm going to try. Can't hurt. We're talking about something they call 'sweat equity,' here. We'd have to fix the place up ourselves, probably do some fund raisers, and meet all codes and regulations."

Single room occupancy (SRO) hotels, for a variety of reasons, mostly economic, had been going by the wayside in America's cities for years. Attempts to revive them for the homeless had run up against codes, bureaucracy, and political interests.

"Does that mean we'd have a real place to live?" asked Lottie.

"Yes," said Red Dog. "But don't count your chickens. It is very preliminary."

"I need to talk to you about that," whispered Patrice.

Red Dog gazed into the still beautiful face, that no amount of makeover by Lottie could disguise. Lottie had not been told the reasons for blunting Patrice's patrician looks, transforming her into "Kat." She probably thought it was a defense mechanism against predatory males.

"In due time, Kat."

"Kat, would y'like this last piece?" asked Margie Johnson.

"No thanks," she answered, deeply moved at Margie's generosity.

Margie had trouble selling it, as every belly was now full and comfortable. Carefully, she wrapped the last piece of pizza in several napkins.

When you are on the street, you do not waste food.

As the Sunday morning sun rose in the sky, Patrice struggled for complete wakefulness. No Mexican coffee this morning. Her stopgap shelter had done the job for an early autumn night. But Red Dog's warning that she, along with the rest of the little compound, would soon have to spend nights in public shelters had made her apprehensive. Too many stories of thievery, physical attacks, and grossly unsanitary conditions had come to her attention. Sometimes it was impossible to find a spot. Then what? Find a grate, perhaps; be sustained by steam on a frigid, gloomy night.

Claude Johnson was sitting in front of his family's shelter, carving a figurine from a piece of driftwood he'd recently found at the lakeshore. A still groggy Patrice sat down beside him.

"Hello, young lady," Claude said by way of greeting.

"You look like you're good at that," observed Patrice.

"Usta make a little money at it."

"Is that what you're doing now? For sale, I mean?"

"Ya. Maybe find me a small shop somewhere takes things on consignment."

"Sounds like a good idea."

"Where you from, Kat?"

Here was her first chance to improvise.

"South Texas."

"Knew it. Heard it in your voice."

"You knew?"

"Kicked around yer neck a the woods when I was in th' service. Spent time in Brownsville when I could get leave. Hadta hitchhike hundreds a miles from Lawton. Tha's in Oklahoma. Fort Sill. There was this lady, y'see. Mexican lady. Kinda high fer me, if y' know what I mean. But I admired her anyway. Her brother had this band played aroun' Lawton.. Some sorta Mexican music. Her dad owned a grocery store in Brownsville, called it a bo-somethin'."

"Bodega."

"That's it."

"Well, anyway. I went fer her in a big way, an' she liked me some, but the brother was kinda mean. An' the daddy, well, he jest sent word that I was to be run off. So I was. Run off. After th' army, I went back to Flat Rock. Margie moved in from a close by town, an' I just kinda fell in love with her. Good woman. Real good woman."

"How long have you been married?"

"Twenty years, I guess. Took us a long time t'have Madge. Margie was purty near forty when we found we'as gonna have a kid. Like t'surprised me t'death. That little kid's been the lighta our eyes, though."

"Claude, y'better come here," Margie said from the enclosure.

Claude Johnson put down the figurine he was whittling, and disappeared inside. Patrice continued to sit on her haunches against the flattened side of a small rock. No one else in the little community had stirred, to Patrice's knowledge.

The morning was a bit breezy, the wind coming off Lake Erie in the way of autumn since time immemorial. It would still be quite warm in South Texas. Today, they would be lucky to have sixty-two degrees in Greater Cleveland. Rain didn't look like it was in the forecast.

"Kat, could y'come here please?" asked Margie Johnson.

Patrice approached the cardboard/wooden lean-to, catching a glimpse of a mother's anguished face. "What's the matter, Margie?"

"This ain't right, honey!" she said to the undercover reporter. "Feel Madge's forehead."

A sense of absolute dread enveloped Patrice Orosco. Panic played across Claude Johnson's face.

Madge Johnson was burning up.

"She slept fitful. But I didn't think nothin' was wrong," said Margie.

"Just a little croup. Kids get that alla time."

Madge was so lethargic she couldn't keep her eyes open. Her breathing was rough and labored.

"Can you carry her, Claude?" asked Patrice.

"I can."

"Follow me," said Patrice. "And we'd better hurry."

Patrice in the lead, made a mad dash for Near West Side Medical. She had Harrison Varris' phone number at the clinic. He had call forwarding, as well as a pager, so it should reach him wherever he was.

The three of them were out of breath when they arrived at the closed clinic. Patrice found a nearby pay phone and placed a frantic call to Dr. Varris.

"I'll put your message through, Ma'am, but I don't know how long it will take to reach him," said the disembodied voice from Varris' service.

"It has to be quick!" shouted Patrice. "This is a total emergency. Can you call Dr. Elliot?"

"Dr. Elliot has a cellular. I'll call him now, if you wish to hold the line."

"Thank God they both have the same service," Patrice muttered to herself.

A few moments later, the woman from the answering service was back on the line with Patrice. "I have Dr. Elliot, Ma'am."

"Pudge..." Tension in her voice. "Pudge...there is this little girl. She's got a terrible fever. She's barely responding. We're at the clinic. Her mom and dad have her. Pudge! I can't find Dr. Varris!"

"He's in the clubhouse, Patrice. We'll rush down there right now. Hang on. Try to stay calm, especially around the parents."

"Ma'am, I'm sorry to break in, but I have Dr. Varris on the line. I'll patch him through to you."

"Patrice, this is Harrison. I'm going to send an ambulance. We'll need to take the child to Columbia St. Vincent Charity Hospital. I'll send a cab for you, and the parents if they wish, or they can ride in the ambulance."

Varris sounded winded.

"Is there something I can do now?"

"Try to break the fever, Patrice." The sound of a car door slamming.

"I'm going to hang up in a second, Patrice. The ambulance should be there momentarily. Then I'll get the cab. We are in Pudge's car now, racing to the hospital. Stay with it Patrice. Use water at air temperature. Some kind of cloth. That might start us on the path of breaking that fever."

Disconnect.

There was a convenience store a block-and-a-half away. Patrice sprinted to the store. Fortunately, she'd squirreled away a few bucks in case of an emergency. This seemed to qualify in spades.

Back at the storefront clinic, the apathy of a Sunday shattered by panic, Patrice grabbed Madge and began to apply Perrier by way of a dish cloth. The child was unresponsive.

A small girl with dreadlocks was skipping down the street, bouncing a beach ball. She stopped when she saw three white adults doing something funny to a three year old child in front of the clinic..

"Hey! What you doin'?" said the girl.

"She has a bad fever," said Patrice. "We've got to break it."

"My Mama know what to do for that. I'll get her."

The girl shot toward her house, half-a-block away.

Patrice continued to work with Margie to cool Madge down. Claude held his little daughter. A few moments later, a matronly black woman matching the little girl in dreadlocks stride for stride brought a small plastic swimming pool with two half gallon jugs of tap water. Very quickly, Madge was being bathed in the combined liquid of Cleveland and France.

"I'm Maya," said the woman. "This is my daughter DeShay."

"I'm...Kat," said Patrice. "This is Claude and Margie Johnson. The little one is Madge."

"I know about sick kids, I do," said Maya. "It ain't no fun."

"She seemed to have croup," said Margie Johnson, in a hollow voice.

"This chil' got more 'an croup. She got pneumonia, mark my word!"

"She's not responding," said Patrice, in a shaky voice.

"That the fever," said Maya.

The siren announced the ambulance before it turned the corner. In moments, Madge Johnson was whisked away, her parents riding with her.

"You down on yo' luck?" Maya asked, as she, DeShay and Patrice watched the Johnson's race to the hospital.

Patrice took a long time to respond. "No, but they are. And so are a lot of other people."

"Ain't that the truth!" said Maya. Then she looked closely at Patrice/Kat. "No. You don' look too down on yo' luck. But, if you be thinkin' you are, you know where I live."

Lump throat time. Patrice didn't want to lose it.

"That's extremely kind of you," said Patrice.

"Just the Christian way, chil'"

It seemed like a long cab ride to Columbia St. Vincent Charity Hospital.

Waiting rooms are always crowded in a big city; bustling places where organized chaos reigns. The miracle is the staff somehow manages to deliver quality care in spite of the fact that modern life brings modern emergencies that nature never intended. Like drive-by shootings.

Madge was immediately admitted to the pediatrics ward, where a drip line was set up with massive doses of antibiotics.

Patrice leaned back against her chair, hoping to blink away exhaustion. Claude and Margie were in the room with their daughter. The first order of business, Patrice knew, was to cut the fever.

A voice penetrated her fatigue, wrenching her closed eyes open. "You acted quickly. That's good."

Red Dog.

"Where have you been?" Patrice asked in a neutral voice.

"I was helping Lottie and Darcy over at Hobie's. The word spread fast. Up and down the street. You're one of us, now. Remember what I said. We help each other."

Patrice hadn't been aware Red Dog had sat down beside her until he spoke. She said, "You move like a ghost."

Red Dog laughed. "Long habit."

"Harrison Varris is working on her," Patrice said.

"I know. I just came from the room. They've got her on Ceptra. It's pneumonia."

"What's the prognosis?" asked Patrice.

"The next few hours will tell the story," said Red Dog.

Only one chair in the waiting area was vacant. An elderly gentleman with a cane sat down carefully in the seat, facing Patrice directly. He locked into her gaze after settling himself. His stare was blank. Patrice looked away, startled.

"Better look at me, Sylvia! I ain't goin' away!" boomed the old man.

Patrice stole another look at the old man.

"That's right, bitch! It's me! Thought you'd vamoosed, did you? Not possible, you miserable cunt!"

Red Dog patted her knee. "Don't say anything," he whispered. "To do so would be to confuse him even more."

"Sylvia Whore! Whore Sylvia! If there's a God, he's gonna fry you good!"

The man had a pencil thin mustache, sallow skin, hair a dead gray. He seemed to have collapsed into himself, the way spinal compression in the very old is wont to do. His eyes were filmy.

A woman, elderly herself, bustled up to the waiting area. She exclaimed, "Dad! Where have you been?"

The woman gently helped him to his feet, with considerable effort on both of their parts. A uniformed nurse came up to the two of them, and took the old man by the elbow. "Come, Mr. Dubow. We have to see Dr. Stevenson now."

The elderly daughter approached Patrice, a worried look on her face. "I'm sorry if Dad bothered you," she said, genuine sadness in her voice. "He got away. He can be remarkably frisky at times for a man of ninety-nine."

But Dubow got away from the nurse. "I'm warning you Sylvia!" he roared, "you aren't getting away with it this time!"

"I'm sorry…" the woman said again, rushing to assist the nurse with her father.

Patrice shuddered.

"It's okay," said Red Dog quietly.

"What a vile old man!" snapped a lacquered blonde, three chairs down, aquiline features agitated. "They oughta lock up the geezer!"

"Sooner they lock you up," said Red Dog, turning his gaze directly on the woman. The others seated in the waiting room appeared very uneasy.

The leathery lady gave Red Dog a withering look that might have singed the Norman Rockwell prints on the wall.

"Let's catch some air," said Red Dog, escorting Patrice out of the waiting room, and out of the hospital.

"That kind of got me," said Patrice.

Red Dog grinned. "You've never been called names before?"

She smiled, shaking her head tiredly. "Not that. I could picture my father that kind of old. It just hit me. Ruben Orosco, about a hundred years old, and no longer the man I can turn to for advice. Not that I ever take it. But it's good to have it available nonetheless."

They were strolling on the grounds when Red Dog suddenly put his hand on her shoulder. "I meant it. You really came through. I don't think the Johnson's have any experience with doctors at all. Or sickness. Probably a hardy family in the hills without much medical care, if at all. According to Harrison, another couple of hours and it would have been too late."

"Then she's going to make it?"

"Harrison isn't saying anything. But, yes. I think Madge will make it."

"This is so much for me..." said Patrice.

"It's so much for anybody."

"The streets, and all. Kids getting sick. Knife fights. I don't know if I can take it."

"You're a fighter."

"How would you know?"

"Oh, I've been briefed. You might say, I've seen your file."

They were standing under a chinaberry tree. Patrice stared at the handsome man they called Red Dog. "Exactly what does that mean?"

"In due time."

"You keep saying that."

Red Dog chuckled. "I do, don't I?"

"You're a hard man to figure!"

"Other people keep saying that."

"There's Pudge," said Patrice.

Pudge Elliot had just walked outside the hospital. He was looking toward the parking lot. Patrice and Red Dog caught sight of Randy leading Midge toward her father. Pudge was grinning wildly. Midge looked excited. Randy Elliot reached for her husband. The three of them hugged in front of the entrance.

"The operation is tomorrow," said Red Dog.

"How long have you known them?" asked Patrice.

"Forever. Pudge that is. Randy, maybe five years."

"Will it be a success?"

"I didn't think so, at first. But somewhere along the way, Randy really did fall in love with the real Pudge Elliot."

"I didn't mean that. I meant, will Midge's operation be a success?"

Red Dog gazed at the three Elliot's, still hugging in front of the hospital. The big guy's eyes seemed to mist a bit. "That little girl's been smiling all of her life. Now it'll just be a whole lot more noticeable."

"I don' know anything yet, Almeda," said Juan Sanchez Prieto. "Been only a couple weeks. These things take time, if you wanna stay vivo, alive."

"You're just chickenshit, like all machismo hombres. Talk a big fight, like a banty rooster with a big voice. I want Shaleen out of the life. I want my daughter to live long and grow old with nietos and nietas. I don't want her to be the fuck doll of whore catchers!"

"Okay...okay. I got good smack today. An' I don' want no fuck trade out. I want scratch. Greenbacks. Entendido?"

Almeda Peres pulled a twenty dollar bill from out of the extreme plunge of the neckline her fuck me dress presented johns; an enticing view of oft squeezed cleavage, tortured by push up bras and rough hands sixteen hours a day. "Ahright, Juan. You're a lousy fuck, anyway."

"You should speak, puta!"

* * *

"You have the ugliest game I've ever seen," said Tom Erickson. "And yet, you are effective. You're up two strokes. Looks like I'm going to have to spring for dinner. Unless I can take you good on the last hole."

"The Serbs, Croats and Muslims of the former Yugoslavia will embrace Mohandas Gandhi first," said Jonathan Tubb.

The Executive from the Newhouse owners group double bogeyed the eighteenth. Tubb managed a very sloppy par, chipping out of a sand trap to within an inch of the cup.

"What did I tell you? Ugly. But effective," said Erickson.

Afterwards, at Dick's Last Resort, where Tubb had a hunger for clams, the two settled into serious talk about the upcoming series that would be made into a book. "Your idea has been given the absolute green light, Tubb. I hope this girl is up to the challenge."

"In the sixties, when Jimmy H. was as popular as a drink of water to a desert-weary Bedouin," said Tubb, "I ran a series on Teamster abuses. Soon, other papers followed suit. In the summer of seventy-two, when Nixon was the saint who opened up the Great Wall of China, I hammered away at Watergate, while the national media remained largely silent. In mid 1991, when President Bush had numbers off the wall, I wrote his political obituary, long before a shaky pulse was felt out on the hustings. I trust my instincts, Tom."

"Do you plan to have her continue with the paper after the series and book are finished?"

"I hope she stays. Frankly, she'll be hotter than Gennefer Flowers' pants. We may not be able to afford her."

"The one problem I have is O'Reilly," said Erickson. "Isn't he a little long in the tooth?"

"So is Walter Cronkite."

Tom Erickson laughed. "You've got cojones, Tubb."

"All my babes have said that," he said, attacking another mouthful of clams.

Timothy O'Reilly nursed a vodka Collins at a back table at Nighttown. His brother, Sean, was on duty, so could not be relaxing to the music of Monsieurs Deutrieve and O'Reilly. Uncle Teddy was clearly in a blue funk, and seemed to be taking the whole thing out on his saxophone, Marcus a willing co-conspirator.

When the matinee dinner set was finished, Theodore O'Reilly joined Timothy at the table. A bottle of Glenfiddich miraculously appeared, courtesy of a waiter.

"Let's hear it," Teddy barked without preamble.

"The camp she's staying at has had some rather exciting things happen in the last day," said Timothy O'Reilly. "A knife fight. A little girl from Kentucky got very sick. She might not make it, according to our sources. Sean is monitoring that as we speak.

"Baptism by fire," said Teddy, taking in some malt whiskey.

"You could say that. We wouldn't want the kid's problem to scare Patrice off the streets."

"You make sure knife fights do not become commonplace," said the old man, a look of extreme worry altering his elfin features.

"Ah, Uncle Theodore. Me an' Sean, we don't like the women folk to be battered on. We can hurt people very bad when we take a mind to."

Theodore O'Reilly smiled warmly, some of the wattage thanks to the Glenfiddich. "I know that, Timothy. As sure as Ireland is green, and the whiskey flows to the souls of the Emerald Isle, I trust you nephew. And sure as rain, that young Sean, though he might learn to control his urges a bit better. I guess what I'm tryin' to say Son, is, if anything happens to Patrice Orosco, I mean anything at all, you won't be workin' security for anyone anymore. You'll be workin' bubble gum machines at the mall. Or peelin' potatoes at a fuckin' British pub! And that is like six kinds of hell to a good Irish lad!"

"I understand Uncle."

Timothy O'Reilly had a wild urge to trade in the vodka Collins for something with a little stout in it. Nah. Had to stay sharp. Soon, he'd be spelling Sean for the night hours. Stakeouts. Nothing like 'em.

Church can be a drag, especially if you are a five-year-old, attending high church. If you are part of a set of twins, it can be bearable, at least until you are caught.

Naturally, Virginia Compton observed Tina and Tonya acting up amongst the children's choir.

"You will spend the afternoon doing chores, children. Until you can learn to pay respect to the Lord by acting as proper young ladies," said the redoubtable Miss Compton.

She escorted the young beauties to the Suburban, parked close to St. Thomas Episcopal Church in Shaker Heights. Why disciplining these children for such an infraction should still be necessary was beyond the comprehension of the strangely stern, yet freethinking nanny.

"Doesn't the Lord ever play?" asked Tina Devereaux, face screwed into an expression of pure wonder.

Inside the Suburban, Compton turned to peer over the bench seat at the fiesty twin. "Certainly not during Communion, young lady!"

"But it was so funny!" insisted Tina.

"When Reverend Dalminster spilled the wine down Mrs. Dougherty's dress!" supplied Tonya. "It got her boobs all wet!"

"Children!" roared the nanny. "We'll have respect!"

"I think," said Tina, "the Lord was playing with Reverend Dalminster! I think the Lord tipped his hand, and made him spill the wine!"

"Because the sermon was so boring," said Tonya. "It put Mr. Dalrymple to sleep!"

"And he was snoring," said Tina. "Sawing logs, as Grand-pere would say. Grand-pere would have laughed! I know he would! He's not stuffy, like you are!"

The charge stabbed Virginia Compton like a driven nail. "I'll tell you what," she said after a moment's recovery. "If you promise me you'll never act up in church again, we'll go get a banana split!"

"At 31 Flavors?" asked Tina.

"Sure," said Virginia Compton. "I think I'll have one, too."

"Maybe you're not so stuffy, after all!" said Tonya.

"She's stuffy," said Tina. "She just likes banana splits."

Virginia Compton steered the large wagon expertly through the streets of Shaker Heights to the business district. So much for her resolve to add a little bit more traditional discipline to the eclectic, creative mix necessary in the modern world to prepare children for real life.

Sometimes things were so confusing.

* * *

Lieutenant Nelson had seen about enough vector screens for one day. Never at ease with computers, the thirty-year veteran of the police wars nevertheless understood that computers were the wave of the future. With an angry snap, he slapped the machine to silence.

One stale doughnut remained from the daily dozen he packed from home. He began to gnaw on it, running it down his throat with equally stale coffee. Over the years he'd come afoul of weight tables published by police command. Once he'd been threatened with dismissal for failing to shed pounds. The next morning, Nelson cheerfully put in his resignation. Considering the fact that Edgar Nelson was considered the finest investigator in the history of the Cleveland police department, his resignation was torn to smithereens by a wiser head, the Chief himself.

Edgar Nelson had a problem. How do you run any kind of investigation based on unbelievably slim information? Really, no proof at all. Just a lot of...air. And yet...Edgar Nelson had spent a career functioning on gut feeling. "Woman's intuition," his late, bemused partner, Arthur Jimms had once said off the top of his head. The phrase stuck. "Edgar's woman's intuition, again," went the chorus of squad room banter whenever Nelson locked his teeth on another spindly case.

This time, the case was razor thin.

"Give me Jesperson," Nelson barked into the phone, mouth full of old-fashioned.

Ned Jesperson came on the line, as if he'd been sitting on it, in spite of having a secretary. Well, Jesperson was private, and he could afford a secretary, unlike the Cleveland Police Department. Even a Detective First Grade had to work Ma Bell's invention himself or herself.

"Listen, Jes, I wonder if you could back paper this Kremintz. Don't you have a few contacts out Reno way?"

"Could be," said the laconic Jesperson, one of Cleveland's most famous faces because of his TV spots. Not that he ever said more than two words in any of them.

"Could be? Could be?" roared Nelson through the mouthpiece. "What does that mean?"

"I'll call," said Jesperson, cutting the connection.

Edgar Nelson stared at the now silent earpiece. That Ned Jesperson was a strange sort went almost without saying. Nelson had once asked him how he could investigate anything when the entire town knew who he was from a hundred paces.

"See me comin', they spill beans," he'd replied.

Nelson's quandary called for using a private license for a very simple reason. He had no witnesses, no complaint, no crime within his jurisdiction, no probable cause in connection with any malfeasance whatsoever.

And yet, Edgar Nelson knew, without the slightest inkling of doubt, that the onetime Clevelander, Stanley Kremintz, had been murdered via a Cleveland connection. It had started with three separate anonymous phone calls. Then there followed a Manilla folder containing certain documents. That's when his nose became "...as tender as a sirloin."

Five former employees...

Gone freelance, but still working for the company as independent contractors...

Five dead former employees...

Five dead former employees, broke as hell, accounts emptied, assets invisible...

Something stank...

That's when Edgar Nelson called in longtime pal Ned Jesperson to investigate the home front. Now it was time to expand the investigation to Reno. To Atlantic City. To Las Vegas. To Miami. To Newport.

Five dead former Cleveland computer wizards.

Five random home invasions, resulting in homicide.

Sure. And Cleveland's infamous Laos Boys are really just Boy Scouts.

Edgar Nelson would nail that frog!

Fancy pants Maurice Devereaux wouldn't know what hit him when three hundred and fifty pounds of Detective First Grade landed on his ass...

Patrice Orosco couldn't keep her gaze off of Red Dog. For his part, he seemed to be photocopying the entire environment, with the exception of the girl he'd street-named Kat. The two were sipping hot tea in the cafeteria at Columbia St. Vincent Charity Hospital. The sun was slipping to the west, bringing with it chilly air, a persistent foretoken of an autumn to come.

"I like it," Red Dog was saying. "Not too many people really do a good job moving pianos. Pianos are incredibly sturdy, yet vulnerable instruments. One wrong move, and you wreck thirty-thousand dollars worth of grand piano."

He rubbernecked as he said this. No eye contact.

It unnerved Patrice.

"What make do you like best?" she asked, trying hard to find a conversational gambit.

"You mean as a pianist, or a piano mover?"

"Both," she said. 'Look at me,' is what she wanted to say, but dared not.

"Well, the old Everett was great from the standpoint of a piano store and its movers. The posts were steel, and so held a tune very, very well. Fewer complaints, if the store wanted to economize on piano tuning. You know, tune it on the floor of the store and not send a technician out to the home. The tone left something to be desired, though. Yamaha bought the company in 1973, and it has improved in tone since then. If I were to talk only about tonality, I'd say Schimmel is my favorite. Even over Bosendorfer. That, however, is highly subjective. If I had to talk about domestic pianos, it would be Sohmer, over Steinway. Great bell-like treble section. But I'm talking the old Sohmer, when the family still owned it and it was made in New York. After they moved to Connecticut, well, I think they started to go down hill. All the old piano makers were dead or retired by then. All the great craftsmen. Sohmer had one shortcoming, however. The action was too soft. Better, from the standpoint of dynamics to have a stiffer action. A Steinway action. So, if I were to practice up, and play a concert somewhere, I'd prefer the Steinway. Sohmer wasn't a concert instrument, anyway. And the Steinway, you couldn't beat the ballsy bass."

Now he looked at her. It was painful. He hadn't noticed before. Not until they'd been seated and the first of the Earl Grey crossed his lips. The shock was electric, like a cattle prod. Patrice Maria Orosco could have been Cherie Devereaux's look-alike cousin. It was in the eyes.

"I've got to go," he said abruptly, stalking out of the cafeteria.

A stunned Patrice sat silently watching him march out of the building.

Claude Johnson looked up when Patrice entered the room and smiled. "She's going to make it," he said hoarsely. Margie was fast asleep, slouched in the room's other chair. "Doctor said we beat the grim reaper by on'y a couple hours. Large thanks to you, Kat."

"You didn't do too shabby yourself, Claude. You ran lickety-split with Madge in your arms."

"Ran track back in the holler in middle school. Woulda in high school, but I hadta quit. Needed to work, after Dad's heart attack."

Madge Johnson looked angelic in the hospital bed, tubes everywhere.

"Someday, things is gonna be better," said Claude Johnson. "I know they gonna be, or there ain't no God nowhere. An' I know there is. Surely."

One floor away, Midge Elliot was playing with Tickle Me Elmo when Patrice entered her room. The room seemed to be a storage area for a busy florist.

Those Midge Elliot eyes danced!

"I knew you'd come," said Midge.

"Try keeping me away."

Pudge Elliot entered the room, a strawberry shake in one hand.

"Hello, Patrice. Harrison says you did your good deeds for the year, today."

"I guess it was a close call."

"All too close." Then he turned to his daughter. "Here's your shake, Princess. Last thing you can have. How was dinner?"

"Not good, Daddy. Not like Mommy makes."

"What can I say? Hospital food! Toxic!"

"Does that mean yucky?" asked Midge, a certain light in her eyes.

"Pretty much."

"We can have dinner at home pretty soon," said Midge. "Maybe I'll cook for you Daddy. You like the pancakes I make!"

"Best I ever had, Princess."

Pudge could not keep the tears from his voice, the mist from his eyes. "Don't cry, Daddy…"

#

CHAPTER 13

Friday, October 4, 1996

Comebacks Part of City's Sports History: Cleveland sports fans know The Choke.

They know victory so tantalizingly close you can almost taste the gold. And then comes the fumble, the strikeout, the interception, the whatever.

> Brian E. Albrecht
> Plain Dealer Reporter

"Nobody expects you to spend twenty-four hours a day on the street, Treece," said Theodore O'Reilly. "You've gotta let your hair down and enjoy yourself. Didn't you like singing at Nighttown?

Patrice nodded. A & B Diner's ham and eggs were getting cold.

"You missed the Woodie Guthrie Hootenany Tribute Concert at the Odeon on the evening you took to the streets, all because you wanted to stay in character and remain on the job. Thank heavens you came with me to the Cleveland Orchestra's Opening Night Celebration last month, and the farewell to The Grand Old Lady last week."

Patrice smiled. "Both were really something. I have a passion for music halls and stadiums anyway. I can't believe they are tearing down Cleveland Stadium. Cleveland Municipal Stadium?"

"We usually just say The Stadium. Or refer to it as the Grand Old Lady. Built in 1931. Housed two straight football championships in two different leagues, did you know that?"

"The Browns, ya. First in the All-America Conference, 1949, and the National Football League, 1950."

"That's correct. But, actually I was referring to the Cleveland Rams, 1945, National Football League, and the Cleveland Browns, 1946, All-America Conference. In fact, the Browns won all four All-America Conference championships, plus the NFL title in '50."

"You're kidding? The Rams, in Cleveland?"

"From '37 through '45, then they spent the next 49 years in Los Angeles, before that broad took them to St. Louis."

"Now, Teddy,"

"Nobody respects women more than I, but when you have owners like Schott in Cincy, and Georgia girl in St. Louis, it gives women a bad name."

"Just like men?" asked Patrice.

"As a matter-of-fact, yes. Why should a woman stoop to the level of the Steinbrenner's, the Al Davis', or the late Charley O. Finley? Or Bill Bidwell. Or Robert Irsay, or Art Fucking Modell?"

"Mustn't be aggressive..." said Patrice, eyes crinkling.

"Hell with that! We're talking being damnable!" roared O'Reilly.

"Shouldn't be a bitch..." teased Patrice.

"Female owners ought to remember Joan Payson in New York! That lady had class!" Was Theodore O'Reilly's voice and blood pressure rising?

"Were you a member of the Dawg Pound?" asked Patrice.

"No. I wasn't good enough. Had to sit in a loge," said Theodore O'Reilly. His eyes misted over. "There have never been better fans than the ladies and gentlemen who sat in the Dawg Pound! Even at their most raucous. Comedians lambasted Cleveland! There has never been a finer city! Home to Bob Hope from the age of four to twenty-one. He even fought here, when he boxed under the name Packy East. Never been a place where a more real America resides! And dammit, we had the finest football franchise there ever was, and we're gonna have it again! By 1999!"

"Why, Theodore O'Reilly! If I didn't know better, I'd think you were trying to sell me on the city, with those smiling Irish eyes of yours!"

"Would I do that?" Amazing, the innocence. "By the way, the song you allude to, 'When Irish Eyes are Smiling,' was written by a Clevelander, a man by the name of Ernest R. Ball."

"You keep at it, don't you?"

"Always, when a man loves his city."

"I wouldn't put anything past you," she said with a sparkling smile.

"Then let me invite you and your family to the Strongsville Community Theatre, tonight. Bradley Glenn will be performing his solo show 'The Suburban Poet.'"

"Your tastes are ever so eclectic," said Patrice.

"Of course."

"Mama would love it."

"Mais oui,"

"Grandma Stella would love it."

"Naturellement. Or perhaps I should say, naturlich!"

"I'll ask them. I'm sure they'll say yes," said Patrice.

"With that, and considering you've managed to finish your breakfast, shall we head to Cleveland Hopkins International Airport? We locals just say Hopkins. Where the big birds fly."

"I get to drive Cherry Red," said Patrice.

"Ah, hell. I ought to just give it to you."

"I would recommend that," said Patrice.

Miss Dandridge appeared healthier than she'd been in years, thanks to medication for a hyperthyroid condition, and a regimen to control low blood sugar.

Another reason that may have improved her energy level was the redheaded, red bearded new music teacher making his third visit to the classroom. Scheduled for Mondays, Wednesday and Fridays, Red Dodge had quickly won over the kids.

"Phenomenal," was the term Milton Thompson III had used after Monday's first music lesson. "We may even be able to raise fees."

"Don't even think about it," Ethel Dandridge snapped back.

119

"But it raises our curriculum to a new level," Thompson answered back impetuously.

Dandridge simply stalked out of the office.

"We could pay him if we had to!" Thompson shouted to Dandridge's receding form.

"Kids," said Red Dodge, after he'd quieted the group seated in a circle on the area rug. "I have a monster idea!"

"I like monsters!" said Jimmy Yonkers, like Red Dog, a redhead.

"I don't!" snapped Claudine Demarco. "They remind me of yucky boys!"

Red Dodge laughed. "Not that kind of monster!" Then he made a monster face. The kids shrieked with laughter. Even Claudine, in spite of herself. "Monster, like in monster trucks. BIG!"

"You mean like those big tires?" asked Tina Devereaux.

Red Dodge smiled. "Exactly, Tina! An idea so big, it'll be bigger than any idea the first, second and third graders have!" Red Dodge had no idea what those grades were doing, since he worked only with the two kindergarten classes, but he figured it would sound good to the kids and perhaps motivate them to perform well.

"How 'bout the fourth graders?" asked Jimmy Yonkers.

"Yeah," said Helen Schmidt. "My brother is in the fifth grade! He's really big. Daddy says he has big ideas!"

"I don't know how big their idea will be, but what if we put on a Christmas show for your families?"

"That's a really big idea," said Tina.

"It's a great idea," said Tonya Devereaux. "We could do it! We'd have to work really, really hard, like Grand-pere says. Work hard and you can do things."

A jab at Red Dog's heart.

"What do you think, kids?" asked Miss Dandridge. "Will you work very, very hard with Mr. Dodge?"

The class cheered enthusiastically. Many confident statements rang through the classroom. Only Claudine Demarco seemed to have reservations.

"If we do this, I think I should get to sing!" said the icy little blonde with the perfect face.

"Everyone will get a chance," said Ethel Dandridge.

"Then it's settled," said Red Dodge. "Monday, we will get started on the music. We'll only have two months to get ready. It will take a lot of work. Today, we should talk about singing."

"I can sing already," said Claudine.

"So can frogs," said Tina.

Titters. Claudine Demarco gave Tina an icy stare.

"Let's concentrate on what Mr. Dodge is saying," warned Miss Dandridge.

"In order to sing properly," said Red Dodge, "you must be able to breathe properly."

"I can't breath when my algies kick up," said Jimmy Yonkers.

"Allergies?" asked Red Dodge.

"Yeah. And I sneeze!"

"Yuck, luggies," shouted Armand Dasher, a handsome, diminutive dark-haired boy.

"Now, children," said Miss Dandridge, barely able to suppress a laugh.

"The first thing we are going to do is to practice deep, or super breathing. We are going to learn how to use all of our lungs."

"My uncle Lenny doesn't have a lung anymore," said Jimmy Yonkers. "Cigarettes blew it away! He puffed, and puffed, for a long time! The doctor said it was all gone!"

"Yuck," said Tina. "You have a funny family, Jimmy."

"My uncle isn't funny! He cries all the time! An' he wants more cigarettes, but my aunt Maeve won't give him any!"

Red Dog's head was in his hands. When he came up for air, he caught sight of Ethel Dandridge. Her eyes were dancing. Suddenly, he knew why she and so many other teachers loved their work so much. "Okay," he finally said, when he'd gained a measure of control. "A singer sometimes has to sing for a long time. It is called holding a note. What would happen if you didn't have enough air to sing for a long time?"

Red Dodge attempted to call on Helen Schmidt, but Jimmy Yonkers beat her to it. "Uncle Lenny couldn't sing a thing! Every time he tried to sing Jingle Bells he coughed his head off, an' it didn't sound much like bells!"

It took awhile, but Red Dodge finally got them on breathing exercises.

Hobie's was sparkling. Lottie and Darcy had proven to have a sure hand when it came to keeping the place humming. Hobie Strauss smiled broadly. The Laundromat was bringing in blue collar people, not just drifters. The customers seemed to want to take care of the place, too. No graffiti had yet to appear on the newly painted walls. The message board was crammed with notices. The business, so recently in ruins under the old, discouraged owners, was now truly becoming central to the Near West Side.

Still, Hobie Strauss was bothered. This was no life for Darcy, cleaning up with her mother every day. She belonged in school. A child needed education. It was the only way to escape the streets.

"Lottie, can I speak with you a minute," Hobie asked, when the last of Lottie's shift finally expired.

"Sure, Hobe. Darcy, here's some quarters. Gimme a lemon lime Slice. Pick a sof' drink, y'sef."

"You are doing an outstanding job, Lottie..." Hobie began, and then cleared his throat.

"But..." Lottie had a certain shrewdness about her that most people missed.

"Lott...Darcy ought to be in school." There, he'd said it. He'd said what had been bothering him for a while now.

"Now, Hobe, don' start in on me now. You know what I think a them guys! They can't even protec' kids in school! Guns an' knives, an' drugs, an' who knows what all! If this were back in my home town, now that'd be differ'nt. I'd have Darcy in school in a New York minute. I would! But here, how I know she won't be killt by some crazy person?"

"I have an idea, Lottie. Let me tell you about it."

"Guess you're gonna tell me, so go ahead."

"Cleveland was one of three Ohio cities to benefit from something called the Stewart McKinney Act. It goes back to '87. Anyway, they can provide tutors, who are actual teachers. There are some shelters in Cleveland that you two could go to, instead of living at that old factory. There, at the shelter, Darcy could be taught. I think it's worth a try, Lott."

"I don' know, Hobe. Once they get their claws in ya, they never let go."

"Who's they, Lottie?"

"You know. Teachers, an' principals, and the board a education, an' those folks. They don' unnerstan' the troubles we got. They don' care."

"Do me this favor, Lottie. Think about it for awhile. There's no hurry. Okay?"

"You're a nice man, Hobe. I'll think about it, okay? But I can't promise anything."

"Fair enough, Lott. Fair enough."

"This is ridiculous! Would you like me to have the accountants do a cost analysis of your investigation?" Maurice Devereaux barked at Todd Englewood. "If that meurtriere is not found, who knows what he will do next!" Devereaux's plush executive office seemed to vibrate. "Mon Dieux!"

Todd Englewood fumed. "Fairly and Tomajac have turned over every stone. According to the letter Stanley Kremintz had squirreled away, Delaney is in Cleveland. But if so, he has gone underground. No sign of him topside."

"Then look souterrain! How difficult can that be?"

"Plenty," said Englewood. "He's foxy, that Coxy. No paper trail. No contacts with friends. Absolutely no sightings. We've papered the town with top quality digital Photostats of his last known picture. We've gone better than that. We've used computer progression to age him. We've changed his looks, again via computer. Facial hair, long hair, no hair. You name it. Nada."

"You should perhaps re-interview his friends," said Devereaux.

"That would be a cold trail. Everything checked out, five years ago. He made no contact with any of them. Personally, I think he's long gone. Might have gone underground with someone, perhaps a woman, a paramour possibly, then skipped town."

"You are naive, Todd. He has some kind of agenda, and it pertains to money. It's always money. He'll strike when you least expect it."

"What do you want us to do, Maurice? Que me voulez-vous?"

"I don't think he has the wherewithal to launch a campaign against us topside, as you say. So look below the surface. Look to the seamy side of Cleveland. Gangs, even. I think he's here. And I think his is a low budget operation. Find him, Todd. And kill him. It's the only way to stop that kind of, meurtriere, murderer. If we let the authorities in on it, he'll just get a slick lawyer, next thing you know, it's s'en aller libre."

"We'll redouble our efforts, Maurice."

"Veuille faire ceci. Redoubler."

*   *   *

"You look strong, son," said the grandfatherly patriarch of the small, but extremely successful furniture business. For years, Deblay's Rent-to-Own Furnishings had served the Near West Side on Lorain Avenue, just down from St. Ignatius High School. "You know how to work?"

Oscar No Name thought a minute. But, of course he did! Who was it helped Mama in the kitchens of West Side eateries? Oscar! Who loved to work with Mama, who always said, 'an honest day's work, for an honest day's pay'? Again, it was Oscar. He might not have had a real job, but he knew how to work!

"Yes, Sir, I worked with Mama! She taught me!"

Enrique Deblay liked what he saw. What the slim, silvered hair merchant saw was a young man who needed a break. Often called on to hire players from the St. Ignatius football factory, it might be time to take a down-and-outer and give him a break.

"When can you start?"

"Right now!"

"I pay five bucks an hour. Paychecks every Friday. No guarantees. You work when I have the work for you. How do I contact you?"

Oscar No Name was stumped.

"Who," asked Deblay gently, "do you know in the business community?"

"I know Lottie. She works at Hobie's," said Oscar, hopefully.

"I know Hobie Strauss well. Fine man. He grew up around here. Worked for me when he played football. I was young then. Just getting started myself. Tell you what. Contact Hobie Strauss, make some arrangements for me to contact you when I need you, and the job is yours."

"Thank you, Sir!"

"On your first day, I'll have to take you to the Social Security office and get you an SS number. That shouldn't be a problem. Okay?"

"Okay."

When Oscar left the building, it seemed to him that his feet never quite touched the ground.

Inside the cluttered store, crammed with everything from divans to coffee tables to futons, a bustling office crew was preparing monthly billings for its customers.

"Why did you do that, Pop?" asked a nervous, thin man who looked just like a younger version of Enrique Deblay. "I don't think the guy has two brain cells to rub together."

"Stephano, Stephano. How little you understand the rhythms of life. And to think, someday, all of this will be yours! It crunches my mind!"

Few experiences in life are as heartfelt as comings and goings at a busy, cosmopolitan airport. Most every emotion comes into play. Anxiety not the least.

Wouldn't you know it? Grandma Stella was in the lead, traipsing down the concourse, drinking in stimuli that batters deplaned travelers. If Stella Orosco was in the lead, one might imagine the distractions that were catching the eyes of Ruben, Audrey and Yolanda.

"Liebchen!" shouted the delightful old lady when she spotted Patrice. She rubbernecked around the huge, open space, looking for her son, daughter-in-law and grandchild. "Sie wussten nicht was zu tun. I told them, what you do is find your luggage before a dieb finds it for you! And he'll keep it, including the schlupfer!"

"Grandma Stella," said Patrice, taking in a big breath, and hugging this very precious person in her life. "God, how I've missed you!"

Ruben, Audrey and Yolanda appeared, as if by magic.

"Esta la comida?" barked Ruben.

"Essen!" shouted Stella. "That's all that junge ever cared about! Food! Always food! So what does he do? He builds a restaurant, and he chains his old mother to it! Schandlich!"

"Tengo ganas de comer!" said Ruben Orosco. "Let's find one of Patrice's diners and eat! Enough already."

"Do we have to eat at a diner?" asked Audrey.

"Hello, Mother," said Patrice.

"Hello, Dear. I do hope you pick a place that is at least clean."

Yolanda hugged Patrice. "Hi, Big Sis! I never knew I'd miss you like this. There's nobody to fight with on weekends like when you used to come home."

"Yol. God, I missed you, too," said Patrice. "The day hasn't gone by when I haven't thought about you and your senior year. And I'm not even around to enjoy it."

More debarking. An even more crowded concourse. "All right," said Ruben, "are we going to take up residence here, or what?"

"Come on, all," said Patrice, leading the way to the carousel, and then hopefully, out of the congested terminal. "Let's get the luggage, and then I have a surprise waiting for you."

The surprise was Theodore O'Reilly, waiting in Cherry Red, which he insisted on driving so Patrice could visit with her family. When he drove into the parking lot of The Palazzo on Detroit Avenue, Audrey breathed a sigh of relief.

"Mr. O'Reilly," she said, "I believe you to be a man of great taste."

"Definitely!" said the Elfin One. "And I'm really going to indulge in good taste for dinner tonight. I'm going to have a Polish dog."

"Good grief..." said Audrey.

There are tantalizing choices of pasta at The Palazzo. Run by the granddaughters of the woman who founded it, the decor can only be said to be full-throated, like a good Chianti.

Of course, Audrey was in her element. She gave a running discourse on the cuisine, much to the delight of Theodore O'Reilly. Ruben seemed amused. He devoured his meal on twenty different levels. The gourmet, the gourmand, the wily restaurateur.

"What do you think, Mutter?" he asked at one point. "Should we feature an Alfredo?"

"Northern Italian is good," said Stella. "It blends in well with the German dishes."

"And what food do you prefer, young lady?" asked Theodore O'Reilly of Yolanda Orosco.

The teenager thought for a moment. "A Big Mac does nicely. You can always trust Taco Bell. In a pinch I can handle Dad's restaurant. The price is right, that's for sure."

"Gracias, Mija! Nos vermos e diario! Every day, I tell you!" Ruben implored the table with puppy dog eyes. "And I never knew my own daughter so hated my food! It's as if Ich kenne sie nur vom sehen. I must only know her by sight! This daughter! Big Macs!"

"Your food is good, Ruben," said Audrey simply. "I've always told you that. And I've eaten absolutely everywhere. Lord knows, I don't cook. But she's a teenager, Dear. You must remember that."

"I didn't say I didn't like Dad's food," said Yolanda. "But, when you have to eat it every day of the year..."

"Well, I miss it," said Patrice. "I haven't been on my feed lately. I want a fajita, the way only Papa and Grandma Stella can make them. And, heaven help us, before leaving my apartment, I became hooked on Mexican coffee!"

"You look so...so...dunn, thin, Liebchen!" said Stella.

"Yes. La Flaca!" said Ruben enthusiastically, as if he'd just diagnosed a new syndrome.

"We will fatten you up. A little fett on a Fraulein, das gut!"

"I can't really eat at home, guys," said Patrice. "I've got to give this a few weeks, or so. I have to be able to write from real experience. Even this lunch, as great as it is, I can't be feeling homelessness with a belly this full." She looked down at her plate. Her fettucini Alfredo was mostly history. Ruben and Stella looked wounded. "However, perhaps a fajita tonight won't hurt anything."

Huge, beaming smiles from Papa and Grandma Stella.

"I wouldn't mind being in on one of those fajitas," said Yolanda demurely.

"Ah! So my Mija tries to make nice, now! After wounding her old father a little earlier. Grease the way for more free meals at Padre Orosco's for she and her many friends! Most of the town are friends! Most of them eat free! Never own a restaurant, Senior O'Reilly. I mean, never! The profits they go up in smoke, into the bellies of ungrateful young people!"

"Mostly into the bellies of your cousins and their friends," said Audrey. "And don't let him fool you, Mr. O'Reilly. At the prices he charges, it is so profitable he could feed half of Reynosa for free and still break even."

"Now, my novia, my darling wife, stabs me with a driven nail! Accuses me of gouging diners in my humble cafe. Dios mio!"

Theodore O'Reilly insisted on paying for everything.

"All right," said Ruben Orosco eventually. "But the next time, it is my treat, or you will have to fly out to McAllen and eat at Padre Orosco's just to even up the score."

"Would it be any good?"

"Muy bueno, Senior."

Teddy caught Patrice in the parking lot a few moments before her family caught up with them. Ruben insisted on paying his respects to the cook. Audrey seemed mesmerized by the romantic ambiance of the Palazzo, and Yolanda visited the little girls room.

"They're fabulous," said O'Reilly. "Are they always like this?"

She smiled. "Oh, yes. We prattle back and forth in three languages. Lots of give and take. People often find us a bit bizarre. Do you?"

"Hardly. No Irishman would."

"You've got a point, there. Here they come. Better get them settled into my apartment, then let them rest off the jet lag for a bit, while I check out the street. When are you going to pick me up?"

"How about six? That'll give us time to catch something to eat. Polish dog for me. Then, after Bradley Glenn's performance, how's about we entertain your family at Nighttown? Have they ever heard you sing?"

"Only in school choirs."

"Then, they are in for a treat."

Her family gave Patrice their imprimatur almost the second they saw her apartment.

"I don't know how you can stand being away from this place and on the street," said Yolanda after the grand tour.

"It's what I do, I guess."

The two sisters were alone in the front room, with parents and Grandma Stella having opted to lay down for a nap. Theodore O'Reilly had gone away on an errand, but would shortly return to take Patrice back to the streets for the remainder of the afternoon. Yolanda seemed to want to say something. Not really knowing how to do it, she just blurted it out.

"What would you say if I went to UTSA?"

"I'd say good."

"And followed in your footsteps?"

Patrice thought about it for a moment. "Ordinarily, Yol, if you asked me what you should do, I'd say do what you feel comfortable with. Since I know you would be comfortable with some kind of writing career, I'd say I would expect you to pursue it. The only thing that surprises me is UTSA. I always thought you were leaning toward Baylor."

"Not anymore."

"What changed your mind?"

"I called Mel and Martha."

Patrice smiled. "That would change anybody's mind!"

A literate listener might have used poetic allusions to describe the strains coming from the seven foot Schimmel grand piano. Skip Omyer was such a man; literate, sensitive, tough-minded, a man who could make interconnections. He immediately thought of Robert Service, and The Shooting of Dan McGrew:

...he clutched the keys with his talon hands—my God! but that man could play.
Were you ever out in the Great Alone, when the moon was awful clear,

And the icy mountains hemmed you in with a silence you most could hear;
With only the howl of a timber wolf, and you camped there in the cold,
A half dead thing in a stark, dead world, clean mad for the muck called gold;
While high overhead, green, yellow and red, the North Lights swept in bars?—
Then you've a hunch what the music meant...hunger and night and the stars.
And hunger not of the belly kind, that's banished with bacon and beans,
But the gnawing hunger of lonely men for a home and all that it means;
For a fireside far from the cares that are, four walls and a roof above;
But oh! so cramful of cosy joy, and crowned with a woman's love—

Red Dodge slowly rose from the piano, Beethoven's haunting Sonata No. 14 in C-Sharp Minor, Op. 27, No. 2— popularly known as Moonlight Sonata, all three movements—finished. He was seemingly alone in the demonstration room with a dozen grand pianos of various lengths and makes, most new, some vintage. Again that many high quality studio uprights. A small seating area in the middle, for recitals.

Carefully, Skip Omyer withdrew from the room, so as to make his former presence unknown. A man deserves to be alone with his thoughts. Red Dodge, above all.

A complicated man, Red Dodge, thought Omyer. It had only recently come to his attention that the man had no real home. The word he received was no one really knew where he stayed. He got his mail at a drop, that much was certain. A medical clinic.

An undeniably educated man. A man of intellectual substance. A man Omyer truly admired.

Damn good piano mover, too. Passionate about his work. Passionate about his playing, obviously.

Omyer retreated to other parts of the store to do his duties. A good man, a likable man.

In the display room, the hirsute man Omyer knew as Red Dodge continued to stand motionless in front of the piano. Softly, he spoke, as if to the instrument. "That one was for you, Cherie. And it's for our daughters. That one day, God willing, I can be a normal part of their lives. You'd be proud of them, Cherie."

Then, quickly, he slogged out the back door, to make his way resolutely to the old car plant. It was just about time to put the plan into motion. For, no man can live this way forever.

Oscar No Name looked up to see a smiling Patrice Orosco standing over him. He was hungrily consuming a can of beans. His face broke into a beatific grin.

"I got a job, Kat! I got a job! A real job! I move furniture for a living!"

Patrice slipped down on her haunches, smiling warmly at the young man. "You want to tell me about it?"

"I was walking in back of this furniture store, and I saw some guys moving a big couch or somethin' out the back door. So I went in, and asked if they wanted help. Mama would have been proud, Kat. I got the job, just like that."

"Oscar, are you still hungry?"

"Yes."

"How would you like your own take-out pizza?"

"I can buy my own food now. I have a job!"

"That's great, Oscar. But, I'd like to buy you a pizza. You can even pay me back someday, if you want."

"Okay. Can I have pepperoni?"

"Of course."

"That's what Mama liked. Pepperoni. Sometimes we had to eat somethin' else, though. When somebody wouldn't eat it. Some of them pizzas had awful things on them."

"Like anchovy?"

"Yuck…"

Patrice and Oscar started walking to the new pizza parlor on Lorain Avenue. Oscar regaling Patrice with stories about Mama.

"She never hit me, Kat. Never once."

"I don't know why anybody would ever hit you, Oscar."

"Some people hit kids," he said quietly.

"I know, Oscar. I know."

*   *   *

Stella Orosco continued to clean Patrice's kitchen with the obsessive habits thorough women always seem to display, especially in someone else's kitchen. A fine dinner, provisions obtained at a nearby Dave's Supermarket, was already completed and ready to assemble and warm. Fajitas, of course. Trimmings.

Stella was completely oblivious to Theodore O'Reilly's plan to pick up some white soul food. In his case, a Polish dog.

Ruben Orosco had taken delivery of a rental car. Armed with maps, the foursome had managed to negotiate the streets with a minimum of confusion.

Yolanda was busy channel surfing, getting her television bearings.

Audrey had used much of her allotted luggage space for esoteric art books. Her meetings at the Cleveland Museum of Art were still three days away.

Ruben was pouring over the Yellow Pages. Restaurant listings.

"What are you doing, Papa?" Yolanda finally asked.

That was about all Ruben Orosco needed. His face lit up like a football stadium.

"What better place to expand to? This Cleveland! Every nationality in the world resides here!"

"You never wanted to build a chain, Ruben," said Audrey. "You've always said that is the end of quality."

"Maybe I was wrong! You ever think of that? That I might be wrong sometimes? Incorrecto! Erroneo. Falso!"

"Oh, never!" said Audrey.

"Sie haben unrecht von zeit zu zeit…" said Grandma Stella. Then a pause. "Not!" she roared. "Ruben, you are wrong, all the time! Una y otra vez!" She continued to clean obsessively, furiously.

"See! What did I tell you, Audrey! Even I, the finest restaurateur the world has yet seen, sometimes makes mistakes! We will expand into Cleveland. Bring the flavors of the Southwest, and the Rhineland! And maybe Northern Italy! I might also serve some Chinese! Lemon chicken! Moo goo gai pan! These Polish dogs Senior O'Reilly talks about! I'll call it International Orosco's! The profits, they will be en gran escala."

"I won't cook a thing in Cleveland," said Grandma Stella. "Lacherlich!"

"You just did, Mutter! Great fajitas!"

"I mean in a restaurant!" she roared.

"You won't have to. I'll obtain a staff of the finest people! You'll see! And to start things off, we'll all take a cruise, to rest up. Before I begin preparations!"

"I could go to Cleveland State," said Yolanda.

"You'll do nothing of the kind!" roared Ruben Orosco. "It is all decided. UTSA, or in your bedroom for correspondence school!"

"Lacherlich!" roared Grandma Stella.

"Theodore O'Reilly will be picking me up in a little while," said Patrice. "Otherwise, I'd accept your invitation.

Red Dog looked disappointed. "Well, perhaps another time…"

"You can count on it," smiled Patrice. "I like fish and chips."

"It's not much. A lady such as you should dine in fine restaurants."

"I do. A lot. I did today."

"Oh."

"Theodore and I picked up my family at Hopkins."

"You didn't tell me."

"You are a hard man to pin down."

"Perhaps I'll be easier to talk to in the future. In fact, we do need to talk. About your project. I think I may have some information for you."

"Why not tomorrow? I guess I'm mostly taking a day off from being homeless. I felt guilty about it before, but not now."

"Why the change of heart?"

"I felt an emptiness without my family. Now I feel fulfilled. Now I think I can really help the people on the street. First your own spirit must be whole, before you can serve other people."

Red Dog continued to gaze at her.

"What?"

"Oh, nothing…"

"Oh, nothing? You had a certain look in your eye," said Patrice. "A look I've not seen you have before. Or maybe I have."

"It's a very long story," said Red Dog. "When your investigation matures a bit, we'll talk about it. Okay?"

"Okay. At least, this time you didn't bolt from the room."

Red Dog gazed at the car factory ruins. "Not much of a room to run from."

"Have you been running, Red Dog? or whatever your name really is…"

"Not from anything. Not really. To something. I'm running to catch up with my life."

"You'd better go get your fish and chips. Something tells me this is a long story."

"It is that, Kat."

"And you'll tell me in due time."

"There is that, too."

In the near distance, a group of African-American children could be heard playing the dozens.

In a few moments, Theodore O'Reilly appeared, a hundred yards away, piloting Cherry Red. He honked like a teenager.

The game of dozens heated up.

Such a complicated man.

#

CHAPTER 14

Saturday, October 5, 1996

Saved by the Belle: Darkness was closing in.

The Cleveland Indians, facing oblivion in the chilly autumn twilight of Jacobs Field, extended their season for at least one more game with a nerve-wracking 9-4 victory over the Baltimore Orioles yesterday. With the game tied at 4, Albert Belle settled the matter decisively with a towering grand slam in the seventh inning.

> Joe Dirck
> Plain Dealer Reporter

It took dedicated jaw flapping for Patrice to convince her family she wouldn't be sleeping in her apartment.

"Certainly, for just this one night, you can make an exception," said Audrey, as if harnessing the world's logic in one hand. "A night away from the cold, the filth, the hoi polloi."

"It doesn't work that way, Mama. When you have a story to do, you just do it. However, I will be spending Saturday afternoon with you guys. And portions of each day you are here. Having you guys here makes it much easier for me to do what I have to do. But I do need to sleep on the street. It's the only way to get the full story."

The fajitas were outstanding. It took no more than two bites for Teddy to forget all about the Polish dog he didn't get.

When they were ready to head to the Strongsville Community Theatre and the Bradley Glenn performance, O'Reilly won a lifelong friend when he asked Stella for the recipe.

"If you open up a restaurant, you shall pay royalties, young man!" said a laughing Stella Orosco.

Theodore O'Reilly loved the sobriquet, though in all likelihood he was even older than Stella. "No need, madam. I'll make you a full partner!"

"You would steal away Mutter?" roared Ruben Orosco, in mock horror. "Mi Madre? Just to make things taste good? Solamente sazonar la comida?"

With the six of them bunched into Cherry Red, Patrice driving, O'Reilly regaled the assemblage with stories of old Cleveland, Ruben Orosco hanging on every word.

The performance was outstanding. Bradley Glenn absolutely nailed his solo show, "The Suburban Poet," which showed what it was like to grow up white and Catholic in Midwestern suburbia.

After the performance in Strongsville, O'Reilly led the group to Nighttown.

Ruben Orosco was visibly impressed. "What an idea," he said of the dinner house.

When Marcus Deutrieve invited Patrice onto the stage, her family gasped. When she sang Miss Brown to You, an old Billie Holiday tune, the eyes of both parents misted over.

"Rad," Yolanda said after Patrice finished a set. Then she gave her big sister a hug. "You have more surprises than a Cracker Jack box."

"Mija," breathed Ruben Orosco. "I am orgulloso. Proud. You have become artistico. I never knew this. While I was not looking, you have grown up into a mujer completo."

Audrey gazed at her daughter for a very long time. "That was magnificent. Astounding, even. I'm glad I came to Cleveland. You have facets about you we must explore."

"You sing like a bird," said Stella, eyes watering. "But like a very sad bird."

"I guess it's the job I'm doing, Grandma Stella."

"Then it is a job you must complete. Before it eats you from within yourself."

"I think you are right," said Patrice, her own eyes misting over.

"Of course. It is what they call the job description of being a grossmutter."

It was a thoroughly exhausted Patrice Orosco who stumbled into her makeshift shelter just before 3:00 a.m.

"You got in late last night," observed Red Dog, after Patrice emerged from her shelter late the next morning.

"That's true," observed Patrice.

"You always get up at the crack of noon?"

Patrice frowned. "Whenever I can. What's it to you?"

"We street people don't have that luxury."

"Well, pardonez-moi!"

"Oh, God. Do not use French phrases around me, please! I can't stand it!"

"You're a piece of work, Red Dog. Anybody ever tell you that before?"

There was a long silence. Red Dog's eyes seemed to have glazed. Finally, when he turned to Patrice, she'd quite forgotten her remark. "A lady once told me that, yes."

"What?"

"That I was a piece of work. Quite frequently. But, I'd say, with a rather large dose of affection."

"You ready for your long story yet?"

"With you a bleary-eyed, and probably a fuzzy-eared listener? I think not yet."

"Suit yourself," said Patrice.

Borf came up to Patrice. Nuzzling.

"He likes you. He doesn't like many."

"I like him. He's unique."

"He is that. He also has good taste."

"Are you trying to score points?"

"Considering the hole I'm in, that might make good sense, don't you think?"

"You think I dislike you?"

Borf was licking her face.

"You get testy, now and then."

"I've seldom heard that from anyone."

"Maybe I just got off on the wrong foot."

"You did that," said Patrice. "But then, I suspect you've had your reasons."

Red Dog looked deeply into her face. "You may represent my last best chance. And I don't want you to get hurt. And I like you."

"There you go. Becoming a silver-tongued devil. I like that. Beats your own testiness."

"Let's grab something to eat. After you fully awaken, perhaps we will talk."

"Street food?"

"I got some dough. Your choice."

"Find me a diner. And my treat."

"My kind of fare. And with your expense account, I'll take you up on it."

The three of them set out for Lorain Avenue. Red Dog. Patrice. Borf.

"He really, really likes you," said Red Dog. "I guess that means I can trust you."

"You had doubts?"

"Doubts are just one of the many tools that help to keep you alive on the streets."

"Red Dog!" shouted Oscar No Name. "Where you going?"

"You up? Come on with us. Bacon and eggs. Your favorite," said Red Dog. And whispering to Patrice, "Besides, The Plain Dealer can afford it."

"Oh boy," said Oscar, running to catch up with them.

Patrice laughed, and sotto voce, "You really watch out for them, don't you?"

"My God, somebody has to."

"Eureka," said Fairly, from the nondescript gray Chevrolet parked at the curb on Dixon Street. "Stakeouts. Ain't they great?"

"Ya. Like rectal bleeding," said a torpid-looking Tomajac. One should never make the mistake of thinking Tomajac was asleep at the wheel. He'd seen the lanky man enter the clinic through a side door as soon as Fairly had.

Fluidly, the two brawny thugs emerged from the Chevy, and began to cross the street. They found the side door unlocked.

If Pudge Elliot was surprised, it didn't show. Sitting behind his desk, government forms in front of him—the free clinic needed all the funding it could get—Elliot was uncharacteristically placid. He recognized the men instantly, but did not let on.

"Remember us?" asked Fairly.

"Vaguely..."

"Cox Delaney," said Tomajac, ominously. "Now do we ring a bell?"

"Oh, yes. Security from High Data Associates. Has he been spotted?"

"You tell us," said Fairly.

"I haven't seen him. Hope I never do. That asshole killed the only woman I ever knew who was just like a sister to me. Then dumps his twins on my doorstep. 'Bout freaked my girl out. But, then, you remember all of that."

"Of course," said Fairly. "Some might think it strange that you've turned on him so. Growing up together, except for the years he lived in San Antonio."

A thoughtful look crossed Pudge Elliot's face. "You ever been double-crossed, Mr. ah…"

"Fairly. And yes, I have. I didn't like it."

"Then you've an idea how I felt."

"Dr. Elliot," said Fairly in his most affable good guy voice, "I want you to answer me honestly. It is extremely important to Mr. Devereaux. Do you know where Jake Delaney might be?"

With a perfectly timed move, no hesitation, no rush, just as natural as an innocent man would do, Pudge Elliot reached for the Rolodex. A couple of flips, and the card was right there. "This is about three years old. I keep it, just in case, mainly for the sake of the twins, Tina and Tonya. He was in Detroit back then. No reason to think he's not still there."

Pudge copied the address, along with a phone number, on a Post-it Note, and handed it to Fairly.

"Thank you, Dr. Elliot. Boy, I don't have to tell you, Mr. Devereaux is very worried. He thinks Cox Delaney may be planning on snatching the twins."

"God, no," said Elliot, a look of revulsion on his face.

"He's clean," said Fairly, back in the Chevrolet. "Probably really is pissed. He married the woman. Gal with tits. Might have been a problem, finding screaming babies on your porch. Broad doesn't like it, hightails. There goes the nooky."

"Something has always bothered me about the whole thing."

"He immediately called Social Services," said Fairly. "They alerted Mr. Devereaux. He had the babies the next day. No. Elliot is clean."

"I'm not sure."

"Delaney's connection has got to be the brother. We're flying to Detroit, my friend, first thing Monday. And we are going to crack this. Right away. Then, I'm off in a flash."

"Fine, Florida breath."

The Chevy jetted away, heading for 105th Street.

Pudge Elliot was shaken. He'd half expected a visit from the High Data thugs for years. When it finally happened, it rocked him to the core. Had to be Kremintz. Stanley must have broken before they killed him. Yet, Stanley didn't know about Elliot, that Pudge was certain of. Kremintz did know of Delaney's presence in Cleveland. They were backtracking through Cox Delaney's personal history, that much was certain. Making the connections. And that spelled trouble.

Sooner or later, they would find Cox Delaney.

But not through a Detroit connection. Not through Jake Delaney.

Could Coxy, Tubb, Mel Dones and Patrice Orosco make a case against High Data Associates in time? Or would Maruice Devereaux win again? Time to make phone calls. Edgar Nelson answered on the first ring.

Nice to know the constabulary also worked Saturdays.

"Let me hypothesize," Lieutenant Nelson said when Pudge had finished. "With Devereaux actively looking for Cox Delaney, that must mean Delaney poses a threat to him. And, in spite of grandfatherly concern, it doesn't concern the kids. It concerns business. It concerns guilt."

"You're a man of rare perception, Edgar."

"Never did think your buddy did the wife," said Nelson.

"Why?" asked Elliot.

"Besides being too pat, something Delaney said to the clerk the night he bought Death by Chocolate ice cream."

"Can you share it with me?"

A long pause. "Ethically, no."

"Cherie was expecting," said Pudge Elliot.

"Then you know," said Nelson. Then after a pause, "Confirmed by autopsy."

"I didn't know. I guessed."

"Shit," said Nelson. "Well, you didn't hear it here."

"Hear what?"

"You get the picture," said Nelson, as he disconnected.

The next call was to Jonathan Tubb. The Managing Editor took the call in his spa.

"Kremintz blew it, Pudge. Lost it at the tables," said Tubb, after the dentist filled him in on Fairly and Tomajac's visit. "Skimmed. Got caught. Given time, Stanley might have found the keys to at least get Devereaux indicted, and perhaps with that, get Coxy's name cleared."

"And he might not have," said Elliot.

"True. But we still have Patrice. She'll have to go undercover and get inside High Data."

"How is she going to do that?" asked Pudge Elliot.

"High Data Associates is always hiring, Pudge. Anybody would hire Patrice Orosco. In a New York minute."

"Risky."

"Everything is risky."

"You'd better be forthright with her this time," said Elliot.

"Oh, God, isn't that the truth! She'd use my balls for mountain oysters, and burn 'em in the frying!"

"The case of the disappearing cojones."

Tubb's belly laugh rolled through the phone lines. "Listen," said Tubb when he'd recovered, "you're sure that Jake is going to be able to handle this?"

"As you know," said Elliot, "this is the first big mistake they have made. When they get to Detroit, Jake Delaney will be waiting. And ready. He's been ready for a long time. I'll call him now."

Jake Delaney, at fifty-two, fifteen years older than Cox, nevertheless had a familial resemblance that would be hard to miss. Six footer, muscular, carrot top. Just an older version, physically, but much more complex in personality and world view.

Jake Delaney was a successful investor, an avid outdoors man, and a confirmed bachelor. Jake's relationships tended to last about two years, and then on to another woman. All of his ex-paramours left amicably. No one had a bad word for Jake Delaney, not male or female. A man's man. A ladies man.

An angry man.

The phone call caught him by no surprise, unless it was why it had taken so long.

"That is good news, indeed," said Jake Delaney, after Pudge had filled him in. "We'll be ready."

"Been in touch with Coxy?"

"Every week. Like clockwork."

"So how you goin' to set the trap?" asked Elliot.

"You don't need to know, Pudge."

"You're right."

Detroit, Michigan

"Jimbo, Jake here. It's mice in the trap time."

Jim Montrose was an African-American autoworker, and former platoon mate of Jake Delaney's. Lifelong friends. Each would place his life in the hands of the other in an instant. Montrose still worked for GM because he liked it. He'd risen to line foreman, and shop steward. In his private life, he'd made a fortune in his spare time investing, often along with Jake Delaney. His wife, Denise, could give Julia Child tips. Many a time, the bachelor Jake Delaney had been saved from Big Mac starvation by a Denise Montrose meal.

"You want the full setup?"

"You got it, bro."

"I've got some time coming. I'll have it ready by tonight," said Jim Montrose.

"Come to daddy," said Delaney.

"Oh, they'll come," said Montrose with a bitter laugh. "Pity it took so damn long. But, as the frogs say, "Mieux vaut tard, que jamais.""

Cleveland

The woman, who knew what her name was? she went by Deargirl, was more retro sixties than natural nineties, or so she often said. A toke here, a toke there. Grateful Dead. She ate Ben and Jerry's ice cream. Of course, Cherry Garcia.

At the moment, she was examining a carving. A delicate jackrabbit.

Nuances you seldom see in a carved figurine. Throwing back her long blonde hair, she riveted her sparkling blue eyes on Claude Johnson. "How many of these can you deliver me? I don't mean just rabbits. I want dear, and all of the forest creatures you can think of. I can move them wholesale all over the country. Of course," she said, pointing around the shop, "I'll retail them here, as well."

"I might be able to give you a dozen a month," Johnson said, scarcely believing his luck.

"That'll have to do, I guess," said Deargirl. "At that rate, I think I can keep you going for a year. After that, maybe we'll switch to Pegasus and such."

"Who?"

Deargirl laughed. "We'll talk about that when we get to it."

"Yes, ma'am."

Claude Johnson left the boutique in a daze of euphoria.

Things did not go so well for Oscar No Name Something or Other. After a bracing breakfast with Red Dog and Kat, he went to his new place of employment to see if they had any work for him. They did.

On his first assignment, he dropped a lamp, shattering the ceramic piece to smithereens

Oscar dissolved to tears.

Stephano Deblay blew six ways to Sunday. "You fuckin' jerk," he roared, "you're outta here. Your fuckin' ass is fired!"

Enrique Deblay took that moment to walk through the rear bay. Seeing his son and new hire standing by the furniture van, with the smashed lamp, he quickly sized up the situation.

"Stephano. Go to my office," he said quietly.

With a sulking cant to his walk, Stephano Deblay stalked back into the building.

"You know, son," said Enrique Deblay, "the same damn thing happened to me on my first day moving furniture. I was in high school. I dropped a mattress down a flight of stairs. The mattress smacked into an expensive vase. The lady pronounced it vaz. The vase shattered to a million pieces. The lady swore like a sailor. Then she hauled off and whacked me right on the nose." Enrique Deblay shook his head in amazement at the memory.

Oscar was wide-eyed.

"Then you know what? I got back to the store, walked into the showroom, and sat down on a recliner. Well, earlier in the day, I'd got myself a haircut. Barbers back then used to slather your hair in oil. Well," Deblay had a large chunk of laughter in his voice now, "my hair could have greased a Mack truck. The back of my head left a terrible stain on the cloth upholstery. What's worse, the recliner was due to be delivered that afternoon. The store lost a customer."

Oscar wanted to ask Deblay what happened next, but the words wouldn't come. Deblay picked up on that.

"Know what?"

Oscar shook his head in wonder.

"The owner of the store, a guy about my age now, said if I wanted a good recliner at cost, I could have it. Otherwise, he'd sell it to someone else at cost. Then, if I later wanted a recliner, I'd have to buy it at the employee's discount, which would be higher."

"I'm fired," Oscar managed to say.

Enrique Delbay laughed. "If I allowed everyone Stephano fires to be fired, I'd have no one to work. Certainly not Stephano. He doesn't know how. And my friend Oscar does know how to work. Right?"

"Mama taught me. She did," said Oscar, nodding.

"I've got more lamps like that in the basement. You want to fetch one? I'll go with you myself on your first delivery. We'll have fun. I always do!"

Oscar high-stepped to the basement, in search of a mauve shag lamp.
When Enrique Deblay reached his office, he roared, "Stephano!"
But the surly son had left the building.

Margie Johnson squinted at the address on the slip of paper. A sixth grade
education was not much, but she could read some. And really, that's all it takes to
do the work, the man had told her.

"We are the biggest," said the recruiter, a Mr. Edwards. "RP Coatings
Corporation ships millions of screws every week all over Greater Cleveland.
People are making fabulous money. You get a buck-fifty for every 1,000 screws
and washers you put together. That adds up fast."

Margie met Mr. Edwards at a fast food stand, while she was buying cheap
burgers for her family. Claude had brought home twenty dollars from Deargirl's
boutique. Nice escape from street food. She thought they'd be eating at St.
Malachi's that night. But meanwhile, bellies were hungry.

"Everybody's doing it," added Mr. Edwards. "You might as well earn some
money for your family."

Hot button words.

"All right, mister. But it better be on the up and up. If this is shady, an' no
money comes to us…"

"I assure you, ma'am, this company has been around awhile. Let me give you
an address, you can go get your first shipment, and be in business today."

That meant both she and Claude would be making money. Things were
looking up. Maybe they could get an apartment real soon.

Leaving Madge with Lottie and Darcy, she took public transportation to
Cuyahoga Heights. Margie was now on foot. Where was RP Coatings
Corporation? The river was just to the west of her. Things seemed as foreign to her
as if she had landed in Paris. She had never been east of the Cuyahoga before.
Perhaps she should ask around.

The boy on the bike.

"Young feller," she hollered. "Can you tell me where I c'n find that screw
place, RP Coatings?"

"Two streets over," said the youngster, who happened to be a high school
football player. A very honest, forthright young man. His name was Tony. An
outspoken youth. Much admired for his penchant for telling it like it is. At this
time he fought a terrible inner fight with himself. Should he tell this Appalachian
transplant the truth? That the whole thing might be a scam? His father had told him
as much. The company was taking advantage of poor people big time. Many of the
workers ended up making less than a buck an hour. Shame. But Tony at last
decided not to say anything. A buck an hour might be the difference between eating
and not eating for this lady. "Good luck," he finally said, "just go left here, you'll
run right into it."

Tony had a miserable feeling that he'd done the lady a disservice.

"I shall scout the city, Mija," said Ruben Orosco to his oldest daughter. "I shall
find the perfect property. Perfecto! Would you like to come?"

Theodore O'Reilly had just dropped Patrice off at home, and then sped away in Cherry Red, a date with the Indians and Orioles at Jacobs Field for the playoffs.

"I thought I might take a little time off, and drive Yolanda around to the malls," said Patrice. "A little sisterly bonding."

"Oh," said a clearly disappointed Ruben Orosco.

Audrey was off meeting with friends from the art world, so Ruben went with his mother to get the lay of the land just in case International Orosco's became reality.

In the now seldom driven Cherokee, Yolanda kept up a chattering update about her senior year, interrupted by a week or so in Cleveland. "And you wouldn't believe what the volleyball team Captain did. Emily Parsa. She went and got herself preggers, just before college scouts swooped down on McAllen."

"That'll make it tougher," said Patrice. "But not impossible."

"I suppose not. Say, you had Jeremy Devoe in history, didn't you?"

"No. Manny Gonzalez."

"Oh. Well, anyway, Jeremy Devoe went home at lunch three weeks ago. He never did that. Caught his wife in bed with some businessman. Shot 'em both in the head, and then gut shot himself. And lived. Now he's in the prison ward of the hospital. Probably have to go to trial. They say he's on suicide watch."

"Jeez..."

"See what happens? You leave the area, and it all falls apart," said Yolanda, with a bit of a hitch in her voice.

Patrice parked the Jeep in a parking garage near Tower City.

"What the matter, Yol? You've been in a funk since you arrived."

"You remember Benny Benitez?"

"Your on-again, off-again boyfriend?"

"He's decided to go the Washington State University. I'm afraid it's going to be over for us."

They were walking by the shops. "I know a great clothing store here," said Patrice. "I didn't know you were that interested in Benny."

"I wasn't," said Yolanda. "But now that I may never see him again, I've been thinking of him a lot. A lot."

"They say sometimes absence makes the heart grow fonder," said Patrice.

"You think so?" asked Yolanda. "You mean, he might realize that he really had something back home and almost let it go?"

"It might work out that way."

"Wow. That puts a whole different spin on it."

Patrice was holding up a tank top that was half price, and perhaps perfect for the balmy South Texas autumn. "What do you think, Yol?"

"It would look good on you," said Yolanda Orosco.

"How would it look on you?"

"We're the same size."

"Maybe Benny would like it," said Patrice. She took it to the cash register and produced a Visa card.

"You're buying that for me?"

"That's what big sisters do. Next, we'll go to Strongsville. I saw the SouthPark Center when we went to that community theater. I want to check it out."

"God, why not? If I'm going to get some new clothes out of this, drive on."

"Don't press your luck, little sister."

The bar was darkly cast, the inadequate lights a blessing to the class of drinkers who viewed libation as a solitary affair. It was also a good place for Pudge Elliot to meet Cox Delaney.

"The clinic is too risky. I have no idea how many thugs your old daddy-in-law might throw at you."

"As many as he sees fit, I'd imagine. I'm not altogether comfortable with Jake trying to snare those two."

"He'll have help."

Delaney slowly shook his head. "Nothing has worked so far. And I didn't even know you had Edgar Nelson on your side, whoever he is."

"The best," said Elliot.

"I really thought Stanley might be able to do what I started."

"Kremintz was undone by a fatal flaw. Greed. Gambling."

"Jonathan Tubb has stayed with this all along, I know," said Delaney. "So has Mel Dones, from afar. And yet, Maurice has proven to be coated with Teflon. Absolutely nothing has stuck. Remember about two years ago when the Justice Department almost started a probe?"

"Yes."

"And yet, somebody managed to sidetrack the whole investigation. How can he do that? As rich guys go, Maurice Devereaux is almost garden variety. I doubt that he is a billionaire, though he's probably on his way, if things keep going well for him. How does he keep managing to obscure his malfeasance?"

"Good question. There's another problem."

The beer was flat. The flickering candles seemed to work with the powers of depression to blur any light that might shine at the end of a tunnel.

"There are always problems."

"They have papered the town. With Photostats of computer likenesses of you, my friend. Enhanced. Aged. Everything from clean-shaven to shaggy. Remarkably, they don't particularly favor you."

"There were very few pictures of me. And what there was, I'd say, were quite bad. Neither Cherie nor I were much into snapshots, at least until Tina and Tonya came along. Then things changed. Cherie began to take pictures of the babies as if she were Richard Avedon."

"Even so. Some street person might make the connection. Lead the thugs right to your cardboard shanty. I'm thinking you should get out of town and let your friends do the work."

"Never. I'd almost welcome a rematch with those guys. I could have punched their tickets that night. Should have."

"You reacted naturally. You grabbed your babies and came to my place. You knew they'd be safe. Even though you must have known Devereaux would get them."

"What I didn't think about was my fingerprints on that automatic rifle."

"They had you there."

Two steelworkers, hard hats perched atop graying heads, entered the bar and found a table a little ways from Elliot and Delaney. They were quickly served.

"I think we should leave," said Pudge.

They headed toward the restrooms at the back, but bypassed them, and instead headed outside into an alleyway.

"When do we meet again?" asked Delaney.

"There must be hundreds of out-of-the-way watering holes in the West Side. You know my clinic hours. Give me a call. We'll find a place to meet. Make it in a few days."

The two headed in different directions.

Perhaps, just in time.

Fairly and Tomajac entered the bar only seconds after Delaney and Elliot headed into the alley. The two seemed cursed with bad luck. Hunters who run out of bullets just before their prey shows up are usually branded as incompetents. Fairly and Tomajac were not incompetent. They were just thorough. They had thoroughly papered this part of the Near West Side.

Running out of mug shots just half a block from the dimly lit water hole fronted only by a long dead neon sign that read merely "bar."

"This place doesn't even have a name," said Tomajac.

"But they got booze. I need a stiff one," said Fairly.

"I'm going to write down where we left off."

"You do that. Chances are, we end our chase Monday in Detroit. We come back here, knowing the address, and that's it for Delaney."

"I hope you're right, Fairly. I don't like unfinished jobs."

"And I would rather be in Florida."

"I've been thinking. So would I. There must be a lot of work for mechanics in Florida."

"Absolutely unlimited, I would think," said Fairly.

The barkeep slid two steins their way.

The candles continued to flicker.

He lay on the ground in a wreathing heap. Even though pain seemed to be his middle name, he knew he'd eventually be okay. Not that he'd ever be really okay. Not with besbol no longer in his future. Not with a shot rotator cuff.

Juan Sanchez Prieto did not know how long he lay prone in the alleyway, just another derelict in this non-renewed section of The Flats.

Had to make it to where Almeda usually hung out. Under a bridge. Had to tell her. A mother should know.

It might have taken courage to bring himself to his feet, just another loser in the mid-afternoon chill of an early autumn afternoon. Or perhaps, what it actually took, was a certain fatalistic stoicism. A knowing that when you are down, you simply walk low.

Gingerly, Prieto turned a corner. There it was. There was the Main Avenue Bridge. If he could just keep going, he could find her. One step at a time. One foot in front of the other.

He passed a wino. Then a second lover of the grape. An old bag lady. He thought maybe he knew the bag lady. No, maybe not. The cast of characters changed all the time. They packed up, if you could call it that, and simply disappeared.

He was getting close now. Close to Almeda Peres. That poor woman. This wasn't much of a day. In a perfect world, he'd be playing baseball right this minute. The Indians were doing just that. Over at The Jake. Against the Orioles. He, Juan Prieto, should be at second base, or shortstop. Hell, he'd gladly play either. Even riding the pines in a backup role. Nothing wrong with being a utility player. Just as long as you were in The Show. Because Juan Sanchez Prieto knew one thing. If you could make it to the big team, you'd eventually get a chance to show what you were made of.

But it wasn't a perfect world. It wasn't even a very good world. Juan wasn't playing. And Shaleen. Hell, Shaleen. He had to tell Almeda. He had to tell her now. A mother should know.

He was at the bridge. He moved to the spot Almeda usually occupied. She was there! Now he could get this over with. Do what he had to do. What was the decent thing to do. Tell her what happened.

He approached Almeda. Why was she napping in the middle of the afternoon? "Almeda? Almeda? Tal bueno! Se ha quedada dormido!"

Almeda Peres did not move, even after a gentle kick to the sole of her worn left shoe.

"Almeda! Do not do this! Do not do this! Almeda!"

He felt for a pulse.

There was none.

"Almeda..."

Juan Sanchez Prieto could no longer stay on his feet. The many kicks and punches had left him weak. He had tried. Very hard. But in the end, he could not save Shaleen. And worse, Almeda would never know.

It was likely Shaleen would not know either. They had taken her to another city, only they knew where. To a place where she could make them more profit with her body.

And now Almeda. Clutched in her right hand, an empty container of prescription sleeping pills. Next to her body, an empty bottle of cheap whiskey. A woozy Juan Sanchez Prieto suddenly experienced an epiphany. As if Mary, Mother of God herself had spoken into his mind.

Almeda knew. Almeda had known.

And the knowledge had been too much.

#

142

CHAPTER 15

Monday, October 7, 1996

End of Indian Summer: With the season abruptly over and World Series aims dead, fans find consolation in a quiet final trip to Jacobs Field.

The birds are back at Jacobs Field. Not the Orioles, but the genuine article that roosts in the stadium's rafters and niches for most of the year.

Yesterday their calls echoed through the stadium's vacant halls and tunnels, drifting over ranks of empty seats, settling atop a shrouded pitcher's mound as if mocking the futility of humans who tried to call this place "home."

> Brian E. Albrecht
> Plain Dealer Reporter

Who was yammering outside the claptrap shanty? Calling some cat? Let the animal rest. Let her rest!

"Kat," insisted Red Dog in a low, but firm voice, "O'Reilly wants you. He's waiting. You'll have to shake the cobwebs."

"I would predict," said Patrice, in a sleep-soaked voice, "that the hour is very early, and in about half a moment, I'll pummel you for disturbing me."

"Kat."

"Red Dog, you pseudonymous, vexatious cretin, if you don't can it, I'm going to thump you from here to the Cuyahoga."

Red Dog laughed.

Hell hath no fury like a woman cackled at.

Leaping out from the lean-to, Patrice was all over the cachinnating redhead, a tiger-girl thrashing about in semi mock fury. "You...you...dweeb!" she roared, as they tumbled over the hard ground.

That's when Cox Delaney, without thinking, planted a kiss, smack dab on her lips. Anything might have happened. It could have been a martial arts moment. Except for the electric jolt that jobbed the fast awakening Patrice Orosco. She knew she should cut it off. Cut it off, now. But when paralysis strikes, you often do not move. Finally freeing herself, she rose unsteadily to her feet and eyed Red Dog warily. "So, you're a great kisser. Big deal!"

Wide awake drivers are preferred, so Theodore O'Reilly drove Cherry Red to the offices of The Plain Dealer. "When Tubb gets through with you, then it's off to Ruthie & Moe's Midtown Diner. House special. You'll need to eat heartily."

Bleary eyes focused on O'Reilly from the suicide seat. "I want to go to my apartment and clean up."

"Tubb said there isn't time. You can, however, stop in and clean up before we go and eat."

"What time is it?

"Not yet 6:00 a.m. I actually let you sleep an extra half hour."

"How generous."

Jonathan Tubb sat in the conference room, off to the side of the news room, drinking a cup of coffee, and eating a cheese Danish. He was reading the bull dog edition of The Plain Dealer.

Tubb glanced up, as Patrice Orosco and Theodore O'Reilly entered the room. "Shut the door behind you," he said, unnecessarily, to O'Reilly. "See where hizzoner, Michael R. White, is working behind the scenes in the takeover of the Cleveland schools?"

"I'm out of the loop," said Patrice levelly.

"Yes, well. That's why I have you in this morning. To put you, finally, in the loop. I just want to say this, before the bile rises in your throat and you blast me one. Not that I don't deserve it. I had hoped to spare you your next...ah...project. But a man named Stanley Kremintz let us down. All you would have had to do was to write the story. Now, I'm going to be asking you to help make the story."

"Personal journalism," snorted Theodore O'Reilly. "I hate it."

"You're on record as such," said Tubb. "Duly noted. But, when the two gentlemen who are due to arrive get here, perhaps you will see what we are working against, Patrice. Let me assure you, like Mr. Phelps, you have the option of choosing not to accept this...ah..."

"Project?" Patrice supplied, bright eyed. "Wouldn't be an assignment, now would it? Not with options. Just another slow, soft sell job. Complete with waking me in the middle of the night. By way of an obnoxious messenger, I might add. That disgusting Red Dog, whoever the hell he is. Probably an ax murderer, if not an Irish terrorist."

The door had opened silently. "The police seem to agree with you," said the familiar voice.

Patrice wheeled around. "Red Dog. You bastard."

"I'm sorry I had to wake you so early."

"That's not why I'm mad," said Patrice. Then she locked eyes with the handsome carrot top. "Actually, I'm not mad. I guess." She rubbernecked around the room. The man who had entered the conference room with Red Dog was her new friend, Pudge Elliot. "I don't know what I am. I'm confused." Then she looked again at Red Dog. "Did you say the police want you for murder? I hope you didn't do it," she said dryly. "Jeez. A gal sleeps, practically in the open, maybe thirty feet from what could be an ax murderer. Would somebody please tell me what is going on?"

"Patrice," said Jonathan Tubb, "there has been no danger to you while on the streets. I've hired two nephews of Theodore's to watch out for you. They are top notch bodyguards. The homeless stories and book deal are legitimate. I had planned on making a hire to do that project, and to expand our features desk. But, you must know, your reputation precedes you. What you did on the Gulf Coast with the Vietnamese angle. Brilliant."

There it was again. That level, silent, Patrice Orosco gaze. A gaze that would make saints confess their dark side.

"We have another problem," Tubb finally continued. "One we've been working on for five years."

"It's my problem, really," said the man she doubted was Red Dog.

"So," she said, "here's your long story."

"Something like that," said Cox Delaney.

"It's also the problem of any great newspaper that prides itself on good, investigative journalism. We're going to be doing much more of that. As far as High Data is concerned, every source we've had has been nipped in the bud. Transfers, reorganizations that leave our contact in the dark about operating procedures, outright firings."

Tubb paused, for breath and thought.

"Deaths," Patrice supplied, feigning lightness. "Little things like that."

"Well..." said Jonathan Tubb. "I wouldn't put it like that..."

"I would," said Theodore O'Reilly.

"Stanley Kremintz comes to mind," said Pudge Elliot. "Also that computer geek you hired three years ago. Drive-by street gang shooting, my ass."

"Kremintz wasn't an employee," said Tubb with some exasperation. "Just a contact."

"Ya, but you'd need a seance to contact him now," roared O'Reilly.

"Stanley Kremintz might as well have committed suicide," said Tubb. "Skim off the mob, and they will eventually catch on, especially in the computer age. Kremintz was killed because greed did him in. No one else has lost a life in the pursuit of this investigation. Except the geek."

"Okay," said Patrice, "stop right there. What investigation?"

The five of them were seated at one of the three tables in the conference room, this one small and round for intimate meetings.

"Anyone want a a a Danish?" Tubb asked, "Before we enlighten Ms. Orosco."

"It would spoil the great breakfast I'm going to have at Theodore's expense," said Patrice. "Unless you are going to give Fidel Castro and Bill Clinton a run for it with a long boring speech. If that's the case, I'll eat them all."

"I think we can be concise," said Tubb. "Why don't you start, ah, Red Dog. Tell her about High Data Associates' money laundering operation."

He smiled. "First, let me say, Patrice, my real name is Cox Delaney. And, yes, I'm wanted for murder. I am supposed to have shot my wife with a semiautomatic, .223 caliber rifle. Hoping to make it look like a home invasion. Only, a couple of security people from my father-in-law's firm happened to be in the neighborhood and heard the shots, and witnessed my flight. Then, miraculously, my fingerprints were found all over the rifle. A botched killing. Realizing this, I fled to Pudge's house with my babies, left them on the doorstep, and fled to places unknown, with a briefcase full of daddy-in-law's cash, embezzled over a period of time to support me and some paramour on a tropical island, no doubt.

"And now, wonder of wonders, after my father-in-law's hired killer offed a friend of mine who had deeply penetrated his operations, they find out I've been in Cleveland all this time. But they don't know where. Now a couple of his gunsels, perhaps the very ones who killed Cherie, show up at Pudge's clinic, asking about my brother Jake. They will be looking him up soon, obviously to get to me, but they will find a rude reception."

"Where does this involve me?" asked Patrice. "I'm not a private detective."

"If the gunsels spill the beans at Jake's," said Jonathan Tubb, "then you have a great story to write. We'll be getting indictments, confessions; an end to a crooked business. Plus, Coxy will be set free. He can get his babies back."

"If it doesn't work?" asked Patrice.

"Then I want you to go undercover. Go to work for High Data Associates as a computer analyst. Find out how we can bury Maurice Devereaux."

"I found out they were running shadow programs that actually cleansed huge amounts of money," said Delaney. "I have no idea how they knew I'd been inside these programs."

"Traps," said Patrice.

"I had immunization."

"Double blinds. Second, even third sets of codes that have to be sequenced in exactly the right order."

"I know that now."

"What I want to know," said Theodore O'Reilly, emotion in his voice. "Is this girl going to be in danger?"

"Yes," said Delaney.

"Then I recommend against it," said O'Reilly.

"You have to say that," said Patrice. "You care about me. My father would say the same thing. But he also said something else. I descend from warriors and conquistadors."

"Then you'll do it, if it comes to that? Infiltrate High Data Associates?" asked Jonathan Tubb.

"I'm going to go home and take a long, hot shower. Then I'm going to clean up, and dress in a regular way. Then I'm going to go and eat a really great breakfast. Maybe a double portion. Then I'm going to decide if I like the offer. You did say, didn't you Tubb? My salary gets doubled?"

The Jonathan Tubb sputter. But the eyes were dancing.

"I thought you did," said Patrice with finality.

"She did it. She grabbed my cojones, and fried 'em up. Double her salary! And I don't have a choice," grumbled Jonathan Tubb.

"We'll just have to milk the stories harder," said Tom Erickson.

"Maybe syndicate the whole thing. We'll get our money out of it."

"We'd already planned to syndicate the homeless pieces."

"Well, my friend. You'll just have to sell them harder. And for more moola." The Newhouse Owners Group man laughed deeply. "I do think Patrice Orosco has got your number, Tubb. First person I ever knew who did."

"Liebchen!" whooped Grandma Stella. "You've come home!" Stella, herself, had decided her son should drop her back at the apartment early.

"Just to clean up and try to figure out exactly what to do next."

"You don't wissen?"

"It's hard to know what to do, sometimes. Don't you think, Grandma Stella?"

"I've never known," said the old lady, breaking into a bittersweet smile. "You do something, mit fleiss, and you find it is unrecht. You do not do it, and then you find out you have made an even bigger fehler.

"I know just what you mean. Oh, well. I'm going to take a shower now, and dress in something nice. Mr. O'Reilly will be after me in an hour."

Fortified with a quick Egg McMuffin, Cox Delaney made his way to the Thompson School, partly on foot, and partly by public transportation.

He was excited to be working on the Christmas program again. Idly, he wondered how long it would take to get a teaching certificate. One thing he thought he knew: If he ever got out of this mess, he wanted to do something with children. Perhaps he could become a music teacher in the school system.

That was a comforting thought. He'd never felt such peace as when working with the kids in Tina and Tonya's class. Even the difficult ones, like Claudine Demarco.

Thank God for Miss Dandridge. That she'd believed in him, no questions. Did Patrice Orosco believe in him, too? It was hard to say. She always seemed to be faintly irritated with him.

But, the kiss. Indeed, the kiss…

Where the hell had that come from? It was almost as if someone else was inside of his soul. The someone who had once had feelings. Who had once been a viable part of civilization, and not an underground mole traipsing along figurative subterranean tunnels in order to survive.

The kiss.

Time would only tell.

Pudge Elliot was in his office at Near West Side Medical, about to see the Monday patients. He decided to make a phone call in the moments before he'd extract his first tooth.

"Edgar?"

"You caught me," said Lieutenant Nelson.

Edgar Nelson had just had a most distressing phone call from Ned Jesperson. The paper trail on Stanley Kremintz went only so far, and no further. No links. No links whatsoever with High Data Associates.

"It's like his records had contracted Alzheimer's," said the laconic detective.

"Whattaya mean?" Nelson had growled.

"His computers have been picked clean. Sorry."

The conversation with Jesperson might account for Nelson's current dyspepsia. And so early to have dyspepsia. It usually didn't start up until the afternoon.

Now he was a little miffed with Pudge Elliot. "Tell me, Pudge," growled Nelson through the digestive pain, "who made the anonymous calls and sent me stuff through the mails? Was it you?"

"I don't know what you mean," said Elliot.

"I've gotten anonymous phone calls on the Cox Delaney/High Data Associates thing. And I have some documents that purport High Data to be in the money laundering business. Nothing concrete. Just allegations."

"That wasn't me," said Pudge. "When I called you over four years ago, I identified myself. I've called you several times since. Always identifying myself. But I'll say this: Cox has many friends, and I think they wouldn't hesitate to try and enlighten you."

"The last item was mailed just after this Stanley Kreminitz died. Followed by a phone call, to make sure I'd gotten the mailing."

"I don't doubt that. Kremintz had been trying to clear Cox for a long time. He was also a gambler, and basically, a dishonest man. But he had a heart. He knew Delaney wasn't guilty of killing his wife. This I got from Delaney himself. I personally did not know Stanley Kremintz, and he probably had never heard of me."

"So, you think Kremintz was offed by Maurice Devereaux, or his people."

"Coxy is sure of it."

"How many of Delaney's friends do you know?"

"To be honest, not many. Delaney and I are best friends. Always have been. But the people we see in common differ. He's a computer scientist, I'm a dentist. The two worlds don't necessarily overlap."

"So you couldn't organize a powwow, so I could find out what each one knows. People always know things they don't know they know. Get a group together, we might be able to find High Data's weak link."

Elliot thought for a moment. "That's not a half bad idea. I don't really know how I could go about that. You don't just go asking questions around High Data."

"Granted," said Lieutenant Nelson.

"But I'll think about it."

Sean O'Reilly sat in his gray Ford Escort, watching the Mayfield Road apartment. Patrice had been inside for almost an hour. The young nephew of the Elfin One knew his uncle would be returning shortly. That meant a break.

Timothy was off on one of their firm's other assignments. That meant a long day. Long days on stakeout. You got to know the taste of coffee in a real personal way doing this kind of work. Still, Sean liked it. What he didn't like was the cacophony of steel mills. Anytime he felt bored, he just remembered how much he didn't like working in plants.

Here came his uncle, driving that spiffy '57 Chev. He could safely leave his post now. Everything would be fine. Uncle Theodore was almost as good as the nephews. At least, that's what the elder O'Reilly always said.

Sean had Theodore O'Reilly's timetable. Back to The Plain Dealer in ninety minutes. That would afford some time for serious chow work. Where to eat? What kind of food would go down the gullet with the most satisfaction at midmorning? Perhaps a diner. No. Too much like Uncle Theodore. Spaghetti. Yes. Italian. He'd go over to St. Clair Avenue. Angelas Family Restaurant had some good looking young waitresses. Wholesome. Spaghetti and meat balls. Yes.

After the cherry red Chevrolet disappeared, Sean O'Reilly was free to go after the meal of his current dreams. He would be sure to pick up his protective surveillance at the newspaper offices on time. No one quite knew what Patrice would do next. Couldn't be late. Uncle Theodore surely wouldn't.

Sean was an old hand at negotiating Cleveland traffic. He drove with a deft hand. He'd learned at his uncle's knee when he was fifteen. What a time that had been! He and Timothy, becoming studly drivers. Getting to drive a much younger, but no less pristine Cherry Red.

It was just one of those mistakes. The city bus cut him off at just the right instant. The Escort greeted a light pole.

Sean was unconscious.

He was dimly aware of a keening siren. A jumble of sensations tried to penetrate the fog of merciful unconsciousness. One of them was the face of what undoubtedly would be an angry Theodore O'Reilly.

Lottie surveyed the shelter with a jaundiced look that spoke of years of abuse at the hands of her fellow man. In fact, those years came flooding back, as she stood in the basement of a large Congregational Church gazing at row after row of cots.

The false charges, back in the holler. The accusations of being a scarlet woman. The perception that since she was afraid of snakes, she must be harboring the devil inside her soul. For everyone in the holler knew that if your heart was right, and if you had given your entire soul to Jesus, no snake in the world could harm you. Tell that to Joe Pine. Joe fondled the snake, said the prayer, and was dead from snakebite less than an hour later. "No faith," said the pastor, rather stereotypically named Billy Bob Johnson.

Samaritan House, a brand new venture modeled after Pittsburgh's Bethlehem Haven, was set up in such a way that no one would be judged, everyone would have a warm bed and meals. And cleanliness.

The shelter was set up strictly for mothers and their children. Credentialed teachers, in their spare time, came to give regular lessons to the young people at Samaritan House.

Hobie had been gently insistent that Lottie check out Samaritan House. He let her know that nothing would change if she turned it down. "You have to think of Darcy, you know. And remember this, Lottie, if at any time you do not like what is going on, you are free to leave. Free to return to the old auto factory."

As she looked about the now deserted sleeping area, she was aware of a presence at her side.

"It's a good place, you know," said a plain woman with the serene eyes found only in the truly grounded. "By the way, I'm Sister Veronica, and the man you met a moment ago is Brother James. He just went to the store for some provisions. A letter arrived today. Quite anonymous. It contained a money order for two hundred dollars. We rely on the Lord here. Remember, He said, "Consider the lilies of the field, how they grow; they toil not, neither do they spin: And yet I say unto you, That even Solomon in all his glory was not arrayed like one of these. Wherefore, if God so clothe the grass of the field, which today is, and tomorrow is cast into the oven, shall he not much more clothe you, oh ye of little faith? Therefore take no thought, saying, What shall we eat? or, What shall we drink? or, Wherewithal shall we be clothed?"

"D'you worship snakes here?" asked Lottie, with not a little trepidation.

Sister Veronica sighed, suddenly sensing a lot about the woman from Kentucky. "No, dear. We do not. We worship the one true God. In all his attributes. The Father, the Son, the Holy Ghost."

"D'you need t'know now, if we're comin'?"

"We've had a little bit of room lately, with the weather still habitable outside. But you should make up your mind fairly soon."

Suddenly Lottie could no longer keep the pain inside. At first the sobs were gentle, and then wracking. What was she doing? She was as tough as nails. She knew that. So why the bubbling tears, the pitying wail?

Quietly, Sister Veronica placed her arms around the distressed mother, holding her close. The wise woman said nothing. Words would have been quite extrinsic.

The usual kindergarten bedlam. Children as random neurons of uncontrolled, even untapped energy. Pockets of focus, perhaps, but mostly wide ranging areas of slightly modified chaos.

The man known as Red Dodge loved it.

"Okay, guys and gals. Listen up," he said, hoping to gain the slightest measure of control. "When you warm up the voice, you need to keep a low tone, like this. Hummmmmmmm."

It was too much for Jimmy Yonkers. "My Uncle Lenny sounds just like that when he warms up his voice with a heating pad! His throat gets all red and yucky!"

Red Dodge laughed. "Jimmy, why don't you show the class how to warm up your voice?"

"I don't have a heating pad!" said the redheaded tyke.

"Just do the humming thing," said Red Dodge.

"Like this," said Tina. "Hummmmm. Hummmmm. Hummmm."

"Step up to the front. You can be the warm-up leader," said Red Dodge to Jimmy Yonkers.

"I should be the warm-up leader," said Claudine Demarco.

"We'll need you to lead one of the verses," said Red Dodge. "But, first, we must warm up our voices. We have to practice a real easy attack. No top of the lung singing yet. Then we open the throat. We do our breath control exercise, like we practiced before. And we work on holding notes, and keeping our tone."

"When can we sing a song?" asked Helen Schmidt.

"Children," said Miss Dandridge. "We have to take this step-by-step, as Mr. Dodge directs. It's a lot of hard work. Anything worthwhile always is."

"Mrs. Cronemiller says that when I take piano lessons," said Tonya.

Cox Delaney looked at his daughter with something like longing in his eyes. He finally said, "And how right she is!"

Miss Dandridge had to look away. Kindergarten teachers just shouldn't cry on the job.

Her fingers hurt. Assembling screws and washers was just about the hardest thing she'd ever done. Even harder than taking in washing back home. Margie's hands were raw. Red. Sore.

Claude Johnson, whittling a deer figurine, looked over at his frustrated wife. "Honey, whyn't y'stop fer awhile. I'll take up for ya in a minute, when I come to a stoppin' place."

"No, Claude. You got yer work, I got mine."

Madge was playing with a rag doll a few feet away. Except for the three of them, the old factory was deserted.

"Now, honey, we share th' work. You know that. I don't mind."

"This ain't no harder 'an the stuff yer doin'," said Margie. "What if y'cut yer hand? Jus' as hard. What yer doin'."

"I don' think so," he said. "'Cause I like what I'm doin'. Ain't no way anyone gonna like what yer doin'. An' I'm gonna hep ya. That's all there is to it."

"Oh, Claude, I get so tired a this. Always scrabblin' and scrappin' to stay alive. We ought t'go back to Kentucky."

"No, honey. We shouldn' go back. There, we'd be always scrappin' t'make ends meet. Here, we got a chance. We got a chance t'make sumpin' of ourselves." Johnson looked out toward the industrial section of Cleveland Ohio, sometimes called The American Ruhr. "This's where the jobs are. It might be tight now, but sumpin'll open up. I know it will. Surely."

"I hope yer right, Claude."

Madge seemed to be getting into an argument with her doll.

And she seemed to be winning it.

The lunch bunch paid no attention, as the man-boy ordered his individual pizza. Pepperoni. The way Mama liked it. Heavy on the pepperoni. The way Oscar liked it.

It felt wonderful to be buying a pizza with his own money. Enrique Deblay had advanced him twenty dollars against his first paycheck. Mama would have been proud.

She had so many sayings! Things Oscar would never forget all of his life. "Worry is the interest you pay on the trouble you borrow," Mama had often said. That seemed to work for Oscar. Why worry? He was a workingman now.

"We do not quite forgive a giver. The hand that feeds us is in some danger of being bitten." Oscar didn't quite understand that one. Why would somebody bite someone's hand?

"It is not what we have lost, but what we have left that counts." Oscar really believed that. Oscar knew that he had his whole self together. Mama always said, if you were not missing any body parts, you had half the battle won.

The pizza was delicious. He'd nearly eaten half, as he thought about what Mama had told him so many times. "It is not how much dog there is in the fight— but how much fight there is in the dog." Mama must have had Red Dog in mind for that one. Oscar knew he'd learned much from the redheaded man who had taken him under his wing. He knew he could learn from Mr. Deblay, too. Heck! A guy didn't actually have to have a father! Sometimes you could find one, like Mr. Deblay. Or an older brother type, like Red Dog.

Mama had been insistent on one of her sayings. "If you must make mistakes, it will be more to your credit if you make a new one each time." Boy, wasn't that the truth! He would never drop a lamp again! Or anything else. As Mr. Deblay had said, over a cup of coffee in the store's hospitality area, "…always think about what you are doing, and do the things that you are thinking. Then you will make few mistakes."

That one was good enough for Mama to have said it. Maybe she did, though he couldn't remember. One piece of pizza left. He was just about full. He might as well save it.

Then he saw the old man in the brown, threadbare suit, slowly walking toward a Dumpster at the rear of the new Lorain Avenue pizza parlor. The man, like so many luckless drifters, looked hungry. Oscar realized suddenly, without being able to quite understand the nuances, that he himself had seldom noticed that other people were hungry. He had spent so much time in the condition himself.

Oscar left the dining area, and headed toward the Dumpster at the back of the building, the napkin-wrapped pizza slice in one hand.

"Sir?" he asked in a tentative voice. "Would you like a slice of pizza?"

The man could have been anywhere from fifty to sixty-five. Crooked, yellow-stained teeth. Sallow skin covering a gaunt face. An open smile.

"I'd like that," the old man said simply. "I'd like that, indeed."

The old man thanked him for the pizza and made his way down the street, to wherever he customarily ate his meals; the Dumpster search now abandoned.

Oscar began to make his own way down the avenue toward the old car factory. Without fully realizing it, he had become a slightly different person in some barely definable way.

Back at the apartment, Patrice decided to crash for a couple of hours. When she wasn't getting her rest, she was useless. She quickly slipped into a deep sleep.

Two hours later, nearing mid-afternoon, she awoke to a quiet, but full house. Ruben was back from his exploration of Cleveland real estate. "Mutter!" he exclaimed, "You should have stayed with me. "Fantastisch! I have found the most wunderbar location in the entire world for International Orosco's!"

Audrey, back from morning meetings at the Cleveland Museum of Art, looked hopeful. "I think it's a good idea, Ruben. Other restaurateurs have expanded, and they haven't the product you can produce."

"I still think it's lacherlich!" said Grandma Stella. "Concentrate on what you have. We work too hard as it is."

"That's just it, Mutter!" said Ruben. "We should step out of day-to-day operations, and build a company that will outlast us! Then we can sort of retire! A little bit."

Yolanda, with the wakeful world for the first time this day, yawned. "Does that mean I can eat at your place when I go to Cleveland State?"

"You don't like my comida! And you are not going to go to Cleveland State! So get that out of your mind!"

"I like your food. I just like Big Macs, too. And I'm going to apply this week. To Cleveland State."

"Ingrato!" roared Ruben Orosco.

"It's good," said Audrey. "It's best to apply to more than one."

"Thanks, Mama," said Yolanda.

"You can take some art courses," Audrey said brightly.

"I'm going to take journalism type courses," said Yolanda, "and follow in Patrice's footsteps."

"Here we go!" bellowed Ruben Orosco. "De neuvo. Otra vez! One more daughter to scare out the life from my body! One more worry that will clutch what little hair I have left and rip it from my scalp!"

"People," said Patrice. "I have an announcement to make."

She told of the plan that might have her applying to High Data Associates, and the possible riskes. She spoke of Cox Delaney and his problem. She outlined the new story she would be doing, simultaneously with the completion of the homeless series. She spelled out every last detail.

When she had finished, Ruben Orosco had his head in his hands. "No por Dios! I absolutely forbid this lunacy! No daughter of mine is going to be cannon fodder for such monstruous! You do not raise daughters for such nonsense! You cannot allow such things!" Ruben Orosco looked about the room, locking eyes with each family member in turn. "What would you people think of me if I endorsed such risky business?"

Audrey sighed. "Oh, Ruben. I'd think you'd finally ditched the ridiculous Latin machismo that so hampers your people! I'd think you had finally learned to trust your daughter!"

"Damn straight," said Yolanda. "Way to go, Mama."

"That does it!" roared Ruben Orosco. "We are staying in Cleveland for the duration! While I get the new restaurant up and running. Yolanda! You'll catch a plane for home. Today!"

"I can hook up by computer to the school and keep up my work in that fashion. Maybe even take an AP course at Cleveland State."

"As a consultant to the museum," said Audrey, "I can find plenty of things to keep me busy."

"Let the cousins handle things at home," said Grandma Stella. "Besides, now that you are going to be a chain, I'm going to retire!"

Patrice laughed warmly. "Look at you guys! Is this some kind of family, or what?"

"It is some kind," said Ruben Orosco. "I just do not know what kind."

Theodore O'Reilly was still around the offices of The Plain Dealer, when the call came in. His face went white. Sitting in the controller's office with Mick Mulligan, he asked short, pointed questions of the caller, and seemed to get short, pointed answers back.

"What happened, Theodore?" asked Mulligan quietly, after O'Reilly had hung up the phone.

"That crazy Sean. If it isn't one thing with that boy, it is another. He went and got his back broke in a car accident."

"Is he going to be all right?"

"They think so."

"That's the main thing," said Mulligan, chewing on a meerschaum pipe. "The lad is going to be fine, so why the very long face?"

"That, my man, is going to put us light on covering Patrice."

"I see."

"As for Sean, he has broken everything there is to break. Whether it was football, skiing up in the cheese state, or just plain tomfoolery. I shall not worry unduly. But keeping an eye out on Treece is now more important than ever."

"I see what you mean," said Mick Mulligan. "You'll need to get Timothy to assign one of his men."

"Those hot sketches? They have no operative at all with wits about him to outfox a swine. Timothy and Sean are the best, but the rest, they couldn't guard a henhouse from the hens."

"Ooh. That's bad."

"The reality or the joke?" asked O'Reilly.

"Both," said Mick Mulligan.

"Come on, Yolanda. There's someone I want you to meet."

"I hope he's good looking."

"She is."

"You're not going Lesbo on me, are you?"

Patrice laughed. "Lame," she said. "And politically incorrect."

"But you chuckled."

It took only a few minutes to reach Shaker Heights in the Jeep Cherokee. Yolanda rubbernecked at the upscale neighborhoods. Luxury cars passed by on the streets.

"I wouldn't mind living here," said Yolanda.

"I'd prefer Strongsville," said Patrice. "Great mall."

Patrice parked the Cherokee at Pudge's Woodbury address.

"This is the most delightful little girl. They brought her home from the hospital a little while ago. She reminds me of you," said Patrice.

"Really?"

"She has your indomitable will and clean, clear look at life."

"What?"

"I've always admired you, Yol. You are the person who has inspired me more than anyone else in the world. Midge is like that. She lifts up my spirits."

"What you are saying is precisely the way I feel about you," said Yolanda.

"There you go. As the old song says, '...we belong to a mutual admiration society."

Randy Elliot met them at the front door, dressed in a blue caftan. "Welcome," she said with a bright smile. "Midge is waiting for you."

Midge Elliot was playing in her room with an entire phalanx of dolls. An open toy doctor's kit suggested she might be playing hospital.

Her eyes were dancing.

"Midge, this is the wonderful sister I told you about. Yolanda, meet my friend Midge Elliot."

"Hi, Midge. I've heard all about you. It's great to meet you," said Yolanda.

"You look just like Patrice," said Midge with sparkling eyes.

"I've heard that before," said Yolanda with a grin.

"I have a surprise for you," said Patrice, handing the little girl a luminous foil wrapped package.

"And I have one for you. As soon as I open the package!"

Midge's fingers worked deftly to unwrap the gift. Her eyes gleamed even more when she saw what it was.

A junior miss makeup kit.

"Wow," said Midge. "I've always wanted this."

The little girl crawled up off the floor of her room, leaving her hospital staff grouped about the carpet, undoubtedly going about their business. She stood tall. Shoulders back. Head held high.

"I want to show you something," she said, with barely concealed excitement.

The left side of her face formed a most beautiful smile.

Patrice thought, surely, the most beautiful smile she had ever seen.

Detroit, Michigan 5:30 p.m.

The Lear jet tapped down gently on the tarmac. The busy Detroit Metropolitan Wayne County Airport hosted about a thousand arrivals and departures daily. The company plane, at the beck and call of High Data Associates executive personnel twenty-four-hours a day, seven days a week, three-hundred-and-fifty-eight days a year (even pilots need paid holidays), taxied to an even stop in front of a VIP club at the south end of the airport.

Soon, drinks in hand, Fairly and Tomajac were resting up, waiting for the delivery of a Ford Escort. No limos once again. They would spend a tranquil night at the Pontch—Crowne Plaza Hotel Pontchartrain—their usual haunts while visiting Detroit. They might even do the tourist thing this evening. Belle Isle sounded just right, a thousand acre island park in the Detroit River. Fairly, especially, loved to hike the wooded trails, as well as the half-mile beach. He'd sometimes play the nine-hole golf course. The golf, however, was too much for Tomajac. "Hit a little ball. Chase it. Hit it again. Chase it. That sound exciting to you?"

"Of course. It awaits me in Florida. And if you go down there, you'll take it up too. It's the national sport in the Sunshine State."

"I'm going to eat before I do anything," said Tomajac, eyeing the VIP club lounge, where serviceable steaks could be had. "But not here. I was thinking, more like, The Whitney. I'm ready for pasta and seafood."

"Sure you wouldn't settle for doughnuts?"

"Not this time, orange juice breath."

There would be plenty of time tomorrow to visit Jake Delaney at his home near Wayne State University.

Later, after the superb meal at The Whitney, in the beige Ford Escort, hand-delivered by a scrawny African-American young entry-level male car rental factotum, Tomajac began to reflect about the job they were on. He finally asked, "Think we can clear it up, for once and for all?"

"Jake Delaney will want to tell us," said Fairly. "Before the pain becomes too great to bear."

"Think Elliot will tip him off?"

"No, but it doesn't make any difference. There will be no paper trail linking us to Detroit. You know that. Englewood will see to that. Besides, you are going to make it look like an accident."

"I'd still like to do Elliot," said Tomajac.

"Now, there you go again," said Fairly. "Overkill. That trips up more mechanics than you'd care to think about. In fact, I'd say the single greatest cause of getting caught is overkill."

Fairly steered the Escort over the MacArthur Bridge on East Grand Boulevard. Before them, beautiful Belle Isle, home of Whitcomb Conservatory, Belle Isle Aquarium, Belle Isle Nature Center, Belle Isle Zoo, and Dossin Great Lakes Museum.

A perfect spot to refresh oneself before doing an important job.

"You never did like wet work, did you Fairly?"

Fairly emitted a mirthful laugh. "My dear Mr. Tomajac," he said, turning to his partner, "I've always liked it just fine. Just as long as you are the one getting wet."

The two of them were still laughing after they'd begun to traverse the walking trails, nature's awesome twilight possessing the power to shine into the blackest of hearts.

"We've made a good team," noted Tomajac at one point on the trail.

"Indeed we have, Sir. Indeed we have."

#

CHAPTER 16

Tuesday, October 8, 1996

TOBACCO SQUAD NAILS VENDORS: Illegal Sales Easy, Teen Agents REPORT:
A squad of underage agents has sniffed out an important truth that could have deadly consequences for their peers: Buying cigarettes at Cleveland stores is—compared to the odds of kicking a smoking habit—a relative breeze.
Proof lay in the heap of cigarette packs displayed yesterday to a fifth-grade health class at Valley View Elementary School.

Allison Grant
Plain Dealer Reporter

The video camera was so small it could fit in a stickpin. The microphone, even smaller.
"State-of-the-art," said Jonathan Tubb, with satisfaction.
John Wung, a nervous third generation Chinese American high-tech guru, smiled helpfully. Patrice Orosco smiled back uncertainly. It was just the three of them in the conference room.
"I didn't expect spy gizmos," she said. "Is it really necessary?"
Once again, the hour was too early for Patrice's liking, but the hot coffee and cheese Danish helped to ameliorate her mood. She had driven into the Plain Dealer offices in her Jeep Cherokee. Theodore O'Reilly was meeting with his nephews in the hospital, and the plan was for he and Timothy to meet Patrice at Ruthie & Moe's Midtown Diner in an hour.
"The system is foolproof," said John Wung, his smile magnifying tenfold, "the batteries will last as long as you will."
"Is that supposed to reassure me?" barked Patrice.
Wung's smile lost little of its voltage. "I mean the batteries have a good seventy years of service. They aren't even in the marketplace yet."
"John has all the bases covered," said Tubb, with even more satisfaction. "tell her, John."
Wung cleared his throat. "Well, the batteries are a photo-voltaic/hydrogen hybrid that hasn't even been 'discovered' yet. That's because I discovered them. I'm waiting for the right time to market. Perhaps when the public wishes to embrace an all-electric car that has a five-thousand mile range, costs a hundred thousand dollars, but just pennies to recharge. Then I'll cash in."
"Good for you," said Patrice. "Maybe I'll invest. Meanwhile, why am I being outfitted like some character in a cheap spy novel?"
"Patrice," said Tubb, "with Sean O'Reilly laid up in the hospital, I felt we better have a backup position. So, naturally, I thought of John, here. He's a genius."

"And you know," said Wung, once again animated, "they have devices that can sweep a room and weed out virtually any kind of bug?"

Patrice yawned and nodded.

"Don't mind Patrice. She keeps bankers hours," said Tubb.

"Really?" said Wung. "Sounds like you need tai chi in the mornings, about 4:30 or so. Opens up your system. That's how I've been able to become a regular inventing fool."

"I can tolerate cheese Danish, perhaps, but little else this early. So, if I nod off, don't hold it against me."

"You think it's early?" asked Wung. "It's rather late, actually. I've been up for hours. Early bird catches the worm."

"Serves the worms right, for getting up before the birds," said Patrice, publishing another great yawn.

"Uh," Tubb mumbled, "your were explaining about your equipment, John."

"Oh…" The wattage of the smile had slipped some, obviously blunted by being in proximity to one who would snore her life away. How would she ever grasp the beauty of his paraphernalia. "Yes… well… no scanner of any kind can ferret out my systems. Since the devices look like jewelry, you will even pass a body search. But inside the control vehicle, we will have digital quality audio and visual. A wonderful invention, if I do say so myself."

"You planning some kind of digital alarm clock, perhaps? Maybe one that booms and clangs and whistles, and just generally wakes the very, very dead?" Patrice was managing a straight face, which seemed to somewhat confuse John Wung.

"I don't see much of a need for that," Wung mumbled, clearly losing control of the demonstration session. "Who would buy it?"

"The beauty of this equipment," said Tubb, clearly annoyed with Patrice, "is that when you know something, we'll know it."

"That's excellent. But will this stuff also transmit the pain? Like if security goons decide to whap me upside the head?"

"No, no. It's not like that. You are going to be perfectly safe. Are you getting cold feet?"

"Even though I haven't been around here that long, you should know better than that," said Patrice. "It's just that I have done undercover investigative reporting before, and I never went into a job decked out with spy gewgaws and gimcracks."

Wung sort of coughed, or half-choked, hearing his toys so characterized.

"Would you prefer that I just throw you out to the sharks?" asked Tubb. "Sink or swim? Remember, you have the necessary backup to deal with any technology that might be thrown at you, and who knows what technology High Data Associates might throw at you?"

Patrice sighed, ate another Danish, and once again went over the plan. She finally said, "So, this is definitely a go?"

"It all depends," said Tubb, "on what happens in Detroit."

"Okay," she said, resigned to the fate of doing things somebody else's way. "Show me how this… incredibly sophisticated equipment works." She showered John Wung with a beautific smile.

At that moment, John Wung might have named her in his will, judging by the wattage of his smile.

"Thanks for meeting me, Arnold," said Cox Delaney as he took a seat in the cramped office.

Arnold Anderson nodded. "I wish you the best, you know that. By the way, Mel told me he has a group in good ol' San Antone that might want to help you with the yearly budget, once you get it up and running. They cannot, however, spend any funding on startup costs. Not in their charter."

"I understand," said Delaney. "If you speak to Mel Dones before I do, ask him to say hello to his much better half."

"I believe Madge is going to call Martha tonight. I'll pass your message along."

"On second thought, do not breathe the phrase 'better half' within earshot of either one of them. If it was construed that I called Mel Martha's better half, I would never be able to set foot in San Antonio again."

"Good point, Coxy. Niether would I."

"Sean, you just might be the most unconscious sunuvagun that ever sprung from the Gaelic gene pool."

The immobilized Sean O'Reilly was obviously in pain. The criticism hurt that much more. "Uncle Theodore, I couldn't help it. There was this bus. Suddenly, it was just there."

"Now we've had to go electronic in order to cover that girl."

"We would have used electronics along with live surveillance anyway. Timothy will just bring one of the boys onto the case."

"For all of your accident prone self, you and your brother are still the best. I do not trust electronics."

"Uncle Theodore, you need to go modern. Electronics is the thing these days." Sean grunted, a sharp stab of pain penetrating the physical fog induced by drugs in the IV drip. "Anyway, Timothy will see to things, Unc."

"For the sake of St. Patty's butt, he'd better."

In the waiting room of University Hospitals, Theodore O'Reilly met up with his nephew Timothy, a grim look on his face. "Sean says you will take care of things."

"I will, Uncle Theodore."

"You'd better," snapped the Elfin One.

Detriot, Michigan. Midmorning.

"I think you worship doughnuts," said Fairly, himself masticating a powdered offering from the variety pack.

"Maybe not," said Tomajac, as the two of them sat in a supermarket parking lot just off Jefferson Avenue. "I think I'm picking up a taste for bear claws. Yes I'm buyin' 'em next time."

"Be my guest. I'll be eating petit four hours in gatorland."

"You're that sure we'll wrap this up today?"

"Feel it in my bones."

Fairly coughed the Escort to life in Motor City and nosed it toward Woodward Avenue. In a matter of moments, they could see Wayne State University off to the left. Just beyond the university would be Bethune Avenue, home of their prey.

"Nothing like a full belly for full work," said Tomajac.

"Massa Devereaux do want it complete, Erasmus,"

Fairly and Tomajac were quite certain Jake Delaney would be home.

Alone.

Which was not quite the case, of course.

Jim Montrose, hidden inside a dormer, would be ready. It was ridiculously easy to track the men from High Data Associates, from the moment the Lear Jet taxied down the runway of Burke Lakefront Airport in Cleveland, to the moment it landed at Detroit Metropolitan Wayne County Airport.

Montrose's men almost knew the smell of their coffee, certainly the brand of doughnuts they'd consumed moments before heading for Bethune Avenue.

"Your interrogation techniques rusty, Jim?" Jake Delaney had asked the night before, a chuckle in his voice, as he adjusted the electronic monitoring devices installed in honor of the visitors from High Data Associates.

"I wouldn't say so, no. Not so's you notice."

"I heard about how you handled the guy who stalked your sister last year."

"Yeah? I didn't tell you about that one. I was embarrassed."

"Why so?"

"I enjoyed it. Maybe too much."

Jake laughed. Later, as he dealt two cards to replenish his friend's poker hand, he mused, "I hear you broke all ten of his fingers."

Montrose smiled. "And six of his toes."

"Six?"

"I started to get bored."

"I hear ya," said Jake. "Remember in 'Nam, you were walking point, maybe six clicks from base camp, and you caught this gook, began to bang on him, then abruptly stopped?"

"What about it? You gonna ask me, was it the same thing? Did I get fuckin' bored that time?"

"Yes. That's what I was going to ask."

"Yeah. That's it. It's why I gave up boxin' Golden Gloves. After you get a guy well-pounded, you know? It begins to seem like no point in continuin', If you know what I mean."

"Well, Jimbo. Tomorrow, when they stir from their nest, and come up the street and want to bang me around, I hope you do not have a sense of ennui."

Montrose laid a winning hand on the table, scooped some chips into his corner and grinned. "Somehow, Jake. this seems somewhat different. Like it might keep my interest."

Now, as it started to slip past midmorning, Jim Montrose spotted the Ford Escort with the rental plates as it turned right off of John R. Avenue. Behind aviator sunglasses, there might have been a glint in Montrose's eyes. "Pardon the cliché, Jake, but it looks like it's now showtime."

"This is perfect," said Tomajac, as Fairly parked the car across the street from Jake Delaney's three-story house.

"Indeed," said Fairly. "He's probably in there investing up a storm. You got your black box in the trunk, I presume?"

"As the boss would say, naturellment."

"Then he'd say, tres bien! Strip his accounts. Clean him like buzzard at carrion," laughed Fairly.

The two of them glided across the street, up the sidewalk and onto the porch. Fairly jabbed the doorbell.

"I think it will take just one hour," said Fairly with relish.

"Perhaps less than that," Tomajac replied.

*   *   *

Inside the house on Bethune Avenue, Jake Delaney gave one last check of the electronics, and made his way to the front door. Through the gauzy curtains he could barely make out the back lit forms of the burly thugs. Hope Jimbo is ready for this, he thought. There can be no slip ups when dealing with hired muscle.

Jake Delaney's hand had just begun to turn the doorknob when the door burst open with a perfectly timed shoved. He was on his back. Two hundred plus pounds of enforcement on top, High Data Associates style.

"Jake Delaney!" singsonged Fairly. "Jake Delaney! Do you recall our interview in Cleveland five years ago? We have reason to believe you were not truthful to us. Not truthful at all!"

"Would you mind letting me off the floor," Wheezed Jake Delaney. "Then I will answer all of your questions truthfully, if you will do the same for me."

"There!" said Fairly, with a huge grin. "Didn't I tell you Jake Delaney wants to cooperate?"

"You did! You really did!" said Tomajac, matching Fairly's good mood, tit-for-tat. "Dumb me! Now I've ruffled him up a bit. My apologies, Mr. Delaney. Won't you have a seat?"

The three of them sat around at a round oak table. Jake worked at looking frightened. It was a hard act for him to pull off. He was elated. This could be the breakthrough. The evidence he would need to give to Edgar Nelson in Cleveland. The evidence that would right things for his brother. Providing these goons had loose enough tongues.

"Jake," said Fairly, using the first name as a diminutive. "There is a persistent worry that a kidnapping might be just around the corner. And that two children might be in grave danger from a murderer."

"No." said Jake Delaney.

"Ah, good. No, you say. That's great," said Fairly. "Suppose you help us out, then. Give us your brother's address, so we can alert the police."

This wasn't going quite right, thought Jake Delaney.

"My brother didn't kill his wife."

Fairly's smile was benign. "Then he has nothing to worry about." Then very quietly, "Give him up, Jake. For his sake. For the children's sake." And ominously, "For your sake."

"I believe you two killed her. Fairly and Tomajac, is it? And I believe you tried to kill my brother, but he got away. Did I nail it? Oh…by the way. We have electronic surveillance that you cannot disable. Therefore, a quick head shot to dispose of me won't get you anywhere. I tell you this because you continue with the fiction that Cox Delaney killed Cherie. Therefore, it seems unlikrly we will get any incriminating evidence. 'Bout right?"

"Gentleman," said a disembodied voice. "I have trained a very lethal weapon on your carcasses. And I'm so itching to blow you away. Give me a reason."

Without the slightest hint of fear, Fairly and Tomajac looked around to find the source of the voice. Without luck.

"Oh, Jake," said Fairly quietly. "Jake, Jake, Jake." He scanned the room again, an ironic smile on his face. And then to Tomajac, "Can you believe this guy? His brother's stone-cold killer, and he continues to stick up for him, even adding a ridiculous fiction that we offed his brother! Unbelievable! Isn't that aiding and abetting? I don't know for sure, my law's little rusty."

"Could well be aiding and abetting," saidTomajac, "yes, indeed. I'd think about that if I were you, Mr. Delaney. By the way, sorry I crashed into you when the door opened. I thought I heard a voice say 'come in.' No hard feelings, I hope."

Jake continued to stare impassively at Fairly and Tomajac.

Fairly returned the stare, with a mix of amusement, excitement and meaness. "Unless you and your hidden pal plan on murdering us, Mr. Delaney, we have to go. Security has been heightened where the chicken are concerned. I wouldn't advise your brother to try and break into the compound. It wouldn't be healthy."

The thugs headed for front door. "If you decide to cooperate," Tomajac intoned, "give us a call. It will go easier on you. If you don't, and it can be proven you helped your brother, well, I don't have to tell you the trouble you would be in."

And with that they were out the door.

Jim Montose came down the stairs. "What in the hell was that?"

"Hell if I know," muttered Jake Delaney.

"You don't have enough on tape to implicate them for belchin' in public. You have something that sounds very much like your brother offed his wife."

"We better have them watched, at least after they are back in Cleveland."

"For sure. My people can do that."

"I just don't know what to make of it," said Delaney.

*   *   *

"Something spooked you," said Tomajac as they folded themselves inside the Ford Escort.

"Something wasn't right," said Fairly. "I smelled it the minute we walked into his place. It was as if...he were lying in wait. It was a house of silence. Not business as usual. Perhaps he was tipped off. Something might have gone very wrong if he were tipped of, and we had stayed to do what we came for. We might have been trapped."

"I picked up on your change of strategy immediately," said Tomajac. "Another bit of evidence we make a great team."

Fairly had the Escort back on Woodward.

"He had to be tipped off," said Fairly. "You wanted to do Elliot? Let's go back to Cleveland. You can do Elliot."

"Now you're talkin'," said Tomajac.

"That alone might flush Cox Delaney. If not, we'll take another crack at brother."

Jim Montrose's collection of Vietnam vets, some of whom had intelligence backgrounds, tracked Fairly and Tomajac back to Burke Lakefront Airport, they were met on the Tarmac by the High Data Associates limo. Maurice Devereaux, a VO and water clutched in one hand, listened carefully to Fairly's account of the trip to Detroit on the way to company headquarters.

"So we've got to send a message," Fairly concluded.

"Mais, oui," said Maurice Devereaux.

"We've got to do him," said Fairly.

"Se jouer des difficulties. C'est le tour," said Devereaux. "Il est mort."

Tomajac was grinning with satisfaction.

#

163

CHAPTER 17

Wednesday, October 9, 1996

STOKES SAYS RACISM STILL BIG PROBLEM: Forum Focuses on Race and Diversity.

In his lifetime, Rep. Louis Stokes said he had seen many of the barriers of racial discrimination in public accommodations and employment topple under the pressure of the civil rights movement.

But despite the progress and the many freedoms enjoyed by younger generations, America has a long way to go when it comes to eliminating racism and discrimination.

April McClellan-Copeland
Plain Dealer Reporter

"Let's eat in the Warehouse District tonight," said Patrice, as she soaked a doughnut in a cup of Ruben's Mexican coffee.

She was nearly ready to head out the door for the drive to High Data Associates, an eager just out-of-college job seeker.

"This is a girl after my own corazon," said Papa Orosco. "I may be able to strip a recipe right out from under an unsuspecting chef!"

"Lacherlich!" said Grandma Stella. "You make up your own recetas de cocina."

"Naturalmente. One never inquires about a receta de cocina. Tal malo. Very bad form. Instead, one tastes for the recipe. Did the cocinaro use jalapeno; was it pasilla; was the flavor you tasted in the pollo en vino rojo dry red wine? Or just red wine vinegar? Was the pato fresh or frozen? Was the jugo de naranja fresh or frozen? Or was it merely flavoring? After many years, one learns to distinguish such things."

"I want to go with you this morning," said Yolanda.

Patrice bit another chunk of doughnut. She looked at her sister levelly. "You might as well. Give you experience in job seeking."

"Would that be dangerous?" asked Audrey.

"Peligroso?" roared Ruben Orosco. "Then I forbid it! Only one daughter at a time to be placed in jeopardy!"

"Sohn," roared Grandma Stella. "We aren't putting any girl in danger. But they are big girls now! Yolanda is no longer klein madchen. Patrice is now a grown frau." Then, ever so softly. "You must learn to let loose. To let go. To let the vogel spread its wings. It is the naturlich order to Gott's universe."

"Mutter...I know that. But a padre knows in his heart that things are not always seguro. And when a daughter's safety is at stake, little parts of a father's corazon are wrenched into painful knots. You must know this, Mutter..."

"What I know," said Patrice, "is that my appointment with High Data Associates is in forty-five minutes. Ready, Yol?"

"Sure, Sis."

"And Papa," said Patrice. "We will be just fine. I know what I'm doing."

It was nearing noon the day before when Patrice learned from Jonathan Tubb about the puzzling turn of events in Detroit. "Fairly and Tomajac came on like officers of the court," he muttered. "Very strange. No telling what they might do next."

"So, I'm on for High Data," Patrice replied. "What if they don't hire me?"

"Not hire you?"

"They are sounding down right prescient."

"You mean, what if they smell you're a plant?"

"Precisely."

"God, I don't know. You see, that's just it. It's been going on like this for five years. We start to get close, and they smell us out."

"Does this Devereaux know you are after him?" she asked.

"How could he?"

"What if he does? What if he has a plant in this newspaper?"

"Impossible!"

"Who knows about me and the plan to infiltrate HDA?"

"Only the executives from the owners group, and Theodore. Everyone else thinks you're only working on the homeless series."

"Do you know anybody in the forgery game?"

Tubb had to think about it a moment. "I guess I sort of do."

"Get me some ID. Driver's license, credit cards, an employment history they can check out. Resume. As you know, I did study computers. I also used to know a hacker. I 'accidentally' learned a few tricks…"

"Right," Tubb grinned.

"Make the name Kat Garcia. I can pass for Anglo, but I don't like to. Better get my car reregistered in that name. Make some calls. Shouldn't be hard."

"I don't think the company will go for all of that."

"So what. Do it yourself."

Again, the Jonathan Tubb grin. "You're one tough hombre, Orosco."

"No," she smiled winsomely. "Mujer. One tough mujer."

Kat Garcia swished into the offices of High Data Associates, dressed closer to Carmen Miranda than Patrice Orosco. Gone was the Standard English she spoke so well. On board was a barrio patois that sounded like an Hispanic standup comic doing cadenced hyperbole.

"Kat Garcia for a Mr. Upton," she said to a bored receptionist. Was that Marissa Tomei, or Rosie Perez, Patrice was doing?

Yolanda was also in character. The sisters had often mouthed dialogue from various movies, getting the biggest kick out of mimicking Hispanic actresses, who often liked to put audiences on with exaggerated vernacular.

"I'll siddown, Sis," said Yolanda. "Wish I had some coffee."

"There's a coffee bar just down the hall, Ma'am," said the receptionist, who surprisingly, seemed to come to life with caffeine thoughts.

"Gracias," said Yolanda. "Without my coffee…"

While Yolanda was left with java and waiting rooms, Kat Garcia was led into Mr. Upton's inner sanctum. "Mr. Upton is in conference just now, but he should be with you in a short while," said the receptionist, who stood on extremely high heels. "Make yourself comfortable."

Kat Garcia riffled through dated magazines, mostly of the highbrow sort. Forbes. Business Week. And the requisite business publication for high tech companies, Architectural Digest. With the latter, she scanned house plans she wouldn't live in if the alternative was to pitch a Coleman tent.

Mr. Upton proved to have a first name. Stephen. He also proved to be an extremely fit fellow. Obviously played soccer with fellow employees. Handball. Or racketball. Maybe both. Drank cappuccino. Loves tofu. Patrice could tell from the spring in his step.

"Well," said Mr. Upton, glancing at the resume she'd just handed him. "You seem to have all the experience in the world for a just graduated person, Ms. Garcia. Texas Instruments. That's impressive. Know what I think?"

Kat Garcia shook her head nervously.

"I think you're damn near overqualified for this job. It's entry level. You could probably make twice the money elsewhere, or even here if something opens up."

Stephen Upton scanned the rest of the resume.

"Why not hire me now? Then when your better job comes along, I'll be right here."

Upton laughed. "It doesn't work that way, Ms. Garcia. We have many more applicants to interview. I think I'll take your resume on advisement, and give you a call if we decide anything. If so, I'll interview you then."

Yolanda hadn't even finished her espresso when Kat Garcia emerged from the offices of Mr. Stephen Upton, health conscious young executive.

Patrice gave her an almost imperceptible shrug, as they fell together, stride for stride.

"I think I blew it, Yol," said Patrice, as they approached the newly reregistered Jeep Cherokee.

"How?"

"I haven't a clue."

An hour-and-a-half later, three more interviews under his belt, Stephen Upton handed an executive assistant eight resumes, neatly stacked. "Check these out thoroughly, Maxine," he said. "There seem to be some good ones. This is going to be a tough call."

"Got any preferences, Steve?"

"Not really. The ones that check out, I'll call them back in and then go to work sorting it all out."

"Any that are real pretty?"

"Now, Maxy. None as pretty as you."

"That's what I want to hear. And when I don't hear it from you, I'll hear it from my mirror."

The Penthouse Coffee Shop on Center Ridge Road serves up fried shrimp that would make a seafood house envious. Yolanda was biting into one of the shrimp when Patrice burst out laughing. When she finally got ahold of herself, she turned dancing eyes on Yolanda. "Yol, do you remember that scene in the John Wayne movie, his first starring role, I think. The film was The Big Trail. Anyway, John Wayne turns to Marguerite Churchill, and says something like: 'You can get used to someone not liking you. And when they aren't around, you miss 'em not liking you.'"

"I remember."

"Well, there's this man. The cussedest man I ever met. And yet, he is so drop dead gorgeous."

"Like Mike Piazza?"

"No, much different. He's got the reddest hair a man could have, save a careless type who got a bucket of stain dropped on his noggin. And he's so passionate. He cares about people, and takes care of them."

"Go on, Big Sister." Now it was Yolanda's eyes that were dancing; dancing in juicy anticipation.

"He's a great kisser…"

"Yes. Do go on."

"That's about it." Then after moving her eyes off to the side and thinking a bit, "And a whole lot more that I can't put a finger on."

"Mysterious."

"Not exactly. In fact, he's more like an open book. Just a book you can't quite grasp."

"Mysterious."

"Actually, he's very predictable. A man of old-fashioned honor. He'd always be there for you."

"You love him."

Patrice was wide-eyed. Incredulous. "Yol, I don't love him! I think I hate him!"

"You got it bad, Big Sis."

Patrice continued to eye Yolanda askance, as she ripped into the small, defenseless shrimp as if she were Jaws.

Cox Delaney lay on an examination table in one of the treatment rooms at Near West Side Medical. Being an off day at the clinic, neither Dr. Varris nor Dr. Elliot were in. However, trooper that she was, Amy Walker responded to Delaney's rather embarrassed telephone call.

After his second meeting in as many days with Arnold Anderson at the Cuyahoga Metropolitan Housing Authority, he had been on the way to a bus stop, to catch a bus that would place him in the vicinity of Shaker Heights, and the Thompson School.

That's when the rusty nail bit its way through the sole of his shoe.

"Good thing you called," said Walker, as she dressed the foot. "We would not want an infection to set in, or, God help us, tetanus."

"Lockjaw might be a blessing in disguise. There's this person I know. I seem to always be putting my foot in my mouth. Disgraceful."

"What's her name?"

"What makes you think it's a she?"

"You have a certain adolescent, looney look to your eyes. Plain as day."

"Looney?"

"As in moon."

The shot in the butt made him lightheaded, as shots always did.

"Thanks, Amy."

"Anytime Coxy. The foot's gonna be sore. Were you going to do anything?"

"I was on my way to Tina and Tonya's school. We're doing a Christmas show."

"I heard. Pudge told me all about it. I was thinking of doing some shopping today. How's about I drop you off at the school?"

"Are you sure it wouldn't be an imposition?"

"Not at all."

"I was wondering," said Delaney. "Could we pick up a friend?"

"I don't see why not."

Oscar No Name was excited. He'd found out earlier that Deblay's had no deliveries for him until the next day. He jumped at the chance for an outing. Mama sometimes did that. She'd take him to places so that he might learn about the world.

"I wasn't in school much," he said, from the back seat of Amy Walker's Nissan. "But I liked it when Mama could get me in."

"There are some neat kids," said Red Dog, from the passenger's seat.

"How old are you, Oscar?" Walker asked, just after they'd traveled over the Cuyahoga and into the East Side of Cleveland.

"I'm pretty old. Mama said I was a man, now."

"Do you ever get sick?"

"Mama did."

"If you ever need a doctor, Oscar," said Walker, "won't you come to the clinic? Red Dog can show you where it is."

"I walk by it sometimes. But I'll never need to go there."

"If you do, come see us."

Amy Walker took them right to The Thompson School.

"Thanks, Amy. Once again, I'm in your debt," said Red Dog, as he pulled his frame out of the compact car.

"Nonsense." And then to Oscar, "Glad to meet you, young man."

Oscar No Name leaned toward the open passenger side window. "I don't like to get poked."

"He doesn't like needles," said Red Dog. "But if he needs one, I'll go with him. You can then give me a shot, too. That'll take half the pain away."

Oscar No Name grinned. "You'd do that, Red Dog?"

"Of course."

"You're a real friend, Red Dog," said Oscar happily.

As she drove away in the little blue car, Amy Walker couldn't help the tears that slid down her creamy cheeks. It was at times like these that she knew why she volunteered at Near West Side Medical.

The shiny, brand new black van, so familiar a fixture in Shaker Heights, with the pedigree registration, sat basking in the late morning cloudiness; showers were practically guaranteed by the weatherman. The van fit Maurice Devereaux's dictum: "Never, never be en vue."

Inside, Fairly and Tomajac were eating…doughnuts. "Where's the bear claws?" asked Fairly, "I thought you were going to be adventurous."

"Sara Lee doughnuts are the best. I wouldn't pass them up."

"Your hands will be sticky. When you squeeze the trigger."

"Handi-Wipes."

"You are a man of great planning."

The van was parked directly across the street from Pudge Elliot's Woodbury Road house. The two hoped Elliot would make a lunch time appearance, something they knew he was accustomed to do five years earlier, at least some of the time. If not, their day would be chalked up to surveillance time.

"It is something I learned from you," said Tomajac. "With you retiring, who knows who I'll be working with. Or for."

"That's true."

"And if I join you in Florida, we won't be working together. Not with you parked on your duff."

Fairly laughed.

As if stage managed, Pudge Elliot made an appearance, swinging into his driveway in a burgundy Volvo. Also making an appearance at the front door was a busty woman with a little girl.

"This is a shame," said Fairly, with his usual distaste for untidy dispatch.

"What's the difference?" said Tomajac, "Seeing him go down, or finding him bled out on the front lawn?"

"Point well taken," said Fairly.

Ever since surrendering the Valmet Bullpup, stamped with Cox Delaney's prints, Tomajac had been of two minds about his weaponry. While he'd quickly acquired another one, so useful with close work, he'd also become obsessed with a Mauser Model 66SP. Equipped with a scope, the match rifle used a .308 caliber Winchester bullet. When you needed distance for your wet work, the Mauser was wonderful.

Nowadays, Tomajac was just as likely to use an automatic nine for close work. Usually the Wildey Auto Pistol. The advantage, of course, was that the patented gas operation was adjustable for windage and elevation, and could sometimes be useful at a distance.

Now, toward the rear of the black van, through a custom porthole, Tomajac set up with the Mauser, which sported a specially made silencer not found on the legal market.

Elliot was out of the Volvo.

The first rule of shooting is to control your breath. This Tomajac did. Absolute concentration. Exact timing.

The woman remained on the porch, with the little girl.

The dentist moved away from the car. Toward his waiting family.

Steady. Be ready for the perfect moment. A gentle squeeze. A nearly inaudible pop. A sound that would not carry far through a silent wood.

Pudge Elliot dropped face forward on his cobblestone walkway.

From the moment he entered the kindergarten classroom, Oscar No Name knew he had found a special place. Sesame Street characters dotted the room. The alphabet, posted above the blackboard, caught his attention.

Reading readiness.

"This is my friend Oscar," said Red Dodge, by way of introduction. "He has agreed to help me with the Christmas show."

Oscar beamed.

"Hi Oscar," said Jimmy Yonkers. Other voices chorused the greeting.

"I'm going to have Oscar lead the boys, and I am going to lead the girls," said the redhead. "I understand you all have learned the words to Silent Night."

"We know 'em," agreed Helen Schmidt.

A boy named Donnie Ackerman raised his hand. "What if I can't remember the words? Do I pretend to sing?"

Leave it to Jimmy Yonkers! "That's what my Uncle Lenny does! He just flaps his lips, as my mother says, and nothing comes out!"

This struck Oscar No Name as very funny indeed.

"You'll soon know the words, Donnie," said Red Dodge, suppressing the desire to roll on the floor.

"I can teach Donnie," said Tonya Devereaux.

"I just might call on you to do that," he said, with the slightest hitch in his voice. "All right. The boys will start out with this: 'Silent night, holy night.' Oscar will lead that. Then, my girls will come in with: 'All is calm, all is bright.' Remember breath control. Remember to open your throats. Sing from the diaphragm. Remember, we learned that."

"That's really singing from the belly," said Tina Devereaux.

"Yes," grinned Red Dodge, eyes sparkling.

Oscar was really getting into it. He waved his arms, just like a conductor he'd once seen on an electronics store display television from a cold, dark street.

The two groups did surprisingly well, staying remarkably on tune with the first phrases.

Miss Dandridge was smiling.

"That was great. Now, the boys will sing: 'Round young virgin, mother and child,' and the girls will come back with 'holy infants so tender and mild.'"

Oscar led his group of boys like a practiced maestro. Red Dodge brought the girls into it smoothly.

"Now, then," said Red Dodge, pausing for breath himself. "Remember we talked about harmony? Miss Dandridge will play each part, on the piano with one finger. First the boys part. Go ahead Miss Dandridge."

170

Red Dodge sang the boys part: "'Sleep in heavenly peace; sleep in heavenly peace.'" Then he sang the same lyrics, but this time, a third step higher. "Got that girls?"

Sweet little voices chorused "Yes!"

Quite on his own, Oscar boomed, "Got that boys?"

The boys indicated their affirmation, with bellowing "I got it's," and "yes's," and "you betcha's!"

But it was the voice of Jimmy Yonkers that carried the loudest. "I got it, Mr. Oscar!"

Mr. Oscar!

That sounds terrific!

Mr. Oscar!

The harmony of the first stanza left Cox Delaney breathless.

A moment frozen inside time.

Randy Elliot, transfixed on the porch, as if in eternal limbo. The elapsed time between startled, gorgonized synaptic inaction and her leap toward her husband was actually just a millisecond.

"Pudge! Oh, my God! Pudge!"

She was at her husband's side. The sanguinary, starburst spread of the river of life. The motionless recline. "Oh, my God!"

She must do something. The ghastly slowdown. Like a tableau unfolding with laggardly cosmic aloofness. "Help me," she sobbed. "Somebody help me!"

Midge Elliot responded to the materfamilias entreaty with a cool, reasoned detachment. Her father was in trouble. Always, Daddy would rise to the occasion. His hyper nature notwithstanding, Pudge Elliot always acted with the professional detachment imprinted by his job training. That had somehow been stamped on Midge's nature. Or perhaps it had been a lifetime coping with Moebius syndrome. When you have weight on your shoulders, it makes your shoulders strong.

Midge rushed inside the house. To the kitchen. To the nearest phone. She picked up the receiver. She dialed 911.

"My father's sick. He fell down. Please come," she said.

Modern technology allowed the operator to pinpoint the exact location. With efficient dispatch, help began to roll.

A black van, parked forty yards away, partially obscured by trees, slowly started up Woodbury Road. No one noticed.

"My God, Pudge. You've been shot," sobbed Randy Elliot.

Midge moved to her mother.

"It's all right, Mommy. They're coming to help."

Randy and Midge heard the siren's wail.

* * *

"You were magnificent, Oscar," said Red Dog with pride, satisfaction and affection. "If you can coordinate your schedule with Deblay's, you can come with me every time."

Oscar gave his happy smile. The bus was rumbling over the Lorain Carnegie Bridge.

"I like to sing," he said, "but, why do they call you Mr. Dodge?"

"That's a long story, Oscar. I'll tell you about it someday."

"What do you think of the name, Mr. Oscar?"

"I like it. Is that the name you want to pick?"

"I think so, Red Dog. Mama would have liked it."

"How about a first name?"

"I don't know yet."

"No problem. I've always known you'd eventually have to figure out a name for yourself. My advice is to give it time. You're in no hurry."

"No." Oscar turned to Red Dog. "How's your foot?"

"It's sore. Thanks for asking."

"You really would go with me if I needed a shot?"

"In a New York minute, podnuh."

Oscar No Name nodded. "I knew you would."

"I just blew it," said Patrice, perhaps puzzled, definitely angry with herself.

"Not necessarily," said Jonathan Tubb, from the back seat of Cherry Red.

Tubb, O'Reilly and Patrice were parked in the lot of a Dave's Supermarket, drinking cappuccinos. A kind of combination post mortem and confidence building session. The traffic on Payne Avenue was intense, partially the result of a road crew doing repairs.

"There will be a lot of applications," said O'Reilly. "It might take them a few days to get back to you."

"All of the references will come up golden," said Tubb. "I called in a few chits."

"That's great. But if they hire someone else, then what?"

"It gets back to perceptions. Are you going to go with half empty cups, or half full cups?" asked Jonathan Tubb.

"In other words…"

"Be confident, think good thoughts," supplied O'Reilly.

"Couldn't have said it better, myself," Tubb agreed.

Patrice sighed. "Take me back to the streets. I'm going to work on the homeless story some more."

"You don't have to sleep out there anymore," said Tubb. "You've done that enough."

"We'll see," said Patrice.

"Stubborn to the end," said O'Reilly.

She said, "You bet your Irish knickers."

"It's only a matter of time," said Fairly, in Maurice Devereaux's office. "Delaney will be flushed."

"I want that murdering chien cut down," said Devereaux, "like the cur he is. I will avenge Cherie, if it is the last thing I do."

Todd Englewood, shifting his corpulent frame for comfort, nodded in reassurance. "Fairly is right. Delaney will show himself just as soon as he finds out about his pal. I've assigned seventeen of our security men to help Fairly and Tomajac. This chapter will be at a quick end."

"It has been a ridiculous horaire," muttered Devereaux.

"I admit five years is not a reasonable timetable," said Englewood. "But we had nothing to work with. We had no idea he was in Greater Cleveland. Most wife killers would have fled to the Bahamas, or some such spot. But we've now got a handle on this, Maurice."

"Tres bien."

* * *

"I'm Mrs. Delabeckwith," said the ageless woman with the trim body, brown hair untouched by time's grayish transformations. She might have been seventy, but no one was saying. Her eyes held a kind of crinkle, indicating that mirth was acceptable. It took perhaps a nanosecond to observe that Mrs. Delabeckwith loved children.

"I'm Darcy."

"She's new," said Martin, behind thick eyeglasses donated by the local Lion's Club.

There were eight children ready for lessons at The Samaritan House. Sister Veronica lurked in the background, a small smile playing on her lips.

"Darcy, I'm going to let you read this picture book. On every page, there is a letter of the alphabet, with pictures of things that start with that letter. I'm going to ask Martin to be your mentor. Children, what is a mentor?"

"I know!" said Leann, a striking African-American girl with bright eyes. "That's someone you trust who helps you!"

"Yes! Darcy, that's how we do things around here," said Mrs. Delabeckwith. "We each have mentors. We work together in groups, we work alone during private study time, and we work as a class, while I talk about things. And anytime you have a question, feel free to raise your hand, and I will answer the question to the best of my ability."

It sounded exciting to Darcy. She could barely wait for her first day at "school" to end so she could tell her mother about it when she returned from Hobie's.

"Now, all except for Martin and Darcy, it is time to work on the ant farms. Good thing Martin finished his last week!"

Martin beamed.

"Next time, we'll start your ant farm, Darcy," said Mrs. Delabeckwith.

"Real ants?" asked Darcy.

"Yes," said Martin, "but they won't bite you. They're in a glass cage."

Darcy wasn't too sure about the ants. What she was sure of was that she liked Samaritan House. She felt more secure than she had felt since her early days in Kentucky. And it was sure better than the old car factory. After all, there wouldn't be any knife fights at Samaritan House.

Darcy was sure about that.

Juan Sanchez Prieto had wedged himself against the door of an abandoned sew/vac center on Detroit Avenue. A cheap bottle of muscatel gripped in his throwing hand.

He couldn't believe his eyes. Was that Uptown Lady?

Prieto rose unsteadily to his feet. His drunk shuffle was not unlike that of an aged man. He must move within shouting distance. She was moving away rapidly. He might not make it.

Patrice chose that moment to pivot, searching for a used clothing store that supposedly had some children's things that might fit Madge Johnson.

She saw Prieto. She stopped.

"Juan," she said under her breath. He couldn't have heard her, as he made his laborious way up the avenue. He was perhaps twenty yards away.

Patrice began to walk toward him.

"Uptown Lady?"

"Juan…"

They stopped just a few feet apart. Focusing on each other. Though it was even money that Juan Sanchez Prieto could focus on anything, let alone the beautiful journalist.

"You look like hell," she said.

"I've been through inferno. I have caused a death. I have killed my family with my malo. They have found their way back to the Dominican Republic."

"You are obviously not playing baseball," said Patrice.

"With what cuerpo? My body is shot. I cannot throw. I cannot play the game anymore."

"Would you like me to get you help?"

"There is no ayuda. Not for me."

"You are right. Only those who wish to be helped can be helped."

"I may wish many things. A deseo can only come true if it is a possible thing. What I want is imposible."

"There is more than one dream, Juan. There are a million dreams, maybe a billion. All you need is to find a sueno nuevo."

"I cannot dream another man's dream. No one can."

"Make it your own dream. Think about what you want in life. Why you want it. How you can get it. And when you know this, call me at The Plain Dealer. I'll help you in any way that another person can. But you must remember: Only you can find your way in this life. But, you can find that way, as the song goes, with a little help from your friends."

Patrice began walking away from Juan Sanchez Prieto, up Detroit Avenue. Truly, she must be lost. The used clothing store was not on this block.

"Uptown Lady…" breathed Juan Sanchez Prieto, as he watched her retreat. He staggered back to his lonely doorway, again propping himself in an upright position. He sat like that for the longest time.

The muscatel untouched.

*   *   *

Theodore O'Reilly made the trip to the Near West Side with the heaviest heart he'd had in years. He'd just returned to The Plain Dealer offices when Mick Mulligan caught up with he and Tubb at the horseshoe.

Blowers was manning the desk. Mick motioned the two old friends into the conference room. O'Reilly and Tubb exchanged glances. Mulligan was too happy go lucky to be this solemn.

"I'm afraid I've got some very bad news," said Mulligan, clearing his throat. He looked down at the floor.

"Spit it out," barked O'Reilly.

Jonathan Tubb folded his arms against his chest, as if to defensively ward off some disaster.

"Pudge Elliot has been shot." Mulligan continued to look at the floor.

Silence from O'Reilly.

"And?" Tubb finally asked, his voice as weary as a spent marathon runner's wheeze.

"They just don't know," said Mulligan.

"What do you mean they don't know?" This from O'Reilly.

"Mrs. Elliot's sister called for you, Tubb. A Norma Darling. That's what she said. That's all the doctors know. I'd suggest, if you know someone at University Hospitals, give 'em a call."

It took a few calls, but the gist of the information that was available was that a single bullet had lodged to within a quarter of an inch of Pudge's heart. The only thing that prevented the bullet from passing clear through his body was the fact that a rib had slowed it down. Unfortunately, fragments from the rib were also likely to be a problem. Surgery would be performed whenever it was deemed to be safe. The first thing; stabilize the patient.

"I'm sorry, Tubb. He's got maybe a ten percent chance to make it," said the source.

"I've got to tell Coxy and Treece," said O'Reilly, after Tubb filled him in on the source's report. "I'm leaving now. You coming,?"

"I'll stay here. Stay close to the information." He gestured for Blowers to come into the conference room. The short City Editor came to the door. "Blowers, you're gonna man the 'shoe the rest of the day."

Blowers nodded and headed back to the desk, not asking any questions.

Now, parked near the old car factory, Theodore O'Reilly withdrew from his classic Chev, and gazed out toward the ruins, in hopes of seeing Patrice, and hopefully Cox Delaney.

"Hey, Gramps!" said a young punk, the map of Appalachia stamped on his face. "That's the car I want!"

O'Reilly grinned. "It's for sale! A quarter of a mil."

"Don' think it's that much," laughed the kid. He was suddenly joined by a sandy-haired compatriot. "Whyn't you save the hassle, an' turn over the keys, old man?"

Theodore's grin was now truly beatific. "I think you are making a big mistake, young man," he said softly. O'Reilly leaned his small, ancient frame against the fender. "But, if you think you are man enough, to the winner goes the pink slip!"

"You gotta be shittin'," said the sandy-haired punk.

For the first time, O'Reilly regarded the second youth. "No," he said matter-of-factly.

Both punks made a quick move toward O'Reilly. But he wasn't there. A balletic sidestep, a blur of hand, and the sandy-haired kid was motionless on the ground.

The kid from Appalachia hesitated. O'Reilly did nothing. Watching and waiting. "Well?" he finally asked. "You man enough to continue the attack?"

The kid said nothing.

"I suggest," said O'Reilly, "you pick up your friend, and get out of here. And if I find you have bothered anyone else around these parts, I'll have to come after you. And if I do, I'll hurt you bad. Your friend will be okay in a few minutes."

The kid half carried, half dragged his friend.

A few moments later, knowing Cherry Red would be perfectly safe, O'Reilly walked into the old factory compound.

"God, he's awesome," said Timothy O'Reilly, pulling the binoculars away. The empty surveillance van didn't disagree.

Timothy would have come to his uncle's rescue, but he knew from the beginning that it wouldn't be necessary. He knew Cox Delaney would probably not need him either; he even doubted that Patrice Orosco would need him, after reading her dossier. But when Uncle Theodore wanted something, in this case, security for Patrice, and backup for Cox Delaney while Patrice conducted her investigation, then that is what Uncle Theodore would get.

A tap on the passenger side window. A startled Timothy O'Reilly. Then he saw it was Theodore. "Unc," he mumbled.

"Open the door," Teddy barked.

"How did you sneak up on me like that?"

"It wasn't hard, Timothy."

"I saw your little tussle."

"Where's Patrice?"

"At that camp across the way."

"Wrong."

The new pizza parlor seemed to be keeping the early customers, brought in because of specials no pizza eater could refuse. Cox Delaney and Oscar No Name were just two of them. They were finishing up a pepperoni, Oscar with a satisfied look on his face, when Patrice strolled into the restaurant, tired and hungry. She was unwilling to go home just yet, lest she subject Grandma Stella to cooking chores.

That's what it would be, of course. There was no budging the German lady once she'd discovered a kitchen.

"Kat," Red Dog motioned her over to the table.

"Well. Feeding your faces, I see," she said, somewhat mischievously to the Redhead. "Think I'll do the same. After wasting shoe leather, the same thing happens to me. Try as I might, I can't find the store I'm looking for. Hi Oscar! You're looking good, like you've had a real good day."

"Oh, I have, Kat. I can really sing. I always thought I could."

"Maybe you'll sing for me," she said.

"I'd love that!"

"Oscar," said Red Dog. "Why don't you go home and check on Claude and Margie. See how the baby is doing?"

"Sure, Red Dog. I can do that."

"And Oscar. Thanks for the pizza."

Oscar was filled with pride. "It was my pleasure, Red Dog."

"You're a piece of work," said Patrice, after Oscar had left. "On the one hand, you're really wonderful. People like you. Then, you come across to me like some kind of reprehensible chauvinist."

"Ah, chauvinist. Well, haven't you figured out yet that I have been trying to keep you alive?"

She looked deeply into his eyes. "It might be understandable that a man like you, seeing his wife gunned down, might be protective. But, Mr. Delaney, you treated me more like some kind of fragile Mexican rose. That makes me madder than hell."

This time, it was Cox Delaney who looked deeply into her eyes. "I'm sorry. I think I see what you mean."

She was taken by surprise. "Oh. Okay. I accept what I take to be an apology." She coughed. "I'd better order some pizza."

Like a nervous schoolgirl, Patrice Orosco stumbled to the order counter, confused enough to possibly order anchovies by accident.

"Makes sense," said Tomajac. "If the two of them were in frequent contact, it would come at the clinic."

"You're a quick study," mumbled Fairly, as he kept his eye on Near West Side Medical.

"So we concentrate on this side of town. Do the stakeout thing. Wait for Delaney to show."

"Whoever stereotyped mechanics as slow witted sure had it wrong," said Fairly.

"But when they characterized us as frequently hungry, they were right on the button," said Tomajac. "There's a brand new pizza parlor just down the way. I suggest we take a batch of these flyers, work our way to the pizza joint, and chow down."

"God, you make sense sometimes," said Fairly, as the two of them hauled out of the black van.

Patrice savaged a piece of sausage pizza, thick crust.

Delaney grinned. "You eat like a sailor."

"Are you trying to offend me again?"

177

"No. No. Never. It was a compliment. Who needs a woman who daintily consumes, or nearly consumes, a bird's portion?"

"Well, you'll have to wait to laugh at me some more. I'm going to go to the little girl's room."

Cox Delaney watched her retreating form, as she sped for the head, much like an actor appearing in a commercial for a relief product. A few moments later, he felt a shock of the first magnitude. That's when he locked eyes with a familiar burly figure. There was instant mutual recognition.

Delaney leapt from the table and smashed a forearm into the side of Tomajac's face. He followed that up with a vicious kick to the falling head. Wheeling, he spotted the butt of Fairly's gun swinging through the air. Sidestepping, he planted a hard right across Fairly's temple. He was quickly on top of the fast fading security man. He smashed him with shot after shot.

Utter pandemonium inside the pizza parlor.

That's when Patrice, back from the ladies room, pulled Cox Delaney off of the unconscious Fairly. A few feet away, Tomajac was also in lala land.

"Come on," she whispered.

Sirens were now blaring. Out the back door they ran, Cox Delaney on an extremely sore foot. A brisk wind whipped sweat-soaked faces. They zipped for five blocks, through a residential section.

"I don't think they saw you," said Delaney, trying to catch his breath. They were propped up against an old garage that belonged to a condemned property. Refuse and discarded junk littered the lot. The house's windows were all broken out, or boarded up. Everywhere, weeds. It looked like the owner had finally given up on trying to secure the place.

"Who were they?" asked Patrice, though she had a pretty good idea.

"Maurice Devereaux's men. The one I cold-cocked first is the man who killed Cherie."

"My God..."

Delaney nodded, still fighting for breath.

"I'm too old for this kind of thing," he said, as he gently rubbed his painful foot, "sprinting like a halfback."

"You stay here," she said, realizing he was spent. "I'm going to call somebody, and take you to a place where you'll be safe. That obviously isn't around here."

He looked at her with genuine gratitude. "Thanks..."

She stared at him for a few moments.

"No problemo. You'd do the same for me."

"Yes, I would."

#

CHAPTER 18

Wednesday, October 16. 1996

Woman Strangled: The Cuyahoga County coroner has determined that an unidentified woman discovered Monday night in bushes on E. 30th St., south of Payne Ave., was strangled and ruled the death a homicide. Police said the woman was found nude in some bushes in an area frequented by homeless people.

The Plain Dealer

The special phone was installed in Norma Darling's apartment. When it rang, she gave the excuse that Kat Garcia was in the shower. Would the caller wait for just a moment? A quick sprint to Patrice's digs found the journalist fast asleep. Groggy or not, she managed to get to the phone in record time.

"Ms. Garcia? This is Stephen Upton! Congratulations! You're the newest programmer at High Data Associates!"

Bingo!   How did she manage to win out over what had to be scores of applicants?

"In fact, you'll be joining seven new programmers. We are going for an unprecedented expansion at HDA. I didn't know that when you were here, or I could have probably saved you a lot of anxiety. In fact, I could have saved all the other applicants some anxiety. We hired them all."

"Oh…"

"When can you start?"

"Tomorrow?" she managed to croak.

"That would be excellent. We start early, 7:00 a.m. Come to the employees side entrance. We will have an orientation for about three hours, and then it is off to the races."

After Upton signed off, Patrice frowned at Norma Darling. "Looks like they hired just about anybody and everybody. Some big expansion. That smacks the ego. Not winning out over fifty or sixty applicants."

"You got your foot in the door. That's what counts. I'll tell Randy."

Patrice nodded.

"You need some coffee?"

"That would be great," said Patrice, dropping onto a divan in virtual exhaustion. Four hours of sleep just didn't make it for her.

Theodore O'Reilly, who seldom felt he had to practice the craft of cooking, had nonetheless practiced for a week. He was beginning to get terribly antsy for Ruthie & Moe's, or A & B. In spite of that, the solid blue collar food rolled out of his kitchen, and into the dining room. Down his and Cox Delaney's gullet.

"This is getting old, Theodore," muttered Delaney, as he scooped a forkful of scrambled egg. "I need to check on some people."

"All of Ohio City is running lousy with High Data security, not to mention cops," O'Reilly pointed out. "And you are looking as guilty as hell. You sent two men to the hospital, one in critical condition. A man due to retire in a couple of days."

"Tell me about it."

"You show your face, you're gonna get plugged. Those computer generated, enhanced pictures? They've now been enhanced a thousand times. They're a dead ringer for you. Not to mention the Identi-Kit work up on Patrice from witnesses at the pizza joint."

Delaney nodded.

"If the cops get you, you're looking at assault with intent to kill."

"Tomajac was going for his gun."

"To kill you on sight. You know that, I know that. The dumb crumb cops don't know that. They don't want to know that. All except for the maverick, Nelson. That still doesn't explain what you did to Fairly."

"He was trying to brain me."

"Right again. Fairly acted in self-defense. That's what the call will be. Then you nearly beat him to death. Even if Patrice nails them to the wall, you've got some legal problems that might end up sending you to prison."

"I'll die first."

"No you won't. You'll think of Tina and Tonya first, son. That's what you'll think about!"

Amy Walker pulled up in front of the old car factory. She honked once. Oscar came running. Walker smiled at the enthusiasm shown by the young man. "Hello Oscar. Ready to teach those children today?"

"Oh, yes. Until Red Dog gets better. As long as he's sick, with that bad foot, I'm going to take over.

As the Nissan pulled away from the curb, a couple of suits gripping a batch of flyers could be seen in Walker's rearview mirror.

"Would you like to stay at my place, tonight?" asked Walker.

"Can you cook?"

"Some. Probably not as good as your mother."

"No one could. But I bet you cook good, anyway."

"What would you like?"

"I've had a lot of pizza lately. How about fried chicken?

"I think we could manage that."

In the rearview, Walker saw the men talking to the Johnson's. She had a very bad feeling.

Claude Johnson could be canny when he had to be. Now, looking at the dead on likeness of Red Dog, he nodded. He had to throw them off.

"Yeah. I seen him. He stays over 'bout 44th St. Old garage."

The two men looked rather like mathematics professors, but they had a hard edge to them that suggested they did something much more physical.

"When was the last time you saw him?" asked the taller of the two.

"Maybe last week," said Johnson.

Margie could pick up on her husband of twenty years quickly. "Is he a bad man, mister?"

"The worst. He killed his wife," said the second man.

"Here's my card," said the tall suit, handing it to Claude Johnson. "If you see him, call us right away. He's very dangerous."

"Will do," said Johnson.

After the men left, Johnson continued whittling. Margie was working with her second, and last screw shipment. The company was being investigated and had ceased making deliveries to the assemblers scattered around Greater Cleveland.

"You know, Marge, I've never been wrong about a man in my life."

"I know."

"And I'm not wrong now."

"I know, Claude." She put her arm around her husband. "That was quick thinkin'."

He nodded.

"Have I tol' ya I love ya lately?"

Claude Johnson smiled his warm, simple smile. "Not nearly often enough," he said, as he kissed her on the forehead. "An' I reckon I ought t'say it more often m'sef."

Life support looks much the same in any hospital. Tubes. IV's. Monitors. Perhaps a depressing atmosphere, but not when you see the professionals who do their work with efficient dispatch, and often take time to have a positive word for patients and family alike.

Pudge Elliot lay back, worn-looking, survivor of two surgeries. Not out of the woods yet. That's what Dr. Osborn said. If things went the way they were going, he might be upgraded to serious condition in the next twenty-four hours.

It had been touch and go for a week. Randy had spent practically the whole time by his bedside. Midge was with her grandparents, Pudge's mother and stepfather.

Now Pudge was in a deep sleep. Most of the time, he'd been barely coherent during his brief periods of wakefulness. Randy was sprawled on a cot, fitfully sleeping.

Last night, around 11:00 a.m., he'd come to for the briefest moment.

With eyes fluttery, he'd first asked after Midge. Satisfied she was safe with his parents, he asked Randy to warn Delaney.

"Coxy's been taken care of," she whispered. "Don't worry. Everyone is going to come out of this. I'll be by your side."

He nodded, and returned to sleep.

* * *

Jonathan Tubb sat on the vinyl upholstered booth, an amused look on his face. "You've eyed every cholesterol-clogged breakfast that has passed by your line of sight. Why don't you order?"

"I've eaten," snapped O'Reilly.

"Then you're not hungry?"

"Probably not."

Ruthie & Moe's Midtown Diner was still busy with late breakfast patrons. Tubb drummed his fingers on the Formica table. "Okay. Out with it. You're upset. Spill the beans."

A sausage link order, with eggs sunnyside up, hash browns and toast caused Theodore O'Reilly to nearly drool. In exasperation, he waved the waitress over after she'd delivered the manna from heaven to a discriminating customer. "That order you waved by my nose, Francisca? Bring me one like it," he snapped, "and if you do, a really decent tip awaits you."

"Bene," she smiled. That pazzo guy is all right after all, she thought. My, how I love this America! If only popolo would stop trying to get me to eat that spaventoso pizza!

"With Identi-Kit images flocking the Near West Side, I'm afraid that Patrice has blown her cover with HDA."

"Not at all," said Tubb. "In her getup as Kat Garcia, she bears little resemblance to herself."

"At least that's something."

When Francisca brought his order, you would have been hard pressed to guess that Theodore O'Reilly had eaten scrambled eggs and a slice of ham less than ninety minutes earlier.

"You look like you're enjoying yourself," observed Tubb.

"I'm a hog in pig heaven," he growled, fork full of sausage links poised and ready to go down the hatch.

Cox Delaney had had enough. He put on his boots, ran a razor over his beard, and donned a watch cap to at least partially obscure his blazing crimson hair.

With one last look at the memorial to Mary's decorating skills, he left Theodore's immaculate home, locking the door behind him. He stepped out to Grand Road, and looked in both directions. Unsure of what to do, knowing that he must do something, he decided to check on his people at the old car factory. Maybe the time it would take to do that would give him an idea of where to start, what to do.

The stakes had grown enormously. He had gotten to know his daughters. He had met a woman whose image bounced around his mind. And two hit men had seen him and tried to dispatch him quickly to the next world, and been thwarted in the process. But in stopping Fairly and Tomajac, he had implicated himself even more. Everything he had done seemed to play into their hands. And now Pudge might die.

It was as if they couldn't lose.

Tomajac seemed asleep, as he reclined in the chair next to Fairly's bed. The Intensive Care Unit, or ICU, was a tranquil place compared to many sections of Metrohealth. Yet, underneath the purposefully restive atmosphere was a beehive of activity.

Tomajac, having suffered a concussion, had spent three days in hospital himself. Now that he was out, he used every waking moment to watch his friend of many years. A constant, loyal companion.

Fairly stirred. Could it be? wondered Tomajac. Alert to the first nuance of movement, he hovered over Fairly with fraternal concern.

An eye blinked. Then, like a slowly retracting overhead door, Fairly's blue eyes met the surroundings; a sensation to the recently insensate that is ambiguous, amorphous.

"Hey, pal," Tomajac whispered.

"Wha..."

"You rest, my friend," said Tomajac, moved to the point of tears. "I can promise you, I will get him if it is the last thing I ever do."

"Tom..."

"I'm here."

"Wha' happen..."

The tears came. Tomajac couldn't stop them. He hadn't cried since he was a boy. Since his father smacked him for being too sensitive one fine summer day. What year had that been? He couldn't quite remember. He only knew the offense came when Rusty, his dog, had been run down by a truck. He'd broken down then, utterly devastated at the dog's death.

"You're like a girl," his stevedore father had snarled. And then hit him harder than he'd ever been hit in his life.

Now, as if on timed release, the tears came. They came forcefully.

"Tomajac," Fairly managed to whisper. "We'll...get him...together."

Lottie arrived at The Samaritan House just before noon. She would get a good lunch, play with Darcy some, and then go back to Hobie's for afternoon cleaning.

"I'm so proud of Darcy," said a voice behind Lottie, as she knelt at her cot, putting away a sweater.

Sister Veronica.

"Hi Sister."

"Darcy really picked up on the alphabet today," said the elderly woman.

"That's wonderful," said Lottie. "Say, why're you called Sister? Is that like the Catholics?"

"No. A lot of Protestant denominations call each other Brother and Sister. My name is Veronica Hauptmann. You can call me Mrs. Hauptmann, if you want."

Lottie thought a moment. "I kind of like Sister Veronica better."

"So do I. Even just Veronica, if you'd prefer."

"How did y'get doin' this kinda work?"

"Tell you what. Let's get some sandwiches, and I'll tell you how I ended up here."

When they were seated at a picnic table in the eating area, sandwiches in hand, Veronica turned to Lottie. "You see, I came from Denmark. I am a Jew from birth. I was born Veronica Horowitz. I converted to Christianity, without ever repudiating my Jewishness. I've been a member of Jews for Christ for a very long time. I choose to worship at this Congregational Church. And sometimes I even go to temple.

"When I was a girl, during the Second World War, even though we were Jews, we were Danes first in the eyes of King and country. Our religion was not considered to make any more difference than if we were Lutheran.

"After nearly four years of leaving Danish Jews alone, Hitler issued an order to evacuate all Jews in Denmark. That meant we would be relocated to concentration camps, where all Jews knew you would never return. In perhaps two weeks time, all of Denmark's Jews were evacuated...but, by the Danes themselves. A sort of Underground Railroad. We were mostly taken to safety in Sweden.

"It was there that I met a most wonderful man, Erhard Hauptmann. An ex-patriot German, in fact. From Sweden, we tried to help as many Jews in countries such as Poland as we could. Some we saved, some we couldn't.

"We eventually moved to America. First to New York City, and later to Cleveland. My wonderful husband died about ten years ago. That's when I began to work with the homeless."

There was a look of great peace across the lovely lady's face. "So, when I find someone very wonderful like yourself, I know that God has given me another friend. And Lottie, dear, when we make friends with wonderful people, they will be friends for all of eternity."

"That's some fine story," said Lottie in awe.

"And perhaps, one day you will tell me yours."

"Who's our liaison at police headquarters?" asked Todd Englewood, dressed in his usual slimming Armani suit.

Gary and Gerry Orson sat in the fat man's office, having been pulled away from their regular duties, now that Fairly was out of commission.

"Dominick Tavaro," said Gerry Orson.

"The best investigator on the Cleveland police force," supplied Gary Orson, garbed in his button down suit.

"Unless you count Edgar Nelson," Gerry said, robed in a two-piece that matched his brother's, down to the buttons. "And he's being effectively isolated from all HDA business. He stumbles around, but won't get close."

"Nelson never would cooperate," said Gary.

"Wouldn't go on the pad," said Englewood, who liked to make the Orson brothers uncomfortable. Kept them on their toes.

Gerry Orson winced. "It's not like that, Mr. Englewood. You make it sound like we are Mafia or something. These are consultancies we are talking about. Nothing more. But, no, Nelson never would work with us."

Englewood smiled. Such naivete, the Orson brothers. "How are we cooperating with the police?"

"Our security people are working hand-in-glove with Tavaro's people. We expect to run Delaney to ground within the week," said Gary. "We now think he has been living on the street. No wonder we never found him. A man can disappear on the street like a puff of smoke."

"A week is not soon enough," said Englewood. "You've got three days. Mr. Devereaux insists."

Visible tension rising off the nervous integument's of the Orson brothers, like steam from a radiator.

"Mr. Englewood," said Gerry Orson. "We cannot control the success of police investigators! Even with our own security men helping them!"

"Three days!" said Englewood ominously.

The Orson brothers left quickly, agitated to the extreme.

Cox Delaney slowly moved into the clearing of the old auto factory. Claude Johnson recognized him immediately, even clean-shaven and wearing a watch cap. The Kentuckian waved him over. Margie had gone to the store with Madge.

"Some men'ave been lookin' fer ya, Red Dog," he said as he whittled another carving for Deargirl's store.

Delaney nodded.

"Didn't much like the things they 'as sayin'," Johnson said simply.

Delaney gazed off into the distance. "What did you think?"

"I know people, Red Dog. You didn' kill yer wife. I know that. Surely not." He cleared his throat. "I sent 'em the wrong way. Give you some time."

"I appreciate that, Claude."

"Least I could do."

"I came back to tell you I got us a building. We can all own it collectively. Sweat equity, they call it. We talked about it over pizza once, you remember?"

"Surely."

"When I get my troubles worked out, I'll be back for you and your family, Claude."

"Okay. I can do the buildin' trades. I'll be ready when you are, Red Dog."

"I'll see you later," said Delaney, as he began to walk away. Then he turned back, hesitating. "What did Margie say, Claude?"

"She don' believe 'em, either."

Delaney nodded. "That's good." Then a bit of a pause. "Guess I'll be goin'. Don't quite know what to do, but I guess it'll come to me."

Claude Johnson watched Delaney make his way toward Bridge Court, a weary man with a walk of perseverance. Not at all unlike Johnson himself.

Patrice parked the Cherokee at the curbside in front of O'Reilly's home on Grand Road. In a fit of near obsession, she'd fashioned a batch of brownies in her kitchen, with Grandma Stella hovering over every cooking procedure.

"Good that you know you can win a man's herz, Liebchen," said Grandma Stella. "Through his magen."

"I'm not trying to win his heart. You and Yol seem to think I have something for this guy. He's...he's often brutal."

"Any man can be gefahrlich if you kill his frau, and steal his kind."

"I know."

"And, can you be brutal?"

Patrice laughed. "I've been known to deliver pain, now and then."

Now, at O'Reilly's front door, she pressed the bell a half dozen times to no avail. No Cox Delaney. She didn't expect O'Reilly to be home, he seldom was during the daytime, but with the redhead gone, she didn't quite know what to make of it.

He had agreed to hole up for a time, until they could figure out what to do. Now that she would be starting work at High Data Associates, they had a possible chance to make headway. Slim, but possible.

"Delaney..." she whispered to herself. "Where the hell are you?" Clutching the brownies tightly, she walked back to the Jeep and climbed in angrily. "When I get hold of you, Senior, I will show you what happens when you jerk the chain of a conquistador and a krieger."

A week ago, she had run frantically to find a public phone. There are lots of phones around, until you need one. Then you find lines cut to the receivers in booth after booth. "That's it," she'd roared to the open air, after the third booth was inoperable. "I'm getting a cellular. Or even a PCS."

Finally, she'd found a dimly lit blue collar bar with a working phone. It took almost twenty minutes to find O'Reilly. She finally traced him through Mick Mulligan. By the time The Elfin One arrived at the abandoned garage, Delaney could barely walk, his foot was so puffy.

"You look like an elephant used your foot for a road," O'Reilly had remarked, once they'd reached his house.

"I feel even worse," he'd said simply.

Now, sitting in her SUV, she remembered the time her own foot had looked much like Delaney's. In one of his rare times away from the restaurant, Ruben had taken her horseback riding. She must have been eight years old. Yolanda, at four, had been too young, according to Papa, to tag along. Yolanda had nearly cried her eyes out. The disapproving look on Grandma Stella's face. "You have two kinds, Sohn!" she had barked. "Zwei!"

On that long ago Sunday, she had insisted on going barefoot when they reached their destination, the little mesa the Anglos called Flat Rock, but known to Hispanics as Roca Plano. When an outcropping of basalt from an ancient volcanic eruption sliced her right foot, Ruben had been mortified. Lost in his thoughts, he'd been barely aware of his barefoot daughter, now crying piteously, and dripping blood profusely.

"Mija!" he'd screamed. He grabbed the reins of her horse, clutched his daughter with one hand, and sent his painted pony on a fast gallop for his father's rancho. Patrice smiled at the memory. If there was one thing that made Ruben Orosco come unglued, it was a daughter in peril.

A UPS truck across the street shook her out of her reverie. Only one thing to do. Drive to the West Side. If she knew Cox Delaney, and she was starting to get the idea that she did, that's where he would go. Back to where his people were.

The bar was dark. Working men sucking brews paid scant attention to the newly shaven Cox Delaney, sporting a watch cap that daylight might reveal covered shocking red hair. Delaney moved silently to a pay phone located down a rear hallway. Here he might have some privacy.

A quick call to Skip Omyer left him numb. Things were closing in fast. He had to call Jake in Detroit. He dialed direct, listened to the instructions, dropped the change into the maw that could eat up your coins as quickly as an underfed dog.

"Yes..." said the voice. His brother's deep baritone.

"Jako."

"Where are you?"

"I'm in a bar."

"West Side?"

No answer.

"You'd better lie low, bro. You can do nothing topside. Nothing. It's out of your hands. We will expose them. But if they find you, you're dead."

"Listen, Jake..."

"No, you listen, little brother. Your daddy-in-law's crooked company has got gendarmes on the payroll. Do you understand? Not all of the cops, to be sure, just a few actually; but you sure as hell won't be able to tell the difference. And when you factor in the security men the company is throwing at your trail, you've got a major force peering into every corner looking for you. Now, if you have any sense you will go back into hiding."

"Jake. I need some of your men to penetrate High Data Associates. If I can get in there, I might be able to break their codes."

"Not now. If it comes to that, then that's what we will do. First, you are going to let your friends help you, you obstinate bastard."

Silence from Cox Delaney's end of the line.

"Do you understand, bro?"

"I'll give it a little time," said the younger sibling. "And if that doesn't work, then I'm going to do it my way."

Patrice drove up and down Lorain Avenue, used some residential streets to head up to Detroit Avenue, then parked down West 52nd, within sight of the car factory. If it would take a stakeout, then that's what it would take.

An hour later, just as she was about to crank up the Jeep and begin to cruise more of the Near West Side, she spotted two men, dressed in black suits. The men might just as well have been wearing sandwich boards. She knew instantly what they were doing. Door to door they went. The houses old, less than modest; framed bungalows and Craftsman-style working class abodes.

"Shit," she barked to the upholstery. Slapped the steering wheel. They're doing a virtual sweep, she thought. Delaney couldn't possibly slip through that. Then she remembered the car was currently registered to one Kat Garcia. Should she find Delaney, and be seen picking him up, then the car would have blown its cover.

She'd been skeptical when it was suggested the special phone be installed in Norma Darling's apartment. Whatever for? she'd reasoned. Simple, she'd been told. If HDA did their homework, they would find she was a working girl living with Norma Darling. She had her own phone in order to separate costs. Routine. We can't leave anything to chance, she had been told. With that in mind, it was

187

time to get another car. Jonathan Tubb might have something available at the paper. That would be safer.

She drove slowly away from the neighborhood, trying not to stick out in anyone's mind. They were dealing with a colossus. A company with the resources to run anyone to ground. For the first time, Patrice wondered what she had gotten herself into.

"Grand-pere! Do you like my picture?" asked Tina Devereaux.

"Mais oui! Que c'est beau!"

"I'm glad you came home early, Grand-pere. Anyway, I made this for you. It's a cow."

"But you've never seen a vache!" said Maurice Devereaux with wide eyes and an animated face. "How can you make something so ravissant, so utterly charmant, when you have never laid eyes on a vache?"

"We have pictures! Beaucoup images! Granp-pere? Why do cows give milk? Why don't they just keep it?"

Tonya entered the room at that moment. She broke out in a belly laugh. "They can't help it! People take it away. Sweet milk, buttermilk, and chocolate milk! But cows do not give orange juice!"

"C'est verite." said Maurice Devereaux. "Trees give orange juice."

"Not really!" said Tonya. "Trees try to keep the orange juice, unless they throw the oranges to the ground. People take that, too."

"Why do people take things, Grand-pere?" asked Tina. "Why did Daddy take Mommy?"

"I have tried to keep that away from you," said Maurice Devereaux. "Who told you such things?"

"Claudine," said Tonya. "Over and over. For a long time. She says Daddy took Mommy's life."

Maurice Devereaux lapsed into a dark silence. "We shall not speak of such things in this house," he said finally in the sofest of voices. "It is not what we will speak of."

It didn't take long to locate a van from a printer friend of Jonanthan Tubb. The Managing Editor seemed to think it was a good idea. "Maybe the two of us are being paranoid, but should Delaney be spotted with you, and somebody makes the plates, resulting in police inquiries, well, isn't it awful the way kids today grab vehicles and go on senseless joy rides?"

"I hope I'm not going to get anyone in trouble," said Patrice. "'Stolen vans and such. But I've got to find him."

"I'm long since through with worrying about doing things by the book. Those arrogant assholes at HDA have had their way for too long. I'm ready to try anything and everything to bring them down."

"Do you think the police will ever figure out who I am?"

"I hope not. Too many of them are on the take. Forget I said that, or at least don't repeat it. No reason to borrow trouble," said Tubb.

188

"I've got to find Red Dog," she said. "Good old, cussed, Cox Delaney. He's a loose cannon running around, probably thinking he can make something happen."

"Be pretty hard to make something constructive happen, what with being what they once called Public Enemy Number One," said Tubb. He stood up from his chair at the conference table when he saw his friend approaching. "Let me introduce you to Homer Vladic, Patrice."

Vladic entered the conference room after nodding to Blowers at the horseshoe. "Tubb, you thirsty whiskey man! What nefarious plots are you cooking up with this young damsel?"

"Vladic's parents came over here from Yugoslavia, Patrice. But Homer, here, thinks it was Italy. Thinks of himself as Rudolph Valentino."

"Not at all! Cary Grant! Judy, Judy, Judy."

"Oh God," said Patrice. "That's awful. You ought to look up Frank Gorshin. Take some lessons."

"Everybody's a critic," said Vladic. He pulled out a key ring, holding it out to Patrice. "If you crack up my van, whatever you do, don't fix it. Buy me a new one."

Soon, she was back to Near West Side, cruising the streets in hopes of finding a strange, yet attractive man. A man who could be just as charming as he was irritating.

A man, she knew, who had been through seven kinds of hell.

Cox Delaney sat in the dark bar. For all intents and purposes, a steelworker, unwinding after a shift at LTV Corporation, or U. S. Steel. He nursed a stein of Pabst Blue Ribbon. Good blue collar bear, thought Delaney. He had once had tastes working stiffs would think pretentious. Perhaps, after being on the street for so long, he might agree with them.

Why had he gone for Jonathan Tubb's plan? Actually, Tubb and Mel Dones' plan. Maurice Devereaux was untouchable. He knew that now. But, old Coxy. Always had to be a macho man. He had to allow the girl to come up from San Antonio, then hook her into the investigation. Penetrate High Data Associates. Find the key that would unlock the trail of money laundering. Expose that rats nest of corruption. Prove Devereaux had ordered the execution of his own daughter and son-in-law. Get his kids back.

Well, it wasn't going to happen. He knew that now.

And what had his arrogance cost? Perhaps Pudge's life. The last he heard, his pal was still critical. It could still go either way. And to compound matters, he'd also endangered Patrice.

What a strange girl. About as stubborn as...well...as he was himself. Tough lady. Late sleeping lady. What an oddity. He thought about that sleepy, unbelievably beautiful noggin, early of a morning. The way she looked at you as if she had allowed half her wits to remain asleep.

She denied hating him, but he just felt so off balance when she was around, as if she were always measuring him, and he was always coming up short.

And why had he made an ass of himself and kissed her?

Nice going Coxy.

189

*   *   *

Patrice cruised for almost two hours. She made a grid of the Near West Side, places she knew he ranged. The area was roughly encompassed by west 25th, near the river, to West 105th; and Denison Avenue to the south, all the way to the Cleveland Memorial Highway along the lake.

No godamn Cox Delaney.

Why should she care? What was he to her, anyway? Just another good looking—very good looking—over-inflated macho stud, who thought whatever his ideas were, they were the only ideas on the face of the earth. God! She was so tired of men and their macho bullshit! Just like Pablo! He's just like Pablo! The same testosterone choked veins, pumping machismo to every supercharged organ in his body!

She decided to ditch Vladic's van. She parked it in front of Near West Medical. She'd hot foot it over the usual territory that she knew he roamed. Perhaps her grid had been too expansive. Maybe so. Use the shoe leather.

Find that sucker!

"Eight ball, buddy?"

Delaney glanced at the dark-haired, beefy steelworker, still wearing a hard hat. Blue flannel shirt. Open, friendly face.

"Sure. Rack 'em."

A shaded bulb illuminated most of the table, with just the rim obscured by penumbra. Dave Brubeck Trio & Jerry Mulligan was on the jukebox. Limehouse Blues.

"Usta live in Pitt," said blue flannel shirt. "Came over here to keep my job. Work with a Bessemer. Know that?"

Delaney shook his head.

"We blow compressed air through a mass of molten iron. Turns pig iron into steel."

Delaney nodded. He broke with a powerful, true shot, sinking a stripe. He sank two more before being blocked.

Blue flannel shirt ran the table.

"Now, if I were a hustler, I'da played you for a sucker. Won some dough. But I'm not. You can buy me a beer, though. That is, if you let me buy the next one."

Vic Damone replaced Brubeck. Eclectic.

"You hunt? Fish?" asked Blue Shirt.

The barkeep brought two Pabst Blue Ribbons.

"It's been awhile," said Delaney.

"Usually go up Wisconsin way. There's a lake. Moose Lake. Now there's a place a man can go to. Get away from it all. Hunt a little. Fish a little. Drink a little."

"Went to a lake once," said Delaney. "Little lake. Not a Great Lake. Not in Wisconsin, either. Texas. Medina Lake. With my dad and my brother, Jake."

Another Pabst.

After a while, "You were telling me," said Blue Flannel Shirt, "about this lake in Texas."

"Oh. Well... Dad didn't take much of a hand in raising me. Left it up to my mother, and mostly, my brother. I was always looking for a father figure. There's this guy in San Antone, guy named Dones. He's more like my father than my father. I usually went fishing with Dones and Jake. This time, Dones had to go to Austin. He always protected me. Wouldn't let my brother mess around with me. Jake's like, fifteen years older than me.

"But my father went with us this time. Didn't say much the entire trip. Anyway, Jake figures I should learn to swim. So, he does the sink or swim thing. Tosses me overboard. Has this fish net, in case I get in trouble. So, I bob in the water a bit. Kind of go down. Then I bounce to the surface. I'm real scared. When I break water, I look over to the boat. Dad is smoking a pipe. Fishing off the starboard side. Jake is looking at me with something like love, hope, and contempt, all rolled into one. I figure I'll never live it down if I fail him. So, right then and there, I learn to swim. I just start kicking, and paddling, splashing around like there's no tomorrow. 'Cause, as far as I'm concerned, if I didn't pass this test, there wouldn't be."

"How did your father react?"

"Never said a thing."

"And your brother?"

Delaney's smile in the half-lit bar almost penetrated the shadow. "He gave me a bear hug, and bought me a bike the next day."

"Sounds like your brother really loved you."

"He did. He does."

Patrice Orosco had covered any number of blocks. She peeked into business after business, paying special attention to those she knew Delaney might frequent, such as small grocery and drinking establishments. She was careful to avoid the pizza joint. No way would he be that stupid.

She wasn't having any luck.

On a whim, she decided to call Shaker Keyboards. Perhaps his modest stash had run dry, and he'd moved a few pianos to earn some money.

Once again, it proved a chore to find a phone booth. Kiosk after kiosk, vandalized. Tagged by pubescents, marking the territory as if by urinous canines. Day-Glo, metallic, and the ubiquitous flat black preferred by traditional graffiti artists. And always, the severed cord.

Until she came to a cubicle near St. Ignatius High School. A place near where she had first met Juan Sanchez Prieto. Wondrous serendipity. An intact, working, monument to the communications age.

It was nearly dark. Would the manager be in? Perhaps the phone functioned, but the phone book had skipped away, somebody's souvenir.

Call information. When Susie Telephone finally came on the line, she had the cookie cutter voice of every information operator ever cloned by Ma Bell. A voice that said, 'only a dummkopf would interrupt my romance novel.' Like extracting a tooth, Patrice managed to pluck the number.

When the fourth ring had ended its tintinnabulation, a woman came on the line and announced that she was "Betsy, bookkeeping."

"May I speak to the manager?" asked Patrice.

"I'm sorry, we're closed. Mr. Omyer has gone home. I'm just working late, but I'd be glad to take a message."

Patrice let out a long breath. Well, it was worth a try. "Could you ask Mr. Omyer if he has seen…ah…Red Dodge lately?"

"Who is this?"

A long pause. "Just a friend."

"Would you please identify yourself?"

Patrice almost hung up. "I've only known him a short while. But, I guess he has come to mean something to me…or I wouldn't be pounding the pavement trying to find him."

Why had she said that! Was there something sympathetic in Betsy Bookkeeping's voice?

"A lot of people are looking for him, Miss. Including the police. Officers George and Canady were in here, just before we closed. Mr. Omyer left immediately after."

There was an involuntary catch in Patrice's voice. "Could…Could I give you the number of the phone that I'm at, and could you have Mr. Omyer call me?"

"Give me the number."

It seemed like an eternity before the phone jangled in the stall.

"Hello?" asked Patrice tentatively.

"Who is this?" asked the voice.

"I just talked to Betsy."

"Yes."

"You know my question."

"Let me try to understand something. What is your interest in the question at hand?"

"Mr. Omyer. I was introduced to the man you know as Red Dodge in order that I might work on a story on homelessness. It turns out that the story is a great deal more complicated than that. I think he is a good man. I think he is an innocent man. I'm trying to find him. I'm trying to protect him. God knows how I'm going to do it."

"Okay. I believe you. And I believe in him. If being approached by a police detective by the name of Dominck Tavaro was the only equation I've had to deal with, it might be different. But I've also been approached by some goons who represent your friend's father-in-law. Reprehensible sorts, dressed in business suits. No matter how hard they tried to disguise it, they were goons. I've dealt with their kind before in the music business."

"My God."

"Indeed. When the goons returned a second time, they dropped all pretenses. If I didn't give him up, they would fire bomb my store. When I informed Officers George and Canady of the threat this evening, they said I was a liar, was undoubtedly harboring a fugitive, and that it would not go well with me if I didn't cooperate."

"Have you heard from…Red Dodge today?" asked Patrice softly.

"He called. I advised…Mr. Delaney…to stay clear of Shaker Keyboards."

"When did he call? And where did he call from?"

"The call came to me here at my home just a little while ago. From where, I don't know. There was a jukebox in the background."

Patrice sighed. "Thank you, Mr. Omyer."

An autumn sunset. Often a time that men and women rejoice. A harvest season over with, winter stores set in, a time to reflect and grow as a human being.

For Patrice, it was anything but. If it wasn't exactly panic time, it certainly was close to it. Wanted herself for questioning, if Police, or heaven help her, HDA ever made an ID; trying to save a man who had managed to get under her skin in multitudinous ways; stone cold killers hotly chasing them. It was a situation that hadn't been spelled out for her clearly enough. If she had known all of this, she might have turned the damn gig down. Even the job at The Plain Dealer.

Or maybe not.

Cox Delaney would probably have been the first person to admit that he was in his cups. Far too many beers. But, so what. Maybe he deserved to let loose and get soused. What little life he had was now crashing down around him. How can a man clear himself when he no longer had a base of operations, such as it was? He could hole up in people's houses, perhaps, but that was far less attractive than being free to move around. Free to probe for weaknesses.

Ya, right.

What weakness had he found in High Data Associates and Maurice Fucking Devereaux? A man who would kill his own daughter to safeguard his illegal activities. And then be coated with Teflon, impervious to numerous investigations.

The barkeep finally refused to set him up with another beer.

Fine. There were other watering holes. He'd find one.

He stumbled out of the steelworker's bar, and staggered up the street, his new friend in the blue flannel shirt long gone to hearth and home.

It's not fun to be propositioned by a wino. In fact, it's disgusting. Patrice continued up the street to check the next booze hall. Every place she saw reflected its own personality and character. Some establishments seemed legitimate places to unwind after a day at the factory or office, while others were spots where the losers came to blacken their minds into a walking sleep.

The hard part was, she knew she was doing the old needle in a haystack routine. No way could she ask after Cox Delaney. There was an army of men, both public and private, doing just that. She was going to have to rely on a chance encounter.

At one place, she could have sworn she'd run into some security men from HDA. They turned out to be passing out flyers for a dart tourney.

She was getting hungry. She turned into a mom and pop grocery to get some kind of snack. Almost anything would do. She settled for pretzels and a Coke. Satisfying.

Back to the lonely pounding of the sidewalk. "Goddamn, you, Cox Delaney, you sunuvabitch. Where the fuck are you?" she muttered to herself.

The neon streets refused to answer.

* * *

Delaney moved to a doorway. He dropped to the ground. He put his head in his hands. He wept.

He was down to five bucks. He was immersed to the armpits in a walking hell that seemed to swallow some men; many of their own asking, but a few against every scream their souls could muster.

Across Detroit Avenue, his little segue to the ground caught the attention of alert, catlike, urban predator eyes.

Patrice visited a pool hall. An arcade. A strip joint. Three more bars. She even checked out the lobby of a seedy hotel.

No Cox Delaney.

She walked around the corner of West Boulevard onto Detroit Avenue.

There were few pedestrians. Traffic was getting lighter, the homeward commute beginning to lessen. Working-class businesses, some closed for the day, some closed for eternity, faced the dimming streets.

Some movement in an alleyway. Two ruffians, working over a prone wino. This seemed all wrong to Patrice. She sprinted into the alleyway.

"Hey," she roared.

"Get away, cunt, or I'll cut ya," growled a heavyset man, with shaggy hair. His much slimmer accomplice continued to kick the downed wino.

Patrice, like a blur went into a spin move. The heavyset man went down, crashing into his partner, who in turn slammed into the prone victim.

But the big guy was up like a bouncing rubber ball. Clutched in his right hand was a shiv.

Out on the street, traffic continued to whiz by, oblivious to the little tableau; a drama that plays out in urban America every six minutes.

Now the thin man turned away from the downed prey.

A shiv appeared in his right hand.

"Leave. Leave now," said Patrice with cool detachment.

"We're gonna cut ya," said the big man. "Then my friend is gonna cut this guy. Ain't much of a payday. So far, just five bucks. But we'll get yer money, little lady. We sure will."

They began to circle Patrice. In the knife man's crouch. Parry, and thrust. Patrice assumed a martial arts position. This somehow caused the men to laugh.

"Look at that, Max! She's gonna try an' karate us! Doesn't that beat everthing?" said the thin man.

"We slice up karate and kung fu people fer lunch," said his enormous pal.

Patrice timed a knife parry, used a different spin move and brought her boot up against the temple of the thin man. He dropped hard. Motionless.

"Now it's just you and me, lardo," said Patrice. "Let's see how you can slice me up!"

The fat guy turned and ran.

She watched him retreat for a moment, then checked his friend. He'd be out of it for a good long while.

Patrice bent down to check the reclining casualty. The streets had become a hecatomb. The cities, a gory charnel house, fed by human nature run amock. Patrice shivered. But this time, she noted, the quarry seemed to be alive.

The face was clean shaven. The watch cap had slipped off of the head. The hair was that flaming red she had come to know. The face. Different. The same. A shocking, electric jolt of fear, anger, concern.

"Delaney..." she whispered, checking his pulse. Regular. Examine the head. No marks. The breath. A brewery fuming through the slack mouth. "You dumb...stupid...beautiful hunk of asshole man..."

Sole prints on his clothes satisfied her that though he had received a few kicks, and might be bruised and sore for a few days, mostly he was not damaged that badly. Unless you considered the dead brain cells from his alcoholic stupor.

With a heave, she hoisted him onto her right shoulder, in a dead man's lift. Well, she wasn't going to carry him for twenty blocks or so. Have to find a safe spot.

A Dumpster.

Some time later, Patrice Orosco retrieved the still passed out Cox Delaney, stuffing him in the back of Homer Vladic's van.

"You owe me big time, big guy. That's the second time I've saved your bacon, you idiot," she said to unhearing ears, as she crossed the Lorain Carnegie Bridge. And a while later, nearing O'Reilly's Grand Road home, "God, you smell bad, Delaney. I hope your choice of cologne is a little bit better."

Delaney didn't say.

#

CHAPTER 19

Thursday, October 17, 1996

Stadium Turf Fight Remains Unsettled: City officials continued to disagree yesterday about potential restaurant or retail development around the new lakeside football stadium.

In a nine-page memo to the City Council, Frederick R. Nance, the attorney for Mayor Michael R. White on stadium matters, said studies by city officials and stadium architects show there is not enough room for retail development on the site.

Robert J. Vickers
Plain Dealer Reporter

It would not be accurate to say Patrice bounded out of bed at 5:30 in the morning, refreshed and bubbling, another bright day to conquer. Perhaps thinking a statement that included the wreck of the Hesperus, or cats and their proclivity to drag things too much the cliche, a wide awake Ruben Orosco took one look at his daughter, and shoved a cup of Mexican coffee her way. She savored every sip.

"I don't know what I'm going to do with that man," Patrice muttered, as caffeine finally loosened her tongue.

"In our ancestry, you would do nada. You would wait for the muchacho to make a move," said Ruben, between sips of his own brew.

The rest of the house was asleep, late night revelers who'd munched on popcorn and visited an all-night movie theater.

"First Yol, then Grandma, now you, Papa! You all think I love this guy."

"Mija, the last one to know is the one who is in love. Oh! Estar enamorado!"

"Right. In love with a man who smelled like he brews cerveza in his belly! Fat chance!"

Ruben Orosco smiled that paternal smile reserved only for daughters who have become ladies. Proud. Nostalgic for their long gone, miniature selves. Hopeful, that they may one day present nietas to carry on the sublime lineage from wife to daughter to bebe. "You will know, when it is the right time to know."

Patrice was out the door before the rest of the family awoke, recipient of a Ruben Orosco bear hug. "Oh, Papa..." she'd said.

"I must learn confidence in you, Mija. But it is hard to teach an old perro new tricks!"

Patrice would just as soon forget the night before. It was nearly midnight when she'd managed to take her leave from Theodore's Grand Road home. Getting Cox Delaney tucked into one of O'Reilly's guest beds, with much help from The Elfin One, had been a comedy of cumbersome proportions.

Delaney had never been quite coherent, though he'd muttered a long string of unintelligible sputtering.

"Benders happen to the best of us Irish lads," said O'Reilly dismissively. "And this lad has more reason than most to knock back a few."

"He's disgusting," she'd spat.

"Why do you demand perfection from a man?"

Patrice was taken aback.

"Did you require Pablo Morales to be a perfect human being?" pressed O'Reilly.

Tears appeared on her face. That had been happening lately. Why? "How can you say that, Teddy?"

"Cut the lad a break, Treece. He's lived through something few men ever experience. And he's come through it, a noble mon. You seem to expect your men to be knights in shining armor, as they say. Well, men are made of flesh and blood. They all have their faults. Their dark side. Even as you do."

Patrice entered the side entrance, as Stephen Upton had instructed. Once again, she went through the rigmarole all new hires are subjected to anywhere in the world.

The promised three hour orientation period held few surprises. Patrice quickly saw that she was, indeed, overqualified. Seven hours into her shift, four entering routine data into a terminal, she was beginning to think the whole infiltration exercise was a waste.

"Time for a break," Upton suddenly whispered into her ear, just an hour before the end of her shift.

There were a dozen cubicles in the medium sized room. The space looked newly installed, with the smell of drywall, paint and carpeting still fresh. Ten other workers, eight of them female, were busily hacking away at keyboards.

High Data Associates was housed in a sprawling complex in University Heights. Terminals everywhere. Dress was surprisingly eclectic, even for a high tech firm. Patrice was dressed like she'd just deplaned from Miami. Pastels, tropical patterns, a South Florida look to her coif. The entire crew of new processors seemed to fit the public's understanding of Silicon Valley. Only management wore the coats, shirts, ties and ladies business outfits of the conservative corporate world.

In the break room, Patrice noted she was the only one taking a break.

Figures. She waited for the inevitable visitation. She had been dimly aware that Upton had been going to each new data processor throughout the day. She expected to see him momentarily. As if she were a practicing psychic, here came Stephen Upton.

"So what do you think, Kat?" he asked, as he poured himself a cup of coffee from the coffee bar.

She put the Styrofoam cup to her lips. In her exaggerated Puerto Rican accent, "About what?"

"The job!"

A long pause. She gazed to the right, then brought her eyes to meet Upton's. "It's a start, I guess."

"Remember I said you were overqualified?"

197

"You did say that."

"There can be better things for you here. If you play your cards right, you will be the one we promote. If not, it will be one of the other new hires. The job you all will be vying for is extremely creative. We are going to be announcing new services; services based on a technology we are helping to develop. Sound interesting?"

Patrice shrugged. "How can I say not knowing more?"

Upton smiled. "I like that. You are obviously a woman of ambition."

"Everyone's got ambition."

"But some more than others. Right?"

"You could say that."

The man was short, nattily dressed for a police investigator, but with the kind of beady little eyes that still managed to stereotype him. He looked, he smelled, he talked cop.

Dominick Tavaro approached the horseshoe. "Your boss in, Blowers?"

Blowers smiled, rare for him. "He's with Mulligan. You want to wait in the conference room?"

"Sure. Keep up the good work, Blowers."

Sitting in the glass-enclosed meeting room, the cacophony of the modern print media seeping through the open door, Tavaro gazed out at the numberless desks, the frantic movements, the tense demeanor of assembled news hounds. Much like a police station.

Tavaro thought himself a great policeman. That America has never embraced the notion of baksheesh was not his problem. It took extra money to grease the wheels. Dominick himself had a weakness for female flesh. Especially showgirl types. He would cruise the warehouse district, visit The Flats where the strip clubs were, and when he found a face and body that fit his mood, he always had the bread to ease the way to a liaison. How else could a man balance out a life that caused him to have to rub elbows with scum? It's amazing what a woman's body can do to help forget the bloody corpse you investigated only hours earlier.

And could he ever investigate. With informants, plants and tipsters all over Greater Cleveland, it was said if you committed a crime in his bailiwick, you'd better have done it in secret, or Dominick Tavaro would ferret you out with the force of an alligator's jaws.

"Hello?"

"Mr. Tubb. So we meet. At last."

Jonathan Tubb had just entered the conference room. He looked at his visitor in a questioning kind of way. He held out his hand. "I don't believe I have your name?"

"Domincik Tavaro." He held out his shield.

Tubb's eyes opened wide. "Well, this is a pleasure. Of course I've heard of your exploits. All Clevelander's have. Should have recognized you from the many pictures I've published."

"Not to mention sound bites," added Tavaro without irony. He simply assumed people knew his face. He was actually slightly miffed that Tubb had not known him.

"Well, this is certainly a delight for me. I don't get to meet the players these days, not since I was a beat reporter. That was about a century ago."

"I really should have come to see you. Five years ago, in fact. When Cox Delaney murdered his wife."

Jonathan's face remained impassive.

"You were on my list of people who knew Delaney. The problem is, I thought he was dead. I received a report of a redheaded man decapitated in Detroit while hitchhiking. Before I could get a match, the body was mysteriously cremated, in one of those foul-ups that sometimes happen in a Coroner's Office. Unclaimed bodies do not always go to a potter's field in this day and age. His brother said Cox Delaney was on his way to see him, and proceeded to hold a memorial service for him, six days after the mysterious cremation.

"Well, Delaney never surfaced, so I considered the case 'unofficially' closed. The idea is, you can open it up anytime you need to if there is a sighting. There never was. Until now.

"In retrospect, I have a lot of questions. Why would a family not claim a body, and yet hold a memorial service? Doesn't make sense. And stupid me, I didn't think it through at the time. I was just glad to have a closure, unofficial though it was.

"So, here we are, Mr. Tubb. The man is considered unbelievably dangerous. One of the worst stone cold killers I've ever had to investigate. He practically killed a friend of mine. An honest investigator, just doing his job. Nearly beat him to death in a pizza parlor. Would have, but a woman described as a knockout dame pulled him off at the last minute.

"Mr. Tubb. I have to ask you this: And I need an honest answer. If I don't get honest answers, you may be looking at obstruction of justice charges, harboring a fugitive, accessory after the fact. God, I could probably go on, even add destroying parking meters to the list, if that's what it takes. Mr. Tubb, the question I have to ask is this: Where is Cox Delaney, and where is your reporter, Patrice Orosco?"

He handed Tubb police sketches of both Patrice and Cox Delaney, taken from witnesses at the pizza parlor.

Jonathan Tubb had always been quick on his feet. Gazing at the sketches, he looked Tavaro in the eye. "I hope Patrice has found him. That is one of her goals in the pursuit of the homeless story she has been assigned. A short time ago I received a tip that Delaney might be on the streets. She is looking into it. Could be, if this sketch means anything, she found him and saved your friend's life."

"We should have been informed," said Tavaro icily, "the minute you got your tip. For the moment, we won't go into the possible legal repercussions of consorting with a wanted fugitive."

"Sir, we don't do your investigations for you, and you don't do our stories for us. You're the constabulary, we're the Fourth Estate. Look them up at your local library branch."

"You're an evasive bastard, Mr. Tubb."

Jonathan Tubb smiled. "As far as consorting with a fugitive, we think she was an innocent bystander, at most. Probably stopped in for lunch."

"Have Ms. Orosco call me the moment you hear from her. Here's my card. If she doesn't, we'll pull her in as a material witness."

With that, Dominick Tavaro strode out of the conference room, nodding at Blowers on his way through the crammed newsroom.

Timothy O'Reilly continued the dogged surveillance with resolve and consistency. Except, now he had to find a rest room, and he had to find it quickly. No biggie. Patrice had about thirty-minutes left on her first shift at HDA. He had plenty of time to return. His basic responsibility was to make sure she reached her car safely, wasn't followed, and arrived home in one piece. Should she be followed, Timothy would ID the party, and then assess the information with Uncle Theodore, Jonathan Tubb and Edgar Nelson.

He drove the nondescript white van into the nearby White Front Market on Cedar Avenue. He wondered if he would have to talk his way into a rest room. He really had no choice.

A few seconds after Timothy O'Reilly entered the store, the cellular phone attached to the van's console blared an insistent electronic signal. It seemed to bray interminably.

The only witness was a toddler, stupidly allowed to stay alone in a late model SUV, parked next to O'Reilly's surveillance van.

Jonathan Tubb fumed. "Where the hell is Timothy?"

Sitting alone in his Buick LeSabre, cellular phone in hand, and no way to alert Patrice unless he could reach Timothy O'Reilly, Tubb slammed the heels of his hands against the steering wheel in exasperation. Sean's accident looked like it had the potential to foul up the safety net he had so carefully constructed to protect the beautiful journalist.

Coughing the engine to life, Jonathan Tubb decided to head for home. A good meal cooked by Gloria, perhaps clams, sounded good right now. Meanwhile, he would continue to try and alert Patrice through Timothy O'Reilly. If he could get her in time, have her come to his house, they could get her out of the Kat Garcia getup.

Tubb trusted Dominick Tavaro about as far as he could throw him. He had heard rumors for years. If Tavaro was in Devereaux's pocket, it wouldn't do to tip him to their current investigation.

In fact, it would be a disaster.

Tubb never noticed the unexceptional off-white sedan. It paced him, three cars back, all the way to his house.

Maurice Devereaux stood in front of Milton Thompson III. He was not a happy camper. Devereaux, though not an exceptionally large man, seemed to overwhelm Thompson's office with his presence.

The Headmaster looked like he would spring a leak any moment.

"I have a positive identification," Devereaux said quietly. Too quietly. "I know for a fact that Cox Delaney has been teaching music in your school. In my granddaughters' classroom."

"I'm not a detective, Mr. Devereaux. I cannot screen everyone who comes in here to volunteer."

Devereaux leaned across Thompson's desk menacingly. "I'm going to tell you this just once: If you find out anything about his whereabouts, and do not immediately notify me, I will break you, Thompson! Comprendez-vous?"

Milton Thompson III tried in vain to reach for a smidgen of dignity. "Sir, believe me. That is the first thing I would do."

"Then you will be safe, mon ami!"

Still two blocks from his home, Jonathan Tubb managed to reach Patrice's home number. Ruben Orosco answered on the third ring.

"Senior Orosco. This is Patrice's Managing Editor. You must quietly exit through the rear of your daughter's apartment. I understand you have a rental car. That should get you safely out of the way. Take your whole family. There is no time to explain. I want you to drive to The Palazzo and wait for your daughter and I. We will have already eaten. Order anything you wish. It's on the paper. We have to talk."

"Si Senior."

Tubb pulled into his driveway, still unable to raise Timothy O'Reilly on the cellular. It was now five minutes before the end of Patrice's shift.

"Lo cree ud? Do you believe it?" roared Ruben Orosco after he'd hung up the phone. "Patrice has done it again! She's in trouble! Just like Corpus Christi! Estar en apuro is her middle name!"

"What kind of trouble, dear?" asked Audrey.

"Senior Tubb did not say! But I feel it in my huesos! A padre just knows these things!"

"And mothers don't, I suppose," said Audrey.

"Dios mio! It is not the same thing! Have mothers been charged with keeping a hija safe? Nada! It is the padre. And I have failed. An omission of monumental proportions!"

"Would you stop the histrionics for just long enough to explain what Mr. Tubb had to say?" asked Audrey.

A short time later, the family headed in the rented Honda to The Palazzo. Except for Papa Orosco, the menage didn't consider the circumstances to be at all unusual. But then, they knew Patrice. Over the last few years, sneaking out to meet her had become practically de rigueur.

Flooded carburetors in surveillance vans are more than an inconvenience to a party on active stakeout. Such a happening takes you out of the game. That was the case for Timothy O'Reilly. When he emerged from the grocery store—at the exact time Jonathan Tubb was on the phone with Ruben Orosco—only to discover the van wouldn't start, Timothy O'Reilly became an instant picture of frightened frustration. Explaining to Uncle Theodore was going to be painful.

To compound his bad luck, when he sought a gas station on foot, the cellular phone began to ring again in the empty van. He hadn't yet gotten the message. If he had, he might have merely stood out on Cedar Road and flagged Patrice down as she headed home.

As it turned out, she didn't even take Cedar Road.

Timothy O'Reilly would make the decision to take a bladder bag with him in the future.

Kat Garcia left with the phalanx of shift workers beating a hasty retreat for domicile, grocer or watering hole, each to their own preference.

She'd spent her day entering payroll data for a large new client that specialized in parking garages. Boy, was she getting close to the miscreants!

"See you tomorrow, Kat," said her new friend, a portly, smiling girl from Boston named Jennifer who had followed her new husband to Cleveland to take over a junior executive position with Dairy Mart.

"You bet," said the flamboyantly dressed 'Kat Garcia'. "And I'll bring some of my grandmother's tamales. She usually only makes them on Christmas, but you know, I get so hungry for them!"

A rather sticky wicket had come up when Jennifer said she always thought that Puerto Ricans did not eat tamales. Kat said she wasn't sure, but her grandmother was Mexican, so she ate them. Little white lies.

Patrice wondered if she'd bitten off more than she could chew.

When she drove out of the HDA campus, a thought suddenly struck Patrice. Instead of heading home first, she would head to University Hospitals and check on Pudge Elliot. Soon she was heading up Center Road toward Mayfield Road.

Nowhere near Timothy O'Reilly and his dead-in-the-water van.

A surveillance car, a Ford Crown Victoria, with two Cleveland police officers assigned to Dominick Tavaro pulled in front of the Mayfield Road apartments. Patrice would be cordially invited to go downtown and powwow with Tavaro, just as soon as she showed up. If she did. It was assumed she was on the streets somewhere, working on her story.

"Dollar to a doughnut she goes to the paper first," said a stocky uniform, by the name of Tesselback.

"No biggie," said his partner, a burnout case ready to retire named Johnson. "They got that covered, too. Guess she hasn't shown up at the clinic."

The radio squawked. "Units thirty-one, twenty-seven and fifteen. Dispatch. We've run inquiry. Subject has no instate registration. None in Texas. The trail dies six weeks ago. Vehicle in question seems to have been dismantled in September, though that seems highly unlikely. Ninety-six model. Jeep Cherokee. Burgundy. This is to advise that an APB has been issued on female subject, Patrice Orosco, age 22. Black hair, brown eyes, five-foot seven. One-hundred eighteen pounds. Subject is wanted as an accessory to assault, aiding and abetting a fugitive, and unlawful flight to avoid prosecution. NCIC Probe is negative. Dispatch, ten-thirty."

"Ten-four, thirty-one, ten-thirty," said Tesselback into the microphone.

"Don't that beat all," said Johnson in a tired voice. "Phantomizing the vehicle. Sounds like a druggie to me."

"Don't doubt it none. But If we see a burgundy Cherokee on this street, there is gonna be one surprised little lady."

Patrice turned her computer hacker reregistered phantom car onto Mayfield Road, fighting commuter drive time like any other working-class stiff. Oblivious to the APB. Not aware that Dominick Tavaro had made her for Cox Delaney's companion at the pizza parlor beating.

Cox Delaney.

In the past week, while lying low at Theodore O'Reilly's home, he had finally filled her in on all of the particulars about High Data Associates, and the illegal activities he and others had uncovered.

"I was about to run a search of cash flow procedures on all of our overseas accounts," Delaney had said, out of the blue, after one of O'Reilly's white soul food dinners. "A set of lockouts stopped me. As far as I knew, I had access to anything in the company.

"What HDA does is to offer a fully computerized collection system for cash businesses, such as parking garages, movie theaters, even telemarketing, per response television ads, direct sales, you name it. Those companies need not, in some cases, even have an office, certainly not a cash office.

"Like parking garages. Perfect for absentee investors. Our armored trucks collect the money, process it; that is count it, bank it for the owner, do all payroll functions. Pay vendors. In the case of parking garages, you'd have attendants at some of them. They have what is being called 'no touch cash systems,' in which the money, no matter what the denomination, is inserted into a slot, eaten up, like at a money changing machine, and the right amount of cash is dispensed at another slot for the customer. There is no chance whatsoever of an employee dipping into the till.

"Movie theaters work the same way. All you need is someone responsible for opening up the building, staff to project the film and sell the snacks, all with the 'no touch cash system.'

"Drop shipments are interesting. We collect the money, order the product from the shipper, pay the shipper his price, pay the medium for the advertising, take our cut, and send the marketing company their share. That leaves the marketing company free to do the creative end of the business, such as uncovering new product, without having to have a staff.

"Maurice was one of the first, if not the first, to figure out this type of business. He has been very successful at it. When I started the probe that got me into this mess, I wanted to do a kind of pro forma on the overseas stuff. To see if we needed offices in Europe. I never understood why Maurice didn't have any facilities overseas, seeing as he is French. It is a world wide business. Now I think I know. Interpol.

"I could get only far enough into the shadow programs to discover that vast amounts of money were being funneled out of the country, into Switzerland, the

203

Grand Caymans, and other places where banking secrecy is the general rule. We've since confirmed it's money laundering.

"Unfortunately, I left my footprints in the system. The company found out about it, and when I recognized Tomajac the night he killed Cherie, when I cold-cocked him before he could do me, I knew that Maurice had sent them to kill Cherie and I. Killing me is obvious. Why he thought that Cherie would turn on him, just because she might know what he was up to, I have no idea. As it turned out, I hadn't gotten around to telling her anything. She never knew her own father had her killed.

"Actually, I didn't really know anything then. Just that vast amounts of money were being sent overseas, into what were undoubtedly numbered accounts. Since then, I've had a network of cronies working on it. My brother Jake; a man named Stanley Kremintz, who for a percentage of the hot money, would expose my crooked father-in-law; he got plugged for his efforts. All my fault. Just like Cherie's death. Jonathan Tubb, of course, was another who helped me. Then, the man who was more of a father to me than my own father, a man you also know, Patrice…"

Patrice gazed at him impassively.

"…Mel Dones."

The breath had swooped out of her chest.

"I was set up from the start, wasn't I?" she said without rancor. "All the job offers. Being carefully directed to Cleveland."

"Patrice, if you are angry, and I honestly can't tell whether you are or not, but, if you are angry, I am sorry. I really am. I needed you. What you did on the Gulf Coast was amazing. By the way, what exactly did you do? Everybody always refers to what you did on the Gulf Coast."

Patrice had laughed. A deep, throaty chuckle that eased the tensions the two of them had been feeling. "I'm not angry with you, Delaney."

"You know, my friends call me Coxy."

"I'll have to think about that one."

"Are you going to tell me about your exploits in Texas?"

"Sure. Why not? Very simple, really. I went to the Gulf Coast, mostly around Corpus, to try and make sense of the Vietnamese experience in the oyster and shrimp business. How they had run afoul of local oyster men and shrimpers. Whole families worked the business, which made it hard for the native Americans to compete. The family members worked for very little. Combined, the families made more money than they had ever seen before.

"While that caused some problems with the Anglo and Hispanic shrimpers, it was nothing compared to the problems the Vietnamese Dragons caused their own people.

"Eventually, the Dragons tried to warn me off the story. I don't warn too easy. It resulted in three or four attacks on me. I was even shot at. I had some self-styled Ninja-types come after me. I left them in ruins."

Delaney was wide eyed.

"That surprise you? That a girl can protect herself?"

"Should it?"

"Delaney..." she drew his name out, "I'm going to call you that until I figure out something better. The biggest mistake you could make would be to underestimate me."

"Why?"

"Because I come from conquistadors and kriegers—warriors."

Delaney's smile was wide. "I believe you do."

"We have her ID'd to a fare-thee-well," said Todd Englewood to the newly arrived Maurice Devereaux, fresh from bracing Milton Thompson III. "Patrice Orosco made a reputation for herself in Texas, doing investigative pieces, while still a student at the University of Texas at San Antonio. My analysis is they hope to bring us down, and then make a deal with the District Attorney to reduce prison time for Delaney, in exchange for our hides."

Devereaux regarded Englewood for a long moment. "I doubt it. In my experience it is always les argent. They wish to strip us, possibly with computers, then fade away into the woodwork. Disparaitre."

"We must find them, Maurice."

"Exactement! So Todd, why don't you find them?

Patrice was in the middle of the long walk from her parked car to Pudge's room at University Hospitals. Just a nudge from her sensibilities; honed and trained well beyond her years on the Gulf Coast and other spots in Texas, while uncovering stories as a freelancer.

Observant police types, parked in fleet issue cars. In the front, in the rear. For all intents and purposes she was the living, breathing Kat Garcia, Puerto Rican. Maybe part Mexican. The disguise had been serviceable thus far. She continued her progress toward Pudge's room.

Stake out mode. No other explanation. Constabulary dressed in cop suits; there must be a fabric labeled such. Poised in two different open waiting areas, perfect places for lookouts to monitor every entrance, every path to Pudge Elliot's room.

She slipped into a phone booth. She must get word to Delaney just in case he might make the mistake of paying Pudge a visit.

"Where are you?" roared Theodore O'Reilly when he recognized her voice. "Do you know you are wanted by the police? They are ready to throw the book at you!"

She was momentarily speechless. "They identified me? From a lousy Identi-kit sketch?"

"Six ways to Sunday."

"That means I've got to be invisible," said Patrice. "Bye-bye Teddy! I'll stay in touch."

"Treece!" bellowed O'Reilly.

But she disconnected.

To continue her foot journey would be to give herself away, disguise or no disguise.

Unless...

*   *   *

"I'm sorry I'm late," said an out-of-breath Jonathan Tubb.

"Better late than never," said Audrey Orosco.

The family had ordered drinks, but not dinner. The four of them were restless beyond belief, the wondrous atmosphere of The Palazzo all but lost on them.

"Where's my sister?" asked Yolanda.

"I want the whole story," said Ruben Orosco. "Leave nothing out."

"Of course," said Jonathan Tubb. Then he sucked in more air. "For starters, Patrice is wanted by the police for a variety of charges."

"Dios mio..." muttered Ruben. "I knew this Cleveland was wrong for her."

"Um Gottes willen!" brayed Grandma Stella.

"My husband's right," said Audrey. "The whole story, and if you leave anything out, I'll see to it your next paper is in Podunk!"

"When in doubt," muttered Patrice to herself, "do the cliche, thing."

Dressed in a cleaning lady's duds, pushing a cart, Patrice walked to Pudge Elliot's room unmolested.

Randy Elliot was sitting with her wide awake husband. Two sets of eyes registered deep shock.

"I'm Rosie Perez, and I'm your cleaning lady for today!" she said brightly.

As if releasing a pent-up need to laugh, Randy Elliot tittered uncontrollably. Even Pudge seemed amused, masked as he was with medical paraphernalia.

"O'Reilly is trying to find you," said Randy when she finally got control of herself. "It seems as if the police are combing the streets for you."

"I just talked to him," said Patrice. "And he seemed to have the same story. But, enough of me. How are you feeling?" she said turning to Elliot.

He made some attempt to reply.

"They are about to upgrade him to serious," said Randy. "Pudge is going to be all right, Patrice." Deep conviction in her voice.

"Of course he is," said Patrice. "I need my teeth cleaned."

There was a distinct look of merriment in Pudge Elliot's eyes.

Jonathan Tubb excused himself from the table to make a phone call. Finding Patrice was a top priority. They had to establish a new base of operations for her role as Kat Garcia. Obviously, her apartment wasn't going to work.

"Blowers? You see Patrice yet?"

"No," said the diminutive City Editor. He was behind the horseshoe, something that was happening a lot lately. "Where are you?"

"Eating at The Palazzo. Call me if you see her."

"You got it," said Blowers. "Keep me informed."

"I've saved your bacon again," said the voice on the phone. "Your surveillance team is about as competent as a morgue full of stiffs."

"Good work," said Todd Englewood. "I'll send some cars pronto."

"You do that. And send more money. Bacon costs money."

O'Reilly blew his stack when he heard Jonathan Tubb's voice. "You idiot! You and Mel Dones have got to be the greatest idiots in the history of the world! You're going to get that girl killed!"

"Where is she, Teddy?"

"She's with Pudge. And don't call me Teddy!"

"Sorry," said Jonathan Tubb. Then, "No, I'm not. Everybody calls you Teddy behind your back. Probably because you're so adorable!"

Jonathan Tubb finally got through to Patrice.

"Patrice," he said after he'd explained where he was, who he was with, and why she should join them. "I'm very sorry to have placed you in such a situation. I really don't know what I could say that would make it right."

Patrice paused. "First, we've got to make things right for Delaney. Then you can work on ways to make it up to me. I might warn you. It will cost you. Dearly." She winked at Randy Elliot, who gave a thumbs up sign back.

"I figured that."

Patrice decided to park a good deal away from The Palazzo. Her antennae might be paranoid, but if the city was lousy with cops and HDA investigators looking for one Patrice Orosco, then she would turn the tables and look for them.

Which turned out to be as easy as searching for chocolate chips in cookies. A lone stakeout artist, sitting in a Plymouth. Cop issue to the core.

Patrice approached the car. Crouching in the street, facing the rear window, she tossed a pebble at the glass. No reaction.

Okay.

She moved silently, and invisibly away from the surveillance car. Reconnoitering the immediate area, she found what she was looking for.

The heave. A splintering crash. The passenger side window blew out, as her rock found its mark.

She moved behind a large city trash container, sitting two feet from the rear end of the car. The cop bounded out of the vehicle, his gun drawn. He surveyed the street. About twenty yards beyond Patrice was a pair of Dumpsters, evidently serving several businesses.

"Come out of there with your hands up! You are under arrest!" shouted the cop. He was peering into the fast deepening darkness. "If I have to go in after you, it won't go easy on you."

The cop began to stride toward the large containers. With catlike quickness, Patrice tripped him up and delivered a single sharp blow to the head.

Out like a light.

"That'll hold ya," she muttered. "Well, let's see. Now they can add assaulting a peace officer. Assault with intent to do great bodily harm. Destroying government property. Probably hijacking. Perhaps sedition. Who knows? You've become a master criminal, Orosco."

She crossed the street, grateful her exploits had not been witnessed. She entered a side entrance that lead into a hallway that connected to rest rooms and a business office.

And a bank of telephones.

Quickly, by calling the house phone from one of the pay phones in the service corridor, she roused Jonathan Tubb from the table where he was sitting with her family, all of them still nursing drinks. "You've been followed, Tubb. You are attracting cops and HDA security people like a magnet to metal filings. Here's what you do..."

"No, you listen..."

"I'm all through listening. We're playing it my way, now. You lead my family and yourself out of the dining area and toward the rest rooms. Don't even bother to pay. We'll make it up to them at a later time. There are undoubtedly people watching you from inside. Make a potty ruckus. Tell Yolanda to ask a waitress where the rest rooms are. Have my father do one of his dramatic things about bladder control. Head to the rest rooms a little while after the ladies do. I'll be waiting for all of you in the corridor."

After she hung up, she moved to the opposite wall, standing to the blind side of the service entrance, partially obscured by a column. Grandma Stella had just entered the corridor from the dining area, with Yolanda and Audrey behind her, but out of sight, when the outside door burst open.

The downed cop staggered inside. He didn't see Patrice, but he felt her. From behind, she conked him a vicious blow to the head, and watched him hit the ground a second time.

"God, you've got one hard head," she muttered.

"Liebchen!" gasped Grandma Stella. "Is this the kind of work you do?"

Audrey and Yolanda were now by her side.

"Sometimes," she answered, slowly shaking her head as she looked at the once again unconscious cop. "Unfortunately."

#

CHAPTER 20

Monday, November 11, 1996

Out go the Lights: Snowstorm leaves thousands without power; no one injured as jet skids off runway.

Greater Cleveland received an enormous welcome to winter over the weekend as heavy snow downed power lines, caused traffic to come to a crawl at times and sent dozens of residents to emergency shelters in communities east of Cleveland.

Many schools announced they would not open today. Many residents were without heat as power failures cut off furnaces.

At Cleveland Hopkins International Airport, an American Airlines jet slid off a snow-packed runway as it landed last night. None of the 115 passengers or six crew members was injured, officials said.

> Michael Sangiacomo
> Plain Dealer Reporter

Kat Garcia relaxed in the HDA break room, her Boston friend Jennifer by her side. They were brown-bagging it, or as Jennifer sometimes said of her husband's efforts, brown-gagging.

"It can't be that bad," said Kat in her exaggerated patois.

"Maybe worse! Head cheese?" said Jennifer.

"You're right. Brown-gagging."

"The thing is, he gets a discount where he works. So he picked up a lot of expired lunch meats, including this junk. Then he has the gall to use it in my sandwiches. Just because he loves it, doesn't mean I do!"

"I think it's sweet. That he makes your lunch for you."

"He's a sweet guy. He really is. So. Tell me about this man you've been seeing?"

"Well..."

"You haven't even told me his name."

"All I said was there is this guy who has me confused. I didn't say I was seeing him!"

"A gal who looks like you has to be seeing somebody."

"That's what I love. Everybody seems to think I'm an old maid, just five months after graduating. Some of my friends couldn't wait to call the preacher. One gal got married two days after graduation."

Stephen Upton interrupted the girl talk, with that silly grin he seemed to think made him irresistible. "Glad to see you ladies made it through the snow."

"Four wheel drive," said Kat Garcia.

"We only live four blocks away," said Jennifer. "I walked."

Upton briefly shared his grin with the plump girl, and then attempted to drastically up the wattage for Kat's sake. "Ms. Garcia, I'd like to see you in my office, if you don't mind."

He tried the bonhomie approach on the walk to his office, but Kat wasn't buying.   Interpreting her demeanor as hard-to-get charm, Upton felt quite encouraged. "You know, you're going to go a long way in this company," he said as they entered his inner sanctum. "A long way."

Kat regarded him in a neutral fashion.

"I've decided to promote you, Kat. I've been on the phone with your supervisor, Marvin Danes. He says you're the best he ever had."

She had no doubt Mel Dones would come through for her.

"The only thing is, your new job is on the management wrung. You'll have to drop the Miami cool. Wear clothing that better suits your new image. In fact, with that wondrous figure of yours, I'd recommend tailored business suits. You'd look great. I've always admired slim ladies."

Kat continued to regard Upton without reaction.

"Would you like dinner tonight?" he asked.

"I always eat dinner. Every evening."

"When should I pick you up?"

"Never."

"It would pay you to cooperate, Ms. Garcia. Kat. I can do wonders for your career." He placed his hand on her shoulder, very slightly bringing her closer to him.

A moment later, he was reclining on the floor, a swift hand move from the now smiling Kat Garcia flipping him through the air.

"You're fired, Ms. Garcia. Clear out. You've got five minutes."

"I think not, Mr. Upton. I can get, maybe, one-point-two mil for that little shoulder touch. By the time I embellish a little; let's see, an attempted friction dance, whatta they call it? Frottage? Maybe two-point-four mil. But, it's your choice. I get the job, I say nothing. I get canned, I squeal. I retire, with HDA millions in my bank account."

"It doesn't work that way, Ms. Garcia," said Stephen Upton, getting to his feet. "I'm going to call the police right now. You will be arrested for assault and battery."

He was reaching for the phone when Ruben Orosco's daughter cut his feet out from under him. With incredible dispatch, she had him in a full Nelson. Incrementally, she increased the pain until he passed out. That surprised her. No one had ever slipped into a snore before when she applied a full Nelson. "What a wimp," she chuckled. "Course, I knew it. Guys with that kind of 'look at me' grins are always wimps."

Fortunately, Maxine was out to lunch. Fetching an area rug, she rolled the out-of-it executive into a cigar, jerked him to her shoulder, and carted him out the back way, which fortunately was very close to where she had parked the Jeep. She slogged the rug which wrapped Don Juan de Upton through the mounds of snow, and without being seen, stuffed him into the Cherokee. She grabbed a rag, and tied it around his mouth. "I hope your nose isn't clogged," she whispered. "If it is, you're really going to have to huff and puff."

She found a length of rope tucked into the wheel well, and cut it into strips. Soon, Stephen Upton was secured, and hidden from whichever passing eyes and ears might happen by.

"Terrible thing about these lake effect snow storms," she said to the snoozing Upton's rug wrapped form. "Folks often have to go home on really short notice to save their homes. Which you did. By the way Stevie, you'll get good and cold, but you won't freeze to death. I'll get you warmed up at quitting time. Buenas siesta."

For more than three weeks, Patrice had been patiently doing her work at High Data Associates, waiting for an opportunity to penetrate the labyrinthine computer giant. Now she had the chance, but she would have to keep Upton on ice, thanks to his sexual harassment gaffe. There probably would not have been a way to function with Upton on the scene, and the first rule of attack is to take out your nearest enemy.

The day she'd gone to work for HDA had been fraught with peril in every way. If she didn't believe in Murphy's Law before, she did now. Their first problem was to find a place to stay, in order to have a base of operations. Renting an apartment in this day and age can take some time, even with good phony credentials. They settled for a motel, derivatively named The Stardust.

"The paper will cover it," Jonathan had assured the family.

"You're damn right it will," said Patrice.

The next problem was to find a way to strip her apartment of all her possessions, as well as her family's luggage. Timothy O'Reilly had taken one of his investigators over in a van and managed that problem with ease. Stakeout cops never had a clue.

Finally, it might be just a matter of time before Theodore O'Reilly would be interviewed by Dominick Tavaro or one of his minions. With Cox Delaney on board, it might be dicey. So reluctantly, he was moved out of the Grand Road house and installed in one of the motel rooms.

"There's nothing to worry about," Tubb had said. "Singh hates cops and can direct them out of the way, even if they show up here and try to investigate."

"This is what I wanted to grow up and do," said Patrice. "Be a fugitive. Hammer cops senseless."

"You said he didn't see you. They won't be able to prove a thing."

So it had gone. For nearly a month, Patrice commuted to High Data Associates, stayed away from the paper, dressed like Kat Garcia, and holed up with her family in a crumbling motel.

Leave it to Yolanda. "I think it's great," she'd said. "You get to run around like some kind of secret agent, smacking crooked pigs, chasing bad guys, having a gorgeous hunk fall in love with you, even if he is kind of old. How could life be any better? The kids back home will never believe this."

"My hija impersonates a criminal," said Ruben. "Acts like mobsters in Mexico, and lives on the orilla. The edge. Even I cannot believe this, and I remember Corpus Christi where she did much the same thing. Dios mio..."

*   *   *

The two power companies that vie for customers in Greater Cleveland, CEI, Cleveland Electric Illuminating Company, and CPP, Cleveland Public Power, had to contend with massive power outages. CEI might have as many as 160,000 customers without electricity, while CPP could count at least 73,000. Fallen tree limbs covered roads, and even damaged vehicles.

Sitting in his motel room, worried, Cox Delaney reached for the telephone. A minor stroke of fortune got him connected to Hobie Strauss right away. "Hobie," he breathed into the receiver. "It's me. I need to check on some people."

"Hi, guy. Well, you know Lottie and Darcy are at The Samaritan House. So they're safe. Darcy is learning to read really fast. Lottie is doing a bang-up job here. Did you know that Oscar is still working with Deblay's, and Amy Walker has taken him under her wings? He's staying with her. Claude and Margie Johnson, with little Madge, had some trouble finding a shelter, but they finally managed to find a place. Did you know "Cleveland" Sammy?"

Delaney thought he did.

"He was trying to get to St. Malachi's, when he pitched over, dead when he hit the ground. His indigestion turned out to be his heart. I liked ol' Sammy. Used to sweep out for the old owner, but got insulted once too often."

"I'm sorry to hear about him, Hobe. So typical, though. These people, in spite of Harrison and Pudge's best efforts, just don't get the medical help they need."

"That's the truth," said Strauss. "I checked on Pudge. They have him ready to be discharged. Probably tomorrow."

"I heard. I guess Theodore O'Reilly's nephews' company is going to be watching out for Pudge and family. The cops insist on calling it a random drive-by."

"About as random as loaded dice," said Strauss.

"For sure. Thanks, Hobe. You've eased my mind about my people."

"You're a good man, Red Dog. Mind if I keep calling you Red Dog? It has a certain noble quality to it."

"You go right ahead, Hobe. And thanks."

*   *   *

"Hello, Maxine!" said Kat Garcia.

"Congratulations on your promotion! And you can call me Maxy."

This was going to be easy.

"Thanks. Steve had to go home. It seems the snow has threatened his roof."

"Oh? On an A frame?"

Think quick. "Tree limbs."

"I've told him for years that he should get rid of that damn tree. But, no, obstinate man that he is, he keeps it for shade. Maybe he'll think twice now."

"Hopefully," said Kat Garcia.

"We might as well show you to your new office. It's small, I'm afraid, and sparse, but you have your own terminal with absolutely everything you'll need to write programs."

It was small. It was sparse. It was equipped well enough to give her a flying chance to invade HDA's innermost secrets. Now, if she could just remember what her hacker friends had shown her.

When Fairly walked, with Tomajac, into the executive offices of High Data Associates, he was greeted like a hero. Which, to HDA, he was. He had not gained all of his strength back yet, but his week's worth of recuperation at home after spending over two weeks in the hospital had restored him to what he himself deemed to be eighty-percent.

The gentlemen gathered in the Chairman's office, in addition to Devereaux, Fairly and Tomajac, were Todd Englewood and the Orson brothers, Gerry and Gary. Missing was Stephen Upton, who had gone home, according to his secretary, to attend a roofing problem. Also missing was the company's comptroller, a man named Neiderland, who had been snowed in at General Mitchell International Airport in Milwaukee.

"Monsieur Fairly," said Maurice Devereaux warmly, to open the meeting, "you are due a bonus for your efforts on behalf of our company. I am going to give you what my Cajun cousins in Louisiana and Southeast Texas like to call a lagniappe. In addition to the retirement package you have earned, I am going to spring for a round the world vacance. You may leave at once, if you so wish."

"I deeply appreciate that, Sir. And I do wish to take you up on the world vacation.. However, with your permission I would like to first oversee the field operation that brings Delaney to justice."

The French are Latin's, and Latin's have been called people with strong emotions. That characteristic was now deeply evident in Devereaux's face and eyes, as he gazed fondly at Fairly. "That, Monsieur, is why this country is great. Why this company is great. You may also consider your retirement money to be doubled. Tu est riche, maintenant."

"Merci beaucoup, mon ami," said Fairly, himself under his own deep emotion.

With half a day to probe High Data Associates mainframe from her cramped office, Patrice, as Kat Garcia, tried every trick she knew to work the codes. Nada.

Her first assignment was to develop a system for companies that could take a Federal tax break on state taxes paid. Apparently, HDA was poised to offer complete tax services for their clients. They wouldn't merely be the dispenser of funds, they were poised to replace all business functions for certain types of companies.

What a gold mine, thought Patrice.

With just an hour to go before quitting time, she put her mind to the task and finished an IBM compatible system in about forty-five minutes. With luck, she could do her work in the future with such dispatch, and spend the rest of her time trying to break internal codes. And of course, to not make the mistake that Delaney had made, and leave her footprints in the system.

$*\quad*\quad*$

The small man knocked timidly on Todd Englewood's office. He was ushered into the outer office by a secretary.

"You may go right in, Mr. Blowers."

Englewood smiled when he saw the little newsman. "Good to see you," he said, holding out his hand. "I have your check."

Blowers smiled when he read the numbers.

"We might never have made the bitch," said Englewood, "if not for your good work."

"It was a good likeness."

"Do you think she's investigating us?"

"I have no doubt about it."

"What has Jonathan Tubb said?"

"Nothing directly. He's playing it close to the vest."

"Keep your ear to the ground, Blowers."

"Always."

"Let's go, Fairly," said Tomajac with resolve. "If you are going to go in the field again, we had better get a move on it. I'd recommend we cruise the area near the medical clinic. Maybe focus on the homeless themselves."

"They're not going to be out there in this weather," said Fairly. "A better plan would be to get a stack of five dollar bills and visit the shelters."

Tomajac grinned. "And that, my dear Fairly, is why you make the big bucks."

"So do you."

"This is true."

Blowers, who could be considered an employee in every sense of the term, headed out toward the rear of HDA's massive main building. When he spotted Fairly and Tomajac, also on their way out of the building, he walked over to greet the heroes of the firm.

"My favorite newsman," said Tomajac by way of greeting.

The dour little man did not smile. "If you haven't 'interviewed' Theodore O'Reilly lately, I suggest that you do. He's mixed up in this up to his eyeballs."

"Isn't Tavaro going to take care of that?" asked Fairly.

"I'm sure he will, when he gets around to it," said Blowers. "But, you know, you guys can be more creative than Tavaro."

The Latina woman heading to the exit. Something familiar. No one moved with that kind of catlike grace.

Blowers' mind worked at warp speed.

That explains her whereabouts for nearly a month; a month in which she had been a fugitive from the police. Not just the police, but from HDA, his spiritual company. All in a nanosecond, he calculated the kind of money he could make from High Data Associates with this coup. A lot. A whole lot of money. That's just what a man who likes to gamble, an illegal activity in Ohio, needed. Now he could pay off his chits.

"That's her!" shouted Blowers.

*   *   *

Being cooped up can give you more than cabin fever, it can skew your perceptions, rust your judgment, cloud your fear, and cause you to rush pell-mell into the danger zone.

Call it machismo, call it personal responsibility, or just the opposite, reckless abandon; but Cox Delaney could no longer glue his backside to a motel room chair. With a couple of hours left before Patrice was due to leave HDA's campus, he took public transportation to the sprawling company founded by his one-time father-in-law.

When he arrived, trudging through and sloughing snow, he went straight for the journalist's Jeep Cherokee. He jimmied a door. Perhaps he was surprised to see a living, squirming body, rolled up like a mammoth panetella, inside a costly area rug.

But then, again, maybe not. He had the feeling that being around Patrice Orosco was a ticket to a surprise an hour, if not a minute.

Tomajac produced a silenced Interdynamic KG-9 semiautomatic conversion pistol from out of nowhere, amazing considering the size of the weapon. It was part of his growing arsenal, not unlike the constant acquisition of mechanic's tools most grease monkeys collect.

He had the weapon poised to spit its projectiles in the flash of a hand, but Patrice Orosco saw him produce the gat. She went into a barrel roll, near the exit door.

The shots missed their mark.

A millisecond later, she kicked the door open, in the same rolling movement. Then she sprang to her feet, sprinted the gap between building and idle chariots, and dodged between the parked vehicles, heading in the general direction of the Cherokee.

Tomajac, with the quickness of the lifelong athlete, raced to the door and shouldered his way through, clutching the KG-9. He could see the bob of a black-haired head bounce between a Ford pickup and a Chevy Cavalier.

A rain of nines blasted sheet metal and glass. Ricochet echoes.

Tomajac continued to spit death from a barrel. Many bullets smacked the parked cars and trucks. Others pierced snowdrifts, or trimmed winter dormant trees.

The bobbing head could no longer be seen.

#

CHAPTER 21

Monday, November 11, 1996

Snow Could Continue Through Wednesday: Don't put away those shovels if you live east of Cleveland—there is more snow on the way.

Forecasters at AccuWeather Inc. said northeast Ohioans could expect up to 18 inches of new snow through Wednesday on top of the 12 to 18 inches that fell Saturday and yesterday.

> Side Bar
> The Plain Dealer

Just a pickup truck between safety and bullets. Safety in the form of her burgundy SUV. Or was that a conceit? She once escaped machine gun fire in a ratty Honda Accord with the windshield blasted to shards, by driving in a horizontal position. But then, the Dragons couldn't shoot straight enough to hit Yankee Stadium at six paces.

Patrice crouched behind a Lexus, hoping to take advantage of an empty magazine. Well, she wasn't going to grow old squatting in back of a luxury car.

"Hey, asshole!" bellowed a familiar voice.

Cox Delaney!

The redhead had stationed himself about ten feet from the Jeep Cherokee. With his index fingers stuck in his ears, and three digits flapping in the wind. "Ollie Ollie auction! Coming in free! You muthafuckas can't shoot me!"

Tomajac seemed glued to the concrete sidewalk that fronted the employees side entrance, the KG-9 hanging at his side. But only for the merest moment. The heater rose in a gunslinger's arc and sprayed the spot where Red Dog Cox Delaney had been rooted. The redhead dove like a halfback for the end zone, under the protected side of the Jeep.

The diversion worked. While Tomajac was busy with Delaney, Patrice rolled under the driver's side door, the exposed side of the vehicle, and didn't draw a shot until she was nearly under the car. A nine-millimeter slug grazed her right calf, sending a smarting sensation through her right extremity. Now she rolled all the way under the SUV, and began to scramble into the passenger side, just vacated by Delaney, who catapulted between the front buckets, landing heavily on the back bench.

Tomajac had years of experience. If your prey is unarmed, and you have a rod, you rush the quarry, prepared to dispense death through a muzzle. He broke into a dead run, the semi-auto pistol, fully, and illegally converted to an automatic weapon, dangling by his side.

Without rising to window level, Patrice fumbled the keys out of a side pocket in her hipster pants, and inserted it into the ignition.

Tomajac loomed at the driver's side window. He leveled the merchant of death, aimed through the glass at Patrice Orosco, and squeezed the trigger. Squeezed the trigger with venomous hatred. Squeezed the trigger on an empty magazine.

Fairly entered the game. From ten yards away, he pumped six bullets from a .357 Magnum into the radiator. Tomajac quickly worked at exchanging magazines.

But Patrice had the engine running.

Fairly had three left in the clip of his .357 Eagle. These he emptied into the windshield. A massive explosion of glass. Shards blew over Patrice's head, raining on top of Delaney, huddling on the floor. Farther back, fragments came to rest on top of the rug-encased Stephen Upton.

Tomajac finished reloading. Again he brought up the gun, but Patrice began to peel away, depressing the accelerator with her right hand, steering from memory with the other, the position of the parked vehicles imprinted on her mind. But who has a photographic memory?

Before she was a quarter of the way out of the parking area, she bounced off the left rear of a brand new Dodge Dakota.

Tomajac and Fairly raced to their company car.

Hidden in the shadow of the exit, was the excited Blowers. The tableau unfolding before his dancing eyes was positively orgasmic for the diminutive newsman.

Tiny Tyler was a very good investigator. Behind a desk. So inexperienced was he in surveillance work that he made a decision ten minutes before quitting time to go to White Front Market and buy a six pack of Old Milwaukee, which, as Tyler so well knew, was now brewed in Detroit. The suds would help him relax, before turning over his shift to Timothy O'Reilly himself at The Stardust. He would pick up Patrice when she drove by the market on Cedar Avenue.

Which she never did.

When Theodore O'Reilly found out Cox Delaney was not at The Stardust, he instinctively knew what Delaney would do. Jumping into Cherry Red he rushed through Cleveland traffic to reach HDA before quitting time.

He arrived at the moment Patrice drove the damaged Jeep out onto the boulevard. A hail of gunfire chased the fleeing SUV.

"My God..." he muttered.

Out of immediate danger, at least for the moment, Patrice peeked through the shot out windshield to make her way to the road. It would take them a moment to pursue. She knew they would pursue. Now, to outrun them. Sure. With shot to hell wheels.

It was about the time the bullets began to peck away again at the Cherokee that Patrice saw Cherry Red barrel up Cedar. The shooters had now pulled in behind Patrice in a brown sedan, with O'Reilly bringing up the rear, chasing the chasers.

"My God, Teddy! Get away from this!" she screamed.

"That old man is in back of us," said Fairly. "Take him out."

Tomajac twisted around on the bench seat, coiled out the front window and began to pepper Cherry Red.

"Lucky we had this car handy. It's registered to a mechanic out of Florida," said Fairly with a grin. "Makes no difference if somebody makes the plates. Industrial espionage is a terrible thing! Come and shoot up HDA, a fine upstanding company! My word!"

Tomajac now coiled in the other direction and began to chase Patrice with bullet spray.

Before the pursuit moved off the HDA campus, Maurice Devereaux and Todd Englewood approached the exit, where they met Blowers, who seemed to be in a state of rapture.

"They've cornered Delaney and Orosco," said Blowers.

Devereaux brushed past Blowers, "Come on Todd. I'm going to kill him myself!"

Moments later Devereaux and Englewood piled into a black Mercedes.

"Hang on Coxy," said Patrice. "And whatever you do, stay down!"

"Are you all right…Treece?"

"One of that asshole's slugs sliced my leg, but don't worry about it. What I'm worried about is Teddy. He's following. Must have come looking for you. Why'd you come? Pretty stupid wasn't it?"

"You're welcome. Without me, they'd have shot you up."

A short silence. "You're probably right. Thanks."

"No problem. You'd do it for me."

"I am doing this for you."

Another fusillade bombarded the rear of the Jeep.

Cherry Red continued to labor along in the caravan, now four cars strong, with the black Mercedes trailing the '57 Chev. The windshield of the classic car had been blown to Mars, but the engine was sound,

It was starting to snow again. It looked like it might stick. The roads had been kept fairly clear all day, with drifts stacked in the middle of the road. It would be dark soon.

Reaching under the seat, O'Reilly withdrew a Taurus Model Pt-92 Auto pistol, a nine with a 15 shot magazine. "Okay, you jaspers. You might have us outgunned, but I can shoot some."

With his left hand, he reached through the open window and pumped three shots at the streaking brown sedan.

"That codger is firing at us!" roared Fairly. "Can't you take him out?"

Tomajac sprayed a few more rounds toward the wounded Jeep. Then, in corkscrew fashion, nimbly contorting in the space of the window opening, he sprinkled more shots in O'Reilly's direction. Then he stopped suddenly. "Hey! The boss is following! Both of them! Devereaux and Englewood! I might hit them!"

"Then take out Delaney and Orosco," said Fairly, "And do it now! You're supposed to be a good shot. You've been missing badly!"

"How do you hit a target that moves like a Mexican jumping bean?"

"I've been waiting for this with anticiper," said Devereaux. "A man who would kill another man's daughter. A father. He values fatherhood. "Il y tient comme a la prunelle de ses yeux. The apple of his eye. That is right, my dear Todd. That is why I must be the one to kill Cox Delaney. And for good measure, those who have helped him to escape justice!"

The caravan was approaching Beachwood Plaza Shopping Center.

Tomajac's inability to make a telling shot ended just before the entry to the shopping center. With a whoop, he blew out both the front and rear tires of Patrice's Cherokee. The car zigged and zagged its way off Cedar Avenue and into the crowded, snow-packed parking lot.

"Nice going," said Fairly. "Why didn't you do that before?"

Careering into the center, Patrice, barely peeking above the open space where the windshield once functioned, headed for some new construction. It's hard to drive with the tires on one side blown to smithereens. It is even harder to make an overheated engine sputter to any destination. The Cherokee seemed on its last diet of petrol. It's next engine would have to be a horse, and there were none of those around.

"Okay, Coxy! Ride 'em cowboy!" roared Patrice.

With a last burst of whatever energy the motor could muster, Patrice plowed through a stack of building materials, over a pile of debris, and slammed through a section of plywood wall not yet finished. The SUV, now smoking like a Pike's Peak bust, came to rest in the middle of the incomplete structure. Ignoring the squirming, through-a-rag moan of Stephen Upton, the two sprinted out of the dying machine.

It didn't take long for Orosco and Delaney to hot foot it out the other side of the building. "You know something?" huffed Patrice, slogging through the snow in full flight, Cox Delaney beside her. "I really liked that car."

"I suppose you're going to tell me about the guy in the rug?"

"Oh," she said, as they streaked away from the shopping center, across an open field toward an old barn. "That's my boss. He was beginning to be a pain."

The three trailing cars streaked within feet of the stacked lumber and other building materials that fronted one of America's newest emporiums to be. O'Reilly parked some distance away from the HDA people, and sprang from Cherry Red, ready for action. Fairly and Tomajac began to sprint toward their victims, both of their guns dangling by their side.

"Stop!" shouted Theodore O'Reilly, crouching behind the left front fender of Cherry Red, his pistola aimed toward the rushing gunsels.

Still running, Tomajac twisted to his left and sprayed the classic car with more missiles, O'Reilly dodging out of the way.

"Shit," growled O'Reilly, partially under his car. "Hold out your gun, shout stop to a man with an automatic weapon, holding only a modest rod. Well, maybe not so modest as that, but why not also add, 'put your hands up.' Real effective O'Reilly."

In the midst of this soliloquy, shots rang out from behind Cherry Red, from the vicinity of the black Mercedes.

"Oh, hell. Surrounded at the OK corral, am I? Let's see what a diet of nines will do!"

O'Reilly messaged eight shots in the direction of the Mercedes.

"Forget him!" shouted Devereaux. "When he shows his face, Tomajac will cut him down!"

Englewood tucked the .38 back into his waist band. He wasn't used to shooting at people, leaving that up to his minions, so the suggestion went well with him, especially after O'Reilly answered back with his own fusillade.

"How does it feel to play the game?" asked Tomajac as he and Fairly slowly approached the stricken Jeep.

"Something changed when Delaney poleaxed me. That's why I'm carrying now."

They crabbed their way carefully to the vehicle, both assuming the shooter's position. Tomajac spewed fire from the KG-9 into the body of the car. No response. Moving slowly, weapons at the ready, they peered inside.

Empty.

When Devereaux and Englewood sprinted toward the rising shell of a building, O'Reilly jumped into Cherry Red and raced to the other side of the shopping center, where a large number of people were watching from a distance. He stopped in front of a huge discount store, and ran for the nearest telephone.

"Beachwood Plaza Shopping Center," O'Reilly growled into the phone when his party picked up. "It's going down. All the players are there."

"O'Reilly?"

"Who the hell do you think? And hurry. If you don't get here fast, Tavaro will beat you to the punch. He'll find a way to control the scene, and the good guys will not win."

"Gotcha," said Edgar Nelson.

"How's your foot, Coxy?"

"Coxy now, is it? And, yes, it's fine. Been fine for some time."

The old barn had a lot of room to roam, and spots to hide from prying eyes. But not much protection. Bullets would penetrate the old, dry wood like paper.

"Seeing as neither you nor I are armed," said Patrice, "we are going to have to do this by hand. You up to it?"

"I'd better be."

"Then watch me."

Patrice nimbly climbed to a high spot in the barn, moving with arboreal grace.

"How can a sleepy-head like you be such a physical specimen?"

"Careful. Stuff like that caused Upton to have a date with a rug," said Patrice, grinning down at the redhead.

"My sincerest apologies," said Delaney, as he climbed high with only slightly less agility. "I'll be sure to watch my tongue."

"You do that. Meanwhile, climb to the opposite side of the barn door opening. When they come in here, we will surprise them."

*   *   *

Edgar Nelson sped through the streets of Cleveland, worried about his lack of jurisdiction where he was headed. He tacked a portable Mars light to the roof of the unmarked, and hoped to hell he could beat Dominick Tavaro to the scene.

This could not have come at a worse time. Between Cox Delaney's brother Jake, and Nelson's buddy Ned Jesperson, they were beginning to close in on Maurice Devereaux and High Data Associates. They didn't have them yet, and it could still turn out that Devereaux could once again foil an investigation, but really, thought Nelson, a man cannot always conquer Lady Luck. One day, Nelson knew, Maurice Devereaux would try to draw to an inside straight, and then Nelson and the law would have the Frenchman.

Dominick Tavaro was himself racing to a scene. Then the call from Maurice Devereaux, cellular to cellular; the black Mercedes to Tavaro's unmarked. How unlucky could he get? To be on the way to investigate the scene of a double murder in the West one-hundreds, and then have to rush back, all the way past University Heights, to save the bacon of his benefactor.

Well, it came with the territory. If you are going to live the good life, you sometimes have to pay a good price.

He would call Davenport in to take care of the West Side problem. Now, he wondered, who could he trust with the Beachwood scene? Tavaro worked the phone, calling in chits, as he proceeded swiftly to the East Side.

Theodore O'Reilly sped back to the construction site. Standing beside Cherry Red, he surveyed the area, to get a fix on his enemies. He clutched the nine in his right hand.

Then he remembered Tiny Tyler.

Where was that bookish desk man? At the very least, he could have brought the company issue .38 police special into play. Not for the first time, O'Reilly cursed his nephew Sean. Driving like a somnambulant. Either Sean or Timothy on the job, armed to the teeth, would be competition for Fairly and Tomajac, even if you factored in the gun toting executive, Englewood, who had shot at him briefly.

Theodore O'Reilly decided it was time to investigate the construction site. He moved quickly toward the skeletal framework.

Tomajac led the way to the entrance of the old barn, Fairly just a step behind.

"Careful," said Fairly. "We really don't know if they are armed."

"I'd bet your retirement money they aren't," said Tomajac. "They probably ran right through the barn, using it to shield their progress. Then it is a straight shot to Ursuline College for Women."

"Could we pick 'em off from a distance?"

"Be hard."

Maurice Devereaux and Todd Englewood joined the hitters, the four of them standing just outside the aging structure.

"I'm going inside," said Tomajac.

"Wait," said Devereaux.

"If they're not inside, they're running to the college."

"They're inside," said Englewood. "We came in at an angle. We would see them if they were running toward that broad's school. They're not there. No footprints in the snow beyond this barn.

"Then, what are we waiting for?" asked Fairly.

"Monsieur Tavaro," said Devereaux.

"Dominick and his men can make short work of this," said Englewood. "All within the law. Keep our hands clean."

The massive barn groaned, with the weight of snow and years as a burden.

O'Reilly could see four men standing in front of the distant barn. He could see footprints of a number of people leading to the building. He figured they had Orosco and Delaney cornered. Only one thing to do: Even up the odds for Coxy and Patrice. Approach the barn in an oblique manner. It would take some time, but if he arrived quickly enough, he could add his gun to the mix.

He moved west, keeping low, gratified that he was wearing a light colored insulated coat. He could keep warm walking a circuitous route to the barn. And in the deepening gloom, he'd be very hard to see.

The thug waited in an alleyway bordering Cedar Avenue. This was an easy C note. Just a little patience. The only thing problematic was keeping warm. The sizable dump truck had no heater.

The engine rumbled its idle chatter. Traffic was moving into an ever busier commuter rush, as more and more companies, often with staggered quitting times, released their workers to home and hearth.

A perfect vantage point. He would see the unmarked police car almost a block away. It would take perfect timing, but he was confident he could take the guy out. And escape back into the inner city with untraceable plates, worthless to any witnessing eyes.

If they would only move inside, thought Patrice. She would go for the guy with the semi-conversion, take him out, and use him as a shield to bargain with.

A few feet away, also on a high rafter, was Cox Delaney. She hoped he had a mind for combat, like the mind she'd developed at the dojo in San Antonio. For not the first time, she was glad her teacher had emphasized the realities of urban violence, and not just the spiritual values of martial arts.

"Step into my office," she whispered under her breath.

*   *   *

Devereaux had Tavaro on his portable cellular phone. "Hurry up, Dominick. Vite! I want this wrapped up, maintenant!"

There was a crackle. Something unintelligible to eavesdroppers garbled its way from tower to tower and into the receiver. After a moment, into the mouthpiece, he said, "Tres bien." Then he turned to his three associates. "Dominick is making good time. He'll be here shortly. He also let us know he is taking care of a slight problem."

"Nelson?" asked Englewood.

"Mais, oui."

Circling, Theodore O'Reilly fought against snowbanks, slick ice, and growing fatigue as he traversed the lake effect tundra. It was taking longer than he would have liked. Longer than he needed it to take. He had to come up to the barn from behind, and be ready to pounce, gun in hand, to protect Treece.

Sirens.

The big question was, who's side would the arriving authorities be on? The multimillionaire high-tech guru, or a man wanted for murder, and his moll, an out-of-control fugitive who had been working a disappearing act.

O'Reilly shuddered at the thought.

The timing turned out to be perfect. At just the right moment, down went the foot, screech went the tires, and the huge dump truck smashed into the unmarked car with sickening force.

Edgar Nelson never knew what hit him.

With more squealing, the truck backed up, taking precarious purchase on the snow-packed surface, and finally righted itself, pointing west on Cedar Avenue.

There were three witnesses. None of them thought to take down the license plate. It didn't matter, of course. It wouldn't lead anywhere.

Dominick Tavaro shot out of his car, and directed by a bystander, ran toward the old dilapidated barn. Uniforms, arriving fairly early, had kept the crowd out of it. The beat cops had been warned not to go in. The strategy had been simple: Tavaro's own shock troops would be doing the Swat honors. He would have it under control.

Tavaro seemed to take the drifts between the back end of the shopping center and the abandoned barn like a snowmobile. Aided, perhaps, by the packed down path made by all the other players. But there was another element to his swiftness. This was a job that he had to clean up quickly. It just could not see the light of day.

Theodore O'Reilly was now in back of the barn. The enemy had not bothered to reconnoiter the rear sector. Well thank heavens for small mistakes. Crouching low, he gazed up into the barn's interior through a broken slat. It was too dark to see clearly, though he could make out the five men standing at the entrance. Suddenly, the five looked toward the shopping center. Something was happening.

223

O'Reilly slipped to the side of the building and peered out over the packed snow. Five heavily armored police shooters, two of them carting a compact portable light and generator system were plodding through the snow pack on their way to deal sure death to anything that lived inside the crumbling building.

He slowly worked his way along the outside wall to the front of the barn, keeping out of the line of sight. If they started shooting into the structure, it would be all over.

It took only a few moments to set up the portable lights. Attached to a small but powerful Honda generator, it might as well have been mighty stadium lights as far as Patrice and Coxy were concerned. They would either be spared, and forced to surrender to a system most likely stacked against them, or they would be shot dead, courtesy of Dominick Tavaro.

"Do it," barked Tavaro.

The lights streamed into the building, like an explosion in the night sky.

"Nobody there," said Fairly.

"Covered with hay," said Englewood. "Bet on it."

"Fire," snarled Maurice Devereaux.

"We have to do this by the book," said Tavaro. He brought a megaphone to his mouth. "If we don't warn them, we will not be able to stand up to the inquiry."

"Do what you have to do. But do it," said Devereaux.

"They are considered armed and dangerous," said Tavaro. "We cannot risk sending men in there. They are stone-cold killers."

Devereaux gave him a malicious look. "Il se fait tard."

"Patrice Orosco. Cox Delaney. Come out with your hands up. You have ninety-seconds to surrender, or we will be forced to shoot."

There was no movement inside. The megaphone could be heard inside the barn, but it did not penetrate all the way to the shopping center.

Patrice clung to the top rafter of the old barn. To her left, Delaney had done likewise. With their adversaries so close to the building, there was no way to communicate. When it became clear that the police were up to something, both of them had climbed higher. When the lights came on, they were glad of their caution. Both remained in darkness, the illumination missing their huddled forms.

"Are you sure this will stand up?" Fairly asked Tavaro.

"Do you take me for a fool? When the investigation discovers their guns, their smoking guns, it will be cut and dried.

"They may be unarmed," said Fairly.

Tavaro looked at him with contempt.

"Oh, I get it. Sorry about that. I guess I really am ready to retire."

Fairly was as aware of throw downs as the next law enforcement type. He was also aware of how badly he still hurt. How badly he wanted to go to Florida with his money.

Ninety-seconds of reprieve. Then eight rounds from two Saturday night specials, fired into the air, a rhythmic pattern that sounded like two desperadoes engaged in a gunfight of their own making.

Then an answering bombardment. Bullets splattered all through the barn, high to low, left to right. Into the floor of decomposed hay. Into the ceiling. The HDA men had taken cover. Playing their roles to the hilt.

Theodore O'Reilly almost rushed the crooked cops and HDA executives, armed with just a nine. Almost.

"Nobody could live through that," said Fairly, leading the way into the decrepit barn, followed by Tomajac and Tavaro. A moment later, Maurice Devereaux followed, with Todd Englewood on his heels.

"We've got 'em boys," said Tomajac, "Now let's find the bodies."

Patrice Orosco dropped from the sky like some kind of Deus ex machina, grabbing Fairly in a left arm choke hold. Her right hand stripped his .357 Magnum. "Careful, podnuh," she whispered into his ear. "I'll hurt you forever, if I have to." Then to the rest of the assemblage, "Do not make a move. At this point in time, I really don't care if I kill you or not. Oh, and that old cliché. Drop your guns, or Big Daddy Maurice will be the first to go."

Inside the barn, guns were dropped. Outside, Tavaro's five man Swat team stood at the ready, automatic rifles ready to fire.

The only man to move was Maurice Devereaux, as he began to slowly approach her.

"Give me that gun, jeune fille. And I may yet let you live."

Patrice brought the gun around to spit a disabling bullet his way, but she didn't quite have time. Cox Delaney dropped from the rafters and grabbed his one-time father-in-law, pinning the old man's arms behind him.

"You murdering son-of-a-bitch," said Delaney loudly, his face just millimeters from Devereaux's ear. "You had your own daughter killed, and tried to have me iced as well. Are you getting this Tavaro?"

Theodore O'Reilly slipped into view, adding his own gun to the standoff. He said, "Where's Edgar Nelson?"

"I'm quite afraid Edgar will not be joining our party," said Tavaro. "It seems he suffered an unfortunate accident."

"Did he now?" asked O'Reilly.

With almost no motion, Tomajac had produced a small ankle gun which he proceeded to place against O'Reilly's temple, as he slapped the nine from the little man's hand with his other mitt. Patrice had no time to react.

"The codger buys it, if you don't drop that gun," Tomajac barked.

"I think not," said Patrice. "If you shoot, you die. Then Devereuax dies, then Tavaro dies, then Fairly dies. Have I got your names right? I think so. Crooked, murdering assholes, all."

"I'm running out of patience," said Devereaux. "Drop that gun, Ms. Orosco, or you will die."

"Shut up!" shouted Delaney. "Why did you do it, Maurice? Why did you have your own daughter killed? I can understand going after me, after I stumbled onto your little, make that big, scam. But Cherie? Killing Cherie?"

"You truly are insane," said Devereaux. "I would never have had Cherie killed. Nor would I have had you killed. I would have neutralized you in other, more subtle ways."

"He's right, Coxy," said Theodore O'Reilly. "Todd Englewood put out the contract on you and Cherie. He was afraid Cherie would turn on the company, and cost him billions."

Maurice Devereaux looked at the back-lit Todd Englewood, and even with the shadows, he could see that it was true.

"For all of your qualities, Maurice, you lacked just one thing," said the portly Englewood. "Resolve. The resolve it takes to do whatever has to be done, no matter how painful it might be."

"You had my Cherie murdered," said Devereaux, his voice breaking.

Englewood suddenly produced his overlooked weapon and shot Devereaux through the heart. Delaney switched his hold to a frontal purchase, using the dead Frenchman as a shield. Englewood got off one more shot Delaney's way, aimed for the red head, before Patrice smoked a shot between the corpulent number two man's eyes.

Theodore O'Reilly, with a nifty move, had thrown Tomajac off-balance. Meanwhile, Dominick Tavaro suddenly turned and raced out of the barn at an oblique angle. He shouted at his own personal Swat team, located behind two huge snow-covered boulders perhaps twenty yards in front of the barn. "Shoot them!" he roared.

There was only the slightest hesitation.

A volley of shots once again peppered the barn.

Sirens. Four-wheel-drive Sheriff's Department vehicles. The reports ceased abruptly. Tavaro's Swat team fled toward the shopping mall, Tavaro himself nowhere to be seen.

Inside the barn, two bullet-riddled bodies were tossed aside.

Patrice Orosco's shellshocked gaze found the permanently retired Fairly prone at her feet. Looking to her left, she saw Delaney towering over the fallen Maurice Devereaux. She heard her voice sounding weak and exhausted. "Coxy? Are you okay? Are you hit?"

"I don't think so. You?"

"I don't seem to be." And then, "Oh, my God..."

Patrice moved slowly to the fallen, bloody body of Theodore O'Reilly, lying next to Tomajac, who appeared to have had the side of his head blown off.

She knelt down, seeking a pulse. There was none. "Teddy..." she sobbed. "Teddy...Teddy...oh my God...oh my God. He's dead, Coxy. Teddy's dead."

The words of John floated into her mind: Greater love hath no man than this, that a man lay down his life for his friends.

#

226

CHAPTER 22

Monday, December 16, 1996

Indians Sell Out Season Again: The Indians, the team that was not on the "A" list for the majority of this winter's free-agent class, yesterday sold out their second straight season in Jacobs Field.

They were the first team in history to sell virtually all their tickets before Opening Day last year. Yesterday's announcement makes them the second team in history to do it.

> Paul Hoynes
> Plain Dealer Reporter

The jet taxied to a smooth stop at Cleveland Hopkins International Airport, greeted by forty-five degree weather with the promise of more showers to come sometime during the day.

The young woman who stood for the slightest moment at the apex of the mobile passenger escalator breathed in deeply, picking up the brisk winter freshness off of Lake Erie. Gazing out at the panoramic Cleveland skyline; the I. M Pei-designed lakefront building; the Terminal Tower; the ghost of the Grand Old Lady, now in the grip of the wrecker's ball; she felt like she had come home.

Patrice Orosco began to descend to the tarmac, puddled and wet, glistening and reflecting sky and structures on its watery surface. Only then did she begin to look for her family, waiting to take her home, to welcome her back from the break she had to take.

They were not readily visible, as she approached the terminal. She gripped a single carry-on bag, which held the necessities demanded by any modern woman.

Inside the terminal, she walked quickly toward the carousel. First find her two pieces of luggage, and then track down her people.

"I missed you," said a quiet, strong voice.

Cox Delaney.

"Hello…"

"I hope you don't mind me coming for you. I had a hard time convincing Ruben. He went on and on about his Mija."

"That's Papa."

They were at the carousel. It didn't take long for Delaney to snap up Treece's baggage.

"What finally did the trick was to point out who better to supervise work on the kitchen."

"That would do it," said Patrice. "How's your building coming along?"

"Well, Jake and his boys are here. Jake is going in with me, fifty-fifty. Now that Common Pleas Court has agreed to the reparations from HDA, I should be getting my money back. Many others will too, with the rest being snapped up by the RICO statute. By the way, I've read the first couple of installments on your homeless series. It's terrific. It tells it like it is. Jonathan Tubb is very proud of you, though he thinks he is in some way responsible for Teddy's death."

"In some ways, we all are."

"I understand why you had to leave," said Delaney, as he ushered her to a Chevrolet Suburban. "I also understand why you couldn't do the story on HDA."

Patrice nodded. "I needed to be alone. With Daddy's new restaurant set to open Christmas day, it worked out fine. I had the house in McAllen to myself. It's easy to fax copy nowadays. They fed me well at Padre Orosco's. So did Mel and Martha Dones. I spent a lot of time with them. They helped me to heal."

They were crossing the Lorain-Carnegie Bridge.

"What are you going to do?" asked Delaney.

"I got lucky. I got my old apartment back in San Antonio. The insurance company replaced my Cherokee. It's at the apartment."

"I see."

Delaney pulled up to an old residential hotel on Detroit Avenue; a building sending mixed signals. On the one hand it looked abandoned, neglected and dead. On the other, it sported a beehive of activity aimed at total resurrection.

"And I'm keeping my place on Mayfield Road."

A spark in Delaney's eye that he couldn't quite conceal.

The two walked up to the building. The first person Patrice saw was Oscar No Name. "Kat!" he squealed by way of greeting. "I'm painting!"

Sure enough he was, under the watchful eye of Lottie and Darcy.

"Hello Kat," said the woman from Kentucky. Darcy waved.

Delaney led her to the rear entrance. "I've got my house on Woodbury for sale. The court gave me that back, too. It's next to Pudge Elliot's house. He's getting along fine. Midge just had her second and last operation. It's a complete success. She was asking about you."

"I'm going to go see her, first thing in the morning," said Patrice.

They walked into the crowded kitchen. Claude Johnson was installing a new stainless steel sink. A man who looked very much like Cox Delaney was helping him.

"Treece," said Coxy, "this is my brother Jake."

"I've heard an awful lot about you, kid," said the older Delaney. "And all of it good. In fact, terrific."

Patrice blushed.

Perhaps Cox Delaney did, too, but with his ruddy complexion, it was hard to tell.

Half a dozen of Jake Delaney's men were scurrying about, working on the rehab.

When Ruben Orosco returned to the kitchen, carrying a detailed floor plan, his eyes brightened when he saw his daughter. "Mija. I am very proud of you! My eyes watered when I read your stories. I even advertised in the special section they gave you."

"Oh Papa," she whispered, as he gave her his patented bear hug. "Thank you, just for being you."

Grandma Stella was fixing a feed for everyone, with Margie Johnson as her aide. She had appropriated a cleaned out room, and Jake had brought in a Coleman stove and several ice chests to help her on the way.

"Your Mama and Yolanda will be here shortly," said Ruben Orosco. "They went shopping. What else is nuevo."

"How's the restaurant coming, Papa?"

Ruben Orosco's face lit up like a Roman candle. "Fantastico! So well, the staff kicked me out! They said they have everything under control, and not to come back until it opens Christmas Day!"

A short time later, Delaney led Patrice out the building's front entrance. "I have something to show you. Will you come with me?"

"Sure."

Delaney drove the Suburban across the bridge and into the East Side. When they reached Superior Avenue, Patrice looked questioningly at the redhead.

"We're almost there," said Delaney.

Patrice said nothing.

"One thing that bothers me a lot," said Delaney after a while, "is Tavaro and his shooters disappearing to who knows where. Probably to a tropical island with a lot of HDA's money collected over the years."

Patrice continued to regard Delaney.

"What?" he finally asked her, as they passed by The Plain Dealer building.

"I was just thinking," she said slowly. "We are going to have to sit down soon, and talk about things. I have to talk about Pablo. And I have to talk about Teddy, and what he meant to me."

Delaney nodded.

"And you have to talk," she said. "I know next to nothing about your family. I want to get to know Jake. Hear about your father and mother. You have an advantage. You get to know my people, and they are self-explanatory. But you, Coxy; you are a '…riddle wrapped in a mystery inside an enigma,' to quote Sir Winston Churchill. You will need to talk about Cherie. You need closure. And I do too."

Delaney nodded again. "You're right," he said simply. Then, "We're here," as he broke out into a broad smile.

He pulled the Suburban into the parking garage at her apartment complex. At first she didn't see it, as it sat parked and gleaming, fully repaired and restored, in her very own space.

Cherry Red.

"When you left, after the funeral, Teddy's nephew Timothy managed to get the car released from the impound. He and Sean had it restored at their own expense. Teddy would have wanted you to have it."

Patrice regarded the beautiful classic.

"He really loved that car," she said, her voice breaking.

"Yes, he did," said Delaney. "And he really loved you, too."

"God, I miss him Coxy." She instinctively buried her head against Delaney's chest. Her tears dampened his gray chambray shirt.

"Now I've got something else to show you," said Delaney, a short time later. He took her hand and led her past her own apartment, and Norma Darling's apartment, all the way to number twelve.

At that moment, Audrey drove by in a new Volvo, Yolanda in the passenger seat. Two beautiful five-year-old redheads in the back seat.

"They're back from shopping," said Delaney, with a look of pure delight on his face. "I can't wait to see their new outfits."

Patrice gazed silently into his face.

"May I take you to dinner tonight?" he asked.

Patrice nodded.

"I'm staying here, just until the house sells, and we get something else. I'm considering Strongsville."

"Great shopping center."

The pasta at The Palazzo was perfection to Patrice. The wine list superb. After a long period of animated conversation, Delaney turned silent for a few moments. "This might not have happened if not for you," he finally said. "Jake's people fell just short of indictable proof. In fact, the proof wasn't found until Justice swooped into High Data Associates after everything went down. Even then, they would never have obtained a warrant without your pocket recording."

"Journalists carry 'em."

"You sure saved my bacon, Treece."

She nodded.

"Do you mind if I call you Treece?"

She shook her head.

"I love you," he blurted.

She looked deeply into his eyes.

"Do I stand a chance with you?" he finally managed to stammer.

She continued to gaze into his eyes, into his soul. And then, very softly, "What do you think?"

"I don't know what to think. Just that I love you."

At thirty-seven, it had been a long while. There were all kinds of obstacles. Perhaps there are impediments to any relationship. The task was to find ways to overcome them. At this moment, Cox Delaney didn't care what it took to conquer whatever the future might bring.

"My father says that the last person to know is the one who is in love," said Patrice. "I didn't know at the time I left. I do now."

"And?"

"Cox Delaney," she said, her voice as musical as a songbird's, her smile as warm as a fine day in summer, "Are you always this slow on the uptake?"

He leaned across the table, in full view of diners and staff, and gave her a lingering kiss. "Let's go put my girls to bed," said Delaney, "before we scandalize the place."

Yolanda was playing Chutes and Ladders with Tina and Tonya when Delaney and Patrice walked into apartment number twelve.

"Daddy!" squealed two little pigtailed redheads.

"We beat Yolanda! In everything!" said Tina.

"She hardly scored any points at all," said Tonya.

"Well, it's not fair," said Yolanda with a pout. "They're experts! How can I compete?"

"It's bedtime, girls," said Delaney with a huge grin. "Tomorrow is a big day. We're going to give our first performance of the Christmas show!"

"All right, Daddy," said Tina. "But you promised you'd read a story to us, and we found a great book!"

"In that case, everybody into the bedroom! Come one, come all! Ol' Daddy is going to read a gripping story!"

"Just like grand-pere, before he died of a heart attack!" said Tonya.

The two little girls piled into their beds. Tina pulled a little blue book from under her pillow. "Here Daddy!"

Delaney took the book. His eyes immediately misted. He sat, Indian-style, on the floor between the two beds, with Patrice and Yolanda finding spots on a large bean bag close to the beds. For a moment he just looked at the book, and then his voice could be heard, full of emotion:

> "A mother held her new baby and
> very slowly rocked him back and forth
> back and forth, back and forth.
> And while she held him, she sang:
> I'll love you forever,
> I'll like you for always,
> As long as I'm living
> My baby you'll be."

#

231

ACKNOWLEDGEMENTS

It is scarcely possible to write a book without having a lot of people assist you with many aspects in the process of developing into a book writer. I would therefore wish to thank the following people for their help: Paul McCoy, my close personal friend who was one of the early readers of the manuscript, and showed unwavering enthusiasm for the project. Paul was also very helpful with computer lab assistance.

Also of great assistance with the more esoteric areas of computer workings was my great good friend Gheorghe Chessler. I cannot emphasize strongly enough what a dolt I am when it comes to technical things. Fortunately, as the song goes, "…with a little help from my friends."

I wish also to especially thank Cleveland authorities on homelessness. They spent many hours on the phone with me; and to them, and their delightful city, I owe a dept of gratitude that words cannot express.

I would also like to thank the Cleveland Plain Dealer, without whose help this book would have never gotten off the ground. I still read the Plain Dealer everyday from their website. At the time the book was in production, I had a subscription by mail. I looked forward to every issue that arrived. I personally believe it to be one of the finest newspapers in the country. I had many a fine conversation with various personnel at the paper during the book's production. I continue to root for the Tribe! One day, they will again win the World Series.

I would be remiss if I did not mention two teachers I had at El Rancho High School, in Pico Rivera, California. The first was Richard Davis, my Freshman English teacher, and later my speech teacher during my senior year. He taught me a love for writing, a reverence for books, and gave me zest for public speaking. Richard, you were terrific! The second was Frank Kerr, my senior English teacher. He was so good he later penned an English textbook. Thank you, Frank.

Another early supporter of my writing was Ron Haggerman. Ron gave me unlimited access to his copy machine, and allowed me to write movie reviews for the video side of his movie theater business.

A big thank you to Mike Slizewski, who brought me aboard as a newspaper columnist in 1991, when he was managing editor for the Siskiyou Daily News. Mike, you were the best. And a fabulous musician, too!

I cannot forget Bob Brewer, who brought me into the media at KTAT in Frederick, Oklahoma, those many years ago…

AUTHOR'S NOTE

I am quite happy to hear from readers. Unfortunately, snail mail will just not cut it. Were you to send it to the publisher, there would be quite a delay, and then it would simply get lost in a daily pile delivered by my good friend, the postal lady—once it did reach me.

On the other hand, if you are online, visit my website at www.askdrpiano.com. There is a link on the homepage where you can send me an e-mail. And I will reply!

I will not entertain story ideas; in fact, I will delete the e-mail without reading or replying. I have a policy of writing only what I generate. Besides, I have book ideas to last a hundred years—yet my doctor holds out little hope that I can take full advantage.

Anyone with a request concerning events or appearances may e-mail me, or the publicity department at 1st Books. Snail mail for that is: 1st Books Library, 2595 Vernal Pike, Bloomington, In 47404.

Should you wish to discuss ancillary rights, such as cinema, by all means send an e-mail. You can bet the mortgage I'll answer those.

ABOUT THE AUTHOR

Vin Smith, known the world over as Dr. Piano, is the Internet's popular theosophic mystic relationship advisor. He has answered thousands of questions from people from scores of countries at AskMe.com and his own Ask Dr. Piano! An accomplished singer, pianist, and ventriloquist, Vin broke into broadcasting in 1962. He is the inventor of a breakthrough countrypolitan radio format that fused inner city music with traditional rural sounds. He has written over 3000 musical compositions in the past fifty years. He has written extensively for magazines and newspapers. He is listed in all who's who publications for a long and distinguished career as a communicator.

Printed in the United States
815700001B